Highlander's Captive

by

Donna Fletcher

Highlander's Captive

Cover art
Kim Killion Group

Visit Donna's Web site
www.donnafletcher.com
http://www.facebook.com/donna.fletcher.author

Table of Contents

Chapter 1
Chapter 2
Chapter 3
Chapter 4
Chapter 5
Chapter 6
Chapter 7
Chapter 8
Chapter 9
Chapter 10
Chapter 11
Chapter 12
Chapter 13
Chapter 14
Chapter 15
Chapter 16
Chapter 17
Chapter 18
Chapter 19
Chapter 20
Chapter 21
Chapter 22
Chapter 23
Chapter 24
Chapter 25
Chapter 26
Chapter 27
Chapter 28
Chapter 29
Chapter 30
Chapter 31
Chapter 32
Chapter 33

Chapter 34
Chapter 35
Chapter 36
Titles by Donna Fletcher
About the Author

Chapter One

"Where is Dawn?" Cree demanded so loudly that every warrior in the Great Hall turned silent and stared at him. He had not seen her since late last night when Sloan had come to their bedchamber to inform him that his sister Wintra had been abducted. He had ordered Dawn to bed and left before making sure she had obeyed him, something she rarely did.

He had been busy with plans to go after his sister and kill the idiot bastard who had unwisely abducted her. Thoughts of Dawn had drifted in and out of his mind throughout the night and he had imagined her tucked safely in their bed sleeping. But sunrise usually found her up and about, after they made love, which they did often, and was what he wished they were doing right now. Of course it would be a quick coupling, but no less satisfying. It never was with Dawn, even though she could not speak a word. It still amazed him that she had survived since birth, nineteen years, without being able to utter a sound. Not a peep, a squeak, or moan, could she manage. Nothing. Yet to him, he could hear her clearly in her gestures, even more clearly now that he was completely and madly in love with her—damn it.

He had never expected to fall in love. He had expected to take a wife and have her produce heirs. Love had never been a consideration. He had had no time for it. Yet this voiceless woman had stolen his heart and he didn't want it back. It was hers to keep forever just as her heart—all of her—belonged to him. He growled low at his foolish musings. He had no time for them, though he wanted all the time he could get with Dawn, if he could find her. Where could she have gone off to? The snow was heavy on the ground and she should be careful, especially now that she was carrying their child.

"Damn," he mumbled, a sudden thought disturbing him. What if she was in trouble and not able to call out for help? He scowled and this time shouted, "Has anyone seen Dawn?"

Heads shook, but no one spoke up.

Cree turned to Sloan. "You haven't seen her?"

"Not since last night."

"Find her," Cree snapped, annoyed he had allowed so much time to pass without checking on her. He hoped that he worried needlessly and she was still abed. She could use the rest being with child, not that she would agree. She was always off somewhere, visiting, helping, disobeying him. "Find her," he said again.

"Afraid you've lost her?" Sloan asked with a smile, which faded quickly when Cree's dark eyes narrowed and his scowl deepened. Sloan turned and hurried off without saying another word. He knew Cree too well to know when to turn silent and retreat.

Cree looked over a small contingent of his warriors gathered in the Great Hall. He would take only twenty of his warriors for now, though it would be more like having fifty warriors compared to other fighting troops. His men were highly skilled, and they would follow him into hell if he asked, though they already had. Endless missions for the King had taken its toll on all of them, but at least it had not been in vein. Now, after constant toil of battle, they had what they had fought so long and hard for—a permanent home. A place they could always return to and where family and friends would welcome them back.

Now, unlike other times, he was reluctant to leave. Now he had Dawn, and she had been through her own hell with her true mother trying to kill her and, in the end, having to take her mother's life to protect herself.

"Cree."

The strong voice cut through his musings and had him turning his head to face Kirk McClusky, Dawn's true father and a good man.

"We want to help," Kirk said, "what can we do?"

"I appreciate your offer, but I would much prefer if you remained here at the keep and watched over Dawn, not an easy task I'm afraid."

"She does have an independent nature, though as her father I don't think that is a bad thing," Kirk admitted with pride.

"You might want to think twice about that since she's now carrying your grandchild," Cree reminded.

"Good point. I'll be sure to be extra vigilant."

Cree was about to tell him that he would need to be when one of his warriors entered the room, stomping the snow off himself. "Snow has started falling again?" Cree asked as the warrior approached.

"Aye, my lord, and if we don't leave soon, they'll be no leaving today at all."

Cree nodded. "Then we leave now."

The warriors stood and filed out of the keep, not a one mumbling or complaining. They would do as Cree ordered and brave the winter storm to help find his sister.

Sloan hurried into the room. "I can't find her and no one has seen her, perhaps she is annoyed that you are leaving and is letting you know it by not bidding you farewell."

"That is not her way," Cree said, knowing his wife would never be that petty. He worried that he would have to delay his departure to make certain his wife was all right, which could cost precious time in finding his sister.

Cree was never so relieved when a minute later Dawn entered the keep, throwing back her snow-covered hood and hurrying over to him. His heart hammered in his chest. She was so beautiful, though not in the common sense. Her features were plain, her nose a bit sharp, her eyes dark and her hair a deep red and straight, without a curl or wave to it. Yet she glowed with a rare beauty that caught his breath and stilled his heart. She was a head taller than most women, slender, with hips that curved perfectly and breasts that were barely a handful, but oh how he enjoyed them. She was—to him—perfect.

"Where have you been?" he demanded as she approached.

She smiled and pulled something from beneath her wool cloak, holding it out to him. She pointed to him and pretended to shiver, and then pointed back at the wool plaid and hugged herself.

"To keep me warm?"

She nodded as she drifted into his arms and snuggled against him. He was so warm and his body so hard. He was the epitome of a Highland warrior; strong, bold, and proud.

He lifted her chin and felt himself stir at the raw passion he always saw reflected in her eyes for him. "I would much prefer it be you who kept me warm."

She tapped her chest, letting him know she felt the same and was unable to take her eyes off him. He was beyond handsome, not a single scar marring his beauty. Even his scowl, she had once thought perpetual, had lessened since they had fallen in love, but did not distract from his fine features. And how she loved his lips, such kissable lips that she forever wanted to taste.

"Damn it, Dawn, you know when you look at me like that I can't resist kissing you." And he knew if he did that he'd pay for it, but the hell with it, he kissed her anyway, and he damn well paid for it. He grew too hard, too fast. It didn't matter, though, it was worth it. Their kiss was as hungry as always, and if he had time he would take her quickly so that the scent of her would be on him and he could breathe deeply of it every time he thought of her. But then that would be constantly.

After reluctantly ending their kiss, he whispered, "I will miss you."

Dawn patted her chest, slipped her arms around his waist, and pressed her body firmly against his, then nodded and rested her head to his chest.

Sometimes her gestures spoke much louder than words. He hugged her, gave her one last kiss, and then eased her away from him and walked out of the keep without looking back. Sloan followed closely behind him.

"He would take you with him if he could," Kirk said, placing a comforting hand on her shoulder.

Dawn nodded and wiped away the single tear that lingered in the corner of her eye. She then patted her chest, brought her hands together as if in prayer and rested them against her cheek.

"You're tired and want to rest," Kirk said, easily understanding her gestures. "Yes, you should rest and later we can sit by the fire and talk."

Dawn smiled and nodded and placed a kiss on his cheek.

Kirk grinned when she stepped away. "I am so very glad that I found you, daughter, and I am glad we will have some time alone to talk and get to know each other even better. Now go rest and I will see you later."

Dawn turned and walked slowly, as if heavily burdened, to the steps and took them unhurriedly, until out of sight. Once no one could see her, she flew up the steps, hurried to her bedchamber and gathered the few items she needed. She then carefully retraced her steps, watching to make certain no one saw her. She wanted everyone to assume she was sleeping. This way she wouldn't be disturbed for hours, and it wouldn't be until much later that someone discovered her gone.

She crept through the keep, staying to the shadows so she would not be seen. She hadn't enlisted anyone's help with her plans for fear that Cree would punish them. She would be responsible for her own rash actions, though to her, her plan made perfect sense. She would join her husband, though she would not make herself known until they were far enough away from the keep so that he could not send her home.

The decision had been an easy one, especially after she had seen how upset Cree had gotten when Sloan had told him that Wintra had been abducted. It was then she understood that he would not return home until he found her, and while she was confident that he would be successful in his quest, it was how long it would take that worried her.

She wanted him there with her as his child grew inside her. He would keep them safe and he would help assuage her fears that the child might be born voiceless like her. It was her greatest fear that she would pass her affliction onto their child. She prayed every day that the child would scream loudly when he slipped out of her. If not?

She shook her head, not wanting to think about it. She wanted Cree with her when the time came, as well as now as his child grew within her. There were many willing and eager to help her, especially her best friend Lila and Elsa, Cree's healer, who had assisted Lila in birthing young Thomas. Dorrie, once a foe, now a friend and Flanna, who had turned out to be more a friend than Dawn could have imagined, were also eager to do their part. The list went on, and she was grateful to have so many friends willing to do most anything for her, even if it meant facing Cree's wrath, but she would not ask that of them.

Old Mary's words had also made her decision that much easier. She trusted the old woman who had been a constant in her life, and her ability to see things that were yet to come. So when the old woman had suddenly appeared out of the shadows as she had walked to Lila's, she had paid heed and listened. Old Mary had warned her that Cree would not find his sister so easily and when she was found, secrets long kept would be revealed.

Dawn had decided to keep her decision to herself. This was for her and her alone to do. She had not spent the night sleeping as all believed. She had made use of the time to gather what she needed and had hid her bundle by the kitchen water barrels, which was where she was headed now. She would change into garments that more suited a young lad than a woman, wrap her legs in the fur strips the warriors wore against the winter cold and twist her long hair up to tuck under a helmet that she had borrowed. Lastly, she would wrap the Carrick plaid around her, finishing her disguise.

Dawn felt her excitement build as she made her way out of the keep without being detected and in no time switched to her disguise. She caught the tail end of the troop as it left the keep and blended in with the other lads who tended the warriors' horses and weapons, keeping her head down against the swirling snow just as they did.

Four hours later with the snow falling more heavily and the cold biting at her, she wondered if her plan had been a foolish one. She had not given enough thought to the weather and how difficult it was to travel in snow. Hadn't she learned her lesson that time she had gone in the snow to save Old Mary? A snowstorm was not something to take lightly, but Cree being gone for several months wasn't something she could take lightly either.

Dawn wrapped her plaid higher up around her face and kept walking. Sooner or later they would stop, and then she could rest.

Hours passed and still they didn't stop, and the snow now pelted them as if it would never end. Dawn worried the snow would swallow them whole, or so it felt that way. The endless walking kept her somewhat warm, but there were parts of her that kept getting nipped by the cold until she could barely feel them.

She continued to tell herself that they would stop soon and she would not waste a moment. She would go find Cree and let him know that she was here. She tried to convince herself that he would be pleased. After all he had told her that he would miss her, so why wouldn't he be pleased to see her?

Minutes suddenly began to feel like hours and too

often she feared she wouldn't be able to take another step. She admonished herself for not giving her sudden plan more forethought. It wasn't wise of her to rush off, but the thought of days and nights without Cree had spurred her into action.

She would brave a winter storm to be with her husband and that was the end of that. She kept pace, or at least she thought she was keeping pace, until she raised her head and saw that the troop was several feet ahead of her.

She stopped and held her hand above her eyes to block the falling snow to try and get a better look. What she saw frightened her and got her moving. The troop had disappeared from sight, the heavily swirling snow blurring her path. She hurried to catch up, but after a few minutes she realized that she could not see the troop at all.

Panic rose in her. No one knew she had joined the troop. No one would search for her. If she didn't catch up with them, there would be a good chance—a very good chance—that she would die in the snowstorm, never to be discovered.

She hurried along, praying as she went that she would come upon the troop. What seemed like hours later, her legs unable to support her any longer, she collapsed in the snow too exhausted to move. She told herself she would take a brief rest and start again and not stop until she caught up with them. She kept promising herself that as she curled up in a ball on the ground and her eyes drifted closed.

Cree rode alongside his troop of men, calling out, "You know the drill. Stay shoulder to shoulder or suffer the consequences." He and his warriors had traveled through many a snowstorm. They all knew that if they didn't stay close—touching—that they could very well fall behind and that would be the end—the snow would claim them.

As he traveled the line, Cree counted. When he got to the end, he yelled reminding the young lads to stay close. With his count accurate, he was about to turn his horse when he saw a sizeable lump of snow in the middle of the road only a few feet behind them. He thought to take a look, but with his count accurate it couldn't be one of his men. Besides, he wanted to get his troop to the abandon croft about an hour away. There would be enough shelter there to get everyone warm and fed and to get a good night's sleep since tomorrow they would travel until they reached the abbey. And that was a full day's ride away.

He turned his horse and rode to the front of the line, thoughts of Dawn weighing heavily on his mind.

Chapter Two

The long abandoned croft was a welcome sight. It had once been a thriving farm and Cree intended it to be so once again, though it would also serve as a sentinel station. He planned on having several of the empty crofts do double duty. He wanted his people and land well protected and early detection of any approach to his land would help with that. He had already had some of his men begin work on the place, so a few of the buildings had seen some repair and would provide sufficient shelter for the night.

Warmth greeted Cree when he entered the cottage and he went straight to the fireplace and held his cold hands out to the heat of the roaring flames. He gave a glance around as his hands warmed. Food and drink waited on the small table he had stepped around to get to the fireplace, while a make-shift pallet lay to the side. Sloan had seen well to his duties and was now seeing to the warriors, though when it had come to battles, Cree had been right there to help with the aftermath of death and destruction.

The image of Dawn suddenly filled his thoughts and chased the horrific memories away. He found himself smiling, something he had been doing more of since Dawn had entered his life. He truly hoped this mission would not take long. He wanted to find his sister, return home to Dawn, and wed her so that she would be officially his. Then he would find a good husband for his sister.

Wintra.

She had been so angry when he had left her at the abbey ten years ago. But what choice had he had? After their mother had died, he had known all too well that he would not be staying to work the land. He wanted more than a small parcel of land that he worked for someone else. Someone who cared naught for him and his sister and would put them out at a moment's notice without thought to their welfare.

It hadn't been an easy decision to take Wintra to the abbey, but it had been a wise one. He wanted her safe until he could provide a permanent home for her. It had taken longer than he had hoped and with the passing years Wintra had grown angrier with him. He wondered what she would do if she ever discovered the secret he and their mother had kept from her. That she was a child conceived of rape and that he was her half-brother. That day his mother had returned from the field, battered and bruised remained forever vivid in his mind. She had refused to tell Cree what had happened, and being just ten years, there hadn't been much he could do about it. When she had begun to grow round with child, it had only proven what Cree had feared—that someone had raped his mother. But his mother would never speak about it. The only thing she would say to him was that it would be better if Wintra believed that she and Cree had the same father and so the lie began. As far as his sister would ever know, they shared the same father and he had died just before she had been born.

He shook the disturbing thoughts away and shrugged out of his fur-lined cloak, tossing it over the only chair in the cottage. He was about to fill his tankard with ale from the pitcher on the table when raised voices outside his door caught his attention.

His hand went to his sword that he had placed against the chair just as the door flew open.

Cree stared for a moment at the figure in the open doorway. He was large, his hooded cloak covered with snow as was the bundle he cradled in his arm. He shook his head free of his hood and Cree was surprised and a bit annoyed to see Torr McClusky, Dawn's half-brother. He had told the warrior that he hadn't required his help and still the man had followed him.

Sloan suddenly hurried in behind Torr. "What are you waiting for? We need to get her warm."

Cree felt his stomach clench, and he shoved the table out of his way to get to Torr and take the bundle from him, realizing it was Dawn.

"Good God, she's ice cold," Cree said, taking Dawn from Torr and with two, long strides was in front of the fireplace. He sat on the chair Sloan had hurriedly placed there and pushed the plaid away from her face that had at least sheltered her from the snow, though not the bone-chilling cold.

Torr appeared beside him, holding his hands out to the flames, the snow on his cloak rapidly melting and puddling at his feet.

"Where? How?" Cree asked, placing his warm hand against her pale cheek, her lips slight blue and her eyes closed as if in... He shook his head. She was not dead. He would not let her die.

"Thanks to my mare who had insisted on prodding the lump in the road that I had thought to avoid, I found her. She must have followed you."

"Two of the lads had mentioned that another lad had gone missing," Sloan said. "I foolishly paid it no heed, since the count of the men was accurate."

Cree thought of the lump of snow that had caught

his attention on the road, and he had ignored. It had been Dawn. She had laid there helpless, a few feet from him, and he hadn't gone to see what it was. If he would have found her, she would be safe now. He silently cursed himself for not investigating it.

"Has she woken at all?" Cree asked.

Torr shook his head. "She stirred some when I lifted her, but she hasn't opened her eyes.

"I have to get her warm," Cree said more to himself than the other two men, realizing that while the wool plaid had offered some shelter from the snow, it had also aided in chilling her. The snow had soaked through the wool, wetting her garments.

Torr reached out to help as Cree lifted Dawn, gently slipping the plaid off her.

Sloan helped, unwinding the fur wrappings at her legs and shaking his head. "It's a deep chill she has caught."

"You need to warm her," Torr said his worry evident in his clipped tone.

Cree grew more annoyed, though contained it. The man did, after all, save Dawn, but he didn't need to be told what he already knew and feared. He had lost men to deep cold before. They would simply drift off and never wake again, and he'd be damned if he'd let that happen to Dawn. He wanted her fully awake when he punished her for being so foolish. But first he would hug and kiss her and be grateful that she was alive, then he would punish her.

"Leave, I will see to her," Cree ordered.

The two men nodded, knowing the best way to get her warm quickly.

"Torr," Cree called out before the man reached the door. "You will tell me why you followed us when I had made it quite clear that I didn't require your help."

"You were clear enough," Torr snapped. "And so is the missive that arrived from the King shortly after you left. I knew you would want to see it right away, so I brought it to you. And good thing I did or my sister would be dead."

Cree cursed beneath his breath, annoyed at the man for being right and grateful to him for following, though he wasn't sure how happy he would be with the message from the King. But that had to wait. Dawn came first. He would not lose her or their child. He planned on having many more children with Dawn. And he didn't care if one or all of them lacked a voice, he would love them regardless just as he did their mother.

He got busy right away, stripping Dawn of her wet garments and rubbing her cold flesh as he went. He had thought that his worry over her would prevent him from growing hard and doing what needed to be done to warm her. But he need not have, for as soon as he touched her, he began to grow hard.

Damn, she was so pale, so cold. How did he make love to her when she was so lifeless?

Touch her; bring her to life.

The words echoed in his head, and he finished stripping her naked. Once he did, he placed her gently on the pallet and covered her with a blanket while he quickly stripped off his clothes, discarding them at his feet.

He took a moment to move the table and chair and drape her clothes over the end of the table closest to the fire. Then he grabbed the edge of the pallet and carefully dragged it, and a sleeping Dawn, over in front of the fireplace. Without delay, he joined her beneath the covers.

He snuggled her against him, her body so cold that it ran a chill through him, and he couldn't stop from shivering. And though her cold flesh continued to chill him, he didn't let go of her. He pressed her even closer against him, letting his body's heat seep into her and hopefully warm her. He rested his cheek against her cold one for a moment before he rained kisses over it and grew upset when she remained unresponsive.

Not a move. Not a flinch. Nothing.

He had grown accustomed to her having no voice, not issuing a sound. But gestures, moving, were her way of communicating and so this silence was more disturbing than ever to him. It was as if death had already claimed her, and that he would not allow.

He eased her to rest on her back and a little more aggressively ran his hand over her cold flesh, squeezing her breasts, pinching her nipples, taking a moment to splay his hand over her stomach where his babe lay nestled, and then he slipped his hand between her legs to massage her thighs before spreading them and thrusting a finger inside her.

A low growl echoed down through his chest, so annoyed was he that she had not responded. He had thought—damn—he thought that her body would spring to life like it always did when he touched her intimately. Fear nipped at him and he shoved it away. He had kept fear at bay, never allowing it to control him and he damn well wouldn't let it sneak in now.

He did what he had wanted to do since he had taken her in his arms. He kissed her. He pressed his warm lips to her cold ones, and though she still did not respond, he did not let it stop him. He continued to kiss her and none too gently. He nipped at her lips, tugging at them with his teeth, hoping to heat them and bring them to life before returning to kiss her again and again. As he continued assaulting her with loving kisses, his finger teased between her legs, working to stir a response from her.

He kept his body close against hers, his one leg draped over one of hers, his chest partially covering one of her breasts, and he sent a silent prayer to the heavens.

When still she didn't respond, he began talking to her.

"I should thrash you for being so foolish, but I won't as long as you wake up and let me love you. I want to love you so badly that it hurts. Feel how hard I am for you?" He took her hand that he thought felt warmer, or perhaps he had wanted to think that, and placed it on his hardened groin, holding it there. "I'm forever hard for you. Do you know that, Dawn? I look at you and grow hard. I but touch you innocently and I grow hard. I see you smile and I grow hard. And when you touch me here," —he squeezed her hand around his thick shaft—"I feel like exploding."

Her hand remained limp, and so he tucked it between his legs where it was nice and warm. And he returned to tease her nipples only this time with his tongue as his hand massaged warmth back into her cold flesh.

He would stop every now and then to threaten or express his love.

"Don't you dare die on me or I'll war with the heavens to get you back."

Still she didn't stir.

"Damn it, woman, I love you and I will not surrender you to death. You belong to me; death cannot have you."

He continued with his touches and his tirades until

with a sigh he leaned his brow to hers and said, "Voiceless or not, I love you and I always will. You are mine; you belong to me."

He felt her stir then and he saw her eyes flutter and he gently slipped over her and into her, his thrusts tender as he continued to stir her back to life. Her body began to respond, and he felt warmth return to her limbs. Relief spread through him and he grew harder knowing that each thrust was like a breath of life to her, so he continued feeding her breath after breath until...

Dawn's body bucked against the exquisite heat that she couldn't get enough of. It chased away the frigid cold that had frozen her. She had feared that she would never move again until little by little warmth had begun to creep inside her. Slowly at first, until it spread into the coldest regions of her body and she began to feel life return to her limbs.

A shot of warmth penetrated her darkness. A kiss. Warm lips pressed against her cold ones. Familiar lips. Cree's lips. She wanted desperately to respond, but at the moment she couldn't. The bitter cold bit down to her bones, and she couldn't move. She had to regain her strength and chase away the iciness that froze her. And those lips were helping to do just that. And those hands? Lord, if they didn't spark a fire that began to spread rapidly.

She swallowed the silent moan that radiated throughout her body as something warm and wonderful and deliciously intimate worked its way inside her ever so determinedly. She had to wake up. She had to. She fought against the darkness and the cold that was slowly fading away. Then finally when she felt a thick hardness slip into her and move ever so gently, she managed, with a struggle, to open her eyes.

Cree was staring at her, a scowl coupled with a smile on his face. "Come for me," he whispered and squeezed her mouth open so that his tongue could dart in and drive her crazy, turn her hot, and make her want to come repeatedly.

His tongue thrust as he thrust, and she managed to move one hand and press it against his muscled arm as she tried to match his rhythm, but without success, her body still too stiff from the cold.

He drew his mouth away from hers and whispered in her ear, "Slow and easy, Dawn, until I thaw you completely."

That sounded good to her, for it was truly difficult for her to move. Besides, she was enjoying being thawed. While her climax was building and making her feel incredibly warm and wonderful, she also felt drained and thought of how delightful it would feel to fall asleep safely in Cree's strong arms.

Her climax sent a shot of heat down to her very core and the second one that quickly followed flamed it even further until it consumed every pore in her body. The third one left her spent and unable to move.

"Dawn?"

Cree's voice was gentle and filled with concern.

She opened her eyes, though she did not want to. She much preferred to go to sleep.

"Answer me or I will throttle you?" he snapped with a brush of his hand along her brow.

She grinned wide and nodded, no doubt looking foolish, but she didn't care. She felt warm, comfortable, and safe. She was with the man she loved. Her eyes suddenly widened, realizing where she was and that she had just made love with her husband. How had she gotten there? Had her husband found her?

"Surprised to find yourself here, naked in my bed?"

She spotted a hint of anger in his dark eyes, but it did not disturb her, since love shined more strongly in them. She nodded, then wrinkled her brow and shrugged.

"Want to know how you got here, do you?"

She nodded again and tapped his chest.

"No, it wasn't me who found you. It was Torr and thank God he did. Whatever were you thinking?"

She shivered, though not from his snappish tongue. He had slipped to her side and the absence of his warm body left her feeling chilled.

"Damn," he muttered and quickly tugged her naked body against his, tossing his leg over hers and pulled her close. Then he yanked the blanket over them, tucking it tightly against her back and over her shoulders.

She shivered once again, though this time from the blessed warmth that began to return.

"Why did you do such a foolish thing?" he admonished.

She had to wiggle herself a bit loose from his tight hold to tap his chest, and then her own before shaking her head.

Cree shivered this time, for he not only understood her perfectly, he felt the same. "You don't want to be without me."

She nodded, reached for his hand and entwined her fingers with his, as if locking them together. She then patted his chest and her own and tapped their entangled hands.

"Always together."

She nodded again, a smile slowly surfacing. She

pointed at him and then to herself and shook her head.

"Never apart."

Her smile spread. He understood her as easily as if she had spoken the words.

Cree felt the same as she did. He never wanted to be parted from her. Not only would he miss her terribly, he would worry that no one could protect her as well as he could. But she could not always go with him. There were times, though he hated to admit it, that they would have to be apart.

Seeing a scowl surface on his handsome face, she pressed a finger to his temple and shrugged.

"You want to know what I'm thinking."

She bobbed her head.

"I would spend every day of my life with you if it was possible, but we both know there will be times—"

She pressed a finger to his lips, then she made a circle in the air with her finger, pointed to him, then her, jabbed it straight down a few times, and then took his hand and slipped it down between their naked bodies to press against her stomach.

"You're concerned with here and now and the babe."

Nodding, she released a silent sigh.

"I promise you that I will be there when our babe is born."

Dawn was well aware that when Cree gave his word, he kept it. He would be there with her for the birth of their child. The problem was how to keep him with her until then. It wasn't that she couldn't survive without him, or could she? He had become like taking a breath to her and when breath ceased so did life. Or perhaps it was that she had finally found love and couldn't bear the thought of losing it. She didn't know what had suddenly made her feel so connected to Cree that she didn't want to be without him. She only knew that the feeling had overwhelmed her, and she intended to pay heed to it.

She reiterated how she felt about them not being apart, at least for now, by pointing to him, then to her, and then locking two fingers together and nodding adamantly.

Cree knew Dawn well. She had an independent nature, going off on her own to do as she pleased, even though there had been times he had warned her against it. So her insistence that they presently remain together did not make sense to him.

He was about to argue the point with her when she shivered again. Their discussion had had him completely forgetting the ordeal she had been through. The debate could wait until another time, though that time would be not far off. He had to go after his sister and bring her home safely, and Dawn would not be accompanying him. He would have Torr and a few warriors escort her home at daybreak, whether she liked it or not.

"You need to keep warm and rest," he ordered, his hands already busy rubbing her back from her neck down to her bottom.

She nestled her face against his chest, and he felt her chest expand against him in a heavy sigh.

It wasn't long before sleep claimed her as he expected it would after what she had been through. Her skin was no longer cold and that was due mainly to the heat of his body, which was why he hated to leave her side. He had no choice though, he needed to see about the message from the King and explain to Torr that he would be returning Dawn to the keep.

He could sneak out before she woke, leaving Torr

to deal with her protests. That, however, was not his way. His word was law and he had made that clear to everyone when he had taken over the Village Dowell. Dawn, like everyone else, would obey his command; she had no other choice.

After slipping into his garments and donning his fur-lined cloak, he went in search of Torr. The snow had eased, though continued to fall. Two large fire pits had been constructed not far from the cottage and smaller ones burned just inside the two lean-tos. His warriors were keeping warm and filling their bellies in preparation of tomorrow's full day ride.

He spotted Torr at one of the fire pits and went to join him.

Torr stood when he saw Cree approach. "My sister is well?"

"She is much improved and sleeping soundly."

The worry creases on Torr's face eased and he nodded. "This is good. I feared that I may have been too late."

"I am indebted to you for saving her life," Cree said, taking a seat on the long, thick tree branch someone had placed beside the fire.

Torr joined him, the log creaking under the solid weight of the two men. "You owe me nothing; she is my sister."

Cree did not intend to argue with him. He was more concerned with the message from the King, though he would see Torr compensated when all this was done.

"The message from the King," Cree reminded.

Torr pulled a rolled parchment from beneath his cloak and handed it to Cree. The missive was written in Latin, the King aware that Cree could read and speak the language, though the King did not know that he was adept at French as well, and various Gaelics. His mother had taught him and had warned him to keep his language skills to himself for then he would learn things others did not want him to hear. Her advice had been wise and had saved him on a few occasions.

He read it, and then read it again. It was not what he had expected.

"Something wrong?" Torr asked as Cree's scowl deepened.

"Do you read Latin?"

"I do."

Cree handed the missive to Torr.

Like Cree, he read it once, then read it again, and then read it a third time. He handed the parchment back to Cree without looking at him.

The two men sat staring into the fire, neither saying a word. Then finally Torr spoke, "I will go find Wintra. You best return to the keep."

Cree nodded. "No one—not a soul—is to know anything about this until I say otherwise."

"Agreed."

"Bring my sister home safe," Cree said as if in warning.

"You need not worry; I will see to her care."

The two continued staring into the flames, neither one looking at the other.

Chapter Three

Wintra's eyes shot open and her breath caught in her throat, preventing her from screaming, and screaming was exactly what she wanted to do. She stared at the face only inches from hers and wondered if she was suffering a nightmare. It was as if she was staring at two different men; one a demon and one an angel. A thin scar ran down the left side of the man's face from above his eye to his chin, while his right side was untouched. His eyes were a piercing blue color that sent an icy chill through her and his large hand weighed heavily across her mouth. But it was the size of him covering the length of her that frightened her the most. Even through his garments and fur coverings she could feel his hard muscles. He was a powerfully built man, and she had no chance against him.

"I have come to rescue you."

She couldn't help but crinkle her brow. What did he mean rescue her? She was safe. That had her wondering where Owen was. Had this brute done something to him? The sun looked to have only risen. Had he gone off to hunt breakfast for them or had the man on top of her harmed him? Anger mingled with fear, and she prayed that Owen was all right.

"Your brother sent me."

Cree.

How she had longed to hear those words, though she would have preferred to hear them nine years ago when Cree had dumped her at Glenburgh Abbey and told her that he would return soon for her. She had waited and prayed every day that he would come for her. Every time the abbey's bell had tolled, she would run to the gate, hoping it was her brother. The worst part was that Cree had returned to the abbey a few times through the years, but had refused to take her with him.

Not yet he had said, though had assured her the day would come when they would be a family again. The last two times he had visited the abbey she had told the nuns to tell him to go away unless he was there to take her with him. He had left and hadn't returned. That had been three years ago and she hadn't seen her brother since.

And now within a week's time a band of warriors had arrived at the abbey claiming they were Cree's men there to take her home, only to learn they had no such intentions. Now this man appears and claims Cree sent her. She did not know who to believe anymore.

"You are safe," he whispered slowly moving his hand off her mouth.

Wintra nodded, remaining silent. She needed to find out what had happened to Owen before she attempted to do anything.

Torr slid off her and to his feet in one easy motion, then reached down to assist her up. She took his hand hesitantly, though he couldn't blame her. She only had his word that her brother had sent him and, having been abducted once, she was probably leery of trusting anyone.

Her hood fell back off her head as she got to her feet with a jolt, releasing a mass of honey gold-colored curls. They sprung out around her head giving her a wild abandoned look and that was when Torr realized what a beauty she was. She would certainly catch a man's breath, perhaps rob him of it, her features were so exquisite. And her eyes were the color green of the hills on a bright summer morning.

She kept her voice low when she inquired, "Where is—" She stopped not sure how to refer to Owen, since this man believed him her abductor. She was grateful when he finished for her.

"Your captor is off hunting."

"And the others?" she asked, though there were no others. The men who had helped Owen had bid them farewell yesterday. They were now on their own.

"How many?" Torr asked, wondering why she was lying to him. It had taken almost two weeks to track them in the snow, but he had eventually picked up their trail. He had followed and watched for a few days. He had been surprised when the six men had left them yesterday and even more surprised when he followed her abductor before dawn and found him meeting with another contingent of warriors. He wondered if her captor had been paid to abduct her for someone else and was about to turn her over to him. In which case, he had to get her out of there as fast as possible.

"A dozen or more."

Torr stared at her. Another lie. But why? Unless—the thought hit him fast and he reacted just as quickly. His hand was over her mouth before she could let out a scream.

She struggled, but it was useless against his strength. She tried to elbow him in the ribs and it did nothing but hurt her, having hit rock-solid muscle. She didn't give up though, she continued pelting him with whatever she could; hands, elbows, arms, feet. It was like hitting a stone wall. Nothing affected him. Her efforts only served to tire her out, and fast.

Torr let her throw her tantrum, knowing her strength would dissipate quickly and when it did... He managed to rip a piece off the hem of her tunic and shove it into her mouth before he bound her in her own cloak. He then flung her over his shoulder and hurried into the woods.

It took him a while to reach his horse, having taken the time to misdirect his tracks. He had no doubt that the contingency of warriors had a tracker with them and that he would soon figure out what Torr had done. It would take some time, though, and by then he would be well ahead of them.

Torr draped Wintra over the horse. She almost sent herself flying off the animal, she struggled so much. He caught her before she fell on her head, stood her on her feet, and grabbed tight hold of her face, pinching her cheeks with his grip.

"You're going home with me and that's final. Why you would foolishly go off with such a vile man is beyond me. But you are going home. I will see to that."

Her eyes narrowed, the green color darkening as if a murky cloud had drifted over them.

He scooped her up and once again draped her over the horse, quickly mounting behind her, and when she began to protest, he gave her backside a hard whack. Her head jerked around and she glared at him as if she wanted to kill him.

"Struggle some more, and it will be a good beating you'll get." He brought his hand down on her backside once again to let her know that his warning held merit.

She let out a muffled cry, in anger or concern he wasn't sure, and at the moment didn't care. There was no telling what her foolishness could bring them, and he didn't intend to wait around and find out. He took off, though it was slow going with the snow-covered ground, but it would be the same for anyone who followed. More snow would help cover their tracks and delay anyone from following, but it would also slow his own pace.

Clouds moved in over an already bleak sky by midmorning, and Torr worried that another snowstorm would hit. If it was a bitter one, they would not survive long without shelter. His concern grew along with the darkening sky.

Wintra was so angry that she would have screamed if she hadn't had a cloth stuffed in her mouth. How dare this man raise his hand to her? And why had he called Owen vile? She hadn't known Owen long, but he had treated her well and with respect, unlike the stranger who touched her in a spot only a husband should. Wait until she told Cree what this man did to her.

Cree.

Whatever was she thinking? She did not want to return to Cree. She wanted to be with Owen. She was no longer a young girl, wanting or needing her brother's love and protection. She was a woman grown and would soon be Owen's wife. Cree would have no say over her then. She would be free to live her life with the man she loved and who loved her.

The thought calmed her and she realized that unless she continued to keep calm and give thought as to how to escape, she would be stuck with this barbarian until they reached her brother. And that was an unbearable thought.

It took some doing, but after what seemed like forever, she managed to dislodge the cloth in her mouth. She didn't know if it was the breath she let out or took in that felt the best, though it did not truly matter. It just felt wonderful not to be gagged.

She took a moment to gather her wits, then turned her head up toward her captor. "Please, I will be good, just get me off my stomach."

"I will have your word on that?"

Wintra wondered how true anyone was to their word, since people had given their word to her in the past and had never kept it, except Owen. He had promised he would return for her and he had. He had also promised that he would love her forever and never leave her, unlike others.

"You have my word," she said and would keep her promise to be good, though she had not promised she wouldn't try to escape.

Torr eased the horse to a halt, slipped off, and lifted Wintra off. He held her a moment so that she could get steady footing, then he unwrapped her cloak that he had tucked tightly around her.

She eased her arms out and with a wince gave a stretch.

"No time to ease your aches," he said, his hands clamping onto her waist and lifting her to the horse to sit sideways. With a strong, quick leap, he mounted behind her.

She lost what little balance she had and fell against him. Again she was reminded of his strength when she hit hard muscle.

He quickly tucked her in the crook of his arm to keep her steady and from striking out at him, not sure if he should trust her word. He had yet to discover her true nature and until he did, he would remain cautious.

After having stared at nothing but the snow-covered ground for what seemed like hours, she found herself glancing up at the sky and one look told her that another snowstorm threatened. She did not know whether to be happy or worry. It would certainly slow them down, but it would also make it more difficult for Owen to find them. Then there was her concern about what would happen if Owen caught up with them. She was well aware of how skilled her brother's warriors were and she feared Owen would not have a chance against this brute of a warrior. His scar alone frightened, but she would not let him know that. What she needed to do was find out more about him and why, after all this time, her brother decided to bring her home.

She began with the easiest question first. "What is your name?"

"Torr."

"You must be one of my brother's best warriors to have been chosen to bring me home."

"Your brother has many fine warriors."

"Yet he chose you."

Torr didn't respond. He knew that she was seeking information, and he could not blame her. He was, after all, a complete stranger whether he was one of her brother's warriors or not. Though she appeared to trust his word, it made him understand just how much she trusted her brother. But then who would dare go against the infamous Cree?

After Wintra realized that Torr had no intentions of replying, she asked a question that had been disturbing her. "Why do you think Owen a vile man?"

Torr shot a question back at her. "How did you come to know him?"

Wintra smiled. "Owen stopped by the abbey on occasion, though what business he had there I do not know. He asked to speak with the person who tended the gardens, curious with their abundant harvest. I was introduced to him and with his many visits we—"

"The fool convinced you that he loved you and could not live without you," Torr finished with a snort. "And of course he knows who your brother is."

"What is that supposed to mean?"

"Owen knows your brother will provide you with a favorable marriage chest."

Wintra gasped. "You think Owen is only interested in my brother's wealth."

"His last wife didn't fair too well after he wed her. She died a week later."

"Owen has never been married."

Torr plastered his nose against hers. "He lies. He always has and always will."

"You know him so well?"

"Well enough."

"Well, I know him better," she argued. "He is a good, decent man who loves me."

"If he truly loved you as he claims he does, he would have done right by you and gone to see your brother and formally request that a marriage agreement be made. But instead, he went behind your brother's back and abducted you."

"He most certainly did not. He and his warriors saved me from those who claimed to be my brother's warriors. With the snowstorm and a friend's keep close by, he thought it was best he take me there. Where we could be properly chaperoned until Cree gave permission for us to wed."

Torr shook his head. "Owen probably set up the

whole kidnapping scheme to make himself look good."

"Owen would never do such a thing?"

"Yes, he would. He's not an honorable man."

"Until that can be proven otherwise, I intend to wed him," Wintra said stubbornly.

She was too angry with her brother to think he would be fair with her, though he had been the most wonderful brother until he had stuck her in the abbey after their mother had died. She had wanted to stay with him. He was all the family she had left, and she felt safe with him. But it hadn't mattered how hard she cried or begged, he had refused to take her with him.

It's best you stay here.

His words still echoed in her head, since he had repeated them each time he had visited her. Would he tell her it was best she not wed Owen? She didn't care; she would wed him anyway.

"Cree will provide proof."

"It doesn't matter. I intend to wed Owen."

"That decision isn't yours to make."

Wintra was furious. Having spent time at the abbey and being dictated to, she yearned to make her own choices, to taste freedom, to live her life as she pleased after so many years of restrictions. She had discussed the matter with Owen and he had assured her that once she was his wife, she could retain the freedom she enjoyed. He would not dictate to her like most husbands. She had been overjoyed with the prospect, and if she was truthful with herself it had been what made her decide to wed him. She was all too aware that it was Cree's responsibility to arrange a marriage for her, and she feared being stuck with a husband who would dictate as badly as her brother and the nuns had.

"Cree will have no choice but to agree to a union between Owen and me. After all, we did spend a night alone together."

"You claim to love Owen, yet you would place him in such danger?"

"What do you mean?

"Once Cree hears that, he will assume Owen took advantage of you and quickly kill him."

Wintra clamped her lips shut tightly. She knew that Torr spoke the truth. Her brother would kill Owen if she led him to believe that they had been intimate. It would be up to Owen to convince her brother how much he loved her and that he would be a good husband and treat her fairly. Surely, Cree would listen and give his consent.

"What is meant to be will be," Torr said, as if ending the conversation.

His words tolled in her head. Her mother had said those very words to her once. *What is meant to be will be.* But she felt that that was resigning one's self to fate, and so far fate had not been kind to her. She would much prefer to make her own choices, live her life her way.

She hadn't realized it was snowing until she noticed her cloak was dusted with white flakes. She looked up at the sky consumed with snow and shivered.

"We need to find shelter," Torr said. "I recall there being a croft not far from here. The sooner we reach it the better, since the snow is falling heavier by the minute."

He was right. Even with pine branches beneath her blanket, the cold from the snow-packed ground had crept up to sting her last night and still lingered in her bones. But the further they traveled in the falling snow, the more difficult it would be for Owen to find her. And she was certain that by now he was frantically searching for her, fearing the worse, and blaming himself for not being there to protect her.

If she could escape and retrace her steps before the snow got bad, she was certain she would meet up with Owen along the way. And even if Torr found them, it would be better for Owen and her to face Cree together.

But how to get away from Torr?

Torr remembered the cottage being near a stream and so he kept his eyes focused on their surroundings. When he finally spotted the water, he guided his horse passed the trees to follow alongside the edge of an embankment.

"I need to stop," she said, assuming he would give her privacy to see to her needs.

"Can it not wait?"

"No, you rushed me off this morning before I had a chance to see to my needs. I cannot wait any longer."

Torr grumbled beneath his breath as he brought his horse to a halt, slid off, and reached up to help her down.

Wintra turned to hurry off when he grabbed her arm.

"I will be going with you."

Her eyes turned wide. "You cannot mean that. I need privacy."

"I will turn my back."

That would not do. He would hear her hurry off and be on her in no time.

"Hurry, the snow worsens by the minute."

He was right. It was now or not at all. If she gave

him a good shove, there was a chance he'd lose his footing and fall and tumble down the embankment. And if she was lucky, he would roll into the stream. Then he would have to seek shelter immediately and get dry before he could do anything, giving her time to make her escape.

Feeling her plan would work perfectly, she pretended to turn, though dug her boots into the snow as she whipped around and gave him a hard shove.

He stumbled, his arms flailing in the air as he fought to regain his balance, and she turned to take off. Suddenly his hand latched onto her shoulder and the movement must have caused him to lose his balance completely, since he went tumbling back, and she was propelled right along with him.

They tumbled down over snow, Wintra trying to push him away as their bodies became entangled. And then they hit the ice cold water.

Torr got to his feet fast once in the stream, wiping the water from his eyes to look for Wintra. She was a few feet away and he hurried over to her and grabbed her by the arm, hoisting her to her feet. She spit and spurted water, having suffered a worse dunking than he had. And it served to anger her even more.

She struggled against his hold, and his cold, wet hand had trouble keeping hold of her. She slipped out of his grasp and when she did, she turned to run, slipped and went down again. Only this time her head hit a rock, knocking her out cold.

Torr muttered several oaths when he saw that she wasn't moving, and he was at her side in an instant. The water around her head was turning red and he hurried to turn her over. Blood ran down the side of her face from what looked to be a head wound. He gave it a closer look and saw that the blood came from a gash at the edge of her scalp. It didn't look too bad, though he couldn't be sure. What he was sure about was that he had to get her out of the water and out of her wet garments and warm or she'd freeze to death in no time.

He shuddered, an icy cold chill running through him. He was wet as well and could just as likely freeze to death if he didn't do something soon. He lifted her, his arms already beginning to feel stiff and draped her over the horse, took the reins, and began walking.

The snow blinded his vision. He had to squint to see a few feet in front of him. He sniffed the air, hoping to smell the scent of chimney smoke, but there was nothing. If he hadn't walked into the broken down lean-to, he would have passed by the cottage.

The lean-to had barely enough room to shelter his horse, but at least it was something. He took his bedroll and flung it over his shoulder, and then lifted Wintra off the horse, hoisting her over his other shoulder and followed the edge of the house to the front door. He pushed at it with his shoulder, since it was partially open and walked in.

The place was empty and had been for some time. There was no one to greet them. No one to help them. No fire to get them warm. He kicked the door shut, placed Wintra on the narrow rope bed with a sparsely stuffed mattress and went to work setting a fire in the cold fireplace. He snapped pieces off already broken furniture, the shards making perfect kindling. Soon, he had a roaring fire going.

He hurried out of his clothes, leaving them at the fire's edge so that they would dry as quickly as possible. He then went over to Wintra and grabbed the two ends of the bottom of the narrow bed and dragged it in front of the fireplace.

The heat of the fire licked at his cold flesh and he didn't care if he got scorched, he wanted to get as close as possible, though he knew the warmth was only surface deep. He and Wintra needed deeper warmth.

He reached out and began to undress her.

Chapter Four

It was the bitter cold that managed to snap her out of the darkness. It had seeped so deeply into her that she didn't think she would ever be warm again. And oh how her head ached. What had happened? Where was she?

It all came flooding back in an instant and the memories flashed through her mind of her failed escape, landing in the cold stream, the struggle with Torr, and the hit to her head.

She suddenly felt hands at her garments. Someone was tugging at them. What was he doing? What did he want? Panic rose and she fought madly to open her eyes and escape the darkness, only to face what?

Fear crept over her like icy fingers pinching her skin and her eyes sprung open. She grabbed the hand before it could touch her again. Her eyes quickly followed the hand up along a naked arm, over a naked chest, to a familiar face. Torr sat completely naked on the bed beside her.

Her panic soared, almost choking her.

Torr yanked his hand free of her pitiful grasp and seeing the fear in her eyes sought to assure her. "We need to get warm. That means getting you out of those wet garments."

It took Wintra a moment to understand what he was saying. Her hesitation made her realize that her mind was not as sharp as it should be, and she also realized that she was barely able to feel her legs. She knew all too well what could happen if one was caught in the cold too long. It had happened to a traveler who stumbled upon the abbey during a winter storm. Several limbs had turned black and he had eventually died.

But the consequences of being naked and alone with Torr also weighed heavily upon her. Owen could refuse to wed her. And she didn't want to think of what her brother would do. Death actually might be more preferable.

She pushed his hands away. "The fire will warm me and dry my garments."

"Not likely. You need to rid yourself of them and get warm." He stood and held out his hand. "Let me help you get out of those clothes."

She bit at her lip that was beginning to quiver uncontrollably and couldn't help but stare at his naked body only inches away from her, though she properly kept her eyes above his waist. He was all muscle, not an ounce of fat. The men who had stopped at the abbey through the years were never sculpted as he was. Every cut and curve defined his muscles as did the light from the flickering fire. She tried to avoid looking at his private parts. The nuns at the abbey had warned her that the only naked man she was permitted to look upon was her husband and that was only when he bid her to do so.

When ill travelers had stopped at the abbey seeking help, she had been forbidden to help tend or even see them until they were well, out of bed, and walking about. Of course watching the animals had given her some indication of how a man was built, but she had always been curious and with Torr sculpted so magnificently she couldn't resist—she had to take a peek.

The peek turned into a glaring stare so shocked was she by the size of him. It protruded from between his legs thick, large and hard. How could something that large fit in... Heat rushed to stain her cheeks.

"Keep staring at it with that hungry look and you'll find it inside you fast enough," he warned.

Her head snapped up, her eyes turning wide.

"I am an honorable man, but that doesn't mean my body doesn't react to the sight of a beautiful woman."

Beautiful.

A word she had grown tired of hearing. No one had paid her heed when she was young, but as she showed signs of becoming a woman everything had changed. The nuns had warned her that men would seek her for her beauty and women would hate her because of it. The only compliment about her beauty she ever cherished was from her brother. He had returned to the abbey after not seeing her for three years and when he laid eyes on her, he had stared and said nothing for several moments. Then he had taken her hand and told her that she was as beautiful as their mother had been. He had brought tears to her eyes, for the three of them had been such a loving family, and she missed them so badly.

Even Owen's thoughtful expressions of her beauty had not meant much to her and had made her wonder if a man would ever see more than only her beauty.

"Though your stubborn nature does mar your beauty at times," Torr said.

That had her slapping his hands away when they reached out to help her as she struggled to get to her feet. "I am not stubborn."

"So say you as you prove my point."

"You are insufferable," she argued, while continuing to struggle to her feet.

"You will wear yourself out if you don't let me help you," he warned, "and then I'll be left to undress you on my own."

"You will do no such thing. I will dry my clothes, while they remain on me, in front of the fire." She had finally gotten to her feet and the icy chill that shot through her made her shudder. She took an unsteady step, her arms stretched out in front of her, her palms up as if warding someone off, and took two more cautious steps to the hearth.

She pulled her hands back, the heat so hot it felt as if it scorched. She crossed her arms and squeezed them tight to get some warmth and water gushed from her soaked garments.

"They need to come off," Torr said, stepping up beside her, though not laying a hand on her. He turned his bare backside to the flames and smiled. "Naked and getting warmer by the minute."

The truth of his words hit her hard, and she hated him at that moment. Her garments were much to wet to expect them to dry quickly, which meant she would remain chilled much too long. If she wanted to survive, she had no choice but to strip them off and get dry and warm.

"Turn around and do not look," she demanded.

"You bark orders like your brother."

"Then obey me as you would him."

"Get those clothes off fast or I will," he said with a growl and turned.

Wintra didn't doubt for a moment that he would do as he said, so she got busy. She discarded her cloak to the ground in front of the fire. Then she sat on the chair braced against the end of the stone fireplace and tugged off her leather shoes. Once finished, she hurried to stand and struggled out of her tunic, the wet linen stubborn, not wanting to let go of her. After finally getting it off, she draped it over the chair and realized that her chill had grown worse. It seemed that with each garment she removed, she grew colder.

Her hands trembled as she attempted to undo the ties at her chest, the wet wool tight and unbending. She held out her hands to the fire for a moment, and then tried again. No matter how she struggled, the obstinate ties refused to budge.

She grew colder and more frustrated.

"That's it," Torr said turning around.

"You cannot—"

"Cree's sister or not, you don't give me orders, Princess." He slapped her hands away from the tenacious ties.

"I am not a princess."

"Then quit acting like one," he snapped and went to work on the wet ties. It didn't take him long to realize that the wet and cold had fused them together and until they dried they would be staying as they were. And there was no point in trying to slip the garment over her head, since it clung to her body as persistently as the ties. There was only one way to get it off her.

Torr grabbed hold of the neck and yanked. It took a couple of good tugs to split it far enough down where he could strip the rest of it off her.

She stood shivering, and threw her arms across her breasts, her green eyes bright with anger. "That is the only garment I have with me," she said, her teeth beginning to chatter as she spoke.

He muttered several foul oaths and grabbed her

around the waist to turn her around to face the fire. He planted her back against his front, then he shoved her hands away from her chest and began to massage her body as the heat from the roaring flames began to lick her chilled flesh.

The shock of his large hands on her naked body stunned her, and it took a moment before she could find her voice. By then, she realized heat was beginning to spread through every part of her, chasing the chill.

Between her beauty and her stubbornness, Torr didn't know how he would keep his sanity. Then there was her body. Damn if it wasn't perfect. Her firm breasts spilled over in his hands, her waist narrowed to curve over generous hips and her firm bottom begged to be squeezed. Before he had turned her around, he had gotten a good glimpse of the thatch of honey- colored hair between her legs. It sparkled from the fire's light, as if beckoning him to enter and explore.

He had to force himself to concentrate on what needed to be done—get them warm, though if he didn't control his salacious thoughts and desires he would have them both scorching hot in no time.

Torr kept his hands moving up and down the front of her, massaging every ounce of flesh and lingering where she was coldest to the touch. Her nipples were as hard as stones, and he had to fight not to give them a squeeze and fight even harder not to turn her around and suckle them. The thought did have merit. It certainly would warm her blood, since the thought of it was warming his.

He had to do something to distract his thoughts that were anything but honorable, so he turned her around to press her breasts against his chest, foolishly thinking that if he couldn't touch them his ache just might ease. After all, what damage could be down by simply massaging heat down along her back and bottom?

More fool he, since every time he ran his hand over her soft, chilled bottom he had to fight not to cup it and push her up against his growing arousal. What the hell was he thinking? He was far past an arousal. He was hard as a rock and aching so badly that he was getting dangerously close to pushing her down on the bed and laying claim to her. The thought of the bed broke his wicked musings, and he grasped at the chance to step away from her.

His hasty departure startled her, and she lost her balance. He reached out and steadied her with a hand to her arm until she gained firm footing.

"Can you stand a moment while I see to the bed?" he asked.

She nodded, though wasn't sure if she could stand without his help or was it that she was disappointed that she had lost his heat? Or was it his heat she missed? She made herself stand firmly on her own and refused to allow herself to think about his touch. Whatever was the matter with her? She barely knew this man, and her mind and body had turned completely weak and submissive to his touch? Was she absolutely insane? She shivered at the thought rather than the cold.

Torr mumbled a few choice oaths when he saw her shiver. He hurried and flipped the lumpy mattress over to a dyer side, unrolled his blankets, arranged them on the bed, and then turned, scooped her up, laid her gently on the bed, and climbed in beside her, pulling the blanket up over them.

Wintra warned herself to keep her distance, but

Torr had no such thought in mind. He grabbed her, resting her back against him so that their bodies could share the heat. He also draped his leg over hers, tucking them between his two.

She tensed when his arousal poked her backside, and she tried to wiggle away from it.

He gave her body a yank and warned, "Lie still or suffer the consequences."

He needn't tell her twice, she immediately stilled, not moving the slightest bit.

Torr would have loved to massage the cold spots that lingered on her body, but that wouldn't be a wise move. He would let their bodies' heat finish the chore of warming them.

It wasn't long before warmth began to take hold, linger, and spread. With the cold easing and her body beginning to relax, Wintra noticed that her head hurt. She raised her hand to touch where it pained her, but Torr grabbed her wrist before it could reach her face.

"Do not touch there," he warned. "You have a wound at the edge of your scalp and the frigid air stopped the bleeding. If you touch it now, you may start it up again."

Wintra lowered her hand once Torr released it, tucking it back beneath the blanket.

"After we're sufficiently warm, I'll see to the wound for you."

"I can see to the wound myself."

"As you say."

"Why did my brother send you?" Wintra asked, needing to get her mind off the fact that she was lying in bed naked in the arms of a stranger. Besides, she was curious as to why out of all his men, Cree chose Torr for the chore.

"I am the best looking," Torr said.

"Cree would have sent Sloan if looks mattered. No, your scar tells me that you are a seasoned warrior with more than fine skills. My brother evidently respects and trusts you with the chore of returning me to him safely and untarnished."

She was not only tenacious; she was perceptive as well. And she reminded him that he should not take advantage of their present situation.

"But then my brother is greatly feared, and there are few—if any—who would dare challenge him."

"That makes me wonder why that fool Owen would even think to try," Torr said. "Cree would never let you wed such a man."

"Owen loves me. He rescued me from my abductors and has seen to my safety. He has been nothing but honorable."

"Spending the night alone in the woods with you is not honorable."

"And you being naked in bed with me is?"

"Now there's a question to ask yourself. What will Cree do when he discovers that you spent a night alone with Owen and the next day naked in bed with me?"

Chapter Five

Wintra would have bolted out of the bed if Torr hadn't had such a firm grip on her. It would be one thing for Cree to discover that she and Owen had spent a night alone together. It would probably be the very thing that would have him grant permission for her and Owen to wed. However, discovering that she and Torr had been naked in bed together was an entirely different matter. And with her touting how kind and honorable Owen had been, would Cree have no choice but to force a marriage between her and Torr?

"Don't worry I will confirm that Owen was a perfect gentleman and slept on the opposite side of the campfire from you."

"How would you—" The thought startled her silent for a moment, and then she swatted his arm that hugged her stomach. "You were spying on us."

"That I was, so I will be able to confirm that nothing improper happened between you and Owen."

"Nothing improper has happened between us," she snapped.

He laughed. "We are naked in bed together."

"To save our lives."

"And your brother will want to save your reputation."

"He can easily do that by granting permission for Owen and me to wed," Wintra said, though had her doubts.

Torr pressed his cheek to hers. "Owen is not in bed with you naked, *I am.*"

Wintra gave his rib a good jab with her elbow, though it did not seem to bother him in the least. "You would force me to wed you? And you claim to be honorable?"

"I would not force you to do anything unless..."

"Unless what?" she demanded.

"Unless you were too stubborn to see that it was best for you."

With a sharp, unexpected wiggle, she managed to loosen his grip and with a swift turn of her body, faced him. "Too stubborn? What is best for me? And, of course, just like my brother, you would know what is best for me."

"I would."

"You are so sure?"

"Absolutely, and I can prove it."

"Please do."

He brought his face close to hers. "It was best we remained back to front in bed or else the temptation of your hard nipples pressing into my chest and your lips, so damn rosy and plump for kissing would be too damn hard to ignore. And once I started kissing you, I wouldn't stop and you would not want me to stop. Then we would have a much bigger problem."

His warm breath fanned her face and tickled her senses, or was it his words that had her senses befuddled? Why did her skin tingle? She had never experienced such odd sensations with Owen, but then Owen had never even held her hand. Surely, she would feel the same if—

"Oh," she sighed when suddenly an exquisite throb started between her legs. She had felt it on occasion and had talked with one of the nuns about it, thinking there had been something wrong with her. The nun had explained that it was a wicked feeling and that she must ignore it. *Never.* Never must she surrender to it. The only time surrender was permitted was when she wed and wanted to make a child with her husband. She had wondered if they had told her the truth, and then one day a woman, round with child, had come to the abbey. The nuns had told her that the woman had not ignored the wickedness when it had hit her, and she was now carrying a bastard child. Her family sent her away to have the babe, and the babe would be given to a peasant family to raise, and she would be forced to take her vows at the abbey. The birth had been a difficult one and the woman and child had died. The nuns had said it was for the best.

It had upset Wintra for she found it a constant battle to fight the wicked feeling that so often overcame her. She had gotten on her knees and prayed, each and every time the feeling had snuck up on her, until it went away, though it had returned again and again. She had done a lot of praying on her knees. But this—this—felt so heavenly that she could not understand how it could be considered wicked.

His lips brushed hers and the throb increased.

"One taste, just one taste," Torr said more to himself than to Wintra. He had warned himself against it, but he couldn't resist. He needed just one taste to satisfy his curiosity, and then it would be done. He brushed his lips across hers, and damn if they didn't intoxicate. He had to taste her, he simply had to.

As soon as his lips touched hers the throb turned to a merciless beat and the nuns' endless warnings echoed in her head.

Wicked. Wicked. Wicked. Stop!

"Stop!" It was as if the word shot from her mind to her lips.

Torr snapped his head back, her sharp yell feeling like a stinging blow.

"Do not kiss me. Y-y-you have no right," she said stumbling on her words while her chest heaved heavily.

He was no novice when it came to kissing or making love to women. He could tell when a woman was willing and when passion had taken hold of her. Passion had budded in Wintra, but he was not the man she loved.

She turned around without saying a word and lay still. She was relieved that Torr did not reach out and touch her. She feared that if he did she would surrender to the wickedness. And for a moment the memory of that poor woman's continuous cries of pain as she tried so hard to bring her babe into the world surfaced to haunt and warn.

What also disturbed her was the thought that she had been about to surrender so easily to Torr, a complete stranger. Was she one of those women the nuns told her about? The ones who would succumb to the wickedness and spread their legs for any man, even complete strangers?

Wintra hurried to silently recite prayer after prayer. As she did, she began to shiver, not from the cold, for she was still warm from his kisses, but from fear of how she so easily could have surrendered to this man. Another shiver, a stronger one, hit her, thinking of how horrible the consequences could have been. And she promised herself she would never, ever let it happen again.

By how stiff she lay beside him, Torr knew she

would not want him to touch her. But she had shivered too often and this last one had quivered her body much too hard. She still held a chill. She needed warming.

He reached out and grabbed quick hold of her, securing his arms over hers as he drew her back against him. She struggled as he expected she would, and he rested his legs over hers to stop her from thrashing about.

"Stop!" he ordered sharply. "I will do nothing but hold you, so that we both stay warm."

"I have your word on that? My brother's warriors are expected to honor their word. I expect the same."

"You have my word."

The tenseness left Wintra's body, though a spark of it remained. Torr hadn't expected anything less. She trusted him only to a point. It was good that she did, for he did not trust himself. She enticed like no other woman, something he hadn't expected.

"Why do you love, Owen?" he asked to his own surprise.

It surprised her that she struggled for an answer. Why did she love Owen? He had been kind and good to her. He paid her attention when most didn't, and he talked with her as if he was interested in what she had to say. But since there was no one to talk with about falling in love, she wasn't sure how she was supposed to feel when falling in love.

"Can why you love someone be explained that easily?" she found herself asking.

"Love grabs the heart and won't let go no matter how much you fight it."

"You know this from experience?"

"From what I've observed."

"You have never been in love then?" she asked

and wondered why she should be so curious.

"No, love has never struck me, though I wouldn't mind if it did."

"You wish to fall in love?"

"I do, and I hope it is at least half as strong as the love your brother has for Dawn, his future wife."

Wintra found herself speechless for a moment, and then questions poured out. "My brother has fallen in love? He is going to wed? Who is this woman? What is she like? Does she love my brother as he loves her? I cannot believe this."

"Believe it. Your brother has fallen in love with my sister and will wed her soon. Dawn is a kind, loving, wonderful woman and your brother is lucky to have found her. And he is lucky that she loves him."

"My brother is a good man," Wintra snapped defending Cree, though at the moment she was angry with him or was it more disappointment that she felt. Now she understood why he hadn't come for her himself. He was too busy being in love to bother with his sister. She was surprised he had not suggested that she take her vows and remain at the abbey. This way she wouldn't be in his way, interfere with his life, or be more trouble than she was worth to him.

Her heart felt heavy. She loved Cree dearly and missed him terribly. She had thought he felt the same. He had repeatedly promised her that they would once again be family, be together, never to part. Now he would have a wife. Would there be room for his sister in his life?

"I agree. Your brother is a good man, and he will see that you have a good husband."

Torr answered the question on her mind without her having to ask it. She and Cree would never be family again. He would find her a husband and send her away—again.

"I have found a good man to be my husband," she said rebelliously.

"It is not your choice to make."

"My brother can find love, but I cannot?"

"You should discuss that with your brother," Torr advised, attempting to delay the inevitable.

"Discuss?" She gave a defiant laugh. "What is there to discuss? I have no say in the matter. It will be decided for me."

I think not. She wished she could have shouted the words at him, but she wisely kept silent. She would not be forced into a marriage with a man she did not know, who she did not love, and who did not love her.

Owen had claimed to love her. After they had become better acquainted, he had begun to hint at his feelings for her. Until one day, he had boldly admitted that he had fallen in love with her. He had struck her speechless, and she had not been too pleased with what he had said in her wake of silence.

"You are virginal in so many ways that I am sure you do not even know that you are in love with me. I see your love for me in your eyes, and I am honored that one so beautiful would love me."

Did she truly love Owen or had she seen it as a chance to escape the abbey that had grown more confining every day?

"Perhaps the decision would be one that will suit you."

Wintra had almost forgotten that Torr lay wrapped around her that was how natural it felt to be in his arms. She sighed, having grown tired of the worry. "The only decision that would suit me is the one I would make myself."

"Be careful that your mulishness doesn't lose you something that may be good for you."

"I know what is good for me," she insisted.

"As you say," he said as if the matter was settled.

"How long before the clothes dry, do you think?" she asked on a yawn.

"Hours. They are well soaked."

"We will be here through the night then?"

"It would seem likely, especially if the snowstorm continues."

Wintra felt weary. She hadn't slept well last night at all, waking often and at every sound. An odd thing had happened though, and she hadn't given it much thought until just now. When she had finally fallen asleep, her eyes heavy with fatigue, something had stirred her awake. Her vision had been bleary, but she had thought she had seen Owen leaving the campsite. It had been a ridiculous thought, so much so that she had fallen back to sleep without worry. Owen would never leave her alone, unprotected. What then had she seen?

She had been foolish not to shake herself awake and make certain Owen had been there. After all, he had gone off in the morning to hunt for food without telling her. But why would he leave in the dark of night? Where would he be going? Unless it had been to relieve himself. Why had not she been more observant? And should she have been so trusting of Owen?

Suddenly, she wondered if it would be wiser of her to return to her brother. Cree loved her, she had no doubt of that, so would he not want to see her happy? Would he not grant her permission to wed a man of her choosing? Owen had all intentions of speaking with Cree and seeking his permission to wed her, so what did it matter if she simply went on ahead and spoke with her brother about Owen? She could have the matter settled before Owen arrived and all would be settled easily.

With her mind at ease and her body exhausted, though toasty warm, Wintra drifted off to sleep.

Torr could feel when her body relaxed and sleep claimed her. It was as if she melted in his arms, as if she surrendered. He chased away the thought of her surrendering to him. His arousal had finally eased and he did not want it returning any time soon. He had always managed to control his desires rather than give them free rein. It was far less troublesome that way. And as far as beautiful women—they were just as troublesome. Add to that stubborn, and you really had a problem. And that problem was lying in his arms right now, and damn if she didn't feel good there.

The heat from their snug bodies had him finally relaxing, his eyes drifting closed, though he came alert when the wind rapped against the door. It sounded as if the snowstorm had intensified, and he worried that they would be stuck there for days rather than hours. He wanted to get Wintra home, so that Cree could settle the problem.

He smiled as he dozed off, wondering how the mighty Cree would fare against his beautiful, tenacious sister.

Chapter Six

Torr inched the door open to take a look. The snow and wind had eased to a trickle. Once their clothes dried they could be on their way. He shut the door and went to test the garments. His were nearly dry, but Wintra's would take a bit longer. He stoked the fire, and then stood warming his hands.

He didn't know how long he had slept, though the fire hadn't died down that much, so it couldn't have been that long. He was anxious to be on his way. He didn't care for the troop of warriors he had seen Owen with. He did not think it would bode well for him if their paths should cross. While he did not doubt his fighting skills, he also did not doubt that he would be outnumbered. His instinct had served him well in battle and he always paid it heed. And presently instinct was warning him to beware of Owen and his intention regarding Wintra.

Another two days, possibly three due to the snow, and they should be home, or at least on Cree's land. Would Owen dare follow there? And how had he reacted when he had discovered that the woman he loved was gone? Torr's own task had been a simple one, bring Wintra home, but had proven far more a puzzle than he had imagined.

Wintra had been abducted and Owen had conveniently rescued her and decided to take her to his friend's home due to the snowstorm. So why send his men away, leaving him and Wintra on their own, unprotected? Unless he knew another troop of warriors were nearby, though why meet with them secretly?

He turned, his glance falling on Wintra. Her wound still needed cleaning, the blood having caked around the abrasion while some blood had dried along her brow. He hadn't been concerned with it, since it had stopped bleeding rather fast, a good sign. He shook his head as he continued to stare. The blood on her face did nothing to distract from her beauty. He wondered if anything could.

He gave his head a firm shake and turned away from her. This was definitely going to be more difficult than he had thought, and not just for him.

"Torr."

He turned, his name having spilled anxiously from her lips, only to find her still asleep.

"Help me, Torr," she whispered even more anxiously.

She was crying out to him in her sleep, seeking his help, but why him and not Owen? He did not hesitate to go to her, slip beneath the covers, and take her in his arms. She snuggled back against him as his arms closed around her.

"You are safe with me and always will be. You have my word."

It was as if her whole body sighed with relief and relaxed once more.

~~~

Wintra woke with a start. It took her a moment to realize where she was and why. She sat up in bed, holding the blanket over her naked breasts, and stared wide-eyed at Torr.

"You are dressed," she said surprised or was she relieved?

"Your garments are still a bit damp."

"How long before they dry, and how long have I slept?" she asked, lifting her hand to her hair, knowing it must look a sight, but then it always did, the mass of curls doing as they pleased.

He was upon her so fast, grabbing hold of her wrist that she did not have a chance to respond.

"Your wound, remember?" he explained.

She nodded and tugged to free her wrist, and he released it without hesitation. He was proving more and more to be a decent man.

"I will get some snow and melt it so I can cleanse the wound for you," he said and turned to see to the task.

Wintra watched him as he scooped up a worn bucket near the fire and went to the door. His muscled frame was now familiar, very familiar, and she found herself intrigued by it. She studied his every movement. His muscles grew taut as he reached and bent just outside the door, and then he stood tall, his shoulders drawn back and his chest expanding. He was delicious.

Delicious?

Whatever was she thinking? It was as if she was salivating over him as she would over a luscious sweet. *Luscious sweet?* Had she gone completely mad? Good lord, she was one of those wanton women who couldn't control herself. She shut her eyes and shook her head. She was a good woman. Then why did she throb between her legs when she looked at him? She would pray. Prayer would save her. And she would not look at him.

"Is something wrong, Wintra?"

Concern filled his voice, actual concern. He may have been ordered to see to her safety, but his concern for her was his own, and it tugged at her heart. She kept her eyes closed as she answered, "Nothing is wrong; I am fine."

Torr stared at her not sure what troubled her, but knowing something did. "Are you sure?" he asked.

Why did he have to sound so sincere? She could not recall Owen ever sounding as sincere as Torr. One day, when she had been upset, Owen had asked if she was all right, and when she had told him she was fine he had simply accepted her response, not so Torr. He had seemed to sense that she wasn't fine and was concerned enough to ask again.

"Somewhat fine," she corrected.

"Open your eyes, look at me, and tell me what is troubling you."

It was not that he was only firm; it was that he was earnest. And so she opened her eyes, though she silently warned herself against it. As soon as she did, she knew it was a mistake. She almost sighed at the look of worry on his face. He cared how she felt; he truly cared.

"Tell me," he ordered as he set the bucket of snow by the hearth to melt.

She could not very well be honest with him and tell him how attractive she found him. So what then did she say?

She found the words spilling from her mouth before she could stop them. "I find you appealing." She gasped and slapped her hand over her mouth. Whatever was the matter with her? Had she lost her mind? But of course she had or she wouldn't have spoken so recklessly.

Torr stared at her, shocked and amused, though he

kept his smile from surfacing.

Before he could respond, she dropped her hand away from her mouth and tried to explain, make some sense of what she had just said, though she wondered if it was more for herself than him. "It must be the bump on my head. I am not myself. I do not know why I said that."

"So you do not find me appealing?" he asked, a serious tone covering the amusing laugh that threatened to erupt.

"I do," she said so suddenly that she once again shocked herself. Only this time she did not cover her mouth; she shook her head. "It must be the bump to the head," she said again as if it explained everything.

"Then let me clean and have a look at the wound," Torr said.

She looked at him oddly and scrunched her brow.

"Are you in pain?" he asked, though did not wait for an answer. "Lie back and let me cleanse the wound." He did not wait for her to comply. He took hold of her bare shoulders and eased her back on the bed.

She had only known this man for a few hours, and she trusted him so easily? Why? It had taken Owen numerous visits for her to even think of trusting him. What made Torr so different? It was at times like this when she had wished that Cree had allowed her to stay with him. Being cloistered in the abbey had limited her knowledge of men and in some ways life itself. She had come to the abbey an inquisitive child and had driven the nuns crazy with all her questions, which most often had gone unanswered. But she had managed to gain a modicum of knowledge from the various visitors to the abbey, though that knowledge had been limited to certain areas, love and intimacy not having been included.

"Deep in thought or in pain?" Torr asked as he began to gently wash away the encrusted blood from her wound.

"Thought," she answered, finding it much too easy to be honest with this man and finding his concerned touch much too appealing.

"I suppose reflection is commonplace for you, having lived so many years at the abbey."

"It can help at times." *Like now*, she thought when she really needed to divert her thoughts from Torr. He occupied her mind much too often when she should be thinking on her problem at hand.

She winced when he rubbed a particular area.

"Sorry. I hit the bump and the small abrasion in the middle. It has crusted well and should heal in no time, though I would recommend not pushing me down an embankment, especially one close to water."

"It was foolish of me," Wintra admitted. "But you must also admit that your sudden appearance and whisking me away as you did, gave me little choice."

"So now your wound and you and I getting drenched are my fault?"

"You are partially to blame."

"I am not even remotely to blame, Princess."

"Do not call me that and you are too, to blame. If you had taken the time to find out that I was with the man I—I—I—"

"*Love*. The man you *love*, which isn't difficult to say aloud when you truly love someone."

"And you will know without a doubt and be able to say it without a doubt when you find love?" she asked, curious that it should be that easy to accept something that important.

He dabbed away the last of the blood off her

wound and dropped the cloth into the bucket, then took hold of her chin. "When I feel that stab in the heart that love delivers, I'll know it, not doubt it for a minute, and I will move heaven and hell to make certain she is mine."

She stared at the determined glint in his piercing blue eyes. He would protect the woman he loved with his life and think nothing of it. Was he like most men or was he unique? She wished she knew more about men and how they thought and how they loved. She felt woefully inadequate when it came to men and love.

At that moment, her stomach embarrassed her by gurgling.

"You are hungry."

"Aren't you?" she asked, knowing he had not eaten since early morning, and she had not eaten since last night. And even then she had not eaten much. She had been too excited or had it been uncertainty that had had her barely tolerating food?

"The snow has lessened, but food will be difficult to find." He reached down by the side of the bed and seemed to rustle around in something. He came up with a small hunk of bread. "This will have to suffice for now." He broke it in two and handed her a piece.

She took it, keeping one hand against the blanket to once again conceal her breasts as she attempted to sit up.

He reached out, his arm slipping beneath her back and easily lifted her to a sitting position.

The warmth of his hand, the strength of his arm, the ease of his motion, the feel of muscle, all served to tickle her senses. It was ridiculous and disturbing that a simple touch from him could stir her body and all but turn her mindless. She had to focus on something else. She could not let herself linger on him, and she especially, at all cost, had to ignore the spreading tingles his touch had sparked.

"Will we be able to leave here today?" she asked, hoping they would.

"It might not be the wisest choice. Your clothes have yet to dry and by the time we get on the road we wouldn't have much daylight left. An early start tomorrow would be best. Besides, don't you want time for Owen to catch up with you? He must be going out of his mind wondering what happened to you and where you are. If the woman I loved disappeared, I would not stop tracking her until I found her."

"What if she did not want you to find her?" she asked with a surly tongue, annoyed that he was once again pointing out Owen's faults and that he was once again right.

He laughed. "Princess, the woman I fall in love with will be so thoroughly loved that she would not want to be away from me for long."

She bristled at the name or was it that she felt a twinge of jealousy that some woman would know such a powerful and dedicated love.

"Would she not find you tiresome after a while?"

He eyed her strangely for a moment before asking, "Have you found Owen tiresome so soon after falling in love with him?"

"No," she snapped, "of course not."

Did she?

The question took her by surprise. There had been times she had not wanted to visit with Owen when he had arrived at the abbey. Did that mean she did not love as him much as she thought she did?

"Your brother cannot stay away from Dawn. They

spend much time together, and Cree is the one that chases after Dawn when they have been separated for just a short time. He claims it is because she has no voice, an affliction she has suffered since birth, and it leaves her more vulnerable than others. But Dawn is brave and has faced dangerous situations with courage and resolve. So everyone knows it is because Cree's love for her is so strong that he cannot be apart from her for long."

Voice or not, if her brother had fallen in love with Dawn, then she had to be special. "And Dawn? Does she feel the same for my brother?"

Torr grinned. "It is unbelievable how much the two love each other. And it is also wonderful to see that such a powerful love can exist and appear to grow stronger day by day."

Could she honestly say that she felt that way about Owen? Perhaps Torr whisking her away been a good thing. Perhaps she needed time to make more sense of whatever it was she felt for Owen. Perhaps she had wanted nothing more than to be free of the confines of the abbey and Owen could provide that. Whatever the reason, she needed to think on it. Given all that had happened, she wasn't sure how she felt about Owen. And that realization disturbed her.

If she had possibly misjudged Owen's character, then how could she trust herself to trust her opinion of Torr's character? She got annoyed at her brother for keeping her secluded for so long. Suddenly, she was eager to see Cree again, for she had a lot to say to him.

"Will you continue to resist me?"

Wintra's eyes widened and she stared at him speechless.

"Resist me escorting you home," he clarified with

a grin.

She felt ready to scream with frustration. She had learned many things while at the abbey, but few if any had truly helped her prepare for a life outside the convent. In the few short hours she had spent with this man, he had opened her eyes to many things. Not to mention he had sparked wickedness in her that she had thought she had under control.

"Do I really have a choice?" she asked, though more to herself than him.

"Did you ask that of Owen? Did he not take your honor into consideration? Did he not give you the choice of returning home to your brother and properly request a marriage arrangement between the two of you? And didn't his rescue seem a bit too convenient?"

"All valid questions, though what of you?" Wintra demanded. "How do I know if you are truly one of my brother's warriors sent to bring me home?"

"As I told you, I am an honorable man. All you need to do is ask."

So Wintra asked, "Are you one of my brother's warriors sent to bring me home?"

Torr leaned close to her, his mouth barely an inch from hers. "No."

For a moment fear gripped her, and then she realized that Torr had mentioned that the woman Cree loved was his sister. "You are not one of my brother's warriors," she said with confidence, "so why did he send you to fetch me?"

"Your wit is sharp—at times."

She chose to ignore his jibe, instead reminding him of her query. "Why were you sent?"

"Your brother had pressing matters that needed his attention, so I volunteered."

She had actually been surprised when Cree had not been with the troop of warriors that had arrived at the abbey to take her home. Cree had always promised her that he would come for her himself. The thought had never entered her head that anyone would be as foolish as to dare pose as Cree's warriors. But she could see her brother sending one warrior to bring her home. A warrior he trusted without a doubt—a worthy man.

"What matters?" she asked curious to know if these matters actually concerned his soon-to-be-wife.

"Orders from the King that required his immediate attention."

Relief tugged at her heart. She was happy her brother had found love, though worried that she did not matter to him anymore. He was all she had after their mum had died. He had always been a good and loving brother and had taught her many things. Thanks to him she could swim, fish—clean and cook the catch herself—and handle a dagger. She had wonderful memories of hot summer days spent with Cree either fishing or swimming, after chores had been done. He had even proclaimed her a better fisherman than he was.

Another tug caught her heart. She had missed her brother very much and was eager to see him.

She startled when Torr gently tapped the tip of her nose and asked, "Lost in thought again?

"Memories this time."

"Good ones?"

She smiled and nodded. "Very good. Cree always treated me well."

"Then there isn't any reason to think that he would do otherwise now, is there?"

He was right. There wasn't any reason to think

that Cree would deny her happiness with the man she loved. He wanted her happy; he had told her that many times. And Cree was a man of his word.

She sighed. "You are right."

He couldn't stop himself from smiling. She may have agreed a bit grudgingly, but nonetheless she had agreed. Could she actually be a woman who saw reason? His smile grew. Stubborn and reasonable? Now that was a strange combination for a woman.

"I am glad you agree. It will make our journey home that less difficult," he said.

"And the sooner we get there the better." She tucked the blanket around her as best she could and struggled to get to her feet.

Torr's hand was at her arm in an instant to help her and once she was steady, and the blanket tucked more firmly, he let her go.

Wintra went over to the chair that held her clothes and felt them. She turned to Torr. "They are dry, except for the hem, but I can sit by the fire once I am dressed and let it finish drying. Turn around," she said with a twirl of her finger at him.

Another smile he could not hide surfaced. "I have seen all of you already. What difference does it make?"

"That could not be helped. This can. Now be a gentleman and turn around."

"Yes, Princess," he said with a gallant bow before turning his back to her, "though if you need any help..."

She gave up on telling him not to call her Princess. Besides, it was beginning to sound more an endearment than an insult.

"I will do just fine," she assured him, then took a look at her torn grey wool dress.

She slipped it on relishing the warmth, though not for long since she realized after fussing with it that the tear down the middle had rendered it useless. "Now what?" she said aloud without realizing it.

Torr turned, and she grabbed the ripped wool to hold it closed as he approached her.

"The tunic will cover it," Torr said, and shook his head, "though the dress will remain open beneath and will not keep you warm enough."

He rubbed his chin, thinking and admiring the bulge of her breasts where her hands gripped the material closed. He couldn't help but recall the feel of them and gave his head a quick shake. That was not something he needed to be thinking about right now, especially since it was beginning to grow him hard.

"A plaid," he said with relief. "We'll wrap one of the plaids around your midsection and with your tunic over it that should serve to keep you sufficiently warm."

With the fire behind her and Torr in front of her, she was presently more than sufficiently warm. It seemed all he had to do was stand close to her and her body got hot and tingly. And worst of all, she was beginning to like the tingles, look forward to them, and grow ever more curious about them. Could the sensation really be as wicked as the nuns had warned about?

"That is a dangerous way to look at me," he whispered harshly, his face close to hers.

"What way?" she asked, not realizing she was looking any particular way at him.

"As if you want to devour me."

"*I do*," she thought, though she heard the words all too clearly and realized she had said them aloud.

"Your choice, Princess," he said and lowered his

lips to hers.

She did not think about it. She met his lips and the tingles running through her sparked a burst that consumed her entire body and kept her lips hungry on his.

Virginal, eager, excited. That was how she kissed him and damn if it wasn't the most delicious kiss he had ever tasted. He let her have her way, though he guided until his patience, or more so their need, grew too great, and then he took control. He slipped his hand down along her back to cup her backside and press her against him. He then urged her up against his hard arousal as his tongue penetrated her mouth and kissed her senseless.

Wintra thought she would die from the sheer pleasure that continued to grow and devour her all at once. She had startled when his tongue had entered her mouth and at first she thought it wicked and she should not allow it, but the pleasure it brought chased away her doubts and fears. Never—*never*—had she ever thought a kiss could be so delicious or that she would not want it to ever end.

Damn, he would have her on the bed and be inside her in no time if he did not stop kissing her. But damn if she wasn't intoxicating. One taste would never be enough, two might not be either, forget three, he did not want to ever stop kissing her.

A whip of wind against the door tore them apart and sent Wintra's stomach roiling in fright. Her hand released the material and pressed at her stomach, and she shivered.

Torr reached out and with a firm arm around her waist to keep her close and a hand to her ripped garment to try and keep it closed, he tucked her against his side.

Before she could snuggle even closer against him, the door burst open.

Chapter Seven

Owen stood there, his eyes quickly taking in the scene and growing ever wider with anger. "Get your hands off her you wretched beast."

Before either of them could say a word, Owen stepped aside and four warriors hurried in, though there was barely room for them. Torr shoved Wintra away from him, though she grasped at his hand as he did, but he yanked it away just as the warriors descended on him.

"You're making a mistake," Torr said, after not resisting the men, though receiving several blows anyway. "Cree sent me to bring his sister home."

Owen stepped forward then. "I am supposed to believe that when it appears as if you have taken advantage of this poor, innocent young woman?"

Wintra stepped forward. "Torr has done no such thing."

"You are young and virginal and know not what you say. I will take care of everything. You have nothing to fear," Owen said and turned as if dismissing Wintra. "Take him and secure him in the lean-to with his horse. It is where animals belong."

"I have warned you," Torr said as they shoved him toward the door. "When Cree finds out, you will pay."

Owen waved him off, and the warriors shoved him so hard out the door that he fell into the snow.

Wintra hurried to go to him, but Owen shut the

door, stopping her in her tracks. She turned furious eyes on him. "You have no right to treat him like that."

Owen ignored her remark and demanded. "What went on here?"

Wintra stared at Owen, seeing a far different man than the one she had come to know. She had thought him a man with fine features, but not so now. His blue eyes, much paler than Torr's vibrant ones, held a murderous look, as if he fought to control himself. His jaw was so taut that his chin appeared to jut out or had it always been that way? He was also slimmer than she had first thought or was she comparing him to Torr and finding him lacking. And his dark hair, always so perfectly groomed, was in complete disarray making him appear a wild man out of control.

"Answer me, Wintra," he yelled.

She took a step back, keeping a firm hold on her torn dress, his eyes having darted to her breasts. Why was it that she felt much more naked and vulnerable in front of this man, she supposedly loved, than she had in front of Torr?

Her answer came easily. Owen stood in front of her with anger oozing out of every inch of him, whereas, she had seen and felt only concern from Torr.

He took a step toward her.

She raised her chin along with her hand to ward him off. "Not another step."

He heeded her warning and remained where he was and softened his tone as he said, "I do not mean to upset you. I just want to know what this animal did to you."

"Torr is not an animal. My brother sent him to

bring me home and that is where I want to go."

"But our plans—"

"Have changed," she finished. "Now let Torr free, and we will all proceed to my brother's home." Her brow scrunched a moment, and then she asked, "Who are those warriors with you?"

"My friend sent them to escort us to his home." His eyes narrowed and his voice turned firm. "And that is where we will be going. Torr can return home and let your brother know that you are safe with me and that I wish to arrange a marriage between us."

Where had his dictatorial attitude come from? Where had the kind and thoughtful man that she had known gone?

"We will stay the night and leave at dawn," Owen said. "The snow has turned to a trickle and should stop soon. By morning, we should be safe to leave." He walked over to her and took her hand.

She had all she could do but to pull it away.

"I will overlook this discretion and see that you do not suffer for it. I doubt that Torr will admit to Cree that he had his way with you, too fearful of what he would suffer. We will wed and put this unfortunate incident behind us." His tone turned harsh and anger punctuated his words. "And you will be grateful and be an obedient wife."

Fool. Fool. Fool. Dear Lord, how could she have been so blind to this man? And worse what did he truly want from her? She had to get home to her brother. Cree would keep her safe from Owen.

So would Torr.

The thought had her thinking. If she could get to Torr without being noticed and free him, they could escape together.

"Did you hear me, Wintra?" Owen yelled and

grabbed her arm, squeezing it so tight she winced. "You will learn not to have your head in the clouds so much when you are my wife. You will obey my commands without question, starting now." His eyes grew wide and he licked his lips. "Show me your breasts."

She was stunned, though she responded fast enough. "I most certainly will not and when my brother hears ab—"

The harsh slap sent her head reeling to the side and instead of fear rushing through her, anger grabbed hold.

"You will show me more than your breasts before this night is over. I will lay claim to you and your brother will not be able to refuse us marriage, for you will be spoiled goods."

"Though not spoiled by you, and I will make certain my brother knows that." Wintra spat at him and blood hit his cheek.

He hit her again, letting go of her as he did. She fell to the ground, and he grabbed a handful of hair, yanking her head back. "When I return, I am going to spend the next few hours teaching you how to be an obedient wife and your first lesson will be," —he pushed his plaid aside and stroked his enlarged member— "to take me in your mouth and learn how to pleasure me, which you will do at least twice a day from this day on or suffer the consequences."

This time he stunned her speechless. How could he expect such a wicked thing of her? Surely, he was perverse and, if so, what other wicked things would he demand of her? She had to get to Torr.

Owen walked to the door saying, "You had better be naked and on your knees when I return or I will beat you senseless."

Wintra stared at the closed door for a moment, and then shook her head. She had no time to think on what a monster Owen was or why she had never realized it. Another reason why being raised the last few years in the abbey had not been a wise choice.

She quickly wrapped the plaid around her midsection as Torr had suggested, then she slipped on her tunic that hung over her one shoulder, and pulled her boots on. She gathered their blankets, rolled them and tucked the roll under her arm to press tightly against her side. Then she slipped Torr's cloak on and placed hers on top of his before scooping up the broken leg chair that waited to be added to the fire and held it firmly in her hand, making certain her cloak concealed it.

She opened the door, expecting it to be guarded by one of the warriors. "I need a moment in the woods." The warrior did not refuse her; she had not thought he would, though it was a chance she had taken. She had concluded by Owen's actions, defender and protector of her honor in front of the warriors, that they were not aware of his evil nature. And she couldn't be sure if they would believe her if she made them aware of his intentions. So her only reasonable choice was to get to Torr.

"Don't you worry," the guard said as she trailed behind him into the woods, "that animal will get what he deserves."

Did they plan on hurting Torr? Did Owen plan on contacting her brother at all? And what had he told these warriors? She suddenly worried not only for her safety, but Torr's as well. She had misjudged Owen badly. And she not only suffered for her foolishness, but others were suffering as well. No more. She would rectify her folly and be more select when it came to trusting men.

"A moment of privacy, please?" she asked when the guard had stopped in a secluded area.

"I can turn around, but I cannot go off and leave you alone. If anything happened to you, Owen would be distraught. He loves you very much."

The thought that Owen had convinced him of that sent shivers through her and more than ever she wanted to get away from him.

"That will be fine," she said and cringed at what she was about to do to this innocent man. As soon as he presented his back to her, she tossed her cloak back off her arm and, with a prayer on her lips that she didn't do any great damage to the man, swung the chair leg as hard as she could at his head.

He went down with a thud. She gave it a moment to see if he moved and when he didn't she took off, reciting multiple prayers for the fallen warrior. She had kept a sharp eye on her surroundings when they had headed into the woods and had mentally planned her route to the lean-to so as not to be seen. She approached, from behind it, cautiously. She did not know how much time she had before she was discovered missing, so she did not want to waste a moment.

Torr was tied with rope to a worn board that he could easily break with one good yank, but if he did the lean-to would collapse on top of him. Only one warrior stood guard in front, facing Torr, as if at any moment he expected him to break free.

He was so intent on his duties and with the snow-covered ground cushioning her approach, he didn't hear her coming until it was too late.

"We have to get out of here," she said stepping over the fallen warrior to get to Torr. She went to work on the rope, her hands trembling as she struggled to free him.

"Look at me."

His demand was so sharp that she responded without thought.

"He hit you?"

"Please, I want to go home." She hated that she sounded as if she begged him, but the thought of what Own would do to her if she did not get free had reduced her to pleading. She returned to working on the rope and once loosened, Torr managed to free himself the rest of the way.

She slipped her cloak off as he did that, and then slipped his cloak off handing it to him and hurried hers back on. She then repositioned the rolled blankets under her arm since they had done a good job of keeping her warm.

Torr untied his horse and with a gentle hand to the animal's face and softly whispered words, he guided the horse out of the lean-to. He cocked his head at Wintra, directing her to follow, and she stayed right on his heels.

When they were not that far from the cottage, Torr stopped and pressed his face to his horse and whispered something, then he tapped the horse on the backside and the horse snorted and hurried through the snow as fast as he could.

It was then they heard the shouts.

Torr scooped her up and flung her over his shoulder, and then he took a leap over a patch of snow into a bush. They both fell to the ground, though Torr was quick to get to his feet and scoop handfuls of snow to dump on the bush. He then grabbed hold of her hand and hoisted her off the ground and had her tucked behind another bush in seconds.

No soon as he did, then Owen and his men came into sight. Even with the distance that separated them, she could see the fury on his face.

"He took her. Get the horses. We go after them," he ordered, his face burning bright red.

It was not long before the whole troop was barreling down the same path that Torr's horse had taken. They waited a bit longer to make certain no warrior lagged behind or returned, then Torr took her hand, and they hurried off.

They walked for hours until finally Torr stopped and announced, "We rest, but just a bit."

Wintra dropped the blanket roll on the snow and sunk down on it.

Torr hunched down in front of her, taking gentle hold of her chin to glare at the swelling at the corner of her mouth. "What happened?"

Wintra didn't know if she could ever tell anyone what Owen had said to her. She was too embarrassed for being such a fool and thinking he loved her, and she would not dare repeat what Owen had expected her to do.

Torr ran his thumb tenderly over her lips and softly urged, "Tell me, Wintra."

There it was again—concern—and not only in his voice, but in his deep blue eyes as well. She found the words spilling out before she could give it another thought. "He told me that I was spoiled goods and that my brother would have no choice but to arrange a marriage between us. And he demanded that I show him my breasts and when I refused he hit me. Then—" She stopped there, not certain that she could say more.

Torr's heart pounded with anger, though he kept

himself calm. He released her chin and once again urged, "Tell me the rest."

"I cannot repeat the wicked thing he said to me, though I will tell you that he ordered me to be naked and on my knees when he returned."

Anger continued to pound at him, though relief that Owen had not touched her pushed some of the anger aside. Owen was going to suffer for what he had done to her and suffer even more for what he had planned to do to her. He would see to it himself and enjoy every minute of it. But at the moment Wintra was more important to him.

"Your quick thinking saved us both. You are a courageous woman."

"Stubborn," she corrected with a smile. "I knew my only chance of escape and survival was to get to you."

Torr leaned closer, his lips not far from hers. "I will always be there for you, Princess, and I promise I will always protect and keep you safe."

Now that she gave it thought, Owen had never spoken about keeping her safe. And recalling what he had said to her about not allowing her head to be in the clouds was just unimaginable to her. Her mind had wandered since she was young. It was a way for her to learn and work things out. She did not know what she would do if that was taken from her.

Why she asked the question of Torr, she did not know. It just spilled out, which seemed to be the way when she was with him. "Do you mind that my head is in the clouds so much?"

"Your deep thoughts," he clarified with a smile.

She nodded and smiled as well, preferring the way he phrased it compared to Owen.

"Owen accused you of having your head in the

clouds?"

She nodded again.

"Owen is a worthless excuse of a man."

"And what am I for not realizing that?"

"An inexperienced, young woman, which is why there are arranged marriages."

She shook her head. "But I do not want someone choosing who I will wed. Do you?"

"Sometimes we have no choice."

She tapped her chest. "I want a choice. I want to love the man I wed."

"And hopefully you shall." He stood and held his hand out to her. "We need to be on our way."

"Where do we go?" She took hold of his hand, and he helped her to her feet.

"We are heading for your brother's land, though a different route than my horse has taken. Once my horse arrives there, they will know something is wrong and come look for us. Hopefully, we will run into them along the way. The problem is that Owen will either backtrack once he realizes he tracks a riderless horse or he will continue to blindly follow the tracks, in which case we will cross paths somewhere along the way. Either way we are bound to run into one another at some point."

"There isn't any way we can avoid him?"

"There is but it would mean going in a completely different direction. Your brother would no doubt worry when he couldn't find us, but—"

"Owen would not be able to find us either and would tire of his search and give up."

"There would be a very good chance of that."

"But what if Owen went to Cree and convinced him my reputation was shattered and that he would wed me regardless?" Wintra cringed and shivered simultaneously.

"Cree would never believe that of me, though I imagine he would believe it of Owen. Then the fool would be in for a whole lot of suffering. Besides, Cree would never decide anything until he has spoken with you."

"Where would we go?" she asked, the idea tempting, but then so was Torr and that could prove a problem.

"There is a vacated croft that would suit our purpose about two or three days from here. No one would think to look there since it is off any well-traveled paths. It is completely isolated."

The two of them completely isolated for a few weeks, possibly a month? The thought sent the tingles racing through her. This was not a wise idea. She should go straight home to her brother even though there was a chance they would run into Owen. If she stayed alone with Torr, there was no telling what would happen. One thing was sure though, she would be doing a lot of praying. No. She needed to be wiser this time. She needed to get home as fast as possible and see this problem settled.

She looked to Torr and her response was much different than she intended. "Take me to the croft."

Chapter Eight

By the morning of the third day, Wintra was certain she was completely and utterly insane. She had no idea what had made her tell Torr to take her to the croft when her mind had been settled on going home to Cree. No matter how she dissected her decision, she could not come up with a sensible answer. Though when she had laid nestled in Torr's arms the last couple of nights in front of the fire he had built to help keep them warm, she knew it was where she wanted to be. The strength of his arms wrapped so securely around her, and the way he had tightly tucked his fur-lined cloak around them both had made her feel safe and...

There was something else about being in his arms that she couldn't quite grasp. It was as if she looked forward to him holding her, being close to him and wondering—Lord help her—she wondered if he would ever kiss her again. Not to mention that her body forever tingled when near him.

"Wintra!" His arm went around her waist, jolting her to a stop.

It took her a moment to focus and when she did, her mouth dropped open. She had been about to walk into a tree. She sighed. Getting lost in her thoughts was not helping her. Of course neither was trudging through the snow and woods for almost three days now.

He turned her around and as soon as he did, she

rested her head against his chest. His hand went to cup her neck and he lowered his chin on the top of her head to nestle in her wild curls.

"Are you feeling well?" he asked.

I am now, she thought. What was it about this man that had managed to turn her life completely upside down in a matter of days?

"Wintra?" he asked again anxiously.

"Exhausted, cold, and lost in thought as usual," she said with a light chuckle.

"Another few hours and we will be there."

Hours? Could she walk several more hours? It would mean finally being out of the cold and snuggling in a bed with Torr tonight. The thought was enough to give her strength, but also send a tingle through her. And begged to ask the question—what was she getting herself into?

"Then we should keep at it," she said, eager, yet anxious.

Torr reluctantly stepped away from her. He did not want to. He had found he liked having her in his arms. She felt good there, tucked snug against him.

He reached for her hand, taking firm hold of it. "I'm going to hold on to you so that you don't run into any more trees."

Wintra smiled. "I need to stay focused."

"It would be a good idea," he said as he tugged her hand so that she moved closer alongside him as they walked. "What keeps you deep in your thoughts?"

She was surprised by his question. No one had ever asked her that. They simply assumed that she drifted off without rhythm or reason. That was far from the truth, and for the first time she was able to admit aloud, "Loneliness."

Torr turned, surprised at her response. "You had an abbey full of nuns to talk with, and what of travelers who stopped?"

"I was not allowed to speak to any of the travelers unless approved by the nuns. And the nuns lead a very restrictive life. Chores, prayers, and caring for those who sought refuge at the abbey take up most of their day. I learned fast enough that my inquisitive nature would not be tolerated. So I had no choice but to seek my own thoughts."

"You can speak to me about anything, any time" Torr said unable to imagine having no one to talk with. There had always been someone to speak with, family or friends. He had never felt lonely. Actually, there had been moments when he wished he had time alone.

"You may regret offering that," Wintra said with a laugh. "You never know what I might talk about."

"As I said, anything, any time."

Would she truly be able to speak with him about anything? The idea was tempting, very tempting. She would have started there and then, curious to learn more about him, but the effort it took to trudge through the snow made it difficult to keep a steady conversation going.

They soon settled into a comfortable silence, and it wasn't until hours later that they reached the croft. Wintra was never so happy to look down from a slight rise to the cottage below. It appeared a sound structure, the door firmly in place and the shutters as well. It reminded her of the croft where she had been born and had spent the first nine years of her life. Years she would forever cherish in her heart and memory, for it was then she had been the happiest.

Torr released her hand once they reached the

cottage door to clear away the several inches of snow in front. Then he opened it and stuck his head in first before turning, stepping back, and allowing her to enter.

The only light came from the open door and the late afternoon shadows were already beginning to claim that.

"There is wood by the fireplace," she said spotting logs in a basket.

"And a good size bundle out here." Torr brushed off snow from a wood stack by the door. "I will get a fire started with the dry wood, and then bring some logs in to dry."

While he set to work, Wintra opened the shutters on the lone window so that they would have more light, and she could have a better look at the place. There was a small table and two chairs against one wall, a couple of buckets sat empty beside the fireplace, and some baskets lay scattered about. A roughhewn bed with a mattress that needed fresh stuffing was pushed against another wall. It appeared as if the occupants had taken most essentials with them.

Once Torr had the fire going, Wintra pulled the shutters closed, securing the latch that kept them locked. Torr then got to work on bringing in a sufficient bundle of wood and stacked it to the side of the fireplace.

Wintra stood by the table out of his way, not sure what to do or if there was anything she could do. She glanced around and realized what close quarters they would be in, and she quickly asked, "How long?"

"The place will be heated in no time."

"No. How long before we can leave here?"

"Three to four weeks should do it. Owen will

probably have gone to your brother by then and, no doubt, will have started digging his own grave." He watched her pull her cloak more tightly around her, as if attempting to shield herself. Something more had gone on when Owen had been alone with her, and he intended to find out just what it was. "We will know each other well by the time we leave here," he said.

"How well?" she asked.

He walked over to her and took her hand in his. "That is up to you, Princess. Now go warm yourself by the fire. Your hands are still ice cold."

How could a simple touch quiver her body and turn her speechless? She mindlessly nodded her head and did as told.

He walked to the door and stopped before opening it. "I am going to see if I can find us some supper."

Wintra found herself staring at the door after he closed it behind him. Why had she agreed to come here with him? Why had she not taken the chance and gone directly home? She was beginning to think that this situation she was in—alone here with Torr—was far more dangerous than crossing paths with Owen and his men.

And she did not want to think of what he meant when he said it was up to her. What was up to her? If she wanted him to kiss her again, would he? If she wanted him to touch her naked flesh, would he? And why was she having such wicked thoughts?

She shook her head. She had to stop thinking about him.

Pure thoughts. Pure thoughts. She reminded herself just as the nuns so often had reminded her.

She decided that the best thing to do was busy herself. When she kept herself busy, her thoughts did not drift—at least not too much—and for a while she was free of the constant musings that filled her head. She slipped out of her cloak, hanging it on one of the three pegs in the wall next to the door. She set about gathering the scattered baskets and seeing if any were useable and arranged those near the door. And soon she was busy with work and for a while, a quiet mind.

Torr's mind would not still and he laughed to himself, thinking that Wintra's deep thoughts were contagious. But any humor quickly faded when his thoughts lingered on his decision to bring her here. He could not say it was truly necessary, but he felt it was a wise choice, and only time would tell if he was right. He was not sure what would happen here between them, but it would give them time to get to know each other, and he felt that was important.

He stomped his feet to rid his boots and leg coverings of snow, then opened the door to the cottage and entered. Once inside, the door closed, he gave two glances around the room while sniffing the air, surprised to see short, portly candles sitting about the room.

"I cleaned some and found several candles, someone thought beyond use, disposed of in a basket," Wintra said, standing near the hearth. "And what you smell is a pleasant brew."

He titled his head in question.

"I had stitched some bundles of my favorite dried herbs in my cloak, and when I found a usable crock I cleaned it, filled it with clean snow, and set it in the hearth. When the snow melted and the water was hot, I added a bundle of herbs so that we would at least have a nice brew to keep us warm."

Torr smiled and held up a sizeable fish. "And I have us a meal." He went to put it on the table, she had moved in front of the fireplace, to clean when she gave a shout.

"No!" She scrunched her nose. "I just scrubbed that with snow. Please, clean it on the hearth stone."

"Fussy where a fish is cleaned?" he asked, but did as she requested after hanging his cloak on the peg beside hers.

"Blame it on the nuns. To keep me busy, they had me scrubbing everything over and over and now I find it a habit to keep things cleaner than most others."

Torr noticed the pleasant aroma wasn't only coming from the brew. When she walked past him, to give him room by the hearth, a sweet scent drifted off her. He also noticed her face appeared freshly scrubbed, her cheeks rosy, and her hair a bit more tamed than usual. And damn if she didn't look more beautiful than ever.

When he finished cleaning the fish and setting it to cook in the hearth, he took the remains outside to dispose of and to scrub his hands with snow, wishing they smelled a bit more pleasant.

He got his wish when he returned inside.

"I've kept a bucket of sweet-scented water warm for you to wash up if you would like," she said, pointing to a bucket on the table.

Stubborn, reasonable, and now thoughtful, she had a diverse nature, and he liked that.

He scrubbed his hands good and rinsed his face, surprised by how nice he smelled when he finished. After he emptied the bucket outside, he joined Wintra at the table where she had taken a seat.

There was an awkward silence for a few moments, and then Torr decided to ask the question that had been playing havoc with his thoughts, though not before he reached out and placed his hand over hers. "What exactly happened with you and Owen in the cottage?"

His touch offered comfort, his voice concern, but she was not ready to share the details of her encounter with Owen just yet. Besides, she did not want to think about it right now, and she found it easy to tell him that. "I would rather not discuss that now."

"But you will tell me?"

Would she or would she be too embarrassed? She almost laughed. How more embarrassed could she be after having been naked in front of him? Still, though, she feared she would need an extra ounce of courage to discuss it with him.

"You hesitate to answer. Why?"

"It will not be an easy thing for me to discuss with you."

He squeezed her hand reassuringly. "There isn't anything you cannot discuss with me, Wintra. I want you to remember that. Come to me with anything, now and always."

Always. But there would not be an always between them and oddly that left her with a sad ache in her heart.

He slipped his hand off hers, and a chill ran through her. She liked his touch, simple or intimate, it didn't matter. It always felt so wonderful, magical, unbelievable.

Don't fall prey to a man's touch and false promises. Put your trust only in your husband.

The nuns' warning struck her like a cold splash of water in the face. Was she to believe that Torr spoke falsely to her just as Owen had? Was she not to trust any man? And how did she only trust the man who would be her husband when she would not know him at all?

94

"I know that look. You are sinking deep into thought."

The question came too quickly to her lips for her to stop it. "Can any man be trusted?" She was surprised and curious that he laughed.

"That is a question pondered by many."

"Then how do you trust?" she asked perplexed.

"You trust yourself first and you take a chance."

"Your answer confuses more than explains."

"Do you trust yourself, your instincts, your thoughts?" he asked.

She thought a moment, then shook her head. "I never gave it thought."

"Did you trust Owen?"

She opened her mouth to answer and stopped, thinking the question over. There had been remarks he had made that had annoyed her and made her wonder about his true nature. And she shared her revelation with Torr. "Now that I think about it, I would say no, I did not trust him. I suppose I failed to pay attention to my own instincts."

"Most of us do from time to time, though we either learn or continue to remain ignorant to our own trust. And then, of course, there are times we allow passion to overrule all else."

Wintra could not help but think of the poor woman who had died in childbirth at the abbey. She had trusted a man or had it been love she trusted and believed in and in the end it had failed her. She had died along with her baby, unloved.

She was quick to ask, "What of love? Does it not require trust?"

"Above all else love requires trust."

"But what if love fails you? Is it truly trust that fails or your instinct gone wrong or misplaced passion?" She shook her head. "None of it makes sense."

"I think most would agree with you when it comes to love."

"Then how does anyone know when they are truly in love?"

"It would be a good question to ask your brother. You can see the love in his eyes that he has for Dawn and the same goes for her. And Cree is not an easy man to love and—"

"Cree is easy to love," Wintra insisted in defense of her brother. Even though she was still angry with him for sticking her in the abbey, she still loved him and always would. "He is the most wonderful brother and many may fear him, and well they should for he is a fierce warrior, but I am the only one who truly knows his nature."

"I would say that my sister knows him better than you, for she—"

"She cannot know him as well as I do," Wintra argued. "Besides how can she know him so well if she cannot even talk with him?"

"When you meet her you will understand, and when you see Cree and her together you will see love at its strongest." He gave a glance at the fish. "It appears our supper may be ready." He stood to go check on the fish.

Wintra found herself annoyed. No one could know her brother better than she did. She and Cree had always been close—or was that no more? Had these years that separated them changed everything? Or was it that he found someone to love and his sister did not matter to him anymore? The thought made her heart hurt. Cree was all the family she had; she could not lose him.

The thought came swift like an arrow to her heart. He could wed her off to someone and send her away, and she would never see him again. Would he do that? He had deposited her in the abbey, and she had not believed he would. No amount of him insisting that it was for the best, for her protection, had made a difference. She had cried for days and she had cried each time he had come to visit her and would leave her there yet again.

Would she return to him only to have him send her away again?

Another thought hit just as hard. *Trust.* She had always trusted Cree. Never had she feared him or doubted his word. He had never given her any reason to, so why would she question that he would now? He loved her and that would never change. *Trust.* She trusted Cree and she would not let anything damage that trust, not even her anger.

Conversation was limited as they ate since both were hungry and the fish delicious. When they finished and everything cleared away, Wintra rinsed her hands in the warm bucket of water she had kept for herself and offered Torr use of it, which he accepted. He liked the subtle sweet scent that lingered around her, and not quite so much the fish scent that stuck to his hands.

Exhaustion was quickly claiming Wintra, her yawns coming ever more frequently, and the bed looking ever more inviting.

It was Torr who suggested, "Time we get some sleep."

"I could not agree more. My bones are even tired."

"Then it is a good night's sleep you need."

Wintra wasn't thinking of anything but sleep. She

ached all over and wanted nothing more than to crawl into bed and snuggle against Torr to stay warm. The thought sent a quick spark shooting through her, though it faded just as quickly. She was simply too tired to think of anything but sleep.

Torr watched her walk over to the bed, prepared with their blankets. He expected her to drop into bed, her weary eyes closing as soon as her head touched the lumpy mattress. So he was surprised when she stopped beside the bed and started wiggling oddly. It took a moment for him to realize that she was attempting to get out of her torn dress beneath her shift.

He recalled then how he had had to rip it to get it off her. Then he recalled the feel of her naked body and how her skin was as soft as the finest wool. He thought to go help her, but he feared if he started touching her, he wouldn't stop. It was when she struggled to free her one arm that got stuck in the sleeve that he could not just sit there any longer. He went to help her.

"It is stuck too deep, too tight," she said on a sigh.

Where he would love to be—stuck too deep, too tight—inside her. He had to shake the thought away and concentrate on helping her and getting her to bed, though he did not intend on joining her. It would be much too dangerous for him to slip in bed with her now. He was already hard just from the images dancing in his head. He did not need to add to his torment.

He gently got her arm free and stepped away from her leaving her to finish the task, though when the torn garment pooled at her feet he grew that much harder and had to turn away from her.

"Would you put this on the chair for me?" she

asked.

He only half turned and took it from her and took extra time in draping the garment over the chair.

"Hurry to bed, or I will get cold," she said as she slipped between the blankets.

He could not turn around. He could not let himself. If he did, he might not be able to restrain himself. "In a minute," he called out.

"Hurry, I need you," she said in a drowsy voice.

Torr did not answer, her remark much too tempting. He knew that she would soon be asleep and only when she was deep in sleep would he join her. And even then he feared it would be too difficult to keep his hands off her.

He shook his head. He could not touch her. He could not.

Not unless she wanted him to.

Chapter Nine

Wintra woke the next morning with a bit of a chill. She did not have to open her eyes to know she was alone in bed. She had woken once in the middle of the night to find herself wrapped snugly in Torr's powerful arms. She had nestled her cheek against his warm, solid chest and had gone back to sleep, feeling safer than she had in a while.

She opened her eyes as she stretched her arms above her head, expecting to see Torr somewhere in the one-room cottage, but she was not just alone in bed, but the cottage as well. She sat up and looked around again, the fire had been stoked, the room remaining toasty warm, and his cloak was gone.

Food. No doubt he went to find them food.

She swung her feet off the bed and pulled on her boots and wrapping one of the blankets firmly around her, she walked over near the hearth. She shook her head at the sudden thought that she missed the abbey. She had wanted to leave that place since the day Cree had left her there and here she was wishing she was back there, at least for breakfast. Hot porridge sounded good right now.

She scooped her torn dress off the chair and sat. Today she would repair the garment as best she could. The nuns had told her to travel light that her brother would have all she needed when she arrived home. But she had wanted to take certain things with her and having known the nuns would chide her if she appeared weighted down with bundles, she had sewn a few things into the hem of her cloak. Her favorite herbs being one and her stitching needles being another.

Her wool dress was soft to the touch and, though the drab gray color reminded her of the nuns' simple dress, she had always favored it, perhaps because Cree had given it to her on one of his visits. She had been shocked when Torr had ripped it down the middle to get it off her, but not nearly as shocked as to how she felt when his hands had begun to warm her body.

Don't think about it. Don't think about it. She warned herself too late. Images and memories rushed over her along with those wicked tingles. Would they never go away? They pursued her like feverish little bugs nipping at her flesh, though if she was honest with herself it felt more like feverish little bugs tantalizing her flesh.

The door opened then and Torr walked in, fresh snow coating his cloak.

"Snow again?"

"Not heavy, but slow and steady." He deposited his cloak on the peg and set the bucket he carried in front of the hearth. He placed a large, cleaned fish on the hearth stone and turned to look at Wintra and smiled. "I cleaned it outside."

She returned his smile. "As I will remind you, blame my overly cleanliness on the nuns."

"What else should I blame on them?" he asked, and though he meant it teasingly, the way she scrunched her face apparently had her taking his question seriously.

"My curiosity."

He laughed. "I have a feeling you were always

curious."

"My mum would have agreed with you. She had told me that I asked more than my share of questions. But the nuns rarely if ever answered any of my questions and the few they did answer made no sense. So naturally—"

"Your curiosity grew," he finished.

"How could it not?"

"I will not stifle your curiosity, so ask any question you wish."

He made it sound so easy, but it wasn't. She could not discuss just anything with him, especially when it came to intimacy. He wasn't her husband. He was still very much a stranger, though perhaps not as much as before—not nearly as much as before.

She searched for a question that would be permissible to ask, though recalling the shocked reactions of the nuns when she had asked most any question, she had gotten the impression that none of her questions were appropriate.

She found one that had always perplexed her. "Why must a wife obey her husband without question?"

Torr could not help but laugh. "My mother certainly did not obey my father. She was strong-willed and kind-natured and my father loved her dearly. I think it depends on the husband and wife. My mum and da grew up together, and my da had once told me that he knew when he was only a lad that he loved my mum and they would someday wed. I think your brother Cree loved Dawn long before he ever admitted he did. He was just too stubborn to acknowledge it, though I see now that that runs in the family."

She stuck her tongue out at him and damn if he

didn't want to kiss her and spar with the tempting little morsel. He ignored the thought and continued their discussion. "Then there are women who let their husbands think that they obey them when all the while they are the ones in charge. And then there are those who suffer badly at the hands of their husbands and can do nothing about it."

The incident with Owen came rushing back at her, and she shivered at the thought of what life would have been like with him.

"Something disturbs you."

It wasn't a question. He was aware that something troubled her, and she wondered how he had sensed it.

He reached out as he did last night and rested his hand on hers. "Tell me."

She glanced at the fish. "Isn't the fish ready?"

"It can wait."

"As can mine, until after we eat," Wintra said.

"You will tell me then?"

Why not tell him? As he had reminded her, Cree would want to know, and she didn't know if she could tell her brother what Owen had demanded of her. But she was beginning to believe that it would be easier to tell Torr.

"I will tell you," she said.

"And I will take you at your word," he said and turned to see to the fish.

At your word. Given one's word meant one's honor, so she would have no choice but to talk with him after they ate. Perhaps it would do her good to unload the burden she had felt since the incident with Owen. Unfortunately, she felt more burdened than ever since she had badly misjudged Owen. He had played her for a fool and that disturbed her even more.

The meal went faster than Wintra expected, though perhaps not. Perhaps she was simply anxious about talking with Torr. The more she talked with him and the more she watched him move around the room with such ease, the more comfortable she grew with him. The more she believed him a good man and the more she trusted him.

While Torr saw to cleaning his hands in the bucket, Wintra kept refreshed by the hearth, she hurried to get her bone needles from the hem of her cloak. Then she sat in the chair by the fireplace and carefully pulled a thread of wool from the hem of her dress to use to begin her stitching.

Torr thought of asking her what else she had hidden in her cloak, but thought better of it. It would take the conversation away from where he wanted it to go. Another time he would ask what secrets her cloak concealed. For now he moved his chair closer to hers, and waited.

Wintra stopped stitching when the silence grew too heavy for her to bear. She had given her word and he was waiting patiently—damn him—for her to honor it.

She finished a stitch and slipped the needle in the wool to keep it there until later when she could return and do more. She left the dress resting on her lap and looked up at him. Where did she begin? How did she explain? Color stained her cheeks as soon as she recalled Owen's words.

"I will repeat it as many times as necessary," Torr said. "You can tell me anything."

Could she? There was only one way to find out. "Owen thought you had had your way with me and that I was now spoiled goods. He told me that when he returned I was to be naked on my knees and I was to—" She paused a moment at the image that played in her mind and spoke as fast as she could. "I was to take him in my mouth and pleasure him, and I was to do it at least twice a day from that day on."

How Torr managed to maintain his anger, he didn't know. If Owen was in front of him at that moment, he would have snapped his neck without an ounce of remorse. Someway, somehow, he intended to see the lecherous man pay for his actions.

"How could he expect me to do such a disgusting thing?"

"He had no right demanding that of you. It is a degrading act to force upon any woman. But since you forever want to know things, I will tell you this. It is a common act shared between willing partners, but the two people must be willing." Torr said.

"Truly?" she asked, surprised and intrigued. And then the thought hit her. "Do you mean a man does the same to a woman?"

Torr didn't hesitate to answer. "Yes, couples do enjoy tasting each other."

A shiver ran through Wintra at the image of Torr between her legs tasting her. A blast of tingles shot through her, and she felt herself grow wet. Good Lord, she was going to hell.

"Owen had no right to say that to you or to force you to do such a thing."

"But it is an acceptable act?" she asked wanting to make certain she had heard him right.

"Between two agreeable people it is."

"Then husbands and wives do that?"

"If they agree upon it."

She stared at him for a moment, and then blurted out. "Has someone ever tasted you?" She slapped her hand over her mouth soon after the words slipped out.

"You truly are inquisitive. And the answer is yes and more than once, and I quite enjoyed it"

Why the thought annoyed her, she did not know, but she was quick to ask, "And would you expect your wife to taste you?"

"If she wished to, I would quite welcome it."

"And would you taste her?" This time she was too curious to be shocked by her own words.

"I look forward to it."

She grew annoyed again. Why? Was she jealous of what Torr would share with the woman he loved? While what of her? Would her future husband expect that of her? Would he be tolerant if she refused to taste him? The questions raised more questions in her head until she didn't want to think about it anymore. This wasn't something that could be settled right at this moment. At least now she had some prior knowledge and when the time came...

She shivered.

"Cold or did I upset you?" Torr asked.

"I am not sure what to think," she answered, and then smiled. "The nuns would faint dead away if they knew I discussed an inappropriate subject with you."

"I am sure your curious questions probably caused them to almost faint numerous times. And I would not be surprised if they still pray for you daily."

"I was a bit of a problem to them," she admitted. "It was probably the reason they kept reminding me to mind my curiosity and manners when Owen would visit."

"I am surprised that he was allowed to visit with you without Cree's permission."

"It wasn't me he came to visit. He had admired the abundant gardens I so painstakingly tended and asked if he could speak to me. Mother Abbess granted his request and when we spoke he inquired about some of the herbs I grew. We talked briefly, and he bid me good day."

"And did you fancy him when you met him?" Torr wanted to know exactly how Owen had worked his way into meeting Wintra and convincing her that he loved her and wanted to wed her. Something did not seem right about the whole thing, and he knew Cree would be just as curious.

"I thought nothing of it. I simply enjoyed our brief discussion and thought that was the end of it. He returned and requested to speak with me about the garden again, though he mostly discussed the herbs with me, and Mother Abbess granted his repeated requests. There were always nuns nearby. We were never alone."

"Did he ever tell you why he visited the abbey?"

After a moment of thought, Wintra said, "Now that I think of it, he never did, but then I had been warned time and again not to question visiting patrons."

"So he was paying a stipend to Glenburgh Abbey?"

"The nuns were very secretive of abbey patrons, but from what I could gather in snippets of conversations I caught it would seem that he was." She scrunched her brow. "I wonder why?"

Torr wondered the same, though said nothing.

"I was a blind fool for not seeing Owen's true nature," Wintra said annoyed at herself.

"Owen is a man of many talents while you are young and had been cloistered."

"You know him?"

"I know of him. Owen cares about money and

power. He takes what he wants and discards what is no longer of any use to him."

Wintra shivered again. "He would have discarded me when he was done with me."

"Cree would have never allowed it, and if anything had happened, your brother would have killed Owen and not quickly." Torr did not add that Cree would have to have been quick about it because he would have seen to it himself.

Wintra turned her head to stare at the fire's flames. "Dear Lord, I came so horribly close to making a costly mistake. I let Owen convince me that he was in love with me and that we would be happy together. But worse, I let him convince me that I was in love with him." She turned to look at Torr, locking her tears away, refusing to let them fall. "Never again. Never will I let another man make a fool of me."

He smiled. "I would say it was you who made the fool of Owen since you escaped him and freed me."

Her chin went up. "I certainly did."

"And now that you know more about men and love, the choice of who to love will be yours."

"No, no," she argued shaking her head. "I do not know near enough about men or love. You must teach me." She nodded. "That is what we will do while waiting to return home. You will teach me about men and love."

Torr burst out laughing. "Princess, you do not truly want to know about men. And love? I need to learn about that myself."

Wintra took hold of his hand and squeezed it. "But I do want to know about men. I never want to be that vulnerable to a man again. You have been good to me. Honorable. You want nothing from me. I trust you, so who better to teach me? And love? Perhaps we can figure it out together."

Torr yanked his hand away, stood, and walked around to the other side of the table. "You do not know what you ask of me. You told me you found me appealing. I have intimately touched almost every part of you, and we have kissed. I am not a monk who lives a celibate life. I am a man with needs and desires." He slapped his hands down on the table and stared straight at her. "And seeing desire in your eyes for me does not help."

"That's it," she said excited. "That is what you must teach me—how to control my inappropriate desires until I find love. I saw for myself what uncontrolled desire can do to a woman, and I will not let that happen to me."

"What did you see?" he asked.

"A woman was brought to the abbey one night and secluded in one of the many small cell-like rooms. I was not permitted to go near her, but as the weeks and months passed the nuns told me about her, especially since—" Wintra's cheeks flushed.

"Why stop now? If you want to learn, then you need to share everything with me."

She continued before she could stop herself. "Thinking there was something wrong with me, I had spoken to the nuns about a sudden affliction that worried me. I was told to pray whenever I suffered it and that my husband would take care of it when I wed. The nuns made a point of explaining to me that the woman who had arrived at the abbey had surrendered to the affliction before she wed and was now with child. She would give birth to the child, and then take her vows at the abbey. The child would be given to a local peasant family to raise."

Torr was beginning to believe that Cree had made

a terrible mistake leaving Wintra at the abbey with the nuns.

Wintra cringed, drawing her shoulders in as she did. "I can still hear her endless screams when it came time to deliver her baby. It made me think that I never wanted to suffer such pain and what would be the point when—" She turned her head away to once again stare at the flames.

"What happened?" he asked gently.

"She and the baby died, and the nuns said it had been for the best." Tears coated her eyes when she turned to face him, but once again she refused to let them fall. "How could they say that? And what of the man who got her with child? Did he not care about her at all? Or had she been a blind fool like me? Only I was lucky—you came along and rescued me."

Chapter Ten

Wintra bewildered Torr. She was unlike other women; beautiful, stubborn, thoughtful, so very curious and so very innocent that he wanted to wrap her in his arms and protect her. But that wouldn't be what she wanted, and he not only wanted to give her what she wanted, he wanted her to realize her own courage.

"You also rescued me," he said.

She laughed this time. "I have no doubt that you had already determined your escape. If I had not come along when I did, we may have missed each other."

She was a perceptive one, for if she had arrived only a few minutes later to free him, he would have been gone. "I would not have left without you."

"I never doubted you would. Cree sent you and no one disappoints Cree."

"Cree had nothing to do with it."

She stared at him wide-eyed, and her heart beat a bit faster.

He reached out and took hold of her chin. "Know this, Princess, I would have never left you to suffer at Owen's hands. Cree or no Cree."

He would have rescued her no matter what. Her heart filled with joy, though she did not know why, and she did not care. She only knew that it felt good, very good, and she wanted the wonderful feeling to linger.

"I will always protect you," he said and gave her a quick kiss, let go of her chin, and walked around the table not trusting himself to do more than just give her a quick kiss.

Her lips tingled and ached for more. Not to mention the tingles that ran through her and settled between her legs. This was desire and she had to learn to control it, even though she would much prefer to surrender to it.

A thought struck her, not unusual since she was constantly struck by thoughts, though this one truly caught her unaware and startled her. What if her relentless desire for Torr was the fact that she was actually falling in love with him? She had never felt such feelings for Owen. What if this was love? How would she know it?

"What heavy thought has hold of you now?" Torr asked concerned, Wintra having paled suddenly.

She shook her head. "How do you learn about love when you know nothing about it?"

Torr walked back around the table, to sit, though he moved his chair a bit of a distance away from Wintra. Being close to her, simply touching her hand or looking upon her lovely face never failed to arouse him. And it was damn hard being in an almost constant state of arousal.

He settled himself in the chair and said, "I suppose we learn from watching others love. My mum and da loved each other dearly and one would have to be blind not to see it. Cree and Dawn share the same enduring love as does Dawn's friends Paul and Lila."

"I have had no such opportunity to see what you have seen. My da died before I was born, though Cree and my mum told me time and again what a good and loving man he was. And though I was curious to know more about my da, I did not ask my mum since tears always filled her eyes when she spoke of him. And being confined at the abbey certainly did not allow me to learn about love."

She looked away for a moment and Torr knew she was thinking and let her be since his mind also had him deep in thought. This petite woman had changed his life in so many unexpected ways that he was still reeling from the shock of it. He had a duty to do, and he had planned on doing it, but now he wanted more.

"So do you think it is possible to fall in love at first sight?"

Her sudden question startled him, though he had no time to answer since she went right on talking.

"From what you tell me of your parents, it would seem that they both fell in love right away. And I do recall my mum telling me once that she had always loved my da. So that has me thinking that she loved him when she first saw him. Love at first sight then is possible," she concluded.

"Unless of course it is lust one is feeling and once that is satisfied there is nothing else to feel." She wanted to learn, and he wanted her to know the difference, so she could make the right choice when the time came.

Was that what she was feeling for Torr? Lust and nothing more?

"So how do you know the difference?" she asked annoyed, at what, she wasn't sure.

"Not that I know for sure, but I would say that two people in love might drive each other a little crazy, want to be together more often than not, respect and admire each other, would do anything for each other, and, of course, the man would protect the woman he loved with his life.. At least that is my thought on it."

As you protect me.

The thought sent a jolt through her, though she maintained her calm. Could it be true? Could she be falling in love with Torr? She did want to spend time with him. She looked forward to being snuggled in his arms in bed at night. She enjoyed talking with him so very much, especially when—so far—no subject was taboo. She did respect and admire him. And oh how she ached for him to kiss her again. Had love struck her? She certainly had not felt any such things for Owen. She was beginning to realize just how much of a means to an end he had been to her, though when her brother's warriors had arrived to take her home, she had not thought once of notifying Owen about her departure. It had been one of the nuns who had said that she would let Owen know that Wintra had left for home when he visited at the end of the week.

"I never loved Owen," she said, as if saying it aloud freed her of something.

"A good and sensible realization."

"You helped me realize it."

He smiled. "Princess, I have no doubt you would have come to the same conclusion given time."

"I do not want to waste any more time on him, and I want to be ready when love does strike."

He laughed. "I do not think anyone is ever ready when love strikes, but I guess you can give it a try if you want." He stood, stretched, and said, "As much as I enjoy talking with you, I have to go and see about supper for us."

"But it is early yet." She did not want him to go. She was enjoying their conversation and did not want it to end. Another reason to believe she was falling in love with him.

"The skies are heavily gray and night will fall before we know it. I need time to hunt something more than fish."

"Be careful," she urged.

He walked over to her, planning to plant a quick kiss on her lips and reassure her that he would be fine. It did not quite turn out that way.

He bent down to kiss her, and she raised up to meet his lips and that was all he needed. She was eager for him to kiss her, and he did not disappoint her.

His hand went around her neck and held it tight as his lips claimed hers, and good Lord, if she didn't tingle down to the tips of her toes. His kiss was gentle, demanding, teasing, but most of all magical. Sensations rushed through her body, making her legs go weak. If she wasn't sitting, she would have collapsed against him.

The thought of being in his arms, her body pressed against his, his strong arms wrapped around her had her pushing herself out of the chair. And as she did, his arm went around her waist and lifted her up to press against his hard body.

A soft moan tickled at her throat and rose to reach her mouth, though his kiss stifled it. Her arms went around his neck, and she let instinct take hold, or was it love, that had her kissing him as if she knew what she was doing?

It was when she pressed her body hard against his and felt him thick and strong against her that he broke them apart, holding her at arm's length while they both took heavy breaths.

"We need to think about what we are doing here,"

he said.

"At the moment, my thoughts are anything but clear," she said, and then smiled. "You seem to take my breath away."

"You do the same to me, which means I need to leave for a bit. The cold will do me good."

She scrunched her brow and was about to speak.

"Do not ask me why, Princess," he ordered, released her, and hurried out the door.

Wintra dropped down on the chair. She had not wanted him to leave, but she had to agree that it was better that he did. He was right. They had to think about what they were doing here. She could so easily surrender to the lust that consumed her, but she would much rather find out if it was love that had her favoring and wanting Torr as much as she did.

She had to keep things in prospective and keep things proper, though she had no idea how she would manage the latter.

Stop thinking about it. The warning in her head was not as easy to heed as one would assume. She needed a reprieve from her rampant thoughts and the only way to do that was to keep busy. She snatched her dress up off the ground and got busy stitching. Besides, it would be wise for her to remain fully clothed at all times while here with Torr.

She not only wanted the dress repaired, she wanted it done properly and that would take detailed work and that meant precise concentration. She focused on her stitching, and it wasn't long before she was completely lost in it.

Wintra got half the dress done when she realized that the fire's light had faded. That was when she noticed the fire had died down. She hurried off the chair, placing her dress on it and grabbed a log from the stack to add to the fire. It was then she realized how much time must have passed since she needed to add three more logs to get the fire going strong. When she finally had a good fire blazing, she stepped back, rubbing her arms that had chilled considerably.

She cast a glance at the door, wondering how long Torr had been gone and her stomach gave her the answer. It rumbled with hunger, which meant it had been several hours. Had something happened to him? The thought sent a shudder through her, and she did the only thing she knew to do. She walked over to the bed, got down on her knees, and began to pray.

Torr felt the cold and was glad of it. He'd been so heated with passion that he hadn't thought the cold could ever touch him, but it finally had. And now he could return safely to the cottage, or so he kept trying to convince himself.

He had cleaned the rabbit he had managed to catch and he was pleased with the few onions and a turnip he had dug out of the garden that he thought had been picked bare. Luckily or perhaps it had been a smart decision on the farmer's part, to place the kitchen garden where he did. The cottage kept the snow from falling too heavily on the garden, and although he had to battle the hard ground to get at the lingering vegetables, it was worth it. They would feast tonight.

With precious food in hand, he entered the cottage, though came to an abrupt stop just inside the door when he saw Wintra's face buried in the bed and her on her knees. He kicked the door shut, dropped the rabbit and vegetables on the table and went to go to her, but she was off her knees as soon as she spotted him and ran to him.

Her arms slipped beneath his cloak to hug his

waist and she planted her face firmly against his
chest.

His arms went around her to hug her as tightly as
she did him, though after a moment he eased her face
away to look up at him. "What's wrong? Why were
you on your knees?"

"I feared something may have happened to you,
and I was praying for your safe return."

"I appreciate the prayers, Princess, but death itself
would not stop me from returning to you and keeping
you safe."

She pressed her finger to his lips. "Do not tempt
death or surely he will knock on our door."

He pressed his nose to hers. "I will make sure to
let him know he is not welcome here."

Wintra smiled and gave him a quick kiss that so
startled her that she jumped back out of his arms and
stared, shocked by her audacity or was it the shock
that she had kissed him as if it was the most natural
thing for her to do.

"Thank you for the welcome and the prayers," he
said and turned his attention to the food he had
brought back. He would have preferred a lengthier
kiss, but that would have been unwise. And this was
her kiss to give and she gave it freely without thought
or reservation, and he liked that.

Wintra sat down on the bed, her legs a bit too
wobbly to take any steps. Her actions alarmed her,
but they also made her think again on the possibility
that she was falling in love with Torr. And the idea
made her stomach flutter.

"I got us a rabbit and found some onions and a
turnip in the garden, not that the cold ground wanted
to part with them."

Wintra stood, her years at the abbey forcing her to

do her share when it came to every day survival. Everyone had a chore and if one did not do their chore it affected the others, and so everyone shared in the chores so that they all survived quite nicely, or so preached Mother Abbess.

"I will see to the vegetables," she said joining him by the table.

He noticed that she was careful not to step too close to him. He almost laughed since if he wanted, all he had to do was reach out and snatch her around the waist and hoist her against him, or better yet carry her to the bed. But he respected the distance she set between them and turned to scoop up a log and use it to nudge the rod in the fireplace out far enough so that he could skewer the rabbit on it.

When he turned to reach for the rabbit, Wintra was busy rubbing one of the wild onions all over the skinned rabbit.

"It will give it more flavor," she explained.

"Another thing you learned at the abbey?" he asked after scooping up the meat.

"As I've told you, the nuns kept me busy." She took hold of the bucket near the hearth, and then went and slipped her cloak off the peg and onto her shoulders.

"Where are you going?" Torr asked.

"We need clean water and I need to see to..." she let her words drift off hoping he'd understand. Though after the intimate things she had discussed with him, she did not know why it should bother her to let him know she needed to relieve herself.

"I will go with you."

"I prefer the privacy."

"I will give it to you, but I will not let you go out there alone."

"I will stay close to the cottage," she insisted.

"Aye, that you will," he said with a laugh, amused by her stubbornness.

"I can do this myself."

He took her by the arm and opened the door. "That is not the point. I am going to protect you whether you want me to or not."

"But I do not need protecting for this," she insisted once again as he propelled her out the door. "I need privacy."

"You need both, and I will see that you have both."

She yanked her arm free and dropped the bucket. "You are a stubborn man who—"

"Intends to keep you safe," he finished, and then took hold of her shoulders and turned her toward the side of the house and gave her a slight shove. "Now go see to your needs. The light is fading and it grows colder."

She hurried off mumbling beneath her breath, knowing it was useless arguing with him. It took her a few moments to find a good spot and the brief delay had him calling out to her.

"I am fine. I will be a few minutes."

"Call out to me when you are done," he ordered.

For some reason, she smiled. She was not sure why, but that had been the way of it since meeting Torr. At times she found herself feeling happier than she had been in a long time and for no good rhyme or reason.

Love.

She shook her head. This was no time to be thinking about love. She finished what she had to do and turned, then turned back again. Something had caught her eye in the distance by a tree. She strained to see what it was and when she could not quite make it out, she took a few steps closer. When it still was not visible enough, she took several more steps and suddenly froze.

A pair of eyes stared at her from between the branches and she turned and ran, screaming out for Torr as she did.

Torr bolted around the cottage as soon as he heard Wintra scream out his name in terror. His blood ran cold as she continued screaming his name, and he swore to himself that he would never let her go off alone again.

She flew into his arms as he ran to meet her.

"A man! A man!" she said through quick breaths. "Watching me."

Torr scanned the surrounding area and wondered why the man had not followed her, unless he was reporting back to someone in which case they would not be able to stay here, or perhaps he was simply a traveler on his own. He needed to determine for himself what was going on.

"Show me where you saw him," he said to Wintra and took hold of her hand.

She nodded and gripped his hand tightly as she led him back to the spot, coming to a halt a few feet away. She shook her head. "He is still there."

"Where?" Torr asked glancing around.

Wintra pointed as she walked. "He has not moved."

Torr could see the man now and he knew with one glance that he was dead.

Wintra stopped a few feet away. "I think he is dead."

"So do I," Torr agreed. "Do you want to wait here while I have a look?"

She shook her head and held on to his hand. "No, I want to stay with you."

They walked together to the man and stood and stared for a moment. Then Torr released her hand and pulled the man back from where he was braced between the trees. He laid him on the ground, though the man's limbs remained frozen in the same position they had been in.

"I don't know which one did him in, the stomach wound or the cold," he said and turned to Wintra. She was as pale as the freshly fallen snow, and Torr silently cursed himself for letting her see the dreadful scene.

He hurried over to her, wrapping his arm around her and turning her away from the dead man.

But she shook her head, slipped out of his arms, and turned around, pointing to the man, though found it hard to speak.

Torr slipped his arm around her waist. "What's wrong? Tell me?"

Wintra took a deep breath and shivered. "He is one of the men who had been with Owen when he rescued me from my abductors."

Chapter Eleven

Wintra sat by the hearth rubbing her cold hands together and staring at the flames. She could not get them warm enough, and she could not get the vision of the wide-eyed, dead man out her mind.

She jolted when Torr wrapped his hands around hers and started rubbing them. He had moved his chair closer to hers, and she did not hesitate to lean against him. She would crawl into his lap if she could. The strength of him combined with his tenderness was a comfort she more than favored and could use right now, but then curiosity reared its head and questions sprang forth spilling from her lips.

"What do you think happened to him? And why was he alone? Owen had said that his men were needed at his home and that was why they had to leave us. But this area is not anywhere near Owen's home, so where did those men who were with Owen when he found us suddenly come from?"

Her pale cheeks had brightened pink, her wit was quick, and her curiosity as strong as ever, and he was glad to see it. She had paled so badly when she had stared at the dead man that he had thought she might faint. He had kept a strong arm around her waist, her feet barely touching the snow when he had rushed her back to the cottage.

"He met with them in the woods the morning I stole you away from him," Torr said feeling it was time she knew about what he had seen.

She sat up straight. "Why would he do that? Why not have them come directly to our camp and who are they?" She continued as if searching for the answers. "And why send his other warriors home—unless." Her eyes turned wide. "The warriors who left were not his warriors." She shook her head, as if trying to make sense of it all. "What were Owen's intentions?"

"It would appear they were quite different than what he led you to believe," Torr said, Owen's deception a growing concern to him.

"My brother will see to clearing this up and see to Owen," she said with confidence.

"He will at that," Torr agreed.

She slipped her hands out of his and turned to stare at the flames.

Torr did not disturb her. He understood that she needed time with her thoughts, so he let her be.

He was surprised when only a short time later she turned and said to him, "I think it would be better if you took me home as soon as possible. There is no telling what Owen will do or say and without being there to defend myself, I fear what may happen."

"As you wish," he said thinking the same himself. "We can leave at first light."

"How long until we reach home?"

"Five or more days, depending on the weather and our stamina." He did not add that it also depended on whether they ran across Owen and his men.

She nodded and turned her attention back to the flames.

Supper was quiet, neither having anything to say, though Torr urged Wintra to eat.

"I do not know when we will have our next meal. You should eat more to help sustain your strength," he urged.

"My stomach cannot abide another piece," she insisted and shook her head. "My brother will be disappointed in me. I have made a fool of myself and that reflects on him."

"There is no way your brother would ever be disappointed in you and, in the end, it is Owen who will look the fool."

"You are a good man and you have been good to me, and I thank you for that. And I wish to say something, though I hope I am not making more of a fool of myself yet again, but since I find it easy to talk with you, I thought I could—" She shook her head, and then the words rushed from her mouth. "I think I may have fallen in love with you."

He felt a squeeze to his heart, a punch to his gut, and he was struck silent, though it did not matter since she went right on talking.

"I do not know anything of love, but I do know that I miss you when you are not near me and I tingle when you are near me, and I love when you kiss me, whether it be a quick or a lingering one. And I wonder now if it will ever be possible to sleep without you by my side.

"You must understand that this is all so strange to me. I have only met you, so how could I possibly be in love with you? And yet I feel that love has struck me good and solid, and I have no idea what to do about it. And there, I have said what I have meant to and you—" She stopped abruptly as if words suddenly failed her or she ran out of them, or perhaps it was that she feared his response.

Torr stood and walked over to her, turning her chair around, with her still in it, and hunched down in front of her. "Marry me, Princess, for I feel the same about you."

While her eyes turned wide with delight, her words were more cautious. "What if we are wrong? What if it is not love?"

"I do not want to live without you. I would miss your stubborn nature too much," he said with a chuckle.

She gave him playful punch in the shoulder. "I am not stubborn."

"It is your choice. Marry me. I promise you that I will see that we have a good life together."

"This is foolish," she said, though did not want to believe that. She wanted to listen to her body that tingled all over, her heart that beat wildly, and her stomach that fluttered with delight.

"Then we will be foolish together." He kissed her quick. "If I linger kissing you, then we will end up in that bed together, and I will make you my wife this night."

Did she dare let him?

"Again, the choice is yours, but know I would be proud to call you, wife."

It was so tempting to simply fall into his arms and surrender to love, though her once foolish actions had her not only hesitating, but recalling aloud something similar to what Torr had once said to her in regards to Owen. "If you truly love me, you will wait and speak with my brother and arrange a proper marriage."

He smiled. "My own words return to haunt me."

She placed a gentle hand to his cheek. "They are wise words, and as much as I want—and I do want—to have you make me your wife this night, I also want it to be right between us. I want to know for sure that you love me."

"As I said, Princess, your choice, but know this— you are mine and always will be." His hand went to the back of her head and eased it forward as he brought his lips to meet hers.

If his words had not convinced her, his kiss did. And it did not take long before she had to force herself to break away and gently shove at his chest, needing distance from him.

Her teeth nibbled at her lower lip to try and stop the deliciously spine-tingling throb he had left upon her lips. She closed her eyes against it and the sinful, but oh so lovely, sensations that ran through her. If she was not careful, she would find herself dragging him to the bed and—she shook her head. She had made the mistake of thinking herself in love with Owen. And now here she was thinking herself in love again. She could not be foolish again. This time she must be sure.

She grabbed her dress off her lap and pressed it tightly against her chest, and stood. "I need to put my dress on."

Torr did not say anything. He did not have to. Passion smoldered in his eyes, and he quickly turned his back to her. "You will save that dress, for one night I will rip it off you again."

She not only shivered, she grew wet at the thought. And God forgive her, she looked forward to that time.

Wintra hurried out of her shift and into her dress that was not completely finished being repaired, but would have to do. She had managed to stitch closed part of the rip from top to mid-thigh. Her shift would cover the rest.

"You can turn now," she said when she finished.

Torr turned slowly, his blue eyes heavily burdened. "I want you to remember one thing. No matter what happens I love you and nothing will change that."

"How do you know for sure that you love me?"

He laughed. "Only you would ask for proof."

"We barely know each other. How could love have hit us so fast?" She did not truly want to question it, yet she could not help but question it. Could she truly believe that love could strike as fast as lightening? It seemed so unlikely, and yet here she was in love, or so she believed, and did she dare believe?

Lord, she was confused, but wasn't that what love did—confuse?

"I have no answer for you. I cannot explain it. I do not understand it myself, and I do not want to. I simply want to enjoy it, revel in it, and know—not how or why—it is real."

He accepted how he felt without reservation. Wasn't that love? Shouldn't she accept how she felt and not question it or him, but rather enjoy the love she had found, or rather the love that had found her?

"I want to believe that, I truly do, but I seriously misjudged Owen, so how then can I be sure that I am not misjudging—"

He interrupted her, stepping closer, and his arm went around her waist as he said, "I am not Owen promising you sweet nothings. I am a man who, to his great surprise, has fallen in love with you."

He loved her, but was stunned over the revelation, which had her asking, "Why surprised?"

"I was on a mission for your brother, not on a mission to find love," he said, shaking his head as if in disbelief.

"So you are as baffled about this as I am?"

"Baffled? I suppose that fits well with love, since love, at least from what I have observed, can certainly confuse." Torr pressed a firm finger to her lips before she could respond. "The only thing I want to hear from you right now is yes or no to my proposal that we wed. The rest we will sort out as we go."

Her lovely eyes held a hundred questions, and she appeared to struggle for a response.

"Yes, or no," he warned, "or I will kiss you senseless, and it will be you who drags me to that bed and demand I make love to you."

Her eyes rounded wide and a blush tinted her cheeks.

He leaned his head down and whispered in her ear, "Your whole body will blush when I make love to you."

She squeezed her eyes tight against the hungry tingles that ravaged her body. They nipped and feasted ravenously at her most intimate places. Even though she would have preferred to simply let the tingles devour her into surrendering, she had to do this right. She had to make amends for her debacle with Owen. And if it was truly love, then she and Torr could wait, for love would not disappear. It would only grow stronger.

Reluctantly, but firmly, Wintra stepped away from Torr. And just as reluctantly, he let her go.

"I want to say yes, my heart tells me to say yes—" She shook her head. "So I do not know why I hesitate in giving you an answer."

"I will wait. Answer me when you are ready."

"What if—"

"No what if—a simple answer is all that is needed. Now it is best we sleep so that we will be well rested to leave at sunrise."

Wintra agreed with a nod and walked over to the bed. It was better she gave it thought, although she would no doubt think it to death and probably be no closer to an answer than she was presently. After removing her boots, and leaving her garments on, she hurried beneath the blankets, turning her back to Cree. She was relieved when he climbed in and slipped his arm around her, drawing her back snugly against him. She had to admit that she was disappointed he was fully clothed. But it was better that way, less tempting.

It did not take him long to fall asleep. Wintra could tell by his breathing, though his arm remained snug around her. She kept her eyes closed, trying to force herself to sleep, but it was useless. Her mind refused to quiet.

She did not know what had compelled her to tell Torr that she believed she had fallen in love with him. It had been an overwhelming urge that she had not been able to fight. And while she had been thrilled to hear he felt the same, his proposal had startled and frightened her. This being in love was all too new to her, and she was not sure what to make of it.

"Something troubles you?"

She was surprised that Torr was awake, but his whisper was much too soft and filled with concern to startle her. However, she was curious to what had woken him. "I am fine, but what woke you?"

"Your hand that continually squeezes my arm."

Wintra pulled her hand away, realizing she had been doing just that.

"What troubling thoughts keep you awake?" He took hold of her hand and placed it back on his arm, his hand resting over hers and holding it there.

How was it that he could tell when something disturbed her? And how did he find such patience with her never-ending musings? And why did his touch feel so wonderfully enticing?

"No one thought in particular, but rather many that refuse to leave me alone."

"Then tell me all your thoughts so that your mind will finally empty and you can sleep," he said, settling more comfortably around her, as if prepared to spend the entire night listening to her.

The warmth of his body, the weight of his strength, and the thought that he would listen to her endless ramblings made her think that he had to be in love with her, for no man would have such patience. And for some reason that soothed her and her thoughts seemed to fade as her eyes drifted shut.

Torr lay there keeping Wintra close as she slept. This task had turned out far different than he had expected, though he had to admit that it had turned in his favor. Never had he expected to fall in love with Wintra and that he did, still startled him. He could understand her misgivings about being in love after what she had been through with Owen. What he could not understand was that he himself had no such uncertainties. He knew he loved this woman sleeping peacefully in his arms, and there would be no changing that no matter what happened.

He knew there would be hurdles when he returned her home, but they would overcome them. He would see that they did. What concerned him the most was Owen. He knew well of the man and he was a devious one, not to be believed or trusted. He did not do anything out of the goodness of his heart. He did things to fatten his own coffers, and he did not care who he hurt along the way.

Wintra moaned and turned around in Torr's arms to settle snug against him once again and rub her face against his chest, sighing contentedly and resting her head there.

Torr wrapped his arms around her, yawned, and placed his cheek on the top of her head. He had been happy to learn that Wintra did not think she could sleep without him by her side, for he knew for sure that he wanted her in his arms, in his bed, every night.

Chapter Twelve

Wintra could not remember how many days they had been traveling. She thought it had been five, though it could be six. And how Torr knew where he was going she would never know. The snow made everything look the same to her. Thank heaven it hadn't snowed anymore, a few flurries, but nothing more. Her legs ached beyond belief from the constant trudging in the snow. Some areas were not bad while others Torr had to make a path using the strength of his legs so that she could get through to follow him.

Food had been anything but plentiful and it had not been for lack of trying. Last night, or was it the night before—she could not remember—she had fallen asleep before the small fish Torr had managed to catch had finished cooking. He had woken her and made her eat. Not that he had to force her, she had been starving. And she was cold, so very cold that she did not think that she would ever get warm again.

She had not, however, complained about anything to Torr. She had been the one who had wanted to go home, and he had obliged her.

She had been so busy in her thoughts that she did not notice that he had stopped and walked right into his back. He turned, his hand taking hold of her arm and his finger tapping at his mouth, cautioning silence.

She froze, an easy task since she was so cold, and stared at him.

His eyes darted about, and then his hand went to the hilt of his dagger at his waist.

Her heart began to beat rapidly. Had he heard something that had alarmed him? She got her answer when he shoved her behind him.

Could Owen have found them? If not, who approached? Robbers or thugs who would attack innocent travelers? Many such victims had been forced to stop at the abbey for help, some having suffered serious wounds. Her mind went wild with possibilities of what they were about to face one way or another.

She wished the ground was not covered with snow. She could have found a rock or stick, anything that would serve as a weapon. Cree had taught her to use anything she could as a weapon to defend herself. Another reason why she wished she could have remained with him, he would have taught her how to use various weapons to protect herself. She did not like feeling vulnerable, and she intended to do something about it once she was home—if she made it home.

A single rider finally came into view, and she almost breathed a sigh of relief. Torr could easily handle one man. Then all of a sudden men on horses and some on foot poured out of the woods, and her heart sank.

"It is about time you found us," Torr said.

Wintra almost collapsed with relief.

"You hid your trail well."

Wintra stepped around Torr, and took his hand as she stared at Sloan.

"You are well, Wintra?" Sloan asked.

She did not know Sloan well. He had come to the abbey with Cree on only two occasions and they had barely exchanged a few words. "I am well," she confirmed with a nod, "though hungry and cold."

"We are setting up camp not far from here. Come and I will see that you get warm and have food." He went to dismount, but Torr's sharp words stopped him.

"I will see to her care."

Sloan looked from one to the other, nodded, and then signaled to one of the warriors who after being gone for only a few moments returned with Torr's horse.

Torr took the reins, rubbed the mare's face, pressed his face to hers, and then whispered something to her.

Wintra watched how his hands moved over the mare, as if reassuring her and welcoming her back and all she could think was that she missed that touch of his. As shocking as it had been when he had touched her to get her warm, it had also felt incredibly wonderful.

Love.

A reminder of why she felt as she did about Torr?

A loving man. A good man. A trustworthy man.

"You're exhausted and hungry. You need food and sleep, and I am going to see that you get both," Torr said and scooped her up and planted her on the horse. He mounted behind her, and she collapsed back against him, turning into the crook of his arm and laid her head upon his chest. She loved being in his arms, the only problem being that when she was those sinful tingles would attack her and sometimes viciously. Then all she could think of was the both of them naked and touching each other. She definitely was going to hell.

The campsite was a short ride away and as soon

as they dismounted a young lad hurried to see to Torr's horse. Torr in turn saw to Wintra. He took her to one of the three fires and saw that she was seated comfortably on a blanket, then wrapped another blanket around her, tucking it in a fold at her breasts.

She sighed when his fingers brushed her already hard nipples.

Torr leaned down to whisper, "Be careful, your heated passion shows clearly in your eyes and if we were alone I would be hard-pressed not to ignite it some more." He quickly handed her a hot brew, not trusting himself not to kiss her, which was what he ached to do, regardless that Sloan and Cree's warriors where present.

He reached around him and snatched up the bread and cheese he had brought for her and placed it in her lap. "Meat will be brought to you as soon as it is ready. I must go and speak with Sloan."

"And you?" she asked just as concerned for him as he was for her and while she would have preferred him to stay with her, it was wiser that he left. She needed this relentless ache for him to ease, and it would not have a chance of doing that with him so close to her.

"I will join you soon as I finish with Sloan."

"You intend to speak with him about Owen?" she asked.

He nodded.

"You will tell me if there is anything I should know?"

"I will," he said agreeably.

Wintra watched him walk off and wondered if a time would ever come that she would not be racked with tingles when she gazed upon him or he touched her. So why not wed him and be done with it?

Why not? The question echoed in her head and it was one time she wished that she did not think so much. She wished that she would simply accept her love for Torr and accept his marriage proposal without reservation. But that small inkling of doubt continued to nag at her. What if she had misjudged Torr as badly as she had Owen?

She tried to convince herself that there was no rush in making a decision that she would be home soon and...

She sighed, cupping the tankard tighter in her hands. What if Cree did not approve of Torr? What then?

If she was not so hungry, she would have ignored the food, but her empty stomach would not allow that, and it was a good thing. It got her mind off her musings and she finally ate with more gusto than she felt. She also enjoyed the meat a young lad had brought her. Two more tankards of the warm brew and her insides had warmed considerably. Her feet however were still chilled, and she decided she would take her boots off and let the fire dry them while warming her toes. First, however, she needed to seek the privacy of the woods.

She managed to make it to her feet without a groan, though one rumbled in her chest. She did not want to show how much she ached. She was Cree's sister and would show no weakness in front of his men. Cree never showed weakness or had she ever seen him cry, not even when their mum had died or when he had dug her grave and laid her to rest, though he had held her when she cried.

Wintra chased the sad memories away as she walked through the camp to the woods. One of the warriors, guarding the outer edges of camp, stepped in front of her, stopping her.

"I require a moment of privacy," she said.

He nodded and signaled with his hand and in seconds two warriors flanked her.

She was about to argue, but recalling the dead man and his lifeless eyes the last time she had ventured into the woods for the same reason, she decided that she did not mind the two warriors following along. She did not have to ask them to turn away when she stopped. They did so of their own accord, of which she was grateful. Though just to make sure, she retreated a few more steps into the darkness.

With her needs seen to, she was looking forward to returning to camp and getting her feet warm and her boots dry. She took a few steps in the direction she had come—at least she thought she did—but when she did not spot the two warriors, she wondered if she had reared off course. A few more steps and she nearly moaned with frustration.

How could she have gotten herself lost? She could have sworn she had turned back—she shook her head. She had not turned completely around when she had finished. Her only choice, though embarrassing, was to call out so they could hear her and hopefully they would have no difficulty finding her.

"Wintra! Wintra, where are you."

She sighed with relief hearing Torr's urgent shout. She took a few steps forward, following his voice and was about to call out to him, when her foot caught on something and she went tumbling down the hill that she had not realized she had been standing on.

Snow completely engulfed her as she continued to tumble until she finally slammed into something. She rolled onto her back, spitting snow from her mouth, wiping it from her eyes, and taking a breath to calm herself.

"Wintra, answer me!"

She heard the worry in Torr's voice, and she turned with a wince to get to her feet and do as he demanded and found herself staring at the wide open eyes of another frozen dead man. She let out a scream that echoed off the trees like a tolling bell. And she continued screaming as she scrambled to get to her feet. She slipped several times as she did, anxious to get away from the cold, stiff body.

As she finally found firm footing, she was grabbed around the waist and slammed into a hard chest. She did not need to see who it was; she knew it was Torr.

He hugged her tight for a moment, then shoved her at arm's length and, as he kept firm hold of her arms, he looked her up and down and asked, "Are you hurt?"

"No, but he is dead," she informed Torr as she peered past his shoulder.

Torr turned, his hands slipping off her and quickly grabbing one of her hands to hold tightly.

Wintra figured he was not taking any chance of losing her and that was just fine with her, since his strong grip always made her feel safe. She also appreciated the presence of the many warriors who circled them, Sloan included.

"What have we here?" Sloan asked, dropping down on his haunches to take a closer look.

"Another dead man," Torr said and drew Wintra close against his side.

"How did you come across him?" Sloan asked.

"I tumbled down the hill," she admittedly reluctantly, feeling foolish for her misstep.

"You sustained no wounds?" Sloan asked anxiously.

"I'm fine," she assured him even though she felt a bit lightheaded and looked to Torr. "He seems to have the same type wound as the other dead man, and yet he is far from where we found the other body. Do you think someone is tracking and killing these warriors?"

"There is no need for you to worry about this," Sloan said standing straight. "Cree will see to it."

She turned to Sloan, the lightheadedness growing. "It concerns me and, therefore, I will worry about it whether you tell me to or not and as far as my brother—" A wave of nausea hit her so hard that it stole her breath, and she barely called out Torr's name before everything went dark.

Torr felt his heart slam into his chest when he heard his name spill with such urgency and fright from her lips. Then when her body went limp and she was about to collapse, he scooped her up in his arms.

"There will be holy hell to pay if anything happens to her," Sloan said as he hurried with Torr back to camp.

Sloan was right about that, but it would not be only Cree who would be raising hell. Right now, however, it was Wintra that Torr was more concerned with. He had seen people take a tumble, get up, and think nothing of it only to slip into sleep and never wake.

He placed her gently on the blanket near the fire and saw then just how pale she was and fear tightened his gut. He hurried to scoop up a handful of snow and rub it over her face.

"Come on, Wintra, come back to me. You will not leave me now."

Sloan watched surprised by the way Torr spoke to

Wintra. It was as if— No, it could not be. God help him if— He shook his head. The Almighty himself could not help Torr if he had foolishly fallen in love with Wintra.

"Damn it, *Princess*, come back to me," he shouted tapping her cheeks, trying to revive her.

Princess? Sloan shook his head again. *Torr and Wintra?* There definitely was going to be holy hell to pay when they got home. Sloan recalled how Cree would voice his thoughts after visiting with his sister. He had plans to arrange a good, solid marriage for her. Cree would not be happy about this.

Torr kept rubbing her face with snow and demanding she wake as all eyes turned on him.

Her eyes finally fluttered open and with some effort she raised her hand to press against his cheek. "You need not shout. I can hear you. I merely," —she paused trying to clear her jumbled thoughts— "fainted?" She was surprised at her own conclusion. "I have never fainted."

"You rolled down a hill and into a dead body," Torr reminded, relieved to see color returning to her face. "You had a good reason to faint."

Wintra dropped her hand to rest on his chest. "My face is chilled."

"Torr covered it with snow to get you to wake," Sloan said.

She turned her head to glance at him. "I forgot my brother's warriors were here."

Was that disappointment Sloan heard? And Wintra touched Torr with such ease and familiarity. Could she possibly feel as he did for her? How had this happened so fast? Sloan had to smile. The same had happened to Cree, so why not his sister?

"We will see you safely home," Sloan assured her

and stood.

"You will post more guards?" Torr asked, though it sounded more like a command.

"I intend to see to that now." With a nod to Torr, he walked off.

Torr took hold of Wintra's hand that rested against his chest. "Are you in any pain?"

"I am fine," she said, having repeated it so often that it felt like a chant to her.

He leaned down closer, his face not far from hers. "If we were alone I would strip you bare and check every inch of you to make certain."

Images of her naked, his hands roaming over her, exploring, igniting her sensitive flesh, filled her mind. It left her feeling deliciously wonderful, yet terribly vulnerable, especially since in her vision he was completely clothed.

Her remark slipped from her mouth as fast as images had filled her head. "I would permit that— only if you are naked as well." Had she truly just said that? Did she truly mean it? Oh Lord, whatever was the matter with her letting him know that she wanted to see him naked again?

Torr grinned. "I am not asking your permission, Princess, and if you want me naked just ask. I will gladly oblige you."

Her cheeks turned so hot that they probably blistered red, and she wished for more snow to cool them off.

"Tell me you will wed me, and then you will be able to see me naked whenever you want."

She laughed softly and gave him a playful punch in the shoulder. And she found herself about to agree to wed him, but she held her tongue. *Too fast. Too fast.* It was all going too fast since she had left the abbey. She had to take a breath and think. No not think, she thought too much. She needed to let things be—for now.

"You are mine and you know it. Soon you will admit it," he said still grinning. "I would love to wrap myself around you tonight to sleep, but that won't be possible, of course, if we were wed..."

"Go," she said giving him a slight shove. "I need to think."

He laughed. "You never stop thinking."

"I am cursed with a curious mind or so say the nuns at the abbey who are probably at this very moment praying for me."

Torr brushed a damp curl off her face. "I love your curious side. It makes you even more interesting than you already are." He gave her hand a squeeze. "I will be back soon. Do not think. Rest."

Wintra watched him go. Each step he took left her a bit more upset. She sighed and burrowed further under the blanket. Her sole thought and objective for so long had been for her and her brother to be reunited. It had occupied her thoughts day and night. She had taken to devising plans, often nonsensical ones, to escape the abbey and find her brother. But the years had passed and the plans had remained mere thoughts—until Owen.

She wondered now what Owen had truly wanted from her. And try as she might she could not get the two dead warriors out of her mind. Their lifeless eyes haunted her. Were they begging for help or warning that she too could find herself like them—unexpected victims?

Too many possibilities rattled around in her head, and she reached the conclusion that there had to be more to Owen's plan than to simply wed her. There had to be a reason that these two men who had helped him rescue her had been found murdered. She had to settle this matter for herself if she was to keep her sanity. She might not always find answers to her endless questions, but this was one time she intended to get answers, no matter what.

Her busily buzzing thoughts drifted off as sleep laid claim to her. The last thought she took with her, not of death and deceit, but of Torr and how much she wished for his arms around her.

Chapter Thirteen

"The closer we get to the village, the more restless you become," Torr said looking down at her snug in his arms.

"I have not seen my brother in some time, through no fault of his," Wintra was quick to add. "About three years ago, I refused to see him when he visited. The only way I would see him is if he was there to take me with him, foolish on my part since I missed him terribly. I thought in my naïve wisdom that he would give into my demands. I should have known better. And now I wonder how he will receive me."

"Like the sister he has missed as much as you have missed him."

"Or perhaps as the young, witless sister who made things more difficult for him."

"You are far from witless, though closer to stubborn—" He laughed and she punched him, though it felt more like a tap.

"I am not stubborn; I am determined," she insisted.

"Determined is good. Are you determined to love me no matter what? No matter anyone's reaction? No matter what is said or done? Above all else, will you love me as much as I love you?"

His words sent a shiver racing through her. Would their love face that much opposition? But then how could it not? To fall in love in such a brief time was not quite believable. How then did it happen? How did she know with such certainty that she loved this man who held her so lovingly and protectively in his arms?

More questions, few answers, and yet she found herself believing in this unbelievable love. She could not explain it, though she felt it, and she could not explain that either. The thought of being separated from him overwhelmed her with such grief that it roiled her stomach and she grimaced.

"Such a pained face can only mean..." He left her to explain.

"The pain is from the thought of not having you near and as much as I fight the unbelievable that we could love so strongly when only meeting, I cannot ignore the certainty of my love for you."

"Strong enough to wed me?"

"Aye, my love is strong enough to wed you, though I cannot wed you yet. Love may have rushed in to claim my heart, but my mind challenges my heart. I thought myself in love with one man only to realize that I had never loved him and now here I am claiming I am in love again. It troubles, yet excites me, which leaves me completely confused."

"But is your love for me strong enough to stand the strongest scrutiny?"

"You make it sound like I will be facing an impossible task and that my love for you could fail?"

"Could it?"

"Why would it?" she asked, fear prickling her skin.

"We sometimes find ourselves tested by unexpected happenings, and it is the strength of what we know to be true, to be honorable in nature that can help us see the right or wrong of it. I believe love can uncover truths and survive the most difficult challenges. We face a challenge you and I, and I pray that the truth will help us survive."

"Why wouldn't it?" she said. "I may speak at times when it would be wiser for me to keep my thoughts to myself—" his laughter caused her to pause a moment and give him a playful jab—" but I always speak the truth to you as you do to me. No one can take that from us."

"A good thing to know— *and remember*," he emphasized.

Sloan rode up beside them, ending their conversation, though thoughts lingered in her head. She sensed there was more to what Torr was saying than he had voiced and her mind, as usual, went wild with possibilities.

"We will be entering the village soon," Sloan said.

Torr felt Wintra tense against him and he gave her waist a reassuring squeeze.

"I sent a warrior on ahead to let them know we approach," Sloan continued. "They will be waiting for our arrival."

Wintra could not believe it. After all this time, she was finally going to be with her brother.

Not for long. My life is with Torr.

Her thought did not startle as much as she expected. Torr was right about one thing— unexpected things did happen. And she could not help but wonder how many unexpected things were about to happen.

~~~

The village was quiet when they entered, but then it was near to nightfall and most everyone were tucked safe and warm in their homes. Yet Wintra sensed an underlying unease. Was it her arrival that had caused it?

"Owen is here," Torr said as they approached the keep.

Wintra's stomach roiled as she spotted three of Owen's warriors standing at the bottom of the steps of the keep, their eyes remaining steady on her and Torr.

"Owen must have come directly here after finding we led him on a false trail," Torr said.

She feared what lies he may have already told Cree, and how they would affect her and Torr. The one thought that was stronger than all others was for her to get to her brother and tell him the truth about what had passed.

Torr dismounted, and then helped her off the horse. "Do not let this evil man rob you of the joy of being reunited with your brother. That above all else is what is important at this moment."

"That is why I love you so much. You understand me and my maddening thoughts and love me anyway."

"Just to remind you how much, Princess—"

He kissed her and not a gentle, friendly kiss, but a kiss that let all who saw it know that she belonged to him, and it tingled from head to toe and back again. When he ended it, he gave her a minute to clear her senses, then took her hand and led her up the keep steps.

She followed along, though at that moment she would have followed him anywhere.

Wintra stopped a few feet into the Great Hall, Torr halting alongside her and Sloan and some warriors coming to a stop behind them. A nervous quiver ran through her. Cree's warriors milled about while a few of Owen's warriors lingered near the dais, which meant he was close by.

When Owen's warriors spotted her, their heads turned, and just after that Owen's head appeared to the side of a wide set of shoulders.

She cried out as her brother turned around. "Cree!"

Tears stung her eyes and her heart filled with joy at the sight of him. While intimidating to all, he wasn't to her. He was simply her loving brother. She didn't stop her tears from falling, and when he spread his arms wide welcoming her into them as he had done so often when she was young, she did not stop herself from running to him.

Cree hugged his sister tight, happy to finally have her home and he let her shed her tears just as he had always done. Then she would raise her tear-stained face to him and tell him how much better she felt now that he had chased away her fear or sorrow or whatever had been bothering her at that moment. If it was happy tears she cried, she would wiggle out of his arms and tell him that she had planted some happiness on him, and he was not allowed to wipe it away.

She eased herself from his arms, though her hands took hold of his, but before she could say a word Owen stepped from behind Cree.

"There is no need to worry, my dear. I have explained to your brother how much we love each other, and how we are practically wed since we already consummated our love for each other. I also explained how that brute," — Owen pointed to Torr—"forced himself upon you and although you are disgraced I love you and will overlook it. We can wed immediately."

Wintra was horrified by his lies and was about to tell Owen what she truly thought of him when Torr stepped forward.

"You are a liar. You never consummated anything with Wintra. And she does not love you."

"We most certainly did. Wintra gave herself to me willingly the night we spent alone in the woods," Owen said boldly. "She is rightfully mine. All we need is the ceremony to confirm it"

"You are a fool if you think anyone will believe your lies," Torr said, his hands fisting at his sides. "I tracked you and I saw everything that went on that night. You left her sleeping alone while you joined a group of warriors a distance away."

Cree turned his head slowly to glare at Owen. "You left my sister vulnerable to attacks by foe or animal?"

"He is lying," Owen yelled.

"Is he?" Cree asked. "Then tell me how Torr got my sister away from you."

"I offer your sister love and a good life with me," Owen argued rather than answer Cree.

"I do not know your motive for wanting to wed Wintra, but it has nothing to do with love or you would have never hit her or—" Torr never got to finish.

Cree grabbed Owen by the throat and hoisted him up off the ground to dangle in front of him. "You dared lay a hand on my sister?" he demanded, his eyes full of fury.

Owen gasped for breath, his hands uselessly ripping at Cree's to free himself. "L-l-let m-m-me—" He was suddenly dropped to his feet and through heaving breaths he said, "Wintra was hysterical from what Torr had done to her. Slapping her was the only way to calm her."

Wintra was stunned at how easily the lies spilled from Owen's lips. What a fool she had been to believe anything this man had told her. And she was angry that these three men stood here discussing her fate as if she was nothing more than mere chattel to be bargained over.

"Please give me a chance to speak with Wintra alone," Owen begged.

"No," Torr said as if his word was final.

"You have no say in this," Owen said with a self-satisfied smirk. "Cree decides his sister's fate."

"No one decides my fate but *me*," Wintra snapped not able to listen to them discuss her as if she was not there. She took a step away from the three of them. "This is my life," –she tapped her chest— "I will decide what I want."

"Do not be foolish, my dear," Owen said as if speaking to a child. "Men know what is best for women."

A commotion at the door to the Great Hall prevented Wintra from spewing forth what she truly thought of Owen. Warriors hurried out of the way of a large warrior who appeared to be carrying the body of a limp woman in his arms.

Cree rushed forward to take the woman. He hugged her close, his eyes anxious with worry, though Wintra doubted many could tell just how very concerned he was. He concealed his feelings well, though not from her. She could tell how he felt with just one glance.

"What happened, Elwin?" Cree demanded.

"She was visiting with Lila and discovered your sister had arrived, and so she hurried through the village eager to meet Wintra. When her pace slowed, I realized something was wrong, and she turned to me, her face so pale, it frightened me. I caught her before she could hit the snowy ground."

"Get Elsa," Cree barked and Elwin jumped, turned, and hurried off.

Cree carried Dawn over to the large fireplace and sat on one of the benches closest to the fire. She was pale and so limp in his arms that he feared what may have happened to her and their babe. He ran a tender hand over her cheek as he whispered, "Return to me now, Dawn, before I lose my temper."

Wintra watched, upset for her brother, for evidently it was Dawn, the woman he loved, who he held in his arms, and his obvious pain tore at her heart. She turned to Torr and was surprised to see how upset he was as well, then she realized that Dawn was his sister, so naturally he would be concerned for her. She wished she could help the two men she loved the most but felt helpless to do so. Then a sudden thought came to her. "The snow. Would it not help her?"

"Good idea," Torr said and ordered a servant to hurry and get a bucket of snow.

Wintra noticed how everyone in the hall seemed concerned for the couple, their eyes steady upon them. All except Owen and his men, they huddled together whispering.

Wintra moved to stand where she could keep an eye on her brother as well as Owen.

Torr took the snow-filled bucket from the servant when she returned and knelt beside Dawn. "I used snow on your sister when she fainted and it helped."

Cree nodded, though said, "Dawn fainted, no doubt due to our babe, but why did my sister faint?"

Torr rubbed snow over his sister's face as he explained. "She took a tumble done a hill and rolled into a dead man."

"We need to talk."

"That we do," Torr agreed.

Dawn began to stir just as warriors cleared a path to Dawn for a short, round woman.

"She fainted, Elsa, though she is coming around," Cree said as the woman came to a stop behind Torr.

Elsa placed her hand on Torr's shoulder. "Keep rubbing her face with snow." She then reached into the pouch that hung from a knotted belt at her full waist. She pulled out a couple of sprigs of dried leaves and waved them beneath Dawn's nose.

Wintra stepped closer, curious as to what plant she had used. A hand tightened so hard around her arm that she winced with pain.

"A moment to speak with you," Owen whispered in her ear, pinching her arm harder and forcing her to take a step back. "I would not refuse my request or you will take a chance of seeing those you love suffer."

While fear prickled her skin, Wintra felt a modicum of safety here in the Great Hall with everyone around, especially Torr and her brother. And besides, she wanted to let Owen know what she truly thought of him, so she stepped back away with him behind the dais.

"I have plans, Wintra, and I am not going to let you upset them. You will tell your brother that you wish to wed me or as I have said those you love will suffer greatly."

She grew annoyed that he did not let go of her arm, but it did not prevent her from speaking her mind. "At one time, your idle threats would have frightened me, but no more. I see you for who you truly are, a deceitful, manipulative bastard. Now let go of my arm before I scream and bring my brother's wrath down upon you."

Owen leaned close and whispered, "I'll tame that mouth of yours once we are wed."

"Get your hands off her before I do everyone a favor and slit your throat."

Wintra and Owen turned to see a furious Torr standing on the other side of the dais.

"I am talking to the woman I love and will wed," Owen said continuing to carry on the ridiculous charade.

"I think not," Torr slammed his hands so hard on the table that everything on it rattled and a tankard toppled over, ale spilling out.

That brought several of Cree's warriors running over to stand behind him.

Owen wisely released Wintra, and she walked around the dais to Torr.

"What goes on here?" Cree demanded his warriors parting to clear a path for him.

"A few loving words with my intended," Owen said stepping around the dais.

Wintra spoke up before anyone else could. "You are not my intended. I have no intentions of marrying you. I do not love you. I have never loved you. You are a deceitful and horrible man. And if you ever threaten to do harm to those I love again, I will kill you myself."

Cree turned a murderous glare on Owen.

Owen was quick to say, "Wintra, I would never harm anyone you love."

"You are calling me a liar?" Wintra challenged.

"No, I think that this man," —Owen pointed to

Torr—"has manipulated you into believing things about me that are not true, and it has left you confused. I love you and when we wed I will do my best to make you happy."

"You are a fool if you believe you will wed Wintra," Torr said.

"This is no concern of yours and you have caused enough damage already. Stay out of it," Owen hissed.

Cree took a quick step forward, causing Owen to take several hasty and clumsy steps back. It was clear that Cree frightened the man, and he should be frightened. Cree could be cruel in his punishments and oddly enough fair, since any punishment he decreed was well-deserving of the deed.

"My sister does not lie," Cree said adamantly.

Wintra smiled. He believed her, but then they had struck a bargain when they were young and he had caught her in a lie. He had told her that they must promise to always be truthful with each other, for only then could they trust each other. So no matter what, they must never lie to each other. She had kept her word and never spoke another lie to him, and so had he.

"I am sure she doesn't," Owen assured him. "She is upset and under another's influence. I understand and I can help free her. All you need to do is give her to me in marriage."

"No!" Torr said with such command that all eyes turned to him.

Owen sent Torr a murderous glare while he asked Cree, "Will you please inform this cretin that this does not concern him?"

Cree turned to Torr, and they stared at each other for several moments. To Wintra, it appeared as if either permission was sought or an agreement met, and for some unknown reason their silent exchange sent a chill through her.

Cree looked at Owen. "It does concern him."

"And why would that be?" Owen asked annoyed.

Torr turned to Owen. "Wintra is my wife."

Chapter Fourteen

"How can that be?" Owen roared.

Yes, how can that be? Wintra thought as she listened to Owen continue to claim that it was impossible and Torr as well as Cree assuring him that it wasn't. She took a step back away from them, watching and listening as the scene unfolded as if she was stuck in a dream—no a nightmare—she could not wake from. Torr had known this all along and had never told her that he already was her husband.

"What do you mean the king decreed it?" Owen demanded. "Why would he do that? You are lying to me."

"The why of it does not concern you," Cree said in a warning tone. "It is done and cannot be undone."

Her brother's words resonated in her head. *Cannot be undone.* She was wed to Torr whether she wanted to be or not. She had no choice in the matter. He was her husband and would remain so.

She took a sharp step back as the three men continued to argue. Torr shot her a glance and it upset her even more that she had no idea what he was trying to relay to her. She had thought she knew this man, but did she? Was he an honorable man as he had claimed and as she had assumed after spending time with him? But if he was honorable wouldn't he have told her the truth?

Her heart ached horribly. This man she trusted and loved—loved? Did he truly love her or had he

157

made that claim knowing he had no choice? He was as stuck in this marriage as she was. So did he love her out of duty? Each thought made her heart ache more and more.

Owen continued to argue and press for proof of the King's decree, and suddenly Wintra wanted to be anyplace but here. She wished she could suddenly vanish and be alone with her thoughts.

A hand sliding in to hers startled her, and she turned. A woman, taller than her by several inches stood beside her. She had plain, though lovely features and dark, straight red hair that hung past her shoulder.

She smiled at Wintra and gave a nod as if to follow her.

Wintra realized than that it was Dawn, and she immediately asked, "Are you feeling well?"

Dawn nodded and tugged her hand.

Wintra did not hesitate, she went along with Dawn. No one seemed to pay them mind since the argument had grown heated, and Cree's warriors had maneuvered past them to surround him and Torr while several of Owen's warriors hurried into the Great Hall to do the same for Owen.

Wintra was relieved that they left unnoticed, Torr most likely expecting her to stay put until he finished, and then offer her an explanation. Or would he? Would he and Cree expect her to simply accept what the King had decreed? She almost laughed aloud, for again she realized she had no choice. The decision had been made.

They reached the bottom of the keep steps and Dawn hurried her around the side of the keep to a cottage. A woman, stooped from age and with an abundance of wrinkles to prove it, stood in front of the cottage door.

"I had the feeling you needed me?" the old woman said to Dawn.

Dawn nodded and pointed to her lips, and then to Wintra.

She nodded to Dawn and turned to Wintra. "You must be Wintra, Cree's sister. I'm called Old Mary and Dawn would like me to interpret as she speaks."

Wintra nodded, still feeling as if she was dreaming, though now she did not feel so much in a nightmare.

They entered the cottage, a blast of warmth hitting them.

Dawn turned to Wintra and smiled, then patted her own chest before reaching out and patting Wintra's.

"Dawn is very happy to meet you." Old Mary continued interpreting as Dawn continued motioning. "She is happy to have you as a sister and is thrilled that you are here at last. Please sit while she makes a hot brew and she will talk with you."

"Thank you for your kind welcome," Wintra said. "My homecoming is not what I expected, but I am so pleased to meet you."

Dawn smiled and motioned her to take a seat, and Wintra did.

Wintra watched Dawn bustle around the room as if it was familiar to her and perhaps the look on Wintra's face betrayed her thoughts since Old Mary addressed her silent musing.

"Dawn lived here for a while. The sleeping quarters are beyond that curtain," Old Mary said with a nod in that direction.

Dawn stopped, gestured, and Old Mary nodded. "She says that there are clothes in the chest at the foot

159

of the bed, yours to use if you would like."

"Thank you and thank you for bringing me here. It is a welcoming and comfortable cottage," Wintra said, wishing she could reside here away from everyone. She was used to solitude, had learned a great deal about it while at the abbey, though it had been a forced lesson. She had even come to enjoy it at times. So it would be no hardship to have this lovely place all to herself.

"May I help with something?" Wintra offered. "After all you did faint and probably should be resting."

"You fainted?" Old Mary said with a chuckle that surprised Wintra, though her next words explained her reaction. "How did the mighty Cree take it? Bet he was mad as hell that he couldn't do anything about it. He probably threatened you to wake. And no doubt he would rain hell down on heaven itself if you hadn't." She chuckled again and looked to Wintra. "That brother of yours loves Dawn to death. And I do not know how he will ever survive her birthing his babe."

Wintra stared wide-eyed at Dawn. "You carry my brother's child?"

Dawn eyes widened with alarm and her hands started gesturing.

Old Mary reached out, laying her hands over Dawn's. "Dawn is upset that you should find out this way, but it is my fault for not considering that you might not know yet."

"No, it's all right. It's just—" she couldn't seem to finish. It was as if the words stuck in her throat.

Dawn could see the hurt in Wintra's eyes and her heart went out to her. She rested her hand over Wintra's and with her other hand tapped her chest and pointed to her.

"Dawn's urging you to tell her what is troubling you," Old Mary said with empathy in her aged-eyes.

The constriction in her throat dissipated with the two women's heartfelt compassion and she found herself eagerly sharing her concern. "I have a husband I did not know I had, and I now learn I am to be an aunt and strangers knew all this before I did."

"What do you mean you have a husband you didn't know you had?" Old Mary asked while Dawn patted her chest and shook her head.

Wintra looked from one to the other. "Neither one of you knew that I am Torr's wife?"

They both shook their heads.

"No one has heard such news," Old Mary assured her, "for if they did I would have known about it. Nothing gets passed me in this village."

Dawn nodded, agreeing with the old woman.

"I heard them say that the King decreed it. What I do not understand is why the King would do such a thing. Is my brother beholding to him for something?

Dawn began gesturing and Old Mary interpreted. "Torr probably knows why and will explain it to you. He is a good man, not because he is my brother, but because he has proven himself to be. He will make a good husband."

"Because he has to," Wintra said sadly. She was not ready to share the fact that she had fallen in love with him or he with her. Or had he? No doubt she would continue to debate that question over and over since it continued to torment her. And hearing he was a good man and knowing it for herself only proved that he would do his duty and wed her whether he loved her or not.

The door burst open then, startling the women,

and the whoosh of cold wind sent the fire's flames dancing wildly. Cree ducked his head to enter, the width of his shoulders filling the doorway.

"What are you doing here?" he demanded and walked over to Dawn, his arm going gently around her waist and lifting her off the chair to rest against him. "You should be in our bedchamber resting."

Wintra watched as Dawn's hands spoke for her and was surprised when Cree answered her as if she had spoken aloud.

"I understand you wanted to meet my sister and that you feel you are fine, but you fainted—"

Dawn's hand started moving again.

"Presently we are talking about you, not my sister and Torr. I will address that issue when I finish with you," Cree said.

Wintra did not need anyone to interpret Dawn's response, her gesture was obvious when she crossed her arms over her chest and folded her lips tightly in her mouth.

Cree planted his face in front of Dawn's until their noses almost touched. "We are not finished until I say we are finished."

Wintra shivered, recalling that tone of voice. When she was young, it was that tone that had warned her to push no further, obey him or else. She had never bothered or had the courage to find out what *else* meant. So she was surprised when Dawn dropped her arms and started gesturing, not showing a bit of fear for Cree's tone.

"It is not your brother's place to explain to Wintra; it is mine."

Wintra turned to see Torr standing in front of the closed door. He seemed bigger, broader, taller to her, and his scar more dominate on his handsome face.

Had she not bothered to truly see him? Was this man—her husband—standing only a few feet from her the man she had thought he was, or was he a stranger?

He took a cautious step toward her.

She slid off the chair and hurried around to the other side of the table.

He did not like that she was using the table as if it was a shield keeping him at bay. Nothing would stop him from reaching her, certainly not a puny table.

"I want my brother to explain," Wintra insisted.

"No," Torr commanded. "Everyone will take their leave now. It is time you and I talked."

Old Mary hurriedly left the cottage as Cree turned to Torr and said. "I will talk with my sister."

"Tomorrow," Torr said with a warning glint in his eyes.

Cree looked ready to argue when Dawn took his hand and tugged at it.

"All of you go," Wintra demanded, having had enough for one day. "I want to be alone."

Cree slipped his arm around Dawn's waist and led her to the door, though he stopped before opening it. "We will talk, Wintra, and that is not a request." He opened the door and turned to Torr.

"I am not going anywhere," Torr said.

"I do not want you here," Wintra said with an angry snarl.

"It does not matter. I am staying."

"I want to be alone."

"I am staying," he repeated adamantly.

"Cree," she said looking to him for help.

Cree looked to Torr.

"I am her husband and you will leave us," Torr said.

Cree scowled, not caring for what he must say. "He is right, Wintra. I no longer have say over you. You now belong to him." He followed Dawn out the door, closing it behind him.

Wintra turned angry eyes on Torr. "I do not belong to you, and I want you to leave right now."

"I am not leaving. I am staying right here with you."

Wintra's green eyes darkened and turned wide. "You do not mean to stay the night, do you?"

He smiled. "Tonight and all nights to come."

Chapter Fifteen

Torr thought for a moment that Wintra would argue with him, but she did what he did not want her to do. She retreated into her thoughts. Her eyes suddenly lost their anger and her face softened, and he grew angry.

"You will find no answers or solutions in your thoughts. Talk with me," he said, though it sounded more like a demand.

"What is there to say to you? You lied to me. How do I trust you?"

He not only heard the pain of her disappointment, but he saw it reflected in her eyes and it tore at his heart. "What would you have done if I had told you? You would have grown angry as you have just done, and then what? We would not have talked and gotten to know each other. I thought it best you got to know me, discover my nature, and see for yourself if you could care for me."

He made sense, though at the moment she did not want him to. She was much too angry with him. Had he been angry when he had learned that she was his wife? The question hurriedly spilled from her lips. "How did you feel when you learned we were wed?"

It was a good question she asked and one he had not given much thought to. "I had no time to consider it. The message had arrived from the King shortly after your brother left the keep to find you."

"My brother was coming for me?" she asked

surprised, having thought differently.

"Cree had been furious when the news came of your abduction. Warriors were gathered immediately and Cree left with haste. I followed with the message. Cree and I were alone when he read the message. From the look on his face, I feared the news was not to his liking. He handed it to me and I read it, then I told him I would go find you. He agreed, though he truly had little choice, since I was your husband and the decision and responsibility mine."

"When Cree became a warrior, he rarely lived by rules," Wintra said, recalling the obvious change in her brother over the years when he had visited her in the abbey. "He could have commanded you otherwise."

"And take a chance of causing a rift with his sister's new husband? Besides, the King had already seen it done. He had had a proxy marriage performed so that his decree could not be challenged. Your brother also had his warriors and lands to consider, if he had not I imagine his decision would have been different."

She leaned her hand on the back of the chair, her legs having grown much too tired. "What I do not understand is why the King would force a marriage between us?"

Torr could see that exhaustion was quickly taking hold of Wintra. "You are tired and need rest. These are questions better left for another day."

"What I need are answers and I need them now."

"When your brother said it was complicated, he spoke the truth. Leave it for another day when you are not so exhausted."

As much as she hated to admit that he was right; he was. All she wanted to do was slip into bed and sleep—alone. Or did she? She had grown accustomed to having Torr wrapped around her. But now, with him being her husband, he could have his way with her, and the thought sparked her passion to life. How could she be angry at him and still desire him?

"You will be sleeping with me?" she asked.

Torr stood and walked toward her.

She watched him approach, not able to take her eyes off him. His gait was slow and confident, his shoulders broad, and he wore the slightest of smiles on his handsome face. And that was all she needed to see, her body reacted instantly to him, igniting the passion that had sparked in her and turning her legs from tired to weak.

He stopped in front of her and raised his hand to ever so lightly stroke her cheek, chin, and lips. "We are husband and wife and from this night on we share a bed—and so much more."

She almost gasped from the exquisite pleasure his touch stirred in her.

Torr took her hand. "We are both exhausted and need sleep." He moved his hand to her waist and led her to the curtain, pushing it aside so that she could enter.

It was a small, yet welcoming room. A fire glowed and its warmth filled the confined space. A chest sat at the end of a bed that would easily sleep two people. The bedding appeared freshly washed and Wintra wanted nothing more than to sink into it and let sleep claim her, so that she did not have to think another moment about this day, or all the days since she had left the abbey.

Torr stepped away from her and began to disrobe.

"What are you doing?" she asked anxiously and took a step away from him.

"Taking my clothes off."

"Why?

"To go to bed," he said while continuing to undress.

"You are going to sleep naked beside me?'

"I have done it before."

"But it's different now," she insisted.

"Yes, it is. We are husband and wife and have the right to be naked in front of each other. Actually, we had that right when we first met. So your honor was never truly in any danger."

Wintra was about to argue with him when she realized that one more garment and he would be stark naked. Her heart beat a bit faster, and she was about to turn her back on him when she found herself frozen in place.

She tried to keep her eyes from roaming, but it was difficult. He was a fine looking man from top to bottom, and that was where her eyes went from top to bottom and in between, lingering more on the in between. He was such a powerfully built man, his body so tempting that she shivered with the thought of making love with him.

He walked over to her and she took several steps back as he approached, but it did not matter.

His arm snaked out to catch her around the waist and draw her close. "Take your clothes off and come to bed."

She could feel the heat of him through her garments, and it was intoxicating. She recalled how his hands had warmed her naked flesh when she had been so cold and how their bodies had snuggled so intimately to keep warm. He had grown hard then just as he did now. It was obvious he wanted her, and she could not deny that she wanted him.

Her head began to throb, and she turned her back to him, rubbing her temple. She could not think straight. Her mind was filled with jumbled thoughts and nothing made sense. She wanted something—anything to make sense.

She stiffened when his arm slipped around her waist and when he tried to ease her back against him, she held her ground. She was much too vulnerable at the moment, and she had already made decisions she had regretted. She would not do that again.

Torr was hard and aching to make love to his wife, to show her what he felt for her was real, not something forced on him out of duty. Now, however, was not the time—or was it?

"You need sleep," he said, knowing endless thoughts were probably buzzing in her head and the only way she would get any relief was sleep or for him to make love to her.

Wintra did not argue with him. She slipped away from him, relieved that he let her go, and sat on the chest to remove her boots. She wanted desperately to strip herself bare and discard the patched wool dress beneath her shift. But when Torr had scurried her away, her clothes had been left behind.

Then she recalled what Dawn had told her about the clothes in the chest and hurried over to it, dropping to her knees to push at the lid.

Torr was quickly at her side. "What are you doing?"

She wished he would not stand so near to her, especially since he was naked and aroused. She kept her eyes averted, but it wasn't easy since she was on her knees in front of the chest and he was standing at her side. His arousal was much too close to her face. If she turned, her lips would brush it, and she was surprised that the thought actually appealed rather than repulsed her. She would have never believed that she would find the thought inviting after the incident in the cottage with Owen. But then Torr was not Owen.

The thought jolted her for a moment. Torr was nothing like Owen, and she would do well to remember that.

"Dawn told me there were garments in this chest I could make use of. I hope to find a night dress."

He pressed his hand on the lid. "Nothing stops us from sleeping naked together. And that is how we shall sleep tonight—naked together."

The idea that she would feel uncomfortable undressing in front of him disturbed him. It meant that she did not trust him, and that he did not want, and so he would not give her the chance to do so. Not to mention that he ached to have her naked in his arms.

He turned away to add three more logs to the fire, not wanting to glare at her while she undressed. When he turned back around she was still standing as he had left her, fully clothed.

"I feel like a moth too close to a flame?" she said.

He loved that she spoke her mind, and he walked over to her. "You fear I will devour you?"

"Will you?" she asked in a nervous whisper.

He ran his thumb over her lips. "I am your husband."

"You have rights."

"And you have duties."

"You wish me to do my duty tonight?"

This time he brushed his lips over hers. "Do you wish to do your duty tonight?"

She did not know what to think. Odd warmth had

settled over her, and dampness settled between her legs and when he touched her she felt herself throb. She shook her head. "I am confused."

He lowered his hand and splayed it at the apex of her legs, his middle finger resting over her sensitive nub. "Tell me, Princess, do you love me?

"I do," she admitted without hesitation.

"And I love you, so why deny us?"

Her breath caught as his finger slowly began to tease her.

He rested his brow to hers. "The decision is an easy one. You want me and I want you. Therefore..." He stepped away from her, grabbed her tunic and yanked it over her head, and then he ripped the dress she had repaired down the middle and pulled it off her and tossed it into the hearth. The flames eagerly took hold and devoured it.

She was stunned by his actions and yet he had also excited her.

"You have a gorgeous body."

She stared at him. Had she heard him right? He thought her body gorgeous?

Torr saw the surprise in her lovely green eyes and reached out to cup one breast. "You truly do, and I ache to touch you all the time." His hand drifted down along her stomach, to slip into the triangular nest of blond curls. "Tell me you want me to touch you, Wintra."

His intimate touches and suggestive words left her mindless. It was her body that was in now control.

"Tell me, Wintra, tell me you want me to touch you."

A pleading yes rushed from her lips as she moved closer to him, wanting and needing him to do so much more.

His fingers found her precious nub and she jumped at the jolt of pleasure that shot through her. "You are mine, Princess, and always will be."

She grabbed his muscled arms to keep herself from collapsing, her legs having turned limp.

He scooped her up and carried her to the bed and stretched out on his side next to her.

She pressed her hand to his lips as he lowered them to hers. "The nuns warned me that I was to submit to my husband. To lie there and let him have his way, but I feel the need—to touch you."

"Touch wherever you like, kiss wherever you like, taste wherever you like," he said, "for I plan to do the same to you." His hands began to explore her then while his lips claimed a heart-stopping kiss that left her breathless.

Torr could not stop exploring every inch of her. Wherever his hand touched, his lips followed. She tasted as good as she felt and he could not get enough of her.

Wintra grabbed at his arms, the bolts of pleasure shooting through her making it difficult to do anything else but hold on to him. She gasped when he nibbled at her nipples and groaned when his tongue teased them unmercifully. She bucked when his head disappeared between her legs and moaned, thinking she would surely go mad from the endless pleasure he was bringing her. Her eyes drifted closed as she began to moan softly, and then it grew until she was calling out his name over and over.

His own need quickened when he looked at her in the throes of passion, his name echoing from her kissed-swollen lips. He slipped over her, settling between her legs, and he was glad when she opened her eyes. He wanted her to be focused on him as he entered her. He wanted to see her pleasure mount and share in it. He wanted her to remember this moment always, this moment they became one.

Her eyes turned wide when she felt him enter her and the deeper he went the deeper she wanted him to go. Until, she could stand it no more and arched her body, taking all of him deep inside her.

She let out a small cry and Torr immediately stopped moving.

He held himself over her, his taut muscles covered with a fine sheen of sweat. "I caused you pain?"

She shook her head and reached out, trying to pull him closer, though she could not budge him. "No. No." She shook her head again. "I want you as deep inside me as you can go."

He smiled and started a rhythm that Wintra found herself matching, and he went deeper and deeper, the temp growing stronger and stronger. She grasped at his arms and held on for dear life, for she thought she was about to burst.

And she did. The intense sensation hit her so hard the she cried out and Torr moved even harder inside and oh if it didn't feel fantastic.

She launched her hips up pressing into him and squeezing tightly, greedy in devouring every last bit of her powerful climax. Then suddenly she felt Torr burst as she had done and she held onto him and they rode out the last ripples of pleasure together.

It took a few minutes before either of them could move or speak. Then he rolled off her and laid a moment on his back, calming his breathing before he turned on his side to look at her.

"That was so much more pleasurable than I had ever imagined it to be," she said with a sigh.

He smiled. "I am glad I pleased you."

"Did I please you?" she asked anxiously, turning on her side to face him.

"More than you will ever know."

She was about to smile when a yawn slipped out.

"You are exhausted. You need to sleep."

Wintra felt sleep creeping up over her, but she had to ask, "Why tonight? Why make love to me tonight?"

Torr took hold of her chin and held it firm. "To officially seal our vows so that nothing or no one can separate us. I love you, Princess, and I will not lose you."

Chapter Sixteen

Owen had left the Great Hall shortly after Cree and Torr had stormed out realizing their women had left. They were fools to place such importance on women. They were nothing more than a means to an end. They were there to bring a man more land and wealth through marriage and to satisfy his needs whenever instructed to do so.

He snarled as he crept up on the cottage, keeping to the night shadows so that no one would see him. He had worked for months formulating his plan, ridding himself of those who stood in his way and playing a dotting man in love. He would not have it all fall apart. He would not lose the wealth his union to Wintra would bring him. Besides, he wanted the bitch to pay for speaking out in front of all, instead of holding her tongue like an obedient woman should. What did she know about love anyway? She had been raised in the abbey by nuns who should have taught her better manners and obedience, something he would enjoy doing.

It angered him to think that Torr had her before he did. She was a beauty and he would have enjoyed breaking her in to serving his needs. But then he planned on her still serving his needs one way or another.

His jaw clenched when he heard Wintra scream Torr's name and when she did it again, he found himself not only growing more furious, but hard.

"Damn the bitch," he muttered, though did not turn away and leave. He waited and listened, her cries of pleasure exciting him more than he cared to admit. His thoughts drifted to how Wintra would scream when he mounted her. She would beg him to stop, but he would give her a good pounding and when he was done, she would obey his every word. And every night he would do the same to remind her of her place as his wife and—he shook his head. His musings had hardened him so badly that now he would have to find a woman to see to his needs tonight. And she would need to be a willing one at that. He certainly could not do as he usually did and force himself on one, for it would jeopardize what plans he had left.

It disgusted him to think that he would have to be nice to the woman who would spread her legs for him tonight. After all he was the man, the one with the power and he enjoyed wielding it as he liked.

Owen stood staring at the cottage, a snarl distorting his face. It was quiet, not another sound came from it. He should be the one sleeping with Wintra tonight. He should be the one she obeys, but then she will be. She will have no choice. And to make certain of that he intended to not only see Torr dead, but her interfering brother as well.

~~~

Cree's eyes shot open. He had no idea what woke him, but he woke with the express need to keep his family safe. He looked down at Dawn cuddled so comfortably in his arms as she was every night and as she would be every night to come. She belonged to him and that was that, and he loved her beyond reason.

The sun would soon rise and so would he, and though he would prefer Dawn to stay abed and rest, at least for a couple of hours, he knew she wouldn't.

He smiled still amazed that a voiceless woman had stolen his heart. His smile faded as his hand slipped down to rest on her stomach. He felt the growing bump. It had only recently appeared. He doubted anyone could see it yet, and he was glad. It was something Dawn and he shared and no one else. He worried over her and the babe nestled safely inside her. He could not imagine what it would be like for her when the time came to deliver their child.

Her screams would be trapped inside her, for only her to hear. He grew angry at the thought that her agony would be hers alone, and he silently vowed to do something about it. He also wondered if their child would be born voiceless. It did not matter, he would love the child regardless, and Dawn would teach their babe how to cope and live without a voice. But he hoped it would not be necessary. He hoped their child was born with a voice, for he knew Dawn would be distraught if she passed the affliction onto her babe.

Cree felt a slight chill brush his naked arm and realized the fire needed tending. He reluctantly eased away from Dawn and went to add logs and stoke the fire back to life. He would make certain the room was warm for when she woke, though he would not mind heating her body himself.

He grew hard at the thought, and even harder when he thought about how she always welcomed his touches, his kisses, and how much she enjoyed making love with him. He shook his head when he glanced down and saw how hard he had grown. He hadn't had to look, he felt it, and he felt the overpowering need to make love to Dawn.

He shook his head again. She needed to rest. She did not need poking from him. His hand slipped down to stroke his hardness. He could take care of himself, since if he didn't, he would go and wake her and take her much too hard and fast and that would not do. Not now at least, another time when she was fully awake and fully willing, which was usually all of the time.

A moan slipped from his lips at the thought of riding her hard and his hand took on a more forceful rhythm.

Cree startled when Dawn's hand covered his and he turned a quick glance on her. Sleep partially filled her dark eyes and her dark red hair lay wild about her head and shoulders. The contrast of soft and wild struck his gut and groin hard and damn if he didn't want to scoop her up, rush her to the bed, and—

She shoved his hand away and squeezed him hard, then she rubbed the tip of him against her nub and let her head fallback as her mouth opened in a silent groan.

She left no doubt as to how much she wanted him, and he lost all control. He scooped her up, rushed her to the bed and was inside her in an instant. He groaned with the feel of her tight, wet, welcoming sheath.

He told himself to take it slow, don't ride her hard, but when she bucked hard beneath him, he knew she wanted as wild and hard a ride as he did. And he gave it to her.

"I'm going to make you come and then come again and maybe even again," he said and gave a laugh when she nodded vigorously. He nipped at her lips. "God, I love you so much."

She tapped at her chest, and then his, and spread her arms wide, letting him know that she loved him even more.

He almost came there and then, but he wanted her to come first, so that he could make her come again before he exploded in a fury that was building frantically inside him. He pushed up, his muscled arms growing taut as his chest hovered over her.

"Come for me," he demanded, thrusting hard into her and she obeyed willingly.

Dawn heard the scream echo in her head. She squeezed his arms over and over and silently gasped as she felt another climax rush over her and she tossed her head from side to side, the strength of it stealing her breath.

Cree came then. He couldn't stop himself, not when he saw her second climax hit her. He groaned as his climax surged through him and with a final satisfied grunt he collapsed on top of her. After a moment he leaned up, kissed her gently and went to pull out of her.

She grabbed his arms and shook her head.

"Not yet?" he asked, knowing that she liked him to linger inside her for a few moments after he had come. He had learned that she would sometimes climax again, though not as hard but satisfying enough when he did that.

He moved gently inside her and he felt her shudder and her eyes flutter for a moment as one last climax settled over her. He waited a moment longer, and then slipped out of her. He pulled the blankets out from under them and covered them both as he slipped beneath and took her in his arms.

"You are insatiable," he said with a tender laugh.

She looked up at him, smiled, and nodded her head as she tapped his chest.

"It better be only for me," he teased.

She nodded and yawned.

"You're tired," he scolded, though it wasn't Dawn he was scolding. It was himself. He should have been more considerate of her condition and not worn her out.

She shook her head.

He scowled. "Your yawn tells me differently."

She rubbed gently at the lines that had deepened between his eyes, trying to rub away his concern, though she doubted it would work. Cree did what Cree wanted regardless of what others said. But she had grown a bit stubborn herself, though her gentle nature had her handling it differently.

She took his hand and placed it on her stomach, resting hers over it.

His scowl faded some as he said, "The babe makes you tired."

She nodded, patted her chest, and smiled brightly.

"But you feel good."

She nodded, her smile turning natural. She patted her chest again, then placed her two hands together as if in prayer and placed them to the side of her face and closed her eyes briefly, opened them and patted his hand where it lay on her stomach.

"You will rest when the babe needs it."

She nodded again and pressed her hand against his, shaking her head.

"I know you wouldn't do anything to jeopardize the babe, but that does not mean I don't worry about the both of you. So, do not make me worry."

She crossed her heart.

"I will hold you to that promise," he said and kissed her gently.

Dawn enjoyed this early morning time she got to spend with Cree. They would often make love, and then talk. He talked to her as if she had a voice, and she loved him all the more for it.

"My sister is very angry with me," Cree said, "and I do not blame her."

Dawn made no gesture. He needed to talk and she wanted to listen.

"I had other plans for her. I wanted her to pick a husband of her own choosing, possibly fall in love. This was not a homecoming I wanted for her."

Dawn made several gestures and Cree was quick to respond.

"I know Torr is a good man and will treat my sister well, but—"

Dawn interrupted with another gesture.

"You are right," he snapped, "the choice wasn't only taken from my sister. It was taken from me as well. And I don't like it or that I can't do anything about it. She is my sister, damn it. I promised her I would always protect her and keep her safe. Now here she is wed to a stranger. And I do not need reminding that your brother is a good man, to her he is a stranger, and it can be terrifying for a woman to be forced upon a man she does not know."

He cringed, realizing what he had just said and took hold of Dawn's chin. "Were you terrified of me when they threw you in that God-awful shack with me?"

She nodded.

He winced and let go of her chin. "You were brave."

She tapped his chest and pressed her hand to his heart.

"Are you saying I was kind?"

She nodded.

"Are you trying to ruin my reputation?" he

scowled, though his voice teased.

She pressed her hand to her chest, and then to her lips.

"You will keep my secret?"

She spread her hands wide.

"Forever," he nodded, then whispered, "That is how long I will love you—forever."

He kissed her, and they snuggled in each other's arms neither wanting to let go of the other.

Chapter Seventeen

Cree sat in the Great Hall alone. Servants placed food and drink in front of him, but otherwise went about their chores. Dawn had fallen back asleep and to make certain he would not disturb her again, he had dressed and left their bedchamber. She was just too damn tempting not to touch, and he had already touched her enough this morning.

He drank the hot cider, but pushed the bowl of porridge away. He was not hungry. He had too much on his mind. Wintra was a stubborn one, much like himself, but there had always been a time when she would listen or at least talk with him, and he was counting on that time to come again.

What disturbed him more, after giving it thought, was how adamant Owen had been about marrying Wintra, and then threatening her when she had refused. Something did not seem right, and it concerned him.

"Mind if I join you?"

Cree looked up to see Torr standing there, and he gave a nod to the bench opposite him. "My sister fares well?"

Torr nodded, "And mine?"

Cree had to respect him. With two words and no threat, Torr had made it clear that it was neither of the other's concern as long as the women were treated well.

"She is well," Cree told him.

"She fainted yesterday."

Cree would have told him it was none of his concern, but he would not want Torr to do that when it came to Wintra, so he could understand his worry. "Elsa assures me that she is fine."

"Good. I have just found her. I would not want anything to happen to her before I got a chance to know her better," Torr said and filled a tankard with hot cider.

"I understand how you feel. It has been too long since I have seen my sister."

"Then you would not mind if Wintra and I stayed here until your babe is born? I think it would help the situation not to take her away from family so soon while giving me a chance to get to know my own sister."

Cree was more than pleased by Torr's offer, though he found it had never bode well for a mighty warrior to express any degree of gratitude. And habits were hard to break, so while he was more than delighted, he simply said, "You are welcome to stay."

"Thank you," Torr said respectfully, though he had had no doubt that the mighty Cree would refuse him. He had thought about it this morning when he woke with Wintra sleeping comfortably in his arms. It was better they got to know each other here, and then she would have time to reunite with her brother and come to know Dawn. Then when the time came for them to leave, she would be more willing to do so, or at least he hoped she would.

There was one other thing that disturbed Torr and he felt it was important to discuss with Cree, though Cree got to it first.

"Something about Owen disturbs me," Cree said.

Torr was quick to agree. "I feel the same."

"Tell me," Cree urged.

"Owen has an agenda, though I do not know what it is. I believe he had men abduct Wintra, and then he rescued her using a different group of warriors, and now he has another troop of warriors with him. What troubles me the most, is that Wintra found two men dead in the woods. One was from the group that abducted her and the other was from the troop who saved her, and they both had died from stab wounds."

"How did my sister come across them?"

"By sheer accident," Torr said.

"You were not with her?" Cree asked accusingly.

"I was never far from Wintra, but she does require a bit of privacy at times. And I did return here with *my wife* safe and unharmed with the exception of the bump to her head."

"How did that happen?" Cree demanded, not caring in the least that Torr reminded him yet again that Wintra was his wife. He wanted to make certain his sister was safe and always would be, and Torr, so far, had done that.

Torr explained how Wintra had attempted to escape from him and landed them both in a stream and though he didn't go into complete detail about the incident, he felt it was enough to satisfy Cree's obvious concern.

"That sounds like my sister," Cree admitted with a nod. "And it is good to know that you saw and continue to see to her care. Now tell me more about what happened."

It was when Torr explained how Owen had found them at the cottage and what had happened when he was alone with Wintra that had Cree exploding.

"Bring that bastard Owen to me right now," he bellowed, jumping up off the bench and having the few warriors who had entered the Great Hall for breakfast scurrying to obey. He turned an angry glare on Torr, though it was not meant for him. "Do you know anything about this man?"

"He is a sly and deceitful man from what I have heard. He took advantage of a lovely and innocent daughter of a chieftain my father is acquainted with, and ruined her, though made it appear otherwise. He is not one to be trusted."

"How had my sister come to know him?"

"He visited the abbey and had asked permission to speak with her concerning one of the gardens she tended. He cunningly insinuated his way into her life and somehow convinced her that he cared for her."

"I do not understand how the nuns could have permitted this, Cree said annoyed.

"From what Wintra had told me, she was never alone with Owen and he was always proper in his demeanor when around her. So the nuns believed him only interested in what he could learn from her about the gardens."

"The nuns never spoke of him to me," Cree said even more annoyed.

"There was nothing for them to speak with you about. Owen had never approached them about anything other than speaking to Wintra purely out of interest in her garden work. What troubles me is that I think he purposely sought out Wintra with plans to deceive her and convince her that he loved her and that he wished to wed her. The question is why? Did he believe you would bestow an exceptional marriage purse on her?"

"I did intend to, though I spoke of it to no one," Cree said. "Of course, it now belongs to you."

"I nor need it or want it. Wintra is gift enough for

me."

Cree cocked his head and glared at Torr. "You love my sister?"

"Is it not obvious?" Torr asked with a laugh.

"I would say you have not known her long enough to have fallen in love, but—"

"You fell in love with Dawn almost as fast."

Cree grinned. "Though I was a fool and had not realized it."

"Thank the heavens I am not a fool."

"And that you are my sister's husband and I do not make you pay for that remark." Cree turned his attention to Sloan, having seen him enter the Great Hall and hurrying toward them.

Sloan stopped at the end of the table. "You wanted Owen brought to you?"

Cree nodded.

"He departed over an hour ago," Sloan said. "I had assigned warriors to watch Owen and his men, though not let themselves be seen, and to inform me of anything they saw or felt was important. I was alerted to his departure and went to see Owen immediately."

"Did he offer an explanation for sneaking away?" Cree asked, his annoyance now having turned to anger.

"He was much too cordial about it. He apologized for any misunderstanding, and he claimed to not want to disturb you any longer. The strange part was that I did not believe a word he said, so I sent a few men to follow them."

"Good," Cree said. "I do not believe we have seen the last of him."

"My thought as well," Sloan said.

"Join us," Cree offered.

Sloan sat and filled a tankard for himself and raised it looking to Torr. "Congratulations on your unexpected marriage, though it was a relief to hear it."

"Why is that?" Cree asked.

"You should have seen the way he," —Sloan nodded at Torr— "insisted Wintra wake from her faint, and then there was the way she looked at him." Sloan shook his head and laughed. "It was obvious they both loved each other, and all I could think was that you were going to kill him once we got home. So it was a relief to hear that they were wed, and you had known about it."

"My sister loves you?" Cree demanded.

"She does, though I believe there are moments she fights that knowledge."

Sloan snickered. "You are in for it now, especially since she is so stubborn."

"Is she now?" Cree said.

"Aye, she is." Sloan grinned. "But she cannot help being just like her big brother."

"You really do want that tongue of yours cut out don't you?" Cree said, then cringed right afterwards. A threat like that always upset Dawn, and he had tried to curtail using it, but he had said it so often to Sloan, never fully intending to ever do such a thing, that it had become an instinctive reply when Sloan annoyed him.

"I do not worry about that threat anymore," Sloan said still grinning. "Dawn would come to my rescue."

"That she would," Cree admitted with pride, "though she will not come to your rescue when I pick a wife out for you."

Sloan's grin vanished. "That is not funny, Cree. I am not ready to please only one woman."

Cree had been referred to by all as 'my lord' since taking the title of Earl of Carrick, so by Sloan referring to him as he once had, Cree knew he was speaking to him as a friend. "Ready or not, you would be wise to find a good woman before the King commands more marriages to settle the mess the previous Earl of Carrick's wife created."

"What of you and Dawn? Why didn't the King wed you by proxy? Your union would be more important than any other?"

Cree looked to Torr. He had been the only one to see the document. The only one who knew the whole truth.

Sloan saw the look they exchanged. "Good God, you and Dawn are wed as well. Does she know she is your wife?"

"No, and no one is going to tell her."

"Why?" Sloan asked.

"I have my reasons," Cree snapped.

"I am sure Dawn would be curious to know those reasons."

The three men's heads snapped to the side, expecting only to see Wintra, but Dawn stood there as well.

Sloan slipped off the bench, hurrying to stand.

Torr got up more slowly.

Cree didn't move at all.

Wintra and Dawn approached them.

"It is time you see to your duties, Sloan," Cree said dismissing him, and Sloan quickly took his leave.

Torr stepped forward and held his hand out to his wife.

Wintra took it without hesitation, knowing this discussion was meant for Cree and Dawn alone. They left the hall, Torr with a nod to Cree and Wintra with a quick hug to Dawn's hand.

Dawn joined her husband—*husband*—he was actually her husband. The King had decreed it. She sat opposite him.

"Have your say and be done with it," Cree ordered.

She gestured slowly, pointing to him, then herself, and then entwining two fingers tightly and shrugging.

"Yes, you and I are wed good and proper."

She smiled and her hands started gesturing faster.

"I knew it. I knew it, and that was why I did not tell you we were wed. I knew you would then object to wedding me again here at the keep and having a huge wedding celebration. And I want that. I want all to see us wed and I want all to celebrate, for our good fortune is their good fortune."

Dawn's smile faded and she patted her chest and shook her head.

"You never thought of it that way?"

She shook her head again.

Cree reached out and took hold of her hand. "All will look differently upon you now that you are my wife. They all know how much I love you and how happy you make me, and they will be pleased that we have finally joined as one and want to celebrate the wonderful news."

Dawn could not help but have misgivings. After all Cree had taken her as his mistress and now the village was to celebrate her status as his wife. Would the villagers truly celebrate or only do so because forced to?

"I did not plan on keeping the news that we were wed from you. I found out just after Torr brought you half frozen to me. I did not want to tell you then and once you had recovered, Torr's horse had returned and I worried over my sister's safety. Then Owen had showed up and I didn't want to tell you with him here. I wanted time to speak with you about it and about planning a ceremony and a celebration, which I knew you would object to, and I was right."

She nodded, agreeing with him.

He kept hold of her hand as he got up and walked around the table to scoop her up and plant her on his lap after he sat. "I want us to take our vows for all to see. I want everyone to know how much I love you and how very proud I am to have you as my wife. And I want all to celebrate in our joy, in our love, in our future."

Tears clouded her eyes.

"I love you more than any words can express. Marry me, Dawn, and let us celebrate our love."

A tear slipped down her cheek as she nodded, accepting his heartfelt proposal.

Chapter Eighteen

"I was surprised to find you gone when I woke this morning," Wintra said as they walked along the path that ran through the village.

Torr smiled and lowered his voice. "I was concerned as to how tired you were from all that you had learned and been through, and if I had stayed, I would not have been able to keep my hands off your luscious body."

Her steps faltered from his blunt compliment, and Torr was quick to tighten his hold on her, which only worsened matters since it sent her stomach fluttering before it turned to a loud gurgle.

"You're hungry," he said with concern.

"I'm not hungry," she protested, at least not hungry in the way he thought and, besides, she was more famished—famished for him. She turned her head away from him for a moment, her sinful thoughts heating her cheeks. And, of course her stomach had to disagree and gurgle again.

Torr laughed. "You are such a stubborn woman that your stomach must speak for itself."

Embarrassed by her stomach's betrayal, she turned to him with a toss of her chin. "According to you, I have proven time and again how stubborn I am."

He smiled. "Truth be told, I would not have you any other way."

Surprised by his response, she asked, "Truly?"

"Your stubbornness challenges me and that will make for an interesting rather than boring life together. It also helps that I love you."

Her heart fluttered upon hearing him say it without doubt or hesitation. It was as if it came natural to him. He needed no preamble or flowery verse. He stated his love for her simply and honestly.

"I am hungry," she said, though wasn't quite sure how to tell him that it was him she was hungry for.

"Then we will eat," he said and took hold of her hand.

His grip was strong, almost as if he feared letting go and losing her, and her own grip grew a bit stronger, for the thought of him never holding her hand again brought an empty ache to her heart. She loved him and she was happy that she was actually wed to a man she loved, a man she so enjoyed making love with.

"Deep in thought again?"

She nodded.

"Share them with me."

Did she dare take a chance and tell him that she was hungrier for him than for food? Or did she heed the nuns repeated warnings that intimacy was initiated only by the husband?

"They will continue to haunt you if you do not discuss them."

Her brow knitted. "You know me well? How is that?"

He smiled. "You often make your thoughts known by speaking your mind, so it is not that difficult to get to know you, though I wonder what makes you hesitate now."

"I speak my mind around you more than anyone else," she admitted, as if she had just realized it.

"I am easy to talk to."

"So I have learned."

"Then tell me what seems to trouble you," he encouraged.

Her stomach gurgled much too loudly this time and though her cheeks burned with embarrassment, she could not stop from laughing.

"First, I will see that you are fed, and then you will tell me what keeps you from telling me what is on your mind."

They turned around and headed for the keep, though at the bottom of the keep steps Wintra stopped and said, "Dawn and my brother may still be talking and I do not wish to intrude on their discussion."

Torr placed his hands on her waist and gently propelled her up the steps. "Cree would have seen to their privacy by now if he intended for them to remain alone."

Wintra was pleased to see that her brother remained with Dawn at the table in front of the fireplace and pleased that that was where he chose to eat rather than take breakfast at the dais. It made her see that somewhere in Cree still lurked the brother she knew, and he was the one she hoped to talk with.

Dawn's gestures were easy to understand, she eagerly welcomed Torr and Wintra, urging them to join Cree and her.

Torr did not give Wintra a chance to refuse. With a little push of his hand to the small of her back, she took a seat opposite Dawn. Torr climbed over the bench and gave her hip a bump with his so that she would move down to the end and sit opposite Cree while he faced Dawn.

More food and drink were placed on the table and Wintra was grateful for the diversion. There was much she wished to discuss with her brother, but now was not the time or place, though she itched to do so. Cree had no idea how much she had missed him.

Dawn began to gesture and Cree interpreted. "Dawn is pleased that you and Torr will be staying here until the babe is born."

Wintra looked to Torr surprised and yet so relieved by the news. She feared she would be pulled away from her brother before she had a chance to be reunited with him.

"You need time with your brother and I need time with my sister," Torr said, explaining his decision.

Dawn nudged Cree with her elbow, and he scrunched his brow wondering what she implied. She raised her brow at him and tapped his knee under the table.

He watched as she signaled with her hands. She pointed at Wintra and then to Torr and locked two fingers together. He realized what she was saying. The couple also needed time alone, time to discover each other.

"The cottage is adequate for your stay here?" Cree asked.

"I love it," Wintra replied quickly, not wanting to stay anyplace else. It afforded a sense of privacy and solitude. Both were things she had learned to enjoy while at the abbey, and she wasn't ready to give up either just yet.

"In the meantime, perhaps you can help Dawn plan our wedding celebration," Cree said.

"I would love to help," Wintra said enthusiastically and couldn't help but wonder if she and Torr would ever have a true wedding.

"I am gone but a couple of days on a hunt and what do I hear on my return? That I have a new daughter," Kirk McClusky, Torr's father, yelled out as he entered the keep.

Torr stood and his father greeted him with a bear hug.

Wintra stood to be presented to Torr's father, feeling apprehensive. She was surprised to see what a good looking man Torr's father was, though why not? If not for the scar on Torr's face he would be more handsome than most any man. Actually, the scar did little to distract from Torr's good looks. In an odd way it added to his fine features, making him appear a warrior not to tangle with.

"My God, son, she's a beauty," Kirk McClusky said with a genuine smile that startled Wintra as well as the bear hug he gave her. After the hug he held her at arm's length. "I am a lucky man. I now have two beautiful daughters to be proud of."

Wintra could not help but wonder if he knew that she was Cree's sister and so, of course, she had to say something, and bluntly. "I am Cree's sister."

"So I have heard," he acknowledged, surprising her yet again. "And it is pleased I am to have Cree and you join our family. Yes, I am surely a lucky man."

Wintra could not help but smile at the man's sincere joy and the thought flashed through her mind that she now had a father. And once again the thought slipped past her lips. "My father died before I was born. I am pleased to have you as a father."

Kirk McClusky slipped his arm around Wintra's shoulders. "I am so sorry that you never got to know your father, but I would be honored for you to call me Da. And I will do my best to live up to that honor."

A tear tickled the corner of Wintra's eye and she was quick to dab at it with her finger before it could fall and embarrass her. "And I will do my best to be a good daughter."

"I think that will come natural to you," Kirk said and looked to Torr. "You are a lucky man, son."

"That I am, Da, that I am," Torr agreed and reached out to steal his wife away from his father and tuck her in the crook of his arm.

"Join us," Cree said. "We will raise our tankards in celebration to Torr and Wintra."

Before they could, Sloan came barreling into the Great Hall. "A fire at the mill."

Chapter Nineteen

"You stay right here," Cree commanded with a finger in Dawn's face. He then turned to his sister. "And you stay with her."

Wintra was already on her feet ready to help. She was all too aware of how fast a fire could spread. Two small outer buildings at the abbey had been lost to a fire and a third larger one had been saved to the tireless efforts of all the nuns. She had not sat idle that day and she would not sit idle now.

"You cannot command me," Wintra said defiantly.

"But I can," Torr said. "You will stay here with Dawn. And I will not hear another word about it."

Before either woman could protest, the men were gone.

Wintra shook her head. "I cannot sit here and do nothing."

Dawn waved for her to follow, and Wintra was quick to join her.

Once outside, they both stood in shock on the keep's steps when they saw the plume of flame and smoke in the sky. They were about to rush off and help, when Elsa's words stopped them.

"Stay away from the smoke, Dawn, it could harm the babe. If you must help, go to my healing cottage and make ready to help with the injured."

"We will see to it," Wintra assured Elsa, just as concerned for Dawn and the babe as Elsa was.

Dawn and Wintra rushed in the opposite direction of everyone else. And as soon as they entered the healing cottage, a man staggered in cradling his injured arm.

The two women went to work. Healing was not new to Wintra. The nuns had taught her what herbs worked well on various ailments, explaining that it would be her duty to see to her family's care, especially if the man she wed had no healer for his clan. She had quite enjoyed learning the different properties of the many plants, and she hoped to learn more from Elsa while she was here.

Most of the wounds were minor, though Dawn had gestured what Wintra had thought herself, which was that Elsa was treating those more severely injured at the scene until they could be safely transported to her cottage.

Wintra questioned those who sought their help, eager to know if the fire had been contained yet. The last wounded man assured her that it was almost under control and so far the water wheel was still intact, but the mill building itself had sustained some damage.

While Dawn saw to an older man who looked as if exhaustion had claimed him, Wintra took a bucket outside to dump the dirty water and refill it with clean snow to melt by the hearth. She went around back of the cottage when a hand suddenly clamped over her mouth and a strong arm snaked around her waist and began to drag her away.

The hand was so tight against her mouth that she couldn't bite at it, her first thought. And since she was being dragged, she couldn't gain any firm footing, so that left her with only one option. She grabbed one of his fingers at her waist and yanked it back as hard as she could.

He let out a scream as his hand fell off her waist, and the other off her mouth. She didn't waste any time in running and screaming for help as she did.

Dawn heard the screams and ran out of the cottage, the older man trying to keep up with her. She caught sight of Wintra running toward her, the warrior not far behind her.

"Go for help!" Wintra screamed worried that Dawn would attempt to help her and get hurt. "Go! Hurry!"

"Go," the old man shouted at Dawn and gave her a shove as he ran as best he could toward Wintra.

Dawn didn't want to leave either of them, but she was wise enough to know that the quicker she got to Cree, the better chance Wintra had of being rescued. She raised her arm, burying her nose and mouth in her sleeve to keep away what smoke she could as she got closer to the mill.

"Get out of here, Dawn," Elsa yelled when she caught sight of her.

Dawn paid her no heed and Elsa did not stop her. She was too busy tending the more seriously wounded men and women. And Dawn was relieved she had not tried. She had to find Cree or Torr, Wintra's life depended on it.

She stopped, seeing Cree shouting orders and Torr was not far from him at the front line of the brigade tossing bucket after bucket on the last of the fire while billowing smoke plumes consumed an already gray sky.

She needed to get his attention since she was still a distance away, so she did the only thing she could think of, she clapped her hands loudly.

Cree turned at the sound, so out of place in the

chaos, and his eyes widened. Something was wrong. She had clapped to get his attention and her eyes were wide with fright. He rushed toward her.

Her hands were moving before he reached her and he shouted, "Torr."

Torr turned and when he saw Dawn gesturing frantically to Cree, he felt a punch to his gut. Something was wrong with Wintra. He dropped the bucket and when he saw Cree run off as if the devil was on his heels, he quickly followed him.

Torr was beside him in no time.

Cree called out as he kept running, "Someone took Wintra. Behind the healing cottage."

Torr flew past Cree, jumping over mounds of snow and maneuvering around trees. He heard her screams as he turned the corner of the cottage. He shouted her name so loudly that it rang off the trees. "WINTRA!"

When she didn't respond, he shouted her name again and with such power that the woods and all in it trembled with fear.

He heard someone shout as if from pain, and then heard Wintra call out his name loud and clear. He never felt so relieved, though he knew he had to get to her fast. She would not be able to keep the warrior off her for long.

He came upon an old man sitting on a stump, breathing heavy and pointing.

Torr went where the old man pointed.

Wintra let out another scream, and this time her abductor slapped her across the cheek so hard that her head whipped to the side, and she fell face first in the snow. She screamed when he grabbed her by the back of her hair and yanked her up to her feet. Try as she might, she could not strike out at him, since he held her at arm's length in front of him.

"You will learn to behave fast enough," he said with an angry growl.

She did not bother to waste a breath on a response. Instead, she let out another scream, hoping it would help Torr find her.

The warrior cursed profusely as he swung her around.

Torr came upon the scene just as the warrior raised his hand to deliver another stinging blow to Wintra's face. He roared out his rage as he rushed the warrior.

As soon as the warrior caught sight of Torr charging him, he released Wintra in a flash.

She stumbled back as Torr lowered his shoulder and thrust it out to ram into the warrior's gut, his hands going around his upper legs as he did, and then he tossed him over his shoulder to land on the hard snow-packed ground.

Wintra heard the snap, it echoed off the trees. Torr had broken his opponent's neck in one swift move. She watched as he gave the dead man one last glance, and then walked toward her.

She was about to assure him that she was unharmed since he was forever asking how she fared, when he took her in his arms and kissed her with such intense need that it turned her legs weak.

He tore his mouth off hers as his hands reached up to cup her neck and he rested his brow against hers. "I feared I would not reach you on time and that I would lose you. I cannot lose you. It would be like losing a part of myself."

She brushed her lips over his. "What madness has me not only loving you, but needing, aching, for you in a way that is—sinful?"

"I see all is well," Cree said.

She looked to her brother and said, "More than you know."

"It is best we get back to the keep. We do not know who else may be lurking in the woods," Cree said.

Torr was quick to nod and take hold of Wintra's hand. He leaned down and quickly whispered, "Later, I will satisfy your sinful ache."

She shivered at the thought or was it anticipation?

They did not stop at the healing cottage; they went straight to the keep. Once in the Great Hall, Dawn greeted Wintra with a hug.

"The old man who helped does well?" Cree asked, tugging his wife to his side after Wintra assured an insistent Dawn that she had suffered no injuries.

Dawn nodded and gestured that he rested.

"Good, he will be rewarded for his bravery," Cree said and turned to his sister. "Did the man who took you say anything to you?"

"Only that I would learn to obey soon enough," Wintra said. "I assumed he was one of Owen's men, though he wore no plaid that could identify his clan."

Torr spoke up, keeping firm hold of his wife's hand. "It seems odd that a fire raged at the mill at the same time Wintra was abducted."

"I agree," Cree said. "But the question is why would Owen abduct Wintra? He knows she is wed to you, so why would he possibly want her now?" Cree shook his head. "We will speak to Sloan after we see to the mill."

He took Dawn by the shoulders and sat her down on the bench by the hearth. "You will dare not move off this bench until I return." He pressed his finger to her lips, warning her not to argue and looked to his sister and then to Torr.

Torr eased Wintra up against him. "Do not make my heart slam against my chest with worry or my stomach roil with fear because you are too stubborn to obey me. Stay here until I return." He rubbed her cheek, the redness almost gone. "I will send Elsa to—"

She pressed a finger to his lips. "There are others more in need of Elsa than me. I am fine."

He hugged her tight so that he could whisper in her ear, "Good, now nothing will stop me from making love to you tonight."

Wintra lowered herself to the bench when he let her go, his words sparking a passion in her that seemed to sit far too close to the surface all the time. She watched him walk away with the thought that tonight could not arrive soon enough.

Once out of the keep, Torr turned to Cree. "You did put guards on the two of them didn't you?"

Cree laughed and nodded. "You are beginning to know my sister well."

Chapter Twenty

A short time after Cree and Torr left, Flanna hurried into the hall and over to Dawn. She stopped a moment before speaking when she caught sight of two warriors guarding the entrance to the hall.

Dawn grabbed hold of her hand to get her attention. Flanna wore a concerned look and Dawn worried that something was wrong.

Flanna kept her voice low when she said, "I heard that Lila was injured, though I do not know how badly."

That was all Dawn needed to hear. With her cloak in hand, she was off the bench in an instant. She gave a quick glance to the guards at the door and saw that they had begun to approach her. Knowing she would never get passed them, and that they would also prevent her from leaving the hall, she turned and ran to the passageway that connected the hall to the kitchen.

Wintra quickly followed her.

Dawn's heart pounded in her chest with worry. She prayed that Lila was all right. She did not know what she would do if something happened to her. She was more than a best friend. She was like a sister to Dawn.

"Lila is here, Dawn," Old Mary called out to her when she was a few feet from the old woman's cottage.

Wintra had to hasten her steps to keep up with

Dawn. She was through the open door before Wintra made it up the snow-covered path. When she entered, Dawn was hugging a young woman and the woman, her one hand bandaged, was hugging Dawn with just as much fervor.

"You're squeezing the life out of each other," Old Mary said with a chuckle. "And some tears at that. Now sit and have a nice hot brew that will calm you both."

The women did as Old Mary said and Wintra joined them at the table.

Dawn gestured so quickly that Wintra could not understand what she was saying, though Lila's responses helped her follow their conversation.

"A blister is all from lugging the buckets of water. Elsa put some of her special herbal cream on it and has assured me it will be fine. The fire has finally been extinguished, but clean up cannot begin until the last of the embers fade and the debris safely handled."

Old Mary placed a gentle hand on Dawn's shoulder. "Lila will do good."

Lila smiled. "Now tell me. Is it true? Did the King truly wed you and Cree by proxy?"

Dawn wasn't surprised that the news had spread so fast, and she smiled and nodded.

Lila reached out and squeezed Dawn's hand. "I am so very happy for you."

Dawn made several gestures that Wintra did not understand, though Dawn pointed to her, so she assumed that she was being discussed.

Lila stood and bobbed her head at Wintra. It is a pleasure to meet you, my lady."

Stunned at being addressed so formerly and particularly as one of higher birth, Wintra stared at Lila for a moment before shaking her head. "I am

Wintra and would much prefer to be called a friend."

"Like Dawn and me, though we have been best friends forever," Lila said with a smile to Dawn.

Dawn gestured something and tears gathered in Lila's eyes as she interpreted. "Dawn says we are more like sisters."

Wintra found herself envying Dawn. She had never had such a friendship. Her brother had been the closest to a friend that she ever had. The nuns at the abbey had been no more than companions and not very good one at that. Her thoughts suddenly turned vocal and she found herself admitting, "I have always wished for a sister, but with my da having died before I was born that was never a possibility. You are lucky to have each other."

Dawn reached out and took hold of Wintra's hand, squeezing it tight. Then she let go and gestured.

Wintra glanced helplessly at Lila.

"Dawn say she is so very happy to have you as a sister and not only a sister, but a best friend and that you two will share as sisters and friends do, as Dawn and I have done these many years."

Wintra did not know what to say. Not only had she been reunited with her brother, but she now had a sister. And least she forget, she also had a husband as well. Again her thoughts rushed to her lips. "I have a family once again." Tears sprung to her eyes.

Lila spoke as Dawn gestured. "Yes, we are family, and we will always be there for one another."

The women talked and laughed and Wintra found herself enjoying their company. This was what she had missed in the abbey—family and friends. And being the women talked so freely and openly, she decided to ask a question that had been on her tongue for some time.

"Why did the King decide that Torr and I must wed?"

Dawn looked to Old Mary who had stood to rub her gnarled hands near the hearth's flames and gave a nod. She understood the situation better than anyone, besides seeing and understanding beyond what others could.

"It is a convoluted tale, so I will explain as best as possible. Dawn is the daughter of Kirk McClusky and Ann Gerwan, wife of Roland Gerwan previous Earl of Carrick. She used Kirk to get with child, having been childless in her years married to Gerwan. When Lady Ann gave birth to Dawn and learned she had no voice, she knew Roland would suspect an affair with McClusky, since it was known that he had a daughter with the same affliction. She traded Dawn for a normal and beautiful baby—Lucerne. The King promised Cree land, title, and marriage to a noble woman in exchange for Cree's conquering skills. He was to wed Lucerne. Cree, however, fell in love with Dawn and wanted to wed her. Dawn's life was threatened, people started dying, and Lucerne acted wildly due to herbs Lady Ann had given her. In the end, many people had been affected by Lady Ann's desire for power and wealth.

"The King had no choice but to right the wrongs. He had no problem wedding Cree to Dawn since Dawn was now considered of noble blood. But what was he to do for McClusky and the loss of his daughter Dawn all these years? To compensate, he gave Cree's sister," —Old Mary pointed a gnarled finger at Wintra— "you, to Torr, giving McClusky a new daughter and uniting two powerful clans that would no doubt serve the King well."

Wintra did not know what to think and did it

really matter? What was done was done and could not be undone. And did she truly want it any other way? Torr and she may have been forced to wed, but they had not been forced to love.

"She was going to remain here, but it proved more difficult than she had thought, and so Cree permitted her to return to the only place she knew as home, the keep of the previous Earl of Carrick. Lucerne will oversee the care and running of the place for Cree until he appoints a liegeman to take residence there."

"My brother is a good man," Wintra said with pride and the other three women agreed.

"I must be going," Lila said. "I left Thomas safe with the women who watch the children when an incident like this happens, and he needs to be fed. And no doubt Paul will be hungry after such a laborious chore."

Dawn realized then that the two guards probably searched for her and Wintra and gestured that they should leave as well.

"You might as well wait," Old Mary said to Dawn. "Cree is almost here."

That had Lila hurrying to the door, but it flew open before she reached it. Cree stepped in, filling the small space with his potent presence.

Dawn started gesturing and Cree held up his hand to stop her. He then turned to Lila. "You have suffered a wound helping with the fire?"

"A mere blister, nothing more, my lord," Lila said.

"Elsa advises me that you cannot work the wool until the wound properly heals. Find a woman who can help in the meantime."

Lila bobbed her head. "Thank you, my lord." With that she scurried past Cree and out the door.

Cree walked over to his wife and captured her chin between his fingers. "What do you not understand about being told to remain at the keep?"

Dawn ignored his question and thanked him for being so kind to Lila, though it had the affect she had hoped it would.

He let go of her chin, slipped his arm around her waist, and eased her close. "I knew as soon as I found out that Lila had been injured that there would be no stopping you from going to her. And now that you know she is well, we need to return to the keep."

Dawn knew by the tone of his voice that he had more to say, but not here and now.

Wintra knew that tone as well and she worried that what he was not saying might concern Torr. "Where is Torr?"

"He is seeing to another matter and will join us as soon as he can," Cree said.

Wintra went along with her brother and Dawn to the keep, but her thoughts strayed to Torr. Where was he? What was he doing? Was he in danger? Once in the Great Hall, she reluctantly took a seat and waited—much too long.

Warriors came and went, food was continuously being served and the gray skies darkened along with the day and rain began to fall.

Dawn had wisely seen how sitting doing nothing was causing Wintra to worry and she soon had her tearing strips of clean linen for bandages. It wasn't until the table was cleaned and prepared for the evening meal that Wintra's worry returned with a vengeance. Torr had yet to return and she was not just concerned, but fearful that something had happened to him.

When he finally entered the Great Hall, she could

not stop herself from running to him.

He caught her in his strong arms and hugged her tight. "Miss me, did you?" He regretted his teasing remark when she turned tear-filled eyes on him. "What's wrong?"

She sniffled back her tears. "I thought something had happened to you and that you would never return to me."

"Princess," he said and kissed her lips lightly, "the devil himself could not keep you from me."

She sniffled again. "That is good to know since if the devil ever tried to get you, he would know what real hell is when I come after him to get you back."

"Love me that much, do you?" he said, though this time he didn't tease.

"More than you will ever know," she whispered.

"Now that you have assuaged my sister's concern, it is time we talk," Cree said as he approached them. "What have you found out about Owen?"

"His troop grows, though he will be beyond Carrick borders in a day or so, which makes one wonder his intentions."

Chapter Twenty-one

Wintra sighed for the third time. Torr had gone with Cree to his solar to discuss the situation and she had remained at the table with Dawn. That had been two hours ago and Wintra now sat alone. Dawn had grown tired and, with apologies to Wintra for leaving her alone, had retired for the evening. She was feeling the effects of the long day herself and decided that perhaps she would do better waiting for her husband at the cottage.

Her cheeks stained red when the idea of waiting in bed for him—naked—stirred in her mind. Could she do such a thing? Dare she?

Wintra stood, deciding to ponder the idea as she made her way to the cottage. The rain had stopped and the air was cold, and she would not be surprised if snow fell before morning. She hurried along, eager to seek the warmth of the cottage and to determine if she could actually strip and wait naked in bed for her husband.

When she was a few short steps from the front door, her arm was suddenly grabbed and she was yanked back, almost losing her footing. The stench of her assailant stung her nostrils so badly that she thought she would retch. Unlike her earlier attack, this time she was unfettered and nothing prevented her from launching her own attack. She did so without hesitation.

Wintra jabbed him hard in the eye and stomped as

viciously as she could on his foot. While he grabbed for his eye and hopped on one foot, she kicked him in the groin with all the force she could muster. He groaned, grabbed his groin, and went down on his knees.

She grabbed a handful of his hair and yanked his head back. "Who sent you after me?"

He did not respond. She let go of his hand, stepped behind him, and stomped repeatedly on his ankle. He screamed out in pain and fell over on his side. She kicked him in the ribs. "Who?" she demanded, wanting answers.

A hand suddenly rested on her shoulder, and she turned with a tightly clenched fist ready to strike.

Torr caught her fist in his hand before it could connect with his face. "Easy, Princess, it's me."

"I thought you were still with my brother in his solar," she said.

He released her hand and his arm went around her. "I entered the hall as you left, stopping only for a moment to ask Flanna to send supper to the cottage for us. I must admit, I am impressed that you were able to subdue the culprit on your own."

"Supper. The two of us. Alone. How wonderful."

Torr smiled that she was more pleased that he had arranged for supper for just the two of them rather than his compliment over her handling of the situation. But then he was looking forward to their time alone as well.

He called out to three warriors about to enter the keep. "I need two of you to guard this man and the other to fetch Cree. He has retired to his bedchamber."

Two warriors hurried over to him while the third rushed into the keep.

"Let's get you inside. The night grows cold," Torr said.

Wintra refused to budge. "Then you will have to keep me warm, since I will not move from this spot. I will not be left out of the discussion this time."

Torr would not argue with her. She had a right to know what was going on.

"What goes on here?' Cree demanded as he approached.

"I would like to know the very same thing," Wintra said. "Twice in one day I am almost abducted. What is happening, Cree?"

It was not a grown woman he heard ask her, but his little sister who he had failed to protect a few times. And that did not set at all well with him.

Sloan appeared and Cree ordered him to secure the culprit in the shed. The warriors carted the man off moaning and groaning.

Dawn rushed out of the darkness, a fur-lined cloak draped haphazardly over her night dress.

"You were to stay in bed," Cree scolded as he caught her around the waist and settled her against him.

She gestured frantically while looking at Wintra.

"As you can see, my sister is fine. Torr saved her."

"Wintra saved herself," Torr said with a degree of pride.

"Actually," Wintra said looking to her brother. "Cree saved me."

Dawn shivered and Cree ordered everyone into the cottage just as Flanna arrived with food and a pitcher of hot cider. She was quickly dispatched to bring a pitcher of ale.

Once they were seated at the table, the fire stoked

and a blanket wrapped around Dawn due to Cree's insistence, he turned to his sister and said, "As far as what is happening, I do not know, but I intend to find out and put an end to it. But right now—how did I save you when I was not even there?"

For a moment Wintra appeared as if lost in her thoughts, and then she spoke. "Someone grabbed me just as that man did near our farm that day. Only this time, I did what you taught me to do to—I attacked him."

Cree remembered that day all too well. He had been hunting and upon his return home he had come upon a scene that had struck him with gut-wrenching fear. He had spotted a man dragging Wintra away by the arm. She was trying desperately to free herself, but she was no match for his size. Cree had taken off in a run, though did not scream at the man to stop, fearful that he would run off with Wintra into the woods and be lost to him. He had watched as the man knocked her to the ground and was about to rape her. He had never run so fast in his life.

He had thrown his body full force at the man, knocking him off Wintra, then he and the man had fought. Cree had been so furious that he snapped the man's neck. Wintra had run to him afterward and had flung her scrawny little arms around his neck and wouldn't let go of him. Her body had trembled against his as he held her tight, and he had wanted to kill her attacker all over again. She had been his shadow for days on end after that, and he realized then that he had to teach her how to protect herself against someone bigger and stronger, and he had done just that. He also had never left her alone again, and it had been another reason why he had placed her in the abbey.

Wintra shook her head. "I had locked that memory away, not wanting to remember it. But I instinctively remembered what you taught me and I did not hesitate to attack him. But then—" She shook her head again. "I wanted answers. I am so tired of not having answers. I yanked him by the hair and demanded to know who sent him and when he did not respond, I stomped repeatedly on his ankle. He fell over and I kicked him in the ribs and was about to do more. Then Torr was there and I almost punched him, though he was quick to stop me." She shook her head again. "I do not know what happened to me."

"You are angry and rightfully so, and I am so proud to see what a strong and brave woman you have become," Cree said.

Her heart swelled with joy that her brother would speak with such pride of her, but then he had helped make her strong. And she was just beginning to realize that.

"We need to talk with the man who attacked, Wintra," Cree said to Torr.

Torr pressed his finger to Wintra's lips before she could open them. "This will not be pleasant to see. Rest assured, I will tell you everything upon my return. I am sure Dawn would not mind staying with you while you wait." He turned pleading eyes on Dawn.

Dawn nodded and smiled, agreeing.

Torr leaned close to Wintra, pressing his cheek to hers and whispered, "You are not going to win this one, Princess. You are staying put. Besides, I have a promise to keep to you tonight."

Passion rushed in to nip at every bit of her flesh before settling in the most intimate places. She kissed his cheek and smiled sweetly. "Do not be long."

As soon as the door closed on Torr and Cree, Dawn begged Wintra to tell her about Cree and their life on the farm. Wintra, not having had anyone to relive memories with, was only too eager to oblige her.

~~~

"His name is George and he is more than willing to talk," Sloan said when Cree and Torr entered the shack that Wintra's attacker had been taken to.

Cree stepped forward and George, more skin and bones than muscle, cringed and shuffled back on his butt where he sat on the cold ground, wincing as he did.

"I will tell you whatever you want to know," George pleaded.

"I have no doubt of that," Cree said, towering over the frightened man. "Who sent you?"

"Owen McBride of the clan McBride."

Cree didn't have to ask another question. George kept right on talking.

"He ordered me to get Wintra and bring her to him and to do whatever was necessary to see it done. I do not take to hurting women and had no intentions of hitting her. I never expected her to attack me the way she did. She was ruthless, but then she is your sister."

Cree scowled, though inwardly he swelled with pride that Wintra had become such a courageous woman.

George apologized quickly. "I do not mean that in a bad way. I just mean that you are both skilled fighters. And from what I am hearing around camp from the warriors that have been here, is that you are more of a fair man than Owen would have us believe. I do not trust Owen McBride. He is a cruel man. It was a sad day when he married our chieftain's daughter and even sadder day when she died, though talk was that he had her murdered, the poor soul. He treated her so badly, but there was nothing we could do to stop him. His small contingent of men was enough to keep everyone in line. He has brought nothing but grief and poverty to our clan." George bowed his head. "I ask for mercy, my lord. I have a wife and daughter and another child on the way. They will starve, not that we aren't already, but they will not last long if I do not return home to them. Besides, wives who no longer have husbands are used by Owen's men, and I do not want that for my Patricia."

"You have no idea why Owen wants my sister?"

"Everyone knows he wanted her for himself, and we thought it was over once it was learned that your sister was wed. But it is as if he hasn't changed his plans. And then there is his connection to the Earl of Kellmara. For some reason the man seems to support Owen's madness in acquiring your sister as his wife. Kellmara troops are expected any day now." George shivered. "It is whispered that Kellmara is almost as powerful as the King."

"And I am more ruthless than both," Cree said.

George paled and his eyes turned wide.

Cree turned to Sloan. "Take him to Elsa and have her see to his care and see that he stays there the night. Two guards at his door."

"I do not want to go back to Owen McBride. I will pledge my fealty to you and serve you well. I just want to return home and get my wife and daughter and bring them here. We both will serve you well. I am only a farmer, but I know the land and can make anything grow."

"We will see," Cree said and turned walking out the door, Torr following.

The two men went only a few steps when Cree stopped. "What do you think?" he said.

"He speaks the truth," Torr said and told him the same tale he had told Wintra.

Cree scowled. "Why is it that I have not come across this man?"

"He preys on the small, weak and isolated clans, so he will not be noticed."

"Then why would he go after Wintra?"

"Perhaps he now has bigger aspirations."

"George is a farmer," Cree said. "Why would Owen send a farmer instead of one of his warriors to abduct Wintra?"

"Good question. Why would he?" Torr said.

"And why does the Earl of Kellmara support this devil's madness? And why does he send troops to help Owen?" Cree asked more to himself than Torr.

Torr responded anyway. "I care not how strong Kellmara is. Wintra belongs to me and I am not giving her up. She is mine and will remain so forever."

"You love her that much?" Cree asked happy to hear it.

"Even more than that."

"That is good to know," Cree said as they continued walking. "Now options and plans must be discussed, though not tonight. Tomorrow is soon enough."

"What happened to Wintra that day on the farm when a man grabbed her?" Torr asked. He had thought about asking Wintra, but he did not want her to have to relive such a painful event in her life.

However, he had to know.

Cree detailed the whole incident and Torr was delighted to learn that Cree had done what he would have, snapped the man's neck.

Chapter Twenty-two

Wintra stood by the hearth, staring into the flames and heard the door latch shut. Cree and Dawn were gone. She and Torr were finally alone. While she had enjoyed talking with Dawn, she had not been able to keep thoughts of Torr and her naked in bed doing unimaginable, though acceptable, things out of her head. After all she and Torr were wed and their vows consummated. Why then did she feel her thoughts so sinful?

Torr walked over to stand behind her, his arms going around her waist and easing her back against him. "As I promised, I will tell you everything Cree and I learned from your attacker."

She shook her head. "I do not want to discuss that now."

He went to turn her around, but she stopped him with a firm hand to his arm that sat snug at her waist. She needed to speak with him of intimate things, and she did not know if she could face him directly while doing so. Even though they had made love, she still felt vulnerable and unknowledgeable when it came to intimacy.

"What do you want to discuss?" he asked.

She shut her eyes tight and plunged ahead. "Intimacy." Her eyes shot open when he spun her around to face him.

"You have not been shy to speak what is on your mind, another trait I favor in you. And I have told you time and again that you could speak to me about anything, so why does intimacy prove difficult for you to discuss with me?"

"The nuns warned me against talking to my husband about the subject. They insisted it was his domain, and I was to do my duty without question or protest."

Torr could not help but smile. "That would be impossible for you to do. You are much too inquisitive, another part of your nature that I love."

She rested a gentle hand to his cheek. "I am lucky to have you as my husband, for there is surely not another man around who would be so tolerable of my persistent curiosity."

"I am glad that you finally realize my worth," he said, his smile growing. "Now what questions fill your mind?"

She slipped out of his arms and walked nearer to the curtain that separated the two rooms before turning back to face him, his heartening words having given her that last bit of courage she needed. "I thought to wait naked in our bed for you. Is that a proper thing for a wife to do?"

Not only her words, but the image of what she suggested, and that she even thought of doing such a thing, turned him hard. He approached her slowly, though kept a small distance between them. "It is more than proper for a wife to show how much she desires her husband."

Words rushed from her mouth as if she could not stop them or as if she must say them before she lost the mettle to do so. "I desire you so very much that at times I feel as if I will go mad with the want of you."

Torr went to step forward, his hand reaching out for her.

Wintra quickly stepped back, her hand held out to stop his approach. "Please. I have thought of this all night. And I would like to greet you naked in our bed before I lose the courage to do so."

Torr took a step back, more than willing to let her have her way. "Call to me when you are ready."

She nodded and disappeared behind the curtain. Her hands shook as she slipped out of her garments. From what the nuns had told her, she had not been looking forward to performing her wifely duties when she wed, but Torr had changed all that from the very first time he had touched her. And after last night, she knew that she had much to learn or perhaps unlearn as to what was proper and what was not. The only way for her to do that was to embrace her passion for her husband and not be afraid to talk with him about intimacy and learn all she could.

She stood naked. All she had to do was get in bed and call out to him, but she hesitated. She stared at the bed. Could she do this?

Her worries faded and she smiled, for she realized what was most important—Torr loved her and she loved him. She climbed into bed and was about to slip her legs beneath the blanket and pull it up to her waist, but stopped. She wanted nothing separating them this night. Tonight she wanted anything that stood between them stripped away.

Wintra sat with her legs to the side and slightly bent. Her one hand rested on the bed while the other lay against her flat stomach. Her shoulders were drawn back, her chin raised just a notch, and her green eyes bright with anticipation and desire.

"Torr," she called out.

Torr shut his eyes briefly, hearing husky passion in her voice and his groin tightened, not just with need, but with hunger to make love to his wife. He stepped into the other room and his breath caught in his throat.

Wintra was a beautiful woman, but seeing her completely naked in their bed, waiting for him, wanting him, made him see her true beauty and it was not on her face, but in her heart..

He shed his garments as he approached her, wanting nothing to stand between them this night or any nights to come.

Wintra drank in his handsome features from the top of his head to his toes. His body was all hard muscle and form, and she could not stop her eyes from drifting again and again to the spot that proved just how much he desired her. She tingled and quivered at the thought.

He placed one knee on the bed and reached out to stroke her cheek with the back of his hand.

"Your beauty goes far deeper than anyone can see," he said and cupped her face in his hands and brought his lips to meet hers.

Wintra closed her eyes amazed at how gently he kissed her, as if he paid reverence to her. God, but she loved this man.

Torr felt a bolt of passion shoot through him when she placed her hand on his arm. It was such a simple touch and yet it made him feel as if she claimed him. That he belonged to her and no one else.

He ran his lips over hers and whispered, "I do love you, Princess."

Wintra felt tears choke her and though they were happy tears now was not the time for her to cry, so she fought them back and smiled. "Not as much as I love you."

"I don't think so, and I will prove it," he said

teasingly, and then he kissed her with the passion he had held in check.

They slipped down along the bed together and while he continued kissing her senseless, his hands roamed along her body, reveling in the feel of her soft skin and gentle curves.

Eager to taste more of her, he moved to her one breast and, after raining kisses over it, took her nipple in his mouth, rolling his tongue across it.

Wintra moaned with pleasure. She had never thought making love would be so wonderful, or that it got better each time. Another quiver ran through her when Torr moved to her other breast, and she eagerly ran her hands over his back, indulging in the strength that rippled through his taut muscles.

She sighed with frustration when his mouth left her breast, though when he kissed down along her stomach and moved even lower, she thought she would die from the pleasure that shot threw her. The thought struck her then and she knew she had to do it. It would help erase a bad memory and besides, she truly wanted to taste him and see for herself how it felt.

She tugged on him and when he looked up, she said, "I wish to taste you this time."

"Are you sure?" he asked never having expected to hear that from her.

She nodded and eagerly pushed him back on the bed.

He watched as she took him, without hesitation, into her mouth and dropped his head back when after a few moments her sweet, innocent licks turned hungry. As much as he would have loved her to go on and on, he knew he would never last and he wanted to be inside her when he came.

He quickly reached down, grabbed her and turned her flat on her back, and then he moved over her, spreading her legs with his knee and bracing his hands on either side of her head.

She grabbed hold of his arms, the muscles tense, and she whispered, "I need you so badly."

That was all Torr needed to hear, he entered her fast and hard, and he didn't hold back.

She cried out in sheer pleasure and matched his thrusts. They were soon lost in the passion that consumed their souls.

"Torr," she said on a long sigh.

"Surrender to me," he urged.

And she did, crying out his name the intense sensation penetrated and consumed every inch of her. After the initial burst, the sensation rippled through her, fading as it went, and she squeezed every part of her body trying to hold on the very last vestige of it.

Torr's climax hit new heights when he felt Wintra squeeze him tight. It was almost as if she had locked him inside her, and damn if it didn't feel great.

Wintra felt a sense of loss when he slipped out of her, though she was grateful that as he rolled off her, he hooked his hand on her shoulder and took her with him to rest against his side.

"I do not like being apart from you," he said, his breath still a bit labored. "I like you close—very close." He hugged her tighter against his side as if proving he could not get her close enough.

"I like the feel of you inside me," she said.

He grinned. "Then I will be inside you often."

The flames in the hearth crackled and flickered high for a moment highlighting Torr's scar making it appear so much worse than it actually was. Wintra could not help but wonder how he had gotten it. He must have suffered terrible pain and her heart ached for what he must have gone through. Without thinking, she raised her hand to gently run her finger along the scar he would carry for the remainder of his days.

He stiffened, but it did not stop her. She wanted him to know that it did not bother her and never would, though she was curious as to how he got it, and of course the question fell from her lips as soon as she thought of it. "How did this happen?"

Torr hesitated. Many were curious about the scar, but few dared to ask. It was as if the offending mark warned of his status as a fierce fighter. If he could survive such an ordeal, then he was a man to avoid. Dawn, though, had been different. She hadn't avoided him and she had suggested that he speak with Elsa the healer that perhaps she could help him. He had done that already, at Dawn's request, and Elsa had given him a salve to apply to the scar, not that it would erase the scar, but it would ease the appearance over time.

"Your scar does not offend me. It is part of who you are," she said when he did not answer. "Please tell me, I want to know."

"We have just made love. Now is not the time to discuss such a matter."

"You told me that there isn't anything I cannot discuss with you," she said and waited, hoping he would tell her.

He rarely spoke of it. The nightmare of what had happened was bad enough, but it was who had been the cause that he feared would upset her, though she would come to find out eventually. And since he had told her to ask anything of him, then he had to be willing to give her an answer. "I was hunting in the woods near my home when I heard a woman's screams." He stopped a moment. "This is not a pretty tale. Are you sure you want to hear it?"

"Yes, I want to hear all of it."

"I hurried to the screams as fast as I could and came upon a horrific scene. A man was brutally stabbing a woman. I did not hesitate, I attacked him. He was a large man and much quicker on his feet then I would have expected. He was also much more skilled with a dagger than I was. I took a few minor wounds to my arms, and when I think about how he sliced my face, I now wonder if it was a small price to pay, for it saved my life. It had gotten him close enough to me, so that I could catch him in the gut. And I did just that. As he sliced my face, I sliced his gut."

Wintra grew sick at the thought of it, and her heart ached even more for him.

"The woman was beyond help. The only thing I could do was hold her while she died. She looked upon my face and told me she was sorry I had suffered so." He shook his head. "She was dying and she was sorry for me. She also managed to tell me of the man responsible for her own suffering and death."

"It sounds as if she took a while to die," Wintra said feeling her stomach roil, thinking of how the woman had to have suffered as well as Torr, since his wound hadn't received immediate tending.

"An hour or more, I believe. She passed moments before my father's warriors came across me. He had been worried that I had been gone too long and with dusk not far off, he had sent warriors to look for me. Good thing he did, for I had not wanted to leave her body for the animals to ravage. She had been ravaged enough in her young life, barely having reached ten and six years."

"Who was the man responsible for her death?"

Torr stared at her a moment before saying, "Owen McBride, her husband."

Wintra's mouth dropped open in shock.

"It seemed that Owen had convinced her that he loved her and sought her hand in marriage. Her father was chieftain of a small clan and too old and feeble to tend to his duties, so he granted his only child's request. I suspect he thought he had done the right thing and that Owen would see to improving the land and village. Not so. Shortly after they wed, her father died in a fall. Owen began to beat her, among other unspeakable things, and she ran away fearing for her life. The man with the dagger found her and informed her as he stabbed her repeatedly that Owen told him to make sure she suffered for being such an ungrateful wife."

Wintra shuddered, thinking that the poor woman's fate could have been her own. "He is a monster."

"He is a depraved man who appears to stop at nothing to get what he wants and that makes him a very dangerous man."

A thought suddenly hit her and she grabbed his hand and squeezed tightly. "What if Owen plans on killing you, making me a widow so that he gets another chance of taking me as his wife?"

"If I died, Cree would look after you and he would never allow Owen near you," Torr assured her.

"What if the King did?"

"He would have no reason to."

"We do not know that," Wintra said. "A madman is capable of anything and Owen is definitely insane."

"Listen to me," he said bringing their joined hands to his mouth and kissing hers. "Nothing is going to happen to me—"

"You do not know that."

Torr laughed. "After what we shared tonight, nothing—absolutely nothing—will keep me from sharing it with you again and again."

He turned and nuzzled her neck, causing gooseflesh to run down her arms. And his hand slipped over her breast to cup it and give it a tender squeeze. A sigh ran from her lips and she titled her head back to expose more of her neck for him to nibble on.

"God, I love the taste of you," he murmured and feasted on her delicate skin.

Jolts of pleasure shot through her as his thumb teased her nipple, turning it hard.

"I love you, Wintra, and whether we had been married or not, I still would have fallen in love with you from the moment I saw you. You stole my heart, Princess, and now it belongs to you and always will."

She did not mind him calling her Princess anymore, since she realized that he had made her a princess—his princess—from the very first time he had called her it.

Ripples of pleasure began washing over her body and a question shot from her mind straight to her mouth. "We are permitted to make love more than once a night?"

Torr looked at her and grinned. "The only permission we need is from each other. I want to make love again, do you?"

She smiled. "Only," —she slipped her hand down and took hold of him— "if I can touch you this time."

"Touch me as much as you want," he said. "I guarantee that I will respond each time."

The night wore on and Wintra wore out, falling

asleep in Torr's arms. He pulled the blanket over them and before he fell into a much needed slumber, he thanked the heavens for blessing him with such a loving wife.

Chapter Twenty-three

Torr watched his wife sleep contentedly in his arms. He had woken only a few moments ago and smiled at the way Wintra was wrapped around him. Arms, legs, her head on his shoulder, and her hand holding on to his one arm, made it appear that she intended to keep a good hold on him. And he did not mind at all, since he intended to do the same to her.

He glanced at her lips so soft and full and so ripe for a kiss. He reminded himself that she needed some rest after last night and no doubt she had to be sore from as many times as they made love. He had to let her be this morning. He had to.

Her eyes fluttered open and she smiled at him. "Good Lord, I wake wanting you."

"You must be sore," he said, forcing himself not to touch her.

"Not that I can feel." She ran her hand down his chest to between his legs and smiled. "And look, he's already hard and waiting for me."

He grabbed her by the waist and turned her on her back, then settled over her. "You are a wicked woman."

She kissed him quick. "I enjoy being wicked with my husband, but then he is an exceptional lover." She scrunched her brow. "Not that I have anyone to compare him to, nor would I want to, I only know he is—perfect for me."

"And your husband feels the same about you,"

Torr said and was about to kiss her when a pounding knock sounded at the door.

Torr cursed beneath his breath before calling out, "Who goes there?"

"Elwin. I have a message from Cree."

Torr reluctantly slipped on his plaid and only his plaid to let Elwin know that he was busy and went to open the door.

Elwin remained outside as he said, "Cree commands yours and Wintra's presence at the keep immediately. I am to escort you."

"Give us a moment," Torr said and closed the door. He returned to the room to find Wintra getting dressed. "You heard?"

She nodded.

"It must be important if he sent an escort for us," he said slipping into his garments.

"I would rather stay here with you," she said disappointed they had been interrupted, though worried over the summons.

He cupped her face in his hands. "Believe me when I tell you that there is no place I would rather be than here making love to you." He gave her a quick kiss and finished dressing.

Wintra combed her hair and bathed her face with warm water in a bucket left by the hearth. It was a routine she had established every morning at the abbey and one she found she could not do without. It had always made her feel fresh and ready for the day, and it seemed, with her brother's urgent summons, she needed to be ready for what today brought.

Torr grabbed his cloak and hers and after draping hers over her shoulders, he opened the door and as soon as they joined Elwin, he took hold of her hand. Whatever they were about to face, he wanted to make certain Wintra understood that they would face it together.

The Great Hall was nearly empty, the morning meal having been served a couple of hours ago and most of the warriors now off to see to their daily tasks. Cree sat at the table by the hearth with Dawn and Sloan.

Torr slipped Wintra's cloak off her and deposited hers along with his on the end of the bench. Then he slid in beside her at the table, took hold of her hand lying in her lap, laced his fingers with hers and rested their hands on his thigh.

"I received a message from Douglas Hawthorne, the Earl of Kellmara. He requests to meet with me on an urgent matter. His message says it is in regards to my sister Wintra."

A chill so strong raced through Wintra that she shivered. Even as cloistered as she had been in the abbey, she had heard of the powerful Earl of Kellmara. His land extended far and wide, and it was said that the King was even afraid of him. The question that weighed heavily on her mind was already spilling from her lips. "What in heaven's name would he want with me?"

"I do not know, but we will find out soon enough. He will arrive here in a few days. I will leave you to visit with Dawn while I speak with Torr and Sloan in my solar."

Wintra was ready to protest about being left out of a discussion that concerned her when Torr took hold of her face and kissed her.

She scowled at him afterwards, knowing what he was doing.

Torr laughed. "I was wondering when your brother's scowl would show up on your face."

She punched him in the arm, which made him laugh even harder, and she stopped herself from rubbing her small fist, having hit hard muscle and hurting herself more than him.

Torr took her hand that remained fisted and kissed it, which irritated her all the more, since he knew she had suffered more than he, though he was trying to make amends.

"You have yet to eat, so enjoy the morning meal, and I will let you know what goes on as soon as we finish discussing the matter."

Cree watched the exchange between the couple and was about to say something when Dawn squeezed his leg beneath the table. He turned a scowl on her that quickly faded when he looked into the tenderness in her lovely dark eyes. And then she patted his leg, though much too close to his groin, which naturally aroused him.

He leaned down and whispered in her ear. "I expect you to finish what you have just started and sooner rather than later."

Dawn smiled and nodded most eagerly.

The two women watched their men walk off with Sloan and as soon as they were out of the room Dawn gestured to Wintra, as if she was shoveling food into her mouth, and then walked her fingers in the air.

"I should eat and then we should go for a walk?" Wintra asked.

Dawn nodded, walked her fingers in the air again, tapped her lips, and then tugged at her ear.

"We take a walk to see if we can learn anything," Wintra said enthusiastically.

Dawn bobbed her head.

"Are you feeling well enough?"

Dawn's face lit with a brilliant smile, and she

nodded.

"I am so happy for you and my brother. He must have been thrilled when he learned he would be a father. He always wanted a large brood. He had told me that one day we would live in a keep and we would fill it with his children and my children and that there would always be laughter and happiness." Wintra felt her stomach clench. She would not be staying here with her brother. She would be going to live at Torr's home and while she looked forward to a life with Torr, she would miss her brother, especially since she had only been reunited with him.

Wintra chased the troubling thought away. Today she would spend time with her new sister. Wintra rushed her hand out to Dawn's when she caught a pained look in her eyes. "What's wrong? Are you ill?"

Dawn shook her head. She pressed her fingers to her lips, and then rested her hand over that slight bump in her stomach.

Wintra understood her worry right away. "Just because you cannot speak doesn't mean your child will have no voice. Besides, it will not matter to my brother. He will love his child, voice or not, just as he loves you."

Dawn appreciated her comforting words, though unfortunately found no solace in them. How did she explain that she did not wish her affliction on anyone let alone her own child? Her heart would break if her child was born and she heard no cry—not a sound— for her voice would always be trapped inside her, and it was a horrible fate to pass on to an innocent child.

Wintra squeezed her hand. "All will be well. Do not worry." She thought it best to change the conversation and said, "What of your wedding? There is much to do and I agreed to help, so let's start now."

Wintra was glad to see Dawn smile as they talked more of the wedding while finishing their meal. With some decisions made for the special day and the meal done, they donned their cloaks and were out the door.

Yesterday's gray skies and promise of more snow surprisingly never materialized. Instead, the sun was shining and there wasn't a cloud in the sky. Snow was beginning to melt, though no one believed winter was about to leave just yet. Spring was a good two months away, but it was nice to see the sun, if only for a day.

"Where should we start?" Wintra asked.

Dawn gestured for her to follow, and they were soon walking up a path to a cottage. Dawn didn't bother to knock, she simply opened the door. Wintra understood why when they entered. It housed the women who worked on the wool. They seemed a happy group, smiling and greeting them as if they were friends, but then Dawn was.

Sadness washed over Wintra. This was what she had missed all those years in the abbey—family and friends—and she didn't want to ever be without it again.

"Have you come to show Wintra the talented women who spin the wool?" Lila asked.

Dawn gestured something and Lila's hand flew to her chest as if shocked. "You want us to spin special wool to be used for your wedding dress?"

Dawn nodded, smiling, and the women all eagerly agreed and expressed their honor in doing so.

After a brief discussion of what Dawn wanted and insisting she would leave it to them to decide, Lila walked outside with the two women and down the path a few feet.

"You are up to something, Dawn, I can tell," Lila

said quietly.

Dawn looked to Wintra and nodded.

Though Wintra knew Torr would share what he had learned with her, she also knew that village gossip could prove even more helpful. There was a trust among the peasants and it was shared only amongst themselves and never with nobles. She had learned that from the peasants who had stopped at the abbey.

"Have you heard anything about the man who grabbed me yesterday and anything pertaining to Owen or the Earl of Kellmara?" Wintra asked.

Lila kept her voice low. "Gossip has it that the prisoner has asked to stay here in Dowell. He says that Owen cares naught for his people. He lets them starve. He says that the chieftain of the clan died shortly after Owen married his daughter and that the daughter ran away because Owen treated her so brutally. He says she was a good and kind woman always thinking of others before herself. Unfortunately, her body was found in the woods, a distance from her home, and she was returned to Owen. The clan was upset that he did not give her a proper burial. He simply had a grave dug and put her in it without as much as a word being spoken."

Wintra shuddered, wondering if she could be the same woman Torr had come across in the woods. Her heart once again went out to the poor soul.

"You should speak with Flanna," Lila suggested. "She takes food to the prisoner, though he is housed at Elsa's cottage recovering from his wounds." Lila smiled and looked to Wintra. "Gossiping tongues have proclaimed that you are much like your brother, strong and brave."

Wintra thought on Lila's words as she followed

alongside Dawn to find Flanna. She had been told so often now how brave she was that she was finally beginning to believe it herself. She recalled how Cree had told her how heroic she had been when that man had attacked her when she was young. She had fought to get away from him even though her struggles had gotten her nowhere, though Cree had insisted they had. She had delayed him dragging her into the woods and had given Cree time to reach her. It had not mattered to her then. All she had thought about was staying in her brother's strong arms and never leaving them. She had been so relieved when afterwards he had taken her everywhere with him.

That was one of the reasons it had been so difficult for her when Cree had left her at the abbey. She had missed him terribly, and she had felt that he did not want her around anymore, and she had worried that he did not love her anymore. She was just beginning to realize how much he loved her and how hard it must have been for him to leave her there.

Dawn was pleased that she did not need to search for Flanna. She was in the Great Hall when they returned there. It was empty except for the servants she was instructing to be more diligent when scrubbing the tables after meals were finished. She certainly kept the keep clean, more so than anyone would have expected, and Cree had let her know often how pleased he was with her work.

"Is there anything I can get for you, my lady?" Flanna asked with a bob of her head.

Dawn did not want Flanna calling her *my lady*. They were friends, but Flanna had insisted that it was the respectful thing to do. Flanna had, however, agreed to call her Dawn when they were alone.

Dawn looked to Wintra. "We are here to discuss

plans for the wedding celebration."

Flanna beamed brightly, tears rushing to pool in her eyes. "We will make it the finest celebration there has ever been."

Dawn insisted Flanna sit at the table with them to discuss details and make plans. It was during their discussion that Dawn gestured to Flanna that they needed to discuss something else as well.

Wintra did not understand all of Dawn's gestures, but Flanna seemed to have no problem with them. She answered without hesitation.

"George, the prisoner's name is George. He's afraid and worried for his family. He has a wife, pregnant with their second child, and a young daughter. He fears for their safety if he does not return. It seems that Owen's men use the wives who are left without husbands." Flanna lowered her voice. "He said that Owen instructed him to do whatever was necessary to bring Wintra to him."

"What of the Earl of Kellmara?" Wintra asked.

"The only thing I have heard is that Kellmara warriors are expected at Owen's campsite any day now."

Flanna hurried to stand as soon as she caught sight of Cree entering the Great Hall with Torr and Sloan following behind him.

Cree laid his hands flat on the end of the table between where Dawn and Wintra sat. "What are you two up to?"

Dawn smiled broadly and gestured.

Cree's face lit with a smile. "You are planning the wedding celebration?"

Dawn nodded joyously.

Cree summoned Flanna to him with a shout, and she hurried over to the table. "Whatever Dawn wants see that it is done."

"Yes, my lord, and may I say this is going to be the best wedding celebration ever."

"I am sure you will see that it is," he said with a curt nod.

Torr reached down and took his wife's hand, tugging her gently off the bench to wrap his arm around her. "I have missed you," he whispered in her ear as he settled her close against him.

Before she could respond and let him know she felt the same and was wishing for time alone with him, Cree spoke.

"I have had enough waiting. I am taking a contingent of men and going to speak with Owen. Torr will accompany me and Sloan will remain behind. I hope to be back tonight, but we may not return until tomorrow. You two," — Cree pointed to his wife and sister— "are not to go off alone while we are gone. Do I make myself clear?"

Dawn gestured to her husband.

Cree yanked her off the bench and into his arms. "I will miss you too, but do not think you are going to ignore my orders. Understand?"

Torr walked a few feet away with Wintra as Cree continued talking with Dawn.

"Cree is right about this. He cannot wait to see what Kellmara intends, or Owen for that matter. He must see to this, and I must go with him since it concerns my wife."

"You could be in danger as well," she reminded and the thought that she could lose him overwhelmed her with grief. "I do not want to lose you. I love you."

"You sound and look as if you have just realized that," he said resting a gentle hand to her cheek.

"It is not that I have only realized that I love you

since love struck me so hard and fast, and it is not going away—ever. But until this very moment, I did not realize what tremendous heartache I would suffer if I lost you." She tried to laugh, though it sounded more like a croak. "No one would love me as unconditionally as you do. Besides, I could never love anyone as much as I love you."

"Good, for I feel the same about you," Torr said and slipped his hand around the back of her neck and with a gentle yank had her mouth against his in an instant. They tasted of each other like two hungry children receiving a long awaited treat and when he reluctantly brought the kiss to an end, he rested his brow to hers, and said, "I will never grow tired of the taste of you."

"Time to go," Cree shouted.

With another quick kiss to Wintra, Torr turned and joined Cree as he headed out of the Great Hall.

Wintra did not like how empty she felt with each step Torr took away from her and when the door closed behind him, she felt her legs grow weak. She had not known that love could be so wonderful, yet so painful at the same time. And she silently prayed for his safe return, for she knew she would not want to live life without him.

Chapter Twenty-four

Cree despised Owen and he wanted nothing more than to snap the irritating man's neck and be done with him. But until he could determine what Owen was up to, he would have to wait. Eventually though, Owen would suffer a fate of his own making.

"Why would the Earl of Kellmara send so many of his warriors ahead of his arrival if it was only a friendly visit?" Torr asked as he and Cree were escorted into camp by several Kellmara warriors.

As soon as Cree and his contingent of twenty warriors rode off Carrick land, Kellmara's warriors swooped around them. The leader cordially, though firmly, offered to escort them to camp.

Cree kept his temper in firm control. He was furious that Kellmara could think that he could camp just a step beyond Cree's borders and that he would sit there and do nothing about it. But Kellmara had expressed no interest in doing Cree harm, so Cree could do nothing but wait on the man's arrival. He could, however, question Owen.

Cree and Torr both took note of how well organized the campsite appeared, but then Kellmara was known for his warrior skills. And as Cree had learned, being a good warrior was not only about the battle. It was also about keeping your men organized and well trained, and from what Cree could see, Kellmara did just that.

That was why it was easy to see that Owen hadn't

exactly blended well with the Kellmara troops. His campsite was shoddy in comparison as were his men.

Torr voiced Cree's thoughts. "It seems that Owen sits on the outskirts of the Kellmara camp. Not exactly welcomed or accepted."

"What then is Owen doing with them?" Cree asked.

Torr wondered the same himself. "Owen seems tolerated by the Kellmara warriors, but why?"

"There can be only one answer to that—need," Cree said. "Owen knows or has something they need. And it has to do with my sister."

"You have no idea of what it could be?"

"None," Cree said frustration evident in his curt reply.

"I dislike going into a fight blind," Torr said. "It leaves one too vulnerable."

"That is why I sent some of my warriors to gather what information they can. And why we are here to talk with Owen."

"No one is taking my wife from me," Torr reminded adamantly.

"So you have said often."

"And I will continue to say it, shout it if I must, do whatever it takes to make anyone and everyone realize it," Torr said with resolve.

"Let us see if Owen is going to need reminding of that," Cree said as the Kellmara warriors drifted off, after reaching Owen's campsite.

Cree and Torr dismounted and approached Owen who stood by a campfire that looked as if it was in dire need of tending. Two of Owen's warriors stood guard directly behind him, though neither looked intimidating.

"What do you want of me?" Owen demanded.

Cree thought the man foolish before, but even more so now for being under the assumption that he was well protected with the impressive presence of Kellmara warriors. The fool did not realize that the Kellmara men cared naught what happened to him. And they had proved that to Cree when they had drifted off once they neared Owen's camp. It was almost as if they announced aloud to do as you will, we will not stop you.

Torr answered. "What we want you are not capable of giving—the truth."

"The truth?" Owen laughed. "You do not know the truth, but you will soon enough, and I shall be rewarded."

"For being a fool?" Torr asked.

Owen's nostril's flared and his eyes glared with anger at Torr. "We will see who the fool is."

"Why did you send two of your men to abduct my sister?" Cree said as he took a quick step toward Owen.

Not only did Owen jump back, but the two men did as well.

"I did no such thing," Owen claimed. "If any of my men did that, then they did so of their own accord. Return them to me and I shall punish them."

"Why would they do such a thing on their own?" Torr challenged.

"The McBride Clan is mostly comprised of farmers and a few craftsmen. They require nothing more than a simple, boring life. The poor simpletons probably thought that if they brought Wintra here that all would be ended and we then could return home."

"So you deny any part in the attempted abductions?" Torr asked.

"Of course, I do," he snapped. "I would not be so

foolish as to send a farmer to do a warrior's job."

"You were foolish enough to think you could take my wife from me," Torr spat. "Are you still foolish enough to think that?"

"It will not be me who takes Wintra from you, though it will be me who is there to claim her when she is taken from you."

He sounded much too confident to Torr's liking. "What game do you play?"

"A game in which I will be the victor," Owen sneered.

Cree had his hand around Owen's neck before he realized what had happened. "Leave us," Cree ordered with such force at the two guards that they fell over each other as they hurried to obey.

Owen clawed at Cree's hands to no avail.

"Fight me and I'll tighten my hold," Cree snapped and squeezed tighter.

Owen immediately stilled.

"I have had enough of your foolish games. You will tell me what I want to know or suffer the consequences." Cree squeezed at his neck tighter in warning.

Owen nodded as he struggled to breathe.

Cree loosened his hold just enough so that Owen could answer him. "You sent for Kellmara?"

"No, he was already on his way."

"Why?"

"I cannot say. He has sworn me to secrecy. It is for him to tell, not me."

"It has to do with Wintra?"

Owen nodded.

"What is your connection to Kellmara?" Cree demanded.

"I provided information he had been searching

for."

"How did you come by this information?"

"Through the previous laird of the Clan McBride," Owen said coughing to take another labored breath.

Cree released Owen, giving him a shove away from him that sent him stumbling as he walked over to Torr.

"Why not just beat the information out of him?" Torr asked annoyed. This was about his wife and he wanted all the information right now at this moment. He did not want to wait another minute.

"Look around you," Cree whispered. "Kellmara's men stand close and listen. They would stop him from saying anything their chieftain does not want known."

Torr turned away, running a hand through his hair as if frustrated and gave a quick glance around. Cree was right. The warriors had moved closer and made no attempt to hide their presence or that they listened most curiously.

Cree turned back to Owen who had put more distance between them and with a calm that belied his words said, "When this is done, your lands will be mine."

Owen blanched, though squared his shoulders. "When this is done I will not only hold more land, I will hold a title just like you."

Cree took a quick step forward once more and Owen scrambled back out of reach.

"When this is done," Cree said in a harsh whisper, "I will see you dead. You have my word on it." Cree turned and mounted his stallion.

"And I will be the one who kills him," Torr said with a look in his eye that dared Cree to argue with him after mounting his horse.

The two turned and rode off without another word. This time the Kellmara warriors did not escort them out of camp, though they kept steady eyes on them.

Cree's men waited for him on the edge of the camp, alert and ready for anything. The twenty men were not enough to battle the large contingent of Kellmara warriors, but add the fifty that surrounded the camp and the fact that one of Cree's warriors were worth two of any other warrior and that meant the Kellmara warriors were outnumbered.

"Do you think Owen has been promised land and a title or is it his own foolishness that has him believing such nonsense?" Torr said.

"I think that depends on the information he has and how badly someone wants it. And it would seem that the Earl of Kellmara wants it badly."

Torr did not like the feeling that caught at his gut. The King had decreed his marriage to Wintra and only the King could see it undone. So there was nothing for him to worry about, or was there?

Chapter Twenty-five

Wintra and Dawn stood on the keep steps looking out over the village. It was late afternoon, the sky was gray, the air crisp, and light flurries fell. Villagers scurried about busy with their chores and daily routines. All seemed well except that Cree and Torr were two days late in returning home. No message had been received concerning their delay, and the two women were worried.

Sloan did not seem concerned, though he had told them that if Cree had not returned by tomorrow, he would send men to see what had caused their delay.

Wintra tried to convince herself that Torr and her brother were fine that they would return home soon and all would be well, yet nagging doubt would not let go of her. What if the Earl of Kellmara had attacked Cree and his troop and left them for dead? What if at this very moment Torr lay bleeding and helpless somewhere? Endless worries had filled her head and upset her stomach to the point where she could not eat.

Wintra turned her head to look at Dawn when she felt her hand grasp her arm. Dawn was pointing down the length of the village and up toward the rise. Wintra's stomach tightened so badly that she thought she would double over. Was that Torr and Cree coming over the rise? She prayed to the heavens and all who would listen to please let it be so.

Dawn held her arm firm, stopping her from

rushing off the steps and through the village to greet them. She shook her head at Wintra when she tried to yank her arm away and gestured with her one hand.

Try as she might, Wintra could not understand what Dawn was saying. She was grateful when Old Mary suddenly appeared and quickly interpreted.

"It would not be proper for either of you to run and greet the men you love. You must not let others see that you worried over them, for it would cause others in the village to do the same. You must stay strong and remain here on the steps to demonstrate the confidence you have in your men."

Wintra nodded, though wished she could join the village women who ran to greet their men without hesitation. She grew impatient as Cree and Torr rode at a leisurely pace through the village, the villagers crying out hardy welcomes that they had returned home safely. She understood then, watching the scene unfold in front of her, how important their entrance to the village was. The obvious joy and pride on the villagers' faces for the returning warriors left them feeling safe and protected.

Dawn finally let go of Wintra's hand and walked down the steps, Wintra hurrying alongside her. They reached the bottom as Cree and Torr brought their horses to a halt a short distance from them.

Cree dismounted and went straight to his wife, grabbed her around the waist and yanked her up against him and kissed her as if he had not seen her in forever.

Wintra launched herself at Torr, who braced for the impact, catching her petite body in his strong arms and hauling her up against him and kissed her to show her just how much he had truly missed her.

He's home. He's safe. He's mine. I love him. The

litany rang repeatedly in her head and she was forever grateful, for it renewed, over and over, what she needed to hear, know, feel.

"Inside," Cree ordered, "the weather grows colder and I grow hungry." He pressed his mouth close to Dawn's ear. "For more than food."

She smiled, patted her chest, and nodded.

Torr held Wintra back for a moment as Cree and Dawn hurried into the keep.

"I have missed you more than I can express," Torr said, "though I intend to show you how much, later."

"And I shall do the same," she said, "but first for nourishment to sustain us for the long night ahead."

Torr laughed and ran up the steps and into the keep with Wintra close at his side.

Food aplenty was placed on the table as well as drink. Tankards were filled and plates piled high, and the two women sat close to their husbands as if by doing so they could keep them there.

Sloan joined them after seeing to the returning men and raised a tankard to their safe return. The servants even joined in with a cheer.

Cree finally spoke. "We were delayed because one of the warriors sent to see what he could find out about Kellmara met up with us on the way home. He insisted that I see for myself what he had seen, for he did not quite believe his own eyes."

Wintra hooked her arm through Torr's and snuggled closer to him. She worried over what she was about to hear, since in some way it would probably affect her.

"An emissary of the King waits at a campsite for Kellmara to arrive."

"Why would an emissary from the King be with Kellmara?" Sloan asked.

"I do not know," Cree said, "but we will find out soon. Kellmara is not far off. He should arrive by nightfall or morning."

Before anyone could comment, the bell tolled announcing an approaching troop.

Sloan stood. "It appears Douglas Hawthorne, Earl of Kellmara was anxious to get here as soon as possible. I will ride out with the warriors to greet them and escort them to the village."

Torr stood. "And enough time to refresh before meeting Kellmara." He reached his hand out to Wintra to join him.

Cree nodded as he watched his sister hurry out of the keep with her husband. And a thought struck him. "It is a good hour or more before the troop reaches the rise. I should freshen myself and change into clean garments as well."

Dawn smiled and gestured.

Cree grinned. "I was hoping you would want to help me." He helped her off the bench, his hand suddenly going to her stomach. "You have rounded more in the short time since I've been gone. You and the babe are well?"

She nodded and tugged his hand to hurry him along.

He stubbornly refused to move when they reached the bottom of the steps. "You should wait down here."

She planted her hands on her hips and narrowed her eyes at him.

"Do not look at me like that. I have an aching need and damn if I do not want to pound the hell out of you. And that will not do now that you grow round with my child."

She could see he was adamant about it, but she

had missed him terribly and wanted an intimate moment with him whatever way she could get it. But how to convince him? The thought came easily and with his back to those left in the Great Hall, she stepped in front of him confident that no one would be able to see what she was about to do. Her one hand quickly slipped under the new plaid, he had just begun wearing, to grab hold of him and she raised her other hand up to her mouth and inserted one finger in it, then eased it out slowly, and then repeated the gesture over and over as she tugged on him, growing him ever harder.

"Damn it, woman," he seethed through gritted teeth.

She let her hand drop away from her mouth and her tongue slipped out to slowly circle her lips as if showing how much she looked forward to tasting him.

He growled like an angry beast, scooped her up, and took the stone steps two at a time.

~~~

Torr closed the cottage door behind him and held his hand out to Wintra. "Come here."

She drifted into his arms with a smile.

"I want you to know that I will let no one take you from me," he said with such adamant conviction that it sent a shiver through her and faded her smile.

"Do you believe someone will try?" she asked, the thought having gone through her mind as well.

"I have no knowledge that someone will, though it troubles me that Kellmara joins forces with Owen. And Owen seems to believe that he has information that Kellmara wants and I think it concerns you."

Wintra shook her head. "What information can Owen possibly have about me? And why would it concern Kellmara?"

"All good questions which I assume will be answered when Kellmara arrives." He gave her a kiss, lingering a bit longer than he intended. Now was not the time to think of making love to her, but then there was not a time he did not think of making love to her.

Being prudent at what would happen if he remained close to her, he eased her away from him. "I need to wash up a bit and change my shirt."

Wintra was disappointed that he let her go. She loved being in his arms. They were so warm and comforting. And then there was the scent of him, pungent pine and earth mixed with his own muskiness. It always managed to spark her passion.

She shook the thoughts away, wishing they could make love, but they did not have enough time. She saw to getting a bucket and scooping up snow, then placed it close to the hearth for the snow to melt fast so that Torr could wash.

She watched as he stripped off his shirt and tossed it to the table. She took it to hang on the peg and his scents, so potent on it, drifted up to sting her nostrils and invade her senses. She hurried to hang it on the peg and could not stop herself from burying her face in it for a moment and breathing deeply.

With reluctance, she turned away from it to see Torr staring at her strangely. She said what she felt. "I love the scent of you."

He warned himself to stay where he was, to not go any closer to her or he would surely surrender to his growing need and damn if that need wasn't growing harder by the moment.

Wintra had much yet to learn about making love

and passion and all that went with it, but instinct played a big part in it all and when she caught that hungry look in his eyes, she knew exactly what her husband was thinking.

She took a step toward him.

"Don't," he warned. "I will not be able to keep my hands off you."

She took slow steps toward him. "I don't want you to."

"Wintra, you will obey me on this," he chided.

"Do you truly want me to?"

Two more steps and she would be on top of him and by then it would be too late. But then it was already too late.

Torr reached out and snatched her hand, yanking her against him. His kiss was hungry, and she fed it. It wasn't long before he pulled his mouth away, hoisted her up on the table, shoved her dress up, spread her legs and ripped his plaid off to give him room to watch as he plunged in and out of her.

She braced her hands on the table to balance herself and closed her eyes for a moment, relishing every potent poke. Then she lowered her head curious to see for herself and her eyes widened as she watched the thick size of him slip in and out of her with ease, and she groaned, "I am going to come."

"More than once," he urged and took her even harder.

She exploded with such a hard climax that she screamed out his name, and it heightened his own passion that was at its peak and about to burst. But he wanted her to come again and so he kept up the maddening tempo, straining to contain himself for just a moment more.

Wintra thought her heart would burst from her

chest as her desire rose once again and when he grabbed hold of her backside and forced her harder against him again and again, she burst in another explosive climax.

Torr joined her, feeling as if his climax would never end and loving and savoring every minute of it. When he finally stilled, he rested his brow to hers, though did not pull out of her. He was content right where he was and intended to remain there for a bit longer.

Wintra felt the same, for on a labored breath she said, "Do not pull out of me."

"I am staying right where I am."

"Good, for that is right where you belong."

They stayed that way, not moving an inch. The hearth flames toasted Torr's bare backside and Wintra's legs, making them even more content to remain as they were.

"If there were time, I would take you to our bed and keep you there the rest of the day and night."

She smiled. "And I would happily remain there with you."

He reluctantly pulled away from her and carefully lowered her dress and lifted her off the table to place her gently on her feet before he turned away from her. "I need to wash and be ready for Kellmara."

At that moment she had a profound dislike for the man. Why did he have to arrive at the keep now? And what did he want from her? She tried to tell herself that it did not matter. She was Torr's wife and nothing could change that. Then why was she so disturbed by his arrival?

"Do not worry," Torr said, watching her pace in front of the door. "All will be well."

She prayed his words were true.

The sudden toll of the bell letting everyone know the approaching troop had reached the rise startled them both as did the pounding on the door.

"Your presence is requested at the keep immediately," a voice shouted.

"We will be right there," Torr called out and turned to Wintra. "Let us go get this over so that we may return here and enjoy the night together."

"I will be counting the minutes until we are alone," she said eagerly and took hold of his hand.

They left the cottage and she hurried along with Torr into the Great Hall to join her brother and Dawn at the dais to greet the man who had journeyed here in regards to her. Her stomach roiled with worry, and she wished this day was over and that she was in bed with her husband making love. She chased the thought away. She had to keep her mind clear and focused. She had to know what the Earl of Kellmara wanted with her.

"You are to remain seated until I summon you," Torr said to Wintra and she scowled. He could not help but grin. "You are almost as good as your brother with that scowl, though if you show it too often you will be cursed with a bevy of wrinkles."

She poked him in the ribs, her finger hitting nothing but hard muscle. "Then do not make me scowl."

"That's right, it is your fault my sister scowls. She never scowled before," Cree said with a levity that few got to see.

"My brother is right," Wintra said seeing for the first time in many years the brother who had once teased and made her laugh.

"Right or not, I am your husband now and you will obey me," Torr said with a smile, but all who heard knew that it was a reminder that Wintra was his and no one answered for her but him. "Cree and I shall wait in front of the dais to greet the Earl of Kellmara."

Cree nodded letting Torr know he understood, though his scowl let him know that he was appeasing Torr.

The doors to the Great Hall swung open and six warriors, thick in size, entered, their swords hanging heavily at their sides. They scanned the room quickly, then one snapped his hand at a warrior standing guard by the door and a moment later a man walked in.

He was tall with pure white hair that just brushed his shoulders and though age showed on his face, it did so with grace. He was a handsome man with striking blue eyes. His stance was firm and confident, his body more that of a young warrior, muscled and firm, than an aging, seasoned one. And from his intense expression, he was a man who had no intentions of being denied.

"Thank you for receiving me into your home, Earl of Carrick."

"What brings you here, Kellmara?" Cree asked, getting right to the point.

"I have come to take Wintra—*my daughter*— home where she belongs."

Chapter Twenty-six

Wintra was shocked by the Earl of Kellmara's remark, though was even more shocked by Cree's reply.

"So you are the bastard who raped my mother?" Cree said, taking a threatening step toward the man.

Kellmara warriors advanced on their laird ready to protect him, but Kellmara was quick to stop them with a simple raise of his hand. He then took a step toward Cree and in a clear and firm voice said, "I did not rape Colleen. I loved her."

"My mother came home beaten and bruised one day—"

"I only recently found out about that incident and believe me the man responsible has suffered the consequences. I was sent away by my father and thought to return in a few short days with plans of wedding your mother. It was years before I was allowed to return home and by then," —he paused a moment—"I discovered Colleen had died. It wasn't until recently I learned that Colleen had a daughter who would be ten and nine years now. That would make her my daughter and I intend to claim her."

"I have no way of knowing if you tell the truth and I will not turn my sister over to you on your word alone," Cree said.

Torr stepped forward then. "Wintra is not going anywhere. She is my wife and neither of you have say over her."

Wintra listened to the three men argue about her. She wondered for a moment if she was in a nightmare and could not wake, for this surely wasn't real. Her father had died. Cree would never tell her such a lie. This man was not her father. Cree was not her half-brother. The Earl of Kellmara was a charlatan just as Owen had been.

"It does not matter," Torr said. "Father or not, I am her husband and my right comes before all others."

"Not unless the King annuls the marriage," Kellmara said as if it was already done.

Wintra felt a deep chill run through her and she hugged herself tightly as her worry grew, and rightly so. She had learned even while secluded at the abbey that men had power over women and the more powerful the man, the more power he wielded.

"I have petitioned the King to annul your marriage to my daughter," Kellmara said to Torr. "The King has sent an emissary to determine my request and, if he so chooses, the emissary has the authority to grant the annulment posthaste. He will question you both and make the decision over the next few days. Until then, you are ordered by the King to keep your distance from my daughter."

Torr laughed in Kellmara's face. You are a fool if you think that you can keep me from my wife."

Kellmara glared at him. "The King orders it."

Torr's arm shot out, his finger poking Kellmara hard in the chest. "I do not give a bloody damn. No one is taking my wife away from me."

"Wintra should have never been forced to wed you. She is my daughter and deserves better."

Torr clenched his hand into a tight fist, but kept it at his side. "She also deserves a father who cares more about what she wants than what he wants."

"What have you promised the King in exchange for a decision in your favor?" Cree asked, stepping between the two men. "Wait, let me answer for you. You are a powerful Chieftain to the far North where the King has fewer allies and with you as one, it will strengthen his reign and borders."

"I simply presented my petition to the King, no more. I have no sway over what he thinks. But any resistance to the emissaries decision will be dealt with swiftly," Kellmara warned.

"You can count on that," Cree said.

"Now I would like to meet my daughter."

Wintra stepped around the dais, though kept her distance from all three men. She raised her chin and narrowed her eyes at the Earl of Kellmara. "I am not your daughter. I never have been and I never will be. I love my husband and I intend to stay wed to him. And you will have to lock me away to keep me from him. I would advise you to leave now, for I will never acknowledge you as my father."

"You are my daughter for sure, bold and demanding just like me, and your eyes are the same blue as mine. Speak as bravely as you wish, but you will follow the King's command, you have no choice."

"That is where you are wrong. I will not listen to this nonsense and I will not talk with you *ever*. You are a cold, heartless man to come here and make demands of me, especially if I were your daughter. This is no way for a father to show his love for his daughter. So I tell you one last time—leave, or better yet—go to hell."

Wintra walked past Kellmara and one of his warrior's stepped in front of her, blocking her path.

She did not wait. She stomped on his foot as she grabbed his nose, yanked and twisted it. He hopped on one foot while one hand covered his bleeding nose. Then she skidded around him and hurried past the startled warriors and out the door.

"That's my wife," Torr said with pride.

"And my sister," Cree beamed.

"And definitely mine and Colleen's daughter," Kellmara said adamantly.

~~~

Dawn hurried out of the Great Hall through the hallway that led out to the kitchen shortly after Wintra left. The men might admire Wintra's brave tenacity, but Dawn knew just how fragile that tenacity was. She knew that Wintra was now plagued with thoughts and questions, but worst of all she was probably asking herself if it could possibly be true. Was the Earl of Kellmara her father?

It did not take long to get to the cottage that Cree had once assigned her. She had loved its solitude, and the time she and Cree had gotten to spend there. It was a place of comfort and love and Dawn was pleased that Torr and Wintra were making it their home, if only for a while.

She knocked on the front door, hunching her shoulder against the wind that had picked up since nightfall.

"Go away! And do not dare make me repeat myself."

Dawn smiled. Wintra definitely was much like her brother. She eased the door open, using it as a shield since she expected something to come flying at her. She poked her hand passed the door and wiggled her fingers in greeting.

"Dawn?"

Dawn rushed around the door, shutting it closed and securing the latch, not that it would keep Torr or Cree out, but it would discourage others from entering. She turned and looked at Wintra and wasn't surprised to see tears ready to spill free. Dawn spread her arms wide.

Wintra did not hesitate, she ran into them, hugging Dawn tight, grateful she had come and offered comfort.

When Wintra's tears subsided, Dawn eased her down on a chair to sit. She then pulled another chair around next to Wintra's and sat, resting her hand on Wintra's knee.

"It is not possible is it?" Wintra asked, knowing the answer, but wanting someone to deny it. "He can't be my father. He seems a heartless man without true care to how his decisions would affect his daughter." Wintra ran both hands down her face. "It is a nightmare. I am in a nightmare and I cannot wake up. Wake me up, Dawn. I beg you, wake me up."

Dawn did the only thing she could. She squeezed her hand tightly to let her know that this was no dream.

"Do you think Torr will be kept from me tonight? I do not want to sleep without him by my side."

A tepid knock sounded at the door and both women turned inquisitive eyes that way.

"Dawn? Wintra? Are you in there?"

Dawn jumped up, unlatched the door, and opened it, letting Old Mary in.

The old woman rubbed her gnarled hands and shivered. "The wind has a biting chill to it tonight."

Dawn ushered Old Mary over to a chair by the

fire, then the two women brought their chairs around by her as well.

"I had a feeling I was needed here," Old Mary explained, holding her hands out to the fire's heat. "What has happened?"

Wintra explained everything, wiping away a teardrop that fell now and again. "I won't be kept from Torr," she insisted stubbornly when she finished.

"You also do not want to place Torr in a potentially dangerous situation," Old Mary warned. "One that would see harm come to him."

"Never!" Wintra cried, alarmed at the old woman's words. The situation was growing worse by the minute, and the weight of it had her shoulders sagging and her head drooping.

Dawn tapped her arm and when Wintra looked up, Dawn shrugged her shoulders and scrunched her brow.

"What's wrong?" Wintra verbalized Dawn's question before answering it. "The Earl of Kellmara is a powerful man. And if the King feels it would benefit having him as an ally, he will grant Kellmara his request."

"There is that possibility," Old Mary said, "though Torr not obeying the King's command could prove worse."

"I know. I thought the same myself when Torr announced that he did not care what the King had commanded. I may have bravely or foolishly announced that I would not be kept from my husband, but the King's word is final. And if Torr and I do not obey, as the Earl of Kellmara knows we must, we could put not only ourselves in danger, but my brother and all here as well." With the weight of the situation becoming clearer by the moment, Wintra sighed heavily.

Dawn gestured and Old Mary quickly interpreted. "You should speak with the Earl of Kellmara."

"I most certainly will not," Wintra said. "He is a selfish man and cares little about others."

Old Mary continued interpreting for Dawn. "He cannot care for you if he does not know you. If he loved your mother, then he would love the only child he and she had made together. He never got to know you, so he does the only thing he can for you now— he protects you— since he failed to protect your mother. Let him come to know you, love you, and then he will see that you—his daughter—loves Torr, and then he will do anything to see you happy." Old Mary nodded. "Dawn gives you good advice. I would listen to it if I were you."

"What if he does not truly care about me?" Wintra asked, still shy of trusting people after not having seen Owen for whom he truly was. "What if he intends to use me? What if he has intentions of arranging a union to a man that would be more beneficial to him?"

"You will not know that unless you speak with him," Old Mary said.

"It sounds as if it does not matter one way or another, since it is obvious the King wishes to please Kellmara and win his favor. So what difference does it make either way?" Wintra said, fearing that no matter what was done, the outcome would be in Kellmara's favor.

"Where is that tenacity of yours that is so much like your brother's?" Old Mary asked. "You would surrender without a fight for the man you love? Cree would move heaven and hell for Dawn, and Torr would do the same for you, which, again I remind you, can place him in a seriously dangerous situation. So do you fight or surrender?"

Wintra threw her shoulders back as if shrugging off the weight that had rested there. "You're right. It is time to stop feeling sorry for myself and fight for what is not only mine, but what I want."

Old Mary grinned and rubbed her hands together. "Good. And while you do we must find a way to keep you and Torr apart, yet together."

Dawn grinned, tapped her temple, and then her chest.

"You have a plan?" Wintra asked excited. "Tell us."

~~~

Cree had not been surprised to see that Dawn had disappeared shortly after Wintra. He knew she would go to comfort Wintra and he was relieved that she did. He had no choice but to remain here and talk with Kellmara. There was much to find out from him and to find out if he truly cared about Wintra or if this was some type of ploy to use Wintra to his advantage. He had seen it too often with the nobles. Daughters were given away, their fate sealed, in exchange for combining clans and land or to appease an enemy. And he could only imagine the ones that had suffered at the hands of unscrupulous men. If he had a daughter, he would make certain she suffered no such fate. And he would make certain that Wintra did not as well. She loved Torr and he loved her, and he would make certain that the two remained together— no matter what it took.

"You will order your sister to return here so that I

may speak with her," Kellmara demanded of Cree.

"He has no say over Wintra," Torr said. "She is my wife and obeys me."

Kellmara's nostrils flared and his eyes narrowed. "Not for long."

"So say you, but until that is determined Wintra is still my wife and obeys me."

"Need I remind you to stay away from her by order of the King?" Kellmara spat.

Torr gave a cursory glance around the Great Hall. "Where is the King's emissary? Let me hear it from his lips."

"He is at a different camp and will be here in a day or two."

"Until I hear it directly from the King's man, I will obey no such order."

"I would think twice about that," Kellmara warned.

"And I would think twice about taking my wife away from me."

"Are you threatening me?" Kellmara said, taking a step toward Torr, his men quickly following.

"Enough," Cree shouted. "Torr has every right to threaten you. How dare you walk into my home and demand that I turn my sister over to you without proof of anything."

"Watch what you say, Cree, I am a powerful man and not afraid of you."

"You should be," Cree warned, "for you may be powerful, but I am brutal and I have no doubt that the King warned you of that and is the reason why you arrived with a large contingent and have more men waiting in other camps. But be aware of one thing, one of my men are equal to two of yours. They will decimate your warriors, and I personally will see that you never bother my sister ever again."

"Is that a threat?" Kellmara asked fury sparking in his blue eyes.

"It is a promise if you do not conduct yourself in a more cordial manner."

Kellmara was ready to retaliate when he caught movement to the side and he turned to see Cree's warriors lining the side wall two deep. He swerved around to take in the Great Hall and saw that it was filled with Cree's warriors. His men saw the same, their eyes wide with surprise. Kellmara could not believe that that many warriors had entered the room without him or his men hearing or seeing them. And Cree had been right about the King warning him. What Cree did not know was that the King told him he was on his own when he stepped on Cree's land. He would offer Kellmara no help. Now he understood why.

"I suggest we eat and drink and discuss this matter more calmly," Cree said. "Your men must be hungry, as are mine."

Kellmara almost laughed at the way Cree discreetly let him know that his warriors would easily devour the few men that protected him. "That is hospitable of you, Cree."

Though tempers continued to remain high, caution prevailed and the three men took seats at the dais while the warriors in the Great Hall retreated to the tables. Once full, the remaining warriors stood along the walls until a warrior who finished his meal exchanged places with one standing.

As soon as tankards were filled, Cree asked, "How did you come to know my mother? Your land is nowhere near where our farm was."

"What difference does it make?" Kellmara asked

clearly annoyed by the question.

"A big difference, for you have yet to convince me that you did not take advantage of my mother."

"Advantage?" Douglas laughed. "Colleen stole my heart at first sight. She was a beauty, but more than that she never spoke an unkind word. She was like no woman I had ever met and have still not met. I was visiting an old friend of my father's and came across your mother foraging in woods that she was not permitted to forage in. She told me that her young son was sick and she needed some of the plants to help heal him." He paused as if lost in the memory of that day.

Cree clearly recalled it. He had been sick for days with a fever, but he never knew that his mother had taken the chance of foraging on restricted land to help heal him. She had placed herself in danger to save him, and she had placed herself at Kellmara's mercy when he found her.

"What did you do?" Cree demanded, his hand clenching his tankard tightly.

"She was so kind, so apologetic, and pleaded so sincerely for her young son that I dropped to the ground and helped her gather what she needed, and then I saw that she got home safely to you."

Cree's hand relaxed. "I thank you for that."

"But you certainly cannot thank me for falling in love with her, for my love brought her anguish instead of happiness. And I never meant that to happen. I had every intention of wedding your mother and taking you on as my son. My father had other ideas."

"She never spoke of you to me," Cree said.

"She felt it was best not to just yet. I could not blame her. Here I was a mighty chieftain's son claiming to love her and wed her. She had told me I was dreaming that it would never be, but that for now she would love me, for I had stolen her heart when she had thought she would never love again. I intended to prove her wrong, and it breaks my heart and infuriates me that I had given her my word and failed to keep it."

Kellmara turned and looked at Torr. "I will not, however, fail to claim my daughter and protect her."

"And what Wintra wants does not matter?" Torr asked.

"I am her father and will determine what is best for her."

"Good luck with that," Torr said on a laugh. "I thought she was much like Cree, but it appears that she not only got her tenacity from him, but you as well."

"I will talk with her and she —"

Cree and Torr burst out laughing.

"She will talk with you only when she is good and ready to," Torr said.

"He is right," Cree agreed. "I placed her in an abbey to be cared for and kept safe after our mother died since I hired out as a mercenary to help build a better life for us. She was furious and let me know it each time I visited her. Three years ago she refused my visits unless I was there to take her home. Three years and she never wavered. You might be in for a wait."

"She cannot refuse me, I am her father."

Cree and Torr laughed again.

"Your mother had a kind heart. Surely, her daughter has one too."

"She does have a kind heart," Torr said, "but she lingers often in her thoughts, causing her stubbornness to wind up winning out more often than not."

Kellmara looked away as if he was to blame.

"You suffer from the same affliction?" Torr asked trying not to smile, but failing.

"Colleen was the one person who understood my constant musings and helped me to not linger in them. I miss her to this day as badly as I ever have." Douglas shook his head and turned on Torr. "If you claim to love my daughter so much, why didn't you go after her when she ran out of here?"

"Wintra's not only angry with you, but all three of us," Torr said. "And Dawn, Cree's wife, followed after her. She is the best person to talk with Wintra right now. She would understand what she is going through and help her. And if you're thinking it was because I feared you would try to stop me, think again. Nothing would or will stop me from being with my wife."

Chapter Twenty-seven

Dawn rushed into the Great Hall, her hands flying as she gestured.

"Calm down," Cree ordered as he jumped up out of his chair, the sudden jolt sending it tumbling. "I cannot understand you."

Dawn slowed her gestures.

"Wintra is nowhere to be found?" Cree asked to make certain he heard her correctly.

Dawn nodded vigorously.

Torr bolted out of his chair. "Where was she last seen?"

Dawn gestured again.

"At the cottage?"

She nodded.

The Earl of Kellmara was already standing. "We cannot waste a minute. Form a search party."

Cree raised his hand. "Not yet. I want to hear more." He nodded to his wife.

Everyone watched as Dawn gestured.

"Wintra grew upset with what happened here and ran out of the cottage?"

Dawn nodded at her husband and gestured again.

"Wintra wanted away from everyone?"

Dawn nodded again and rubbed her hands nervously.

"That's it," Kellmara announced, "I am going to take my men and search for her."

"Go ahead," Cree agreed. "I will send some of my

men as well."

The Earl of Kellmara gathered his men and hurried out of the keep.

Torr turned to glare at Dawn at the same time Cree crooked his finger at her. "Now come here and tell me the truth."

Dawn grinned sheepishly and approached her husband, her hands gesturing.

"Wintra wanted the Earl of Kellmara otherwise occupied so that he could not keep Torr from her tonight?" Cree asked and when Dawn nodded, he laughed and looked to Torr. "My sister protects you from Kellmara and the King's command while getting her way."

Torr stepped forward. "She is a courageous one for sure, though it was unnecessary. I will allow nothing to keep us apart."

Dawn gestured to Torr.

"No, I do not fear what the King may do if I disobey his orders. And I do not think he truly cares. He appeases the Earl of Kellmara by sending an emissary when he knows full well that Wintra and I are soundly wed by now."

"I agree," Cree said, "but we cannot simply disregard Kellmara. He is a worthy adversary and must be taken seriously."

"I understand that, but I will not bow to his demands. If Wintra truly is his daughter, then he must learn that her husband will suffer no dictate from him. He treats me respectfully or he suffers the consequences. Now I want to find my wife and make it clear that she has nothing to worry about and does not need to concern herself with Kellmara."

Dawn smiled and pointed overhead.

"Here in the keep?" Torr and Cree said

simultaneously.

Dawn nodded and kept pointing her finger up.

"The room at the top of the keep?" Cree asked and after she nodded, he looked to Torr. "Go to her. I will send some warriors to join Kellmara, but I will tell them not to hurry or worry."

Torr nodded and turned to leave, but stopped when Cree called out.

"And you better make certain that my sister understands that her actions are not acceptable."

"I'll leave that to you," Torr said with a grin.

"Coward," Cree said.

"Wise husband," Torr counted and hurried up the steps.

~~~

Wintra paced the room, thinking how much the small space reminded her of her tiny quarters at the abbey and oddly enough she found it a bit comforting. Of course this room had a fireplace, though small and adequate for the room. Her cell-like room at the abbey had no such comfort, which was why she had snuck out and slept in front of the fireplace in the gathering room during the cold winter months. She had made sure to wake before sunrise and scurry back to her room so as not to be caught or else the abbess would have had someone stand watch over the fireplace.

She looked to the door, wishing for a knock. It would either be Dawn telling her that their plan had failed or Torr.

The knock startled her, though not as much as when the door flew open and her husband strode in. She was never so relieved to see him, though he didn't look too happy to see her.

"Do you think me incapable of protecting you?" he asked as he approached her.

She had to laugh, which stopped him in his tracks. "After all we have been through together, how could you even ask me that?"

He walked over to her, his arm capturing her waist in a hug. "Then why hide away, up here, where we cannot be found?"

"Simple. I love you and will not be kept from you," —she pressed her finger to his mouth when he went to speak— "and I know you feel the same and would place yourself in danger to be with me."

He kissed her softly and briefly. "I would battle hell itself to be with you."

"And that is exactly what you could face if you disobey the King, and I will not have it. We simply need to be discreet until this matter can be settled and Kellmara leaves."

Torr shook his head. "No. You are my wife and I will not sneak away to be with you. We are wed good and sound and no one is going to take that away from us, not even the King."

She poked him in the chest. "You claim that I am stubborn, but you are much more tenacious. I will not have anything happen to you. I love you much too much to lose you."

"I think I am just realizing how very much you actually do love me."

"Just now?" she accused, this time with a playful punch to his stomach.

He hugged her closer. "I think you may have realized the same recently yourself."

Wintra tilted her head as if in question and surprisingly said, "You could very well be right. The thought that Kellmara could be my father was not half as upsetting as his intention of annulling our marriage. That he would take from me who I loved most tore at my heart. You are too much a part of me for me to ever let you go, which is why we will make certain that Kellmara thinks we obey the King's command."

The knock startled them both and Torr went to open the door.

Flanna rushed in and looked to Wintra. "The Earl of Kellmara is insisting the keep be searched from top to bottom before he begins his search elsewhere. It seems he feels you will try to trick everyone and remain safely within the keep."

"No doubt something he himself would do," Torr said with a grin to his wife.

"The hiding spot," Wintra said and she and Flanna hurried over to a section of the stone wall.

"What hiding spot?" Torr asked. "And how do you know about it.

"Cree's men discovered a small hiding room upon inspection of the keep after he took occupation of the castle. It is on the wall opposite the fireplace. Dawn told me about it in case we needed to make use of it." Wintra said.

Torr shook his head when the concealed door was finally opened with his help and he got a look at the small space barely big enough for two people. It was dark and musty, not a place you would want to be stuck in too long. He was about to tell her it wasn't necessary for them to hide. He would confront Kellmara and put an end to this nonsense when they heard footfalls on the stairs.

"Hurry," Wintra urged as she shoved him into the confined space and yanked on the metal ring as

Flanna pushed from the outside.

Before he could protest the door closed shut and they were pitched into complete darkness.

Wintra tried to tell herself not to panic when she realized she could not move an inch. The space was so small and the air so musty that she felt as if she needed to gasp for breath. She grabbed hold of Torr's shirt, squeezing the linen in her hands and not dare letting go.

He felt her body grow cold and shiver. She was afraid, and he could not blame her. The confined space would tempt anyone's sanity. And the stale air would not last long. He reached out to grab the metal ring and open the door when he felt her grab his hand to stop him.

"This is—"

She pressed her finger to his lips and her body tightly against his.

Her shiver turned to a tremble, and he wasn't sure what she feared most, the dark confined space or him confronting Kellmara. He decided it was best to let her have her way for now and to let her think that he would hold his tongue when it came to Kellmara.

"For now," he whispered, "you can have your way." And before she could argue with him, he reached for her chin and tilted her head up so that he could bring his lips gently down on hers. At first she seemed reluctant to return the kiss, but he remained patient and determined. He intended to break through her worry and have her relax and fully taste the kiss.

He kept the kiss soft so that she was not compelled to return it, but rather to simply relax and enjoy. He allowed his tongue to gradually slip in and tease hers into responding, which she did with some hesitation.

Her body remained tense and no doubt her mind was overwrought, and they had only been in the room for a minute or more. He needed her to forget where they were, to think of nothing but the two of them.

There was just enough space for him to slip his hand down along her back to her bottom and he gave one round cheek a gentle squeeze as he urged her firmly against him. The kiss had aroused him, growing him hard, but as she fit herself against him and snuggled there, he grew even harder.

He ended the kiss, needing to take a breath and rested his face in her sweet scented hair. She smelled so good, felt so good, and he wished they were in bed so that he could strip her naked and...

The groan that echoed in the small space came from him as her snuggles turned to a deliberate grind against his ever growing arousal. Her hands remained gripped to his shirt and her brow rested against his chest.

"I want you so badly," she whispered.

"Damn," he murmured and with both hands cupping her backside, pressed her to fit against him.

She gasped softly and burrowed harder against him as if somehow she could force him inside her.

He dropped his head back and it hit the stone wall. He growled low in his chest, aching to bury himself deep inside her, aching for this ordeal to be done so that he could make love to his wife without any damn interference from anyone.

He wondered if the room was clear and he could open the door, though right now he did not care who the hell was in the room. He would scoop Wintra up in his arms and walk right past anyone who was there and deliver a good punch to anyone who tried to stop him.

"Torr," she said as if in agony, though pleasurable agony.

It was too dark to see anything, but he knew her blue eyes were steamed with passion and he knew she could not wait.

"I'm going to make you come," he whispered in her ear.

"Yes, please," she begged.

Her soft plea tore at his heart and he silently cursed Kellmara over and over. He should be in bed with his wife, slipping into her and watching her writhe and cry out as she climaxed. The man would pay; he would definitely pay.

Torr held tight to her bottom and rubbed hard against her. Her hand clutched desperately to his shirt and her breathing grew rapid. She kept rhythm with him, pressing as hard as she could against him. He cursed beneath his breath as he grabbed at the sides of her dress and hoisted it up past her hips.

She followed suit, shoving his plaid aside.

Unfortunately the confined space would not let them do anymore. But at the moment Wintra didn't care. At least now nothing separated them, and she welcomed the feel of his shaft rubbing against her already throbbing nub and bringing her closer to climax. It came fast and hard and she gasped as she exploded in a never-ending wave of pleasure.

Torr kept a firm arm around her and a steady rhythm going until he felt her climax ease, and then he slowed to a stop even though he remained hard as a rock.

Wintra still continued to clutch his shirt tightly in her hands. "My God that was fabulous. So much better than—"

"So much better than what?" Torr asked a bit

brisk.

"It is not permissible for me to say."

What the hell was going on? What had she kept from him? "Why?" he demanded as he straightened their garments.

"I should really think before I speak."

"No, you should say what you please. Now answer me."

"The nuns told me it was sinful and I should not speak of it."

Now he was curious and on the verge of furious. "You can tell me anything."

He had proven time and time again that she could. He never belittled her or chastised her over any of her endless questions, so she spoke her mind. "The nuns warned me against urges and how when I got them it was a sin to give into them, but I could not help it. I surrendered many times over. I spent more time on my knees praying for my wicked soul. And they warned me that I was never to do such a thing after I wed that my husband's needs would be enough."

"Do you mean to tell me that the nuns warned you not to pleasure yourself?"

"I was told that good wives do not discuss intimacy with their husband."

"I think we both can agree that that information has been proven wrong, at least where we are concerned," he said. "And one day, Princess, you will show me how you pleasured yourself."

"I cannot," she said with a gasp.

Torr did not need any light to see that she was blushing, the heat from her cheeks when he pressed his against hers told it all. "You can and you will." He kissed her quick. "Now it is time to get out of here."

It was as if someone could hear him, for the stone

wall started opening.

Chapter Twenty-eight

"All is well?" Cree asked with a scowl when the door fully opened.

Wintra tried to hide her heated face against her husband's arm, but there was no hiding her red cheeks against his white shirt.

"All is fine," Torr said, taking his wife's hand.

Cree looked at his sister's flushed cheeks, then to Torr and shook his head. "I do not want to know."

"I had no intentions of telling you," Torr said.

Cree had to remind himself that Torr was Wintra's husband. But to Cree Wintra would always be his little sister and he would always want to protect her. He pushed away thoughts of ringing Torr's neck and focused on the present situation.

"Kellmara?" Torr asked.

"Frantic to find Wintra."

"Then it is time he did," Torr said.

"What are you saying?" Wintra said her eyes turning wide as she stepped in front of him. "We are staying here tonight where we will not be found and can be alone."

Torr took her hand and stepped close to her, planting his nose not far from hers. "We are going to sleep in our own bed tonight, though I cannot guarantee how much sleep you will get."

Wintra blushed, turning her head to look at her brother.

His scowl was deep and his eyes had narrowed.

"It is time for you to leave," Torr said to Cree.

Wintra was shocked by Torr's demand.

"Now!" Torr said with a strength that sent a shiver through her.

"You are lucky that you are her husband," Cree said with an angry growl.

"And you are lucky that I have not spirited her away to my home by now."

"But you would be wise to remember that you are presently in my home," Cree warned.

"And I have respected that, but Kellmara being here changes things and you need to respect that."

Cree nodded. "I am glad to know that my sister's husband is a courageous warrior." He walked to the door and turned. "But do not tempt my patience too much."

"Wait," Wintra called out and walked over to him. She stared at him a moment, not knowing what to say or perhaps not knowing how to ask the questions that troubled her. Then suddenly, as if it came to her, she threw her arms around him and hugged him tight.

Cree did not hesitate to hug her back. He had missed the hugs she had given him when she was a little girl. He recalled how tiny her hand had been in his and how her little fingers would curl around his one finger and squeeze tight. And now she was all grown, little no more.

She looked up at him with teary eyes.

He knew she was looking for an explanation of why he and their mum had lied to her. "Tomorrow?"

"Tomorrow," she confirmed. They would talk tomorrow and she would have her answers then.

Wintra looked to Torr after Cree left. "Nothing I can say will change your mind?"

"Nothing," he said adamantly. "I will not cower to

Kellmara's demands whether he is your father or not. And if it turns out to be that he is your father, I will not have him thinking he can dictate to me. I do, however, appreciate the extent you went to keep me safe."

He walked over to her and leaned down to brush his lips across hers. "But I want nothing more than at this moment to cart you off to the cottage and make love to you."

"We can get there faster if we both run," she said with a smile.

He pulled her close. "And is it the cottage you run to or Kellmara you run from?"

Her smile faded. "I would be lying if I said I did not care if we met up with Kellmara. It is a worry to me that will not go away anytime soon."

"Since I would prefer spending the rest of the night with you rather than arguing with the man who just might be my father-in-law, I will promise you that if at all possible we will avoid him."

Her smile returned and she threw her arms around him, gave him a quick kiss, and then pushed him away and ran to the door, calling out, "I will beat you to the cottage."

"Waiting naked for me?" he yelled and chased after her.

Wintra was laughing as she rushed down the keep steps. She had made it out of the keep before Torr, and thankfully Kellmara was nowhere to be seen. A few short steps and she would be at the cottage.

"Wintra," she heard Torr shout and ran faster, wanting time to undress and be waiting in bed for him.

His second shout had her turning, since he sounded as if he warned and that's when she saw one of Kellmara's warriors headed for her and another warrior going straight for Torr.

She thought fast and grabbed a log from the woodpile by the door and swung it as he came upon her. The blow stung her hand and sent him stumbling, though he did not fall over as she hoped he would. She did not wait until he righted himself, she ran toward the warrior still several feet away from Torr and tossed the log at him. It hit his knees and sent him stumbling, though he got up faster than she expected.

Torr caught up with her and shoved her behind him, ordering her to stay put.

That did not happen. She gathered snow in her hand and stepped in front of Torr to through a snowball at one of the warriors, catching him right in the face.

"Enough!" Kellmara shouted.

The warriors immediately stilled and Torr once again shoved Wintra behind him, this time with a much stricter warning. "Stay behind me or I will beat your bottom red.'

Her eyes rounded like two full moons. "You would not."

"Try me," he said through gritted teeth and turned to face Kellmara.

"Why was my daughter running from you?" Kellmara demanded.

"I was not—" Wintra clamped her mouth shut when Torr turned a murderous glare on her.

"I owe you no explanation since it has yet to be proven that you are Wintra's father, but I will not cause you unnecessary worry until this matter can be settled. She was not running from me. She was trying to beat me to our bed."

Wintra grinned. His comment said so much about

the both of them.

Kellmara turned an angry glare on him. "You dishonor my daughter with such a shameful remark."

"The truth that we love each other so much that we hurry to share our love is shameful to you?" Torr asked anger in his sharp voice. "Or what of the truth? Would you not prefer to know that your daughter is happy with the man she is wed to?"

"Until I can determine that for myself you have been ordered to stay away from her," Kellmara said with the authority of a man used to being obeyed.

"I will not be kept from my wife," Torr warned him.

"Then I have no recourse but to see that you are."

"So you will do to me what was done to you— forcibly keep me from the woman I love and who loves me?"

Kellmara took a step back as if Torr had slapped him in the face.

"What goes on here?" Cree demanded as he came to a stop between Torr and Kellmara.

"It seems that the man my daughter wed is more a ruthless warrior than I thought," Kellmara said. "Tomorrow, Wintra, we will talk." He signaled to his warriors who had grown in number around him, and they followed as he walked away.

Cree turned to Torr. "Is this done for the night now? I will not be summoned again?"

"If you are summoned again it will be because I killed whoever disturbed me this time."

Cree brow knitted and Torr grinned.

With a shake of his head, Cree walked away.

Torr took Wintra's hand and hurried to the cottage before anything else could happen and lowered the latch behind him. When he turned he saw Wintra standing by the hearth, her head downcast, and staring into the flames.

He went to her, lifting her chin. "I would not beat your bottom red."

"I know you meant to scare me silent."

"Not an easy thing to do, though heavy thoughts seem to have hold of your tongue. What is wrong?"

"Do you think it is true that Kellmara was forcibly kept from my mother?"

"So he says, though how he has not gone mad with the thought of being kept from the woman he loved is beyond me. I would do whatever I had to— kill whoever I had to—to make my way back to you."

"I think I will speak with him tomorrow, though first I will talk with my brother."

"And with that settled—" He kissed her.

The kiss quickly turned hungry and they were soon stripping each other's garments off as they made their way to the bed in the other room.

He tossed aside the last of her clothes and nibbled kisses along her soft neck before whispering. "I'm going to touch and kiss every single part of you."

Her eyes widened in alarm. "I'll come before you finish."

"Then I'll make you come again." Torr chuckled. "As you know by now, there are no restrictions on climaxes."

Wintra frowned.

"Why doesn't that make you happy," he said surprised by her response.

"I worry that I will wear you out."

Torr laughed and scooped her up in his arms. "Oh, Princess, I do love you."

He placed her on the bed, going down beside her, then leaned over and kissed her while his hand began to roam over her soft skin. He loved the way her body responded to his touch, moving in welcome with it. It wasn't long before his tongue followed where his hand had been, wanting to taste as much of her as he could.

It didn't take long before she was shouting out his name.

He lifted his head and grinned. "You will bring your father down on us and I do not think he will approve of what I am doing to you."

She clamped her hand over her mouth.

His grin grew as he returned to lovingly tormenting her, and it wasn't long after that they burst together in climax.

They lay spent beside each other.

"I believe the King knew what he was doing when he brought us together," Torr said.

"As long as he does not tear us apart."

He tucked her close to his side. "How many times must I remind you that I am not going to let that happen?"

"How can you stop it? He is the King and his word is law."

"The King's emissary is the one who will decide our fate, not Kellmara. And he will see how happy we are together, and once he realizes that there is a good chance you are with child, then he certainly will not grant an annulment. And I am going to make certain that he knows that you most likely are."

Her hand went to her stomach. "Our babe. How wonderful that would be, though I think speaking with Kellmara may also help. Dawn suggested that I should. She feels that if he truly is my father, he would want to see me happy. And the only way he can do that is if he got to know me."

"My sister is wise beyond her years."

"I do not know how she does it, not being able to speak, and yet she does not let it stop her. And she is favored and respected by the villagers. She is truly a remarkable woman."

"She is and I am so glad that my father and I found her, especially after losing my sister Teressa. She was much like Dawn."

"She could not speak?"

Torr had not thought about discussing with her the affliction that plagued the women of his family. But she had a right to know, so he did not hesitate to tell her. "It seems that most of the women in my family are born voiceless like Dawn. No one knows why. It simply happens."

"So we could very well have a voiceless daughter?"

"Yes. How do you feel about that?"

Wintra let out a hefty sigh and drifted off into thought for a few moments, to Torr not a good sign.

"I will need to learn more about how Dawn gestures so that I may teach our daughter if she should be born that way, though she will have a strong voice just like her Aunt Dawn. I will also make certain she learns how to defend herself as Cree has taught me, though you will also see that she knows how to handle weapons. And, of course, we will have many sons to protect her, though if we have more daughters than sons, then we will teach them to protect one another."

Torr hugged her tight. "God, Princess, I was blessed the day I met you."

She kissed his cheek. "Fate was certainly on our side that day." She yawned.

"You should get some sleep."

"I could use some sleep," she admitted, her eyes growing heavy.

They drifted off together, sleeping the night through.

Wintra woke to see Torr getting dressed. "You leave me?"

"I thought you could use some rest." He leaned down and kissed her quick, not trusting himself to linger.

She frowned when he hurried away from her and to the door though her mind had a quick thought and she laughed and jumped out of bed naked, extending her arms out to him just as he was about to step beyond the curtain. "Are you sure we do not have enough time to—"

Torr turned and had her on the bed and on her back in an instant. And he was inside her just as quickly, all the while cursing himself for not having enough strength to leave when he should have. But then he would have missed sharing the explosive climax they shared.

"You tempt me much too much," he said lifting off her and standing to adjust his garments. "But then you satisfy me like no other."

"Truly?" she asked eagerly.

"Yes, truly." He gave her a quick kiss and headed once again to the door.

"Torr."

He stopped though did not dare turn to look at her.

"I love you."

He turned then. "Not as much as I love you."

Before she could argue, he hurried out the door.

~~~

The Earl of Kellmara's head shot up as Torr entered the Great Hall.

Cree motioned for him to join them at the dais. Torr nodded and took the seat next to Cree, not trusting himself to sit beside Kellmara.

"The King's emissary will speak to both of you today so that we can get this settled immediately," Kellmara said.

"My wife and I are eager to talk with the emissary. I am sure he will see what you refuse to that Wintra and I love each other and are happy together." Torr said in a tone that left no doubt he meant it.

"The emissary will be the judge of that," Kellmara said.

"Enough!" Cree commanded. "My sister will not be going with you, emissary's decision or not, until I have a chance to speak with the King."

Dawn entered the Great Hall then, a smile on her face and her hands gesturing.

Cree scowled and shook his head.

Dawn was persistent and gestured again, pointing to the Earl of Kellmara.

Cree turned to the man. "My wife invites you to our wedding celebration, though I have repeatedly told her that you will not be here by then."

"When is it?" Kellmara asked.

"Two weeks," Cree said.

"I would love to partake in your celebration," Kellmara said, "as long as you do not mind that I extend my stay."

Dawn answered with a shake of her head and a smile.

Cree did not know what his wife was up to, but she was definitely up to something. And as for Kellmara? He was trying to ensure that he would be able to remain here until all was settled with Wintra.

"You are welcome to stay," Cree said, "though all your warriors are not. You do not need the size troops you have waiting elsewhere. Send them home, including Owen McBride."

Kellmara looked ready to argue when he saw Wintra enter the room and quickly said, "As you wish."

Torr stood and went to his wife. She looked beautiful in a dark green wool dress that tied just below her neck, and he liked that she wore no shift over it. She held her hand out to him as he approached and he laced his fingers with hers and gave her a gentle kiss. They walked to the dais together.

Kellmara stood and Dawn noticed the pride in the man's eyes when he gazed upon Wintra.

"You look so lovely," Kellmara said when Wintra drew near.

She was a bit startled by his compliment, though thanked him.

"Torr tells me that you and he are eager to speak with the emissary. He will speak with you today."

"First, I will speak with my brother privately, then with you. Only then will I speak with the emissary," Wintra informed him.

Kellmara was pleased that she would speak with him, though annoyed that she dictated to him. Something he was not accustomed to. "That can be arranged since the emissary arrived late last night and is still abed. You and I could talk after you finish breakfast, giving your brother time to see to daily matters."

Wintra placed her hand to her stomach. "I have no want of breakfast, and if it pleases my brother I will speak with him now."

"It pleases me," Cree said. "We can talk in my solar."

"First, a word with Dawn," Wintra said and did not wait for permission. She stepped away from Torr and hurried over to Dawn, and the two women walked a few feet away to talk in private.

"I told Torr what you said about speaking with the Earl of Kellmara and he feels you are a wise woman. I chose to follow your advice since I agree with my husband. His sister is a wise woman. We can talk after I have spoken to the Earl."

Dawn smiled wide and nodded vigorously, letting Wintra know how much she looked forward to it.

Wintra hugged Dawn. "I will come find you when I am done."

Cree and Torr stood next to each other watching the women.

"I do not trust them. They conspire. I know it," Cree said for Torr's ears alone.

"I would have to agree with you on that. We should keep an extra watch on them."

"I have found that it is easier going into battle than it is keeping watch over the woman you love," Cree admitted.

"Again I agree, but we should at least try."

"I have my warriors keeping an eye on them, but I think, after last night, Kellmara does the same. His warriors now keep a watch on them as well."

"And still the two of them will somehow manage to avoid them all," Torr said, and Cree nodded.

The two women rejoined the men and Cree gave his wife a quick kiss and with a whisper warned her to behave before he took hold of his sister's hand and strode off to his solar.

Chapter Twenty-nine

Flanna stepped out of the shadows as Cree approached his solar, though she did not startle him. He was pleased that he did not always have to summons her. She had the uncanny ability to sense when she was needed.

She bobbed her head. "May I get you anything, my lord?"

"Food and drink," Cree said, then entered his solar.

Wintra walked over to the hearth, extending her hands out to the heat and rubbing them, though her chill went far deeper. She had been eager to speak to Cree about her father, but now that the moment was here she found herself concerned.

Food and drink arrived and right after the door closed behind the servants, Cree approached his sister.

Wintra turned before he got a few feet in front of her. "Is it true? Do we have different fathers?"

Cree pointed to a chair by the hearth. "Sit."

She shook her head. "Why did you and Mum not tell me the truth?"

Cree had promised his mum that he would never reveal the truth to Wintra. But under the present circumstances, he believed she would understand the need for him to do so. "Mum had come home one day beaten and bruised. I had thought she had been raped, but she denied it. Then when she began to round, I knew I had been right. But she had insisted she had not been raped, though she offered no other reason for her being with child. She told me that it would be best for all concerned that the babe be raised believing that my father was also her father, even though Da had been dead far too long for that to be possible. I was a young lad then, though," —he smiled— "old for my years as Mum often reminded me. I did not argue with Mum. She had suffered enough and when you were born she was so happy. I was too. You brought life back into our troubled existence."

"She wanted me then?" Wintra asked, for she had wondered, though only briefly, if perhaps her mum had no choice but to accept her as her daughter just as Torr had had no choice but to accept her as his wife.

Cree reached out and took her hand in his. "Wanted you? She loved you more than anything. She was so thrilled the day you were born as was I. She hugged you all the time and sang to you."

"I remember her doing the same to you—hugging you often."

"Mum was a loving mother and a good woman. She worked hard so that we could survive. She made me promise with her dying breath that I would take you and leave the farm behind, to let someone else toil uselessly on tenant land."

"Do you think this Kellmara could be my father?"

"There was a time that Mum seemed truly happy. She would work the fields, and I would not always be there to help her. She wanted me to learn about weapons and how to defend myself, so she had struck a bargain with an old warrior who had stopped at the farm for water one day. He was crippled with pain from years of fighting and endless injuries, though he bore his suffering well. He would teach me what I needed to know to defend myself in exchange for food and shelter in the small shack on our property. He accepted, and he is the reason I am skilled in weapons and fighting."

"And the reason she would have time to meet a lover," Wintra said, the pieces falling into place.

Cree nodded. "I had thought the same myself when the Earl of Kellmara claimed that he was your father. And it cannot be denied that there is a strong resemblance between the two of you, especially your blue eyes. They are the exact same color."

"Do you think he tells the truth? Do you think he truly loved Mum and planned on returning for her?"

"I want to believe it. I want to believe that Mum had been loved and cherished as she loved and cherished us. Mum kept the truth from you to protect you, and me. There is no telling what someone would have done if it was known you were Kellmara's daughter."

Wintra slipped into the crook of Cree's arm. "I will not go with him, father or not. I will not leave you. I have only gotten you back again, and I most definitely will not leave my husband."

Cree hugged her. "You are not going anywhere. Kellmara is a fool if he thinks he can walk into my home, claim my sister as his daughter and walk off with her."

"But the King—"

"Is indebted to me far more than Kellmara realizes."

"But the King sent his emissary," Wintra said.

"He also told Kellmara that he was on his own when it came to dealing with me, which was a direct message to me."

"Telling you what?"

"That Kellmara was my problem and for me to handle him at my discretion."

Wintra drifted out of his arms and went to the table and poured each of them hot cider. She handed a tankard to Cree before taking a seat by the hearth. Cree sat in the chair beside her.

"I cannot help but feel sad for Mum. She died believing the man she loved and whose child she bore never truly loved her. That he simply used her and then discarded her. I am surprised she could look upon me with such love when I probably reminded her of Kellmara."

"We do not know if she believed that, perhaps she thought he was kept from her. That he had no choice just as she hadn't. Perhaps that was why she was adamant about you not knowing who your true father was. What we do know without a doubt is how much she loved you and that is a good memory to hold on to."

Wintra refused to cry. She would save her tears for later. There were more things to discuss with her brother.

"Now about you leaving me at the abbey."

By the time their talk was done, Wintra felt as if she and Cree had never been separated. And Cree felt that his sister had finally returned home, and he was pleased that Torr had suggested they stay until the babe was born, giving him more time with his sister.

"Will you talk with Kellmara now?" Cree asked, standing and offering his hand to his sister.

She took it and stood. "Not yet. I want to find Dawn and talk with her first."

Cree raised a brow. "Should I be worried?"

Wintra laughed. "When did I ever worry you?"

"Every single day since you have been born."

She laughed again. "And does Dawn worry you?"

"Always, so the two of you together is an endless stream of worry for me."

"And what happens when you have a daughter?"

He took her arm and walked to the door. "I plan on having three or four sons before a daughter that way I will have a small troop to keep her safe."

Wintra laughed again. "What if I have a daughter and she is voiceless?"

Cree stopped and instead of a scowl a worried look crossed his face. "I had not thought of that. The affliction does seem to have roots in Torr's family. I will have more sons and you will need to have several sons as well that way any voiceless daughters we have will be well-protected."

Wintra felt a tug at her heart. Her brother would stop at nothing to protect her and now he would protect her family as well. She looked at him with teary eyes. "I love you so very much."

He lifted her off her feet and hugged her tight. "And I you, little sister, and I am pleased that you are finally home."

Torr was not in the Great Hall when they returned, though Kellmara waited there. Wintra wondered where her husband had gone off to and was quick to ask. "Where is Torr?"

"A warrior brought a message for him and he left without a word," Kellmara said and stood. "We will talk now."

Wintra shook her head. "No, I need to speak with Dawn first, but I shall return shortly." She did not give him a chance to object. She hurried to the door, grabbing a cloak off the peg before running out.

Cree looked to Kellmara. "Wintra will not be dictated to by a man claiming to be her father."

"I am her father," Kellmara said, tapping his chest hard, as if it proved something. "You can see it in our features. There is no way that anyone could deny that Wintra is my daughter."

"Perhaps, but it does not matter what others believe. It is what Wintra believes that makes the difference. If you truly care that she is your daughter and you don't want to see her hurt, then have patience with her and talk with her before making demands of her."

"She is my daughter and must listen to me," Kellmara insisted.

"Was my mother as obedient as you want Wintra to be?"

Kellmara turned away from Cree to walk to the hearth, brace his hand on the mantel, and stare at the flames.

Cree walked over to sit on a bench facing the large hearth, stretching his long legs out for the fire's heat to warm, and waited.

"Believe me or not, though I have no reason to lie to you, but I loved your mother with all my heart. I wanted no other woman but her. I still don't. I mourn her loss every day of my life. She was my sunshine in a very dark world. And I fought the devil himself to get back to her, but my father had many powerful men who were indebted to him and would not dare go against him. He finally grew tired of my endless attempts to return to her and told me that unless I wanted to see her dead, I would obey him. It wasn't until he died that I was free to seek her out once again.

"I cannot tell you of the deep ache in my heart when I discovered she was dead or the joy I felt when I discovered that she had had my child. We had talked

about giving you many brothers and sisters."
Kellmara turned to Cree. "I must say that you do a
father proud. You have grown into a strong,
courageous man."

Cree did not acknowledge the compliment. His
only thought was of his mother and how this man had
loved her and still did. And he knew at that moment
that his mother had loved this man very much. The
thought that they had never gotten to share a life
together infuriated him, for he thought of himself and
Dawn. He did not know if he would survive losing
Dawn, and he wondered how Kellmara had bared it
all these years.

"I would not have known about Wintra if it had
not been for the persistent Owen McBride," Kellmara
said.

"What do you mean?" Cree asked, easing his legs
back.

"Owen McBride arrived at my doorstep one day
and told me I had a daughter. When he told me who
her mother was and that you were her brother, and
then her age, I knew it was a real possibility. I did
some investigating on my own and discovered that he
was right. Owen let me know how much he loved my
daughter and how much she loved him and that they
wished to wed, but she was certain that her brother
would never grant permission. He was hoping I could
intervene and solve their problem."

"You believed him?" Cree asked annoyed.

"I must admit that I did not give it as much
thought as I should have. What was more important to
me was my daughter's happiness. If she loved this
man and wanted to wed him, then I wanted to give
her that. I did not want her to be deprived of the man
she loved as I was deprived of her mother."

"You need to talk with Wintra," Cree said, "and make certain she tells you what Owen did to her in the cottage when he found her."

"Will it anger me?"

"You can count on it," Cree assured him.

"Then I will go take care of the bastard now and be done with it."

"I take it you are talking about Owen?" Torr asked approaching the table.

"How did you know that?" Kellmara demanded, having yet to warm up to Torr.

"I have had two of my men keeping an eye on Owen. It seems that when word reached him that most of the Kellmara troop was being sent home, he grew angry. His departure, along with the few men he had left, came shortly after that."

"Where is he headed?" Cree asked.

"Home, at least it appears that he is," Torr said. "My men are going to follow him."

"Keep me posted," Cree said.

"My wife?" Torr asked.

"Went to talk with Dawn. She should return soon," Cree assured him.

Torr sat to wait.

"A good rest and a good meal is a good start to the day," the gentle voice said.

All eyes turned to the man who had spoken. He was a portly man, bald on top of his head, and what remaining hair he had was shaved short. He stood barely an inch over five feet and he had a round, full face with wrinkles that crinkled at the corners of his eyes when he smiled. And since the wrinkles ran so deep it would seem the man smiled often.

Kellmara straightened to an impressive stance. "Your Emissary, you are well rested?"

"I have rested more than enough so that I may begin my inquiry."

Torr stood and respectfully bobbed his head.

"Will you not greet me, Cree?" the emissary asked.

Cree got slowly to his feet and turned. "You are looking good, old man."

Kellmara and Torr both turned shocked eyes on Cree.

"And you are still as brazen as ever, and I am still grateful to you for saving my life."

Kellmara glared at Cree. "You saved Henry's life?"

"Many years ago," Cree confirmed.

"And my cousin the King was most grateful," Henry said.

"A word, Cree," Kellmara said and stepped a distance away.

Cree joined him.

"You knew when I first arrived here that things would not go my way, didn't you?"

"Let's say that when I learned who the emissary was I knew the King had left matters up to me to deal with."

"Is there any point in Torr or Wintra speaking to Henry?"

"It would appease not only Henry, but the King, and would also alleviate any fears my sister might have that the man she loves will be taken from her."

"I want only what is best for Wintra."

"Then I suggest you ask Wintra what is best for her." Cree turned and rejoined the men at the table.

Henry smiled as Cree approached. "I have suggested to Torr that we take a stroll through the village while we talk since the morning meal was so delicious that I ate way too much. I must meet this remarkable cook of yours Cree."

"Do not think of stealing him away," Cree said. "Turbett belongs to me and he will confirm that."

"A man can dream," Henry said with a chuckle.

Cree placed a firm hand on Henry's shoulder. "Better pleasant dreams than nightmares of what might happen if one should try to take Turbett from me."

Henry laughed and turned to Torr. "Let us go. There is much for us to discuss."

"That there is," Torr agreed and walked off with the man.

Wintra entered as Torr was leaving, and he stopped to introduce her to the emissary.

"I look forward to speaking with you, Wintra," Henry said, cordially.

"I would reserve your opinion on that since your decision means little to me. I intend to remain wed to my husband no matter what conclusion you reach," she said sweetly. "Do enjoy your walk." Wintra gave her husband a kiss on the cheek and walked off.

"She definitely is Cree's sister," Henry said.

Torr nodded with a smile. "And I believe she has much of the Earl of Kellmara in her as well."

"God bless you, my son," Henry said with a laugh and a shake of his head.

Wintra stopped in front of the man who claimed to be her father and said, "It is time for us to talk."

Chapter Thirty

Cree sat enjoying the quiet of the Great Hall and a tankard of ale, his legs once again stretched out in front of the hearth and his back resting against the edge of the table. It had been a busy morning and soon warriors and those in need of food would come here to eat. That he could provide for so many made him feel good. His warriors and their families had suffered enough. And he would do his best to see that they suffered no more hardships. He had had more than his share of battles and he wanted no more. Not that he was foolish enough to believe it would not be necessary to never to go to battle again. Monarchs had a way of making enemies and starting wars. But he intended to do his best to keep him and his warriors from joining the fray.

He heard Dawn before he saw her. He knew her footfalls, though they had changed some since she belonged to him. They had always been a flurry of quick bursts, as if she was in a hurry or fearful of someone following after her. Lately, however, her steps had slowed, as if she finally felt safe.

He stretched his arm out, offering his hand. She rounded the table and laced her fingers with his. He tugged her down on his lap and kissed her, savoring the taste. He got greedy for more and explored her warm, soft neck, nipping in between kisses.

He felt her sigh deep in her chest like the contented purr of a cat. He wanted to make her purr some more, but not here. "Come upstairs with me," he whispered in her ear.

Her shoulders slumped and she frowned, showing her disappointment.

"What is wrong?"

She gestured slowly, her frown deepening.

"Do not worry over Torr and Wintra? All will work well for them."

Dawn raised her brow, shrugged and tapped his chest.

"How do I know? Simple. Fate brought them together, since they are perfect for each other. And fate will let nothing stand in their way, besides fate has me to help her."

She gave him a questionable look.

"Are you questioning my ability to make sure fate gets her way?"

She nodded and gestured.

"You think I keep secrets from you?" he asked as if stricken by her query.

She nodded again and jabbed him in the chest.

He laughed and grabbed his chest. "You wound me, woman."

She tapped his chest several times, tapped his mouth repeatedly, and shook her finger at him.

He laughed again. "I better tell you or else?"

She gave a curt bob of her head and folded her arms across her chest.

"Determined are you?"

Her chin went up to show just how much.

Her smile vanished as his eyes took on a predatory glare before he lowered his lips to her exposed neck and began to nibble at her soft skin.

She reluctantly pushed him away and scurried off his lap, then stamped her foot as her hands went to rest at her hips.

Even though he scowled, he could not keep the humor out of his voice. "Are you challenging me?"

She bobbed her head.

He stretched as he stood and watching his muscles strain against his shirt and seeing passion smolder in his dark eyes turned her legs weak.

Cree snatched her up in his arms before she could stop him, not that he thought she would. He saw at the exact moment desire hit her and he had every intention of satisfying her need, and his own.

"I will hear no more protests. We will finish this discussion upstairs," he said and took the stairs two at a time.

~~~

Wintra watched Kellmara pace in front of the hearth in Cree's solar. He had directed her to sit after they had entered, saying they had much to discuss, but he had yet to start the discussion. He just kept pacing while his brow creased in thought. As she continued to watch him, she wondered if that was how she looked when she drifted off into her musings.

Had she inherited the trait from her father? *Her father.* Was Kellmara truly her father? She had believed that she and Cree had shared the same father for so long that it was difficult to think otherwise. To her, her father was dead. Would she be able to accept this man as her da?

Kellmara finally stopped pacing and looked at Wintra. "I want what is best for you."

"How do you know what is best for me when you do not know me?"

"I would like to rectify that."

"How? By taking my husband, the man I love, away from me?" Wintra asked as if she could not believe her own words.

"I was told you loved someone else."

She sighed, her shoulders slumping. "Owen. I rue the day I met him."

"I am learning that he is not who he claims to be."

"He is a selfish, heartless man."

"He had convinced me otherwise," Kellmara said annoyed. "I should have known better, but I was so overjoyed with the news that I had a daughter that I was not as cautious as I should have been. And when Owen had sent news that he had gotten you out of the abbey and was on the way home with you, I thought he was a man of his word, for he had done what he had promised."

"And what promise was that?"

"He promised to bring you home to me, and he would have if Torr had not interfered."

"You mean my husband."

"A husband chosen for you by the King," Kellmara reminded.

"How did you come to know that?"

"I had petitioned the King to claim you as my daughter. He informed me that he had wed you to Torr by proxy. I then petitioned him to annul the marriage since you were my daughter and for whatever reason he had married you to someone, to now claim it invalid." He shook his head. "But he placated me and sent me on this useless mission, knowing Cree would have his way."

"But the King sent an emissary to do his bidding."

Kellmara laughed. "I have just learned that at one time Cree saved Henry's life. Who do you think the emissary will favor in his decision?"

"Then why do you stay here? Why not return home?"

Kellmara stood in front of her, concern etched in his blue eyes. "I cannot walk away from you when I have just found you. It would be like leaving your mum all over again, and I cannot suffer such pain again. I would like time to get to know you, time for you to accept me as your da."

Wintra did not know how to feel toward this man. One moment she was furious at him for the way he tried to dictate to her and the next her heart went out to him for losing the only woman he had ever loved and discovering he had a grown daughter.

"You could have said that when you first arrived here. I may have been more accepting of you, more willing to talk." He appeared contrite, an expression she doubted he wore often. And it softened her opinion of him—a little.

"My only thought was to see you safe. I had thought that Cree may have placed you in an abbey to be rid of you. And then when I heard that the King had wed you to a stranger, when supposedly Own insisted you loved him—" He shook his head. "My first and only thought was to get to you and protect you."

Wintra's brow creased in thought and it was a few moments before she spoke. "Owen was shocked that the King had wed me to Torr when Cree announced it. You never told him this news?"

"I did not want to upset Owen or you, especially if you loved each other. I thought if I could rectify it, then all would be fine. I never got to share a life with your mother, the woman I loved beyond all reason, and I do not want you to suffer the same horrible fate.

I want to make certain that you have the choice your mum and I never did. I want you to marry the man of your choosing. The man you love and want to spend the rest of your life with. I want you to have what your mother and I only had a brief taste of—happiness."

Tears were hard to hold back, but Wintra did her best. She could not stop from thinking how she would feel if Torr left her never to return and never knowing what happened to him. That was what had happened to her mother. The man she loved had promised to return for her and never did. Had she worried something happened to him? Had she believed he never truly loved her? How had she managed to survive all those years without knowing the truth?

"You get lost in thoughts like I do," Kellmara said, as if it was another sign that confirmed she was his daughter.

She could not stop from saying, "I cannot help but wonder if my mum died thinking that you never truly love her since you never returned for her." She was surprised to see tears sting his eyes, though he turned his head as he fought to control them.

When he turned back to her, his blue eyes glistened with unshed tears. "It is something I think about every day. I pray that she knew I was forcibly kept from her. I pray that she kept hope in her heart, as I did, that we would one day be together. And I pray that she never stopped loving me, for I never stopped loving her."

Wintra hurriedly wiped away the single tear that had fallen on her cheek. Now her heart not only broke for her mother, but for her father as well.

"I know I acted poorly when we first met, but I was concerned that things were being forced upon you that you did not want. I never took the time to ask you what you wanted. I would like another chance. Will you let me be your father? Will you let me love you as much as I love your mother?"

Another tear slipped out and she was quick to wipe it away. "I love Torr and I want him as my husband and, to me, Cree is my brother, not half-brother, but *my brother*. I will let nothing change that and let nothing come between us."

"I am glad to hear that you love Torr and that you are not stuck in a loveless marriage and as for Cree? I am proud of the man he has become and how he has protected and loved you as a good brother should."

"I was a handful at times," she admitted, thinking how she had tempted his patience more often than not.

"I would like to hear about when you were a child," Kellmara said and sat in the seat beside her.

She laughed. "You may not want me as your daughter after hearing the tales I have to tell."

"You are my daughter and nothing you say or do will change my love for you. And I hope someday that you will be able to see me as your da and love me."

Words failed Wintra. Though this man bared his heart to her, he was still a stranger and she needed time to get to know him before she could accept him as her father and begin to love him.

She offered him what she could. "Given time—"

"That's all I ask for right now—time for us to get to know each other. Now tell me about when you were young."

~~~

Clouds moved in over the village and by mid-afternoon it started raining and it wasn't long before it turned heavy. The snow began to wash away and the ground turned to slush. The people took to their cottages, leaving the village to look deserted. At least that was Torr's thought as he hurried toward the keep and out of the rain.

He was eager to see Wintra and hear how her talk went with her father. And tell her of his talk with Henry, the emissary. He hurried into the keep and was disappointed when he did not find her in the Great Hall or anyone else for that matter, except a few warriors who lingered over tankards of ale and conversation.

He hurried to the solar, thinking that perhaps Wintra and Kellmara were still talking, but he found it empty. Where could she have gone? He left her here and surely the rainstorm would have kept her from venturing outside. He shook his head. He should have made the cottage his first stop, for she would go there if seeking solitude. He hurried out of the keep, worried that her talk with Kellmara had upset her.

He entered quietly to find his wife standing in front of the hearth, staring at the flames, deep in thought as usual. He went to her, standing behind her to slip his arms around her waist.

Wintra sighed and rested back against him, placing her hands over his.

"Did your talk with Kellmara go badly?" he asked, feeling the weight of her burden in the slump of her body against his.

"No, though it left me thinking that nothing is what I thought it was and my return home is far from what I imagined it to be."

"What had you imagined it to be?"

"I am not sure," she said shaking her head. "I suppose I thought everything would be as it once was, but what I had not considered was that I am no longer a child, but a woman full grown."

"I will attest to that," Torr said with a light chuckle.

Wintra gently elbowed him in the ribs.

Torr laughed and tucked his arms more tightly around her. "I am glad you are full grown, I am glad Cree kept you tucked safely away in the abbey, and I am glad the King wed you to me. While none of it is what I had imagined my life to be, I am very pleased with what fate has given me."

"I am certainly not ungrateful to fate..."

Torr turned her around to face him. "Yet something troubles you, tell me."

Wintra did not hesitate to share her worries with him. "Fate has been kind to us thus far, but what if fate decided to separate us as it did my parents? The thought of you never returning to me fills me with dread. I cannot imagine life without you beside me."

"I am not going anywhere."

"My father thought the same. He had all intentions of returning to my mother. How did my mother do it? How did she survive all those years without the man she loved?"

"She had you." Torr did not give her a chance to argue, he continued. "A daughter who was part of the man she loved and, therefore, she always had a part of him with her. Do not mourn for what your mother did not have, but rather find solace in what she had surely found joy in—a beautiful and loving daughter and a good and loving son. She lives on in you and Cree, and I am sure Kellmara sees it that way as well. Every time he sees you, no doubt, he sees your mum as well."

Wintra took hold of his hand and turned, tugging at him to follow.

Torr didn't budge. "Where are you going?"

"We are going to bed to make love and to conceive a child. One, may I add, among a whole gaggle."

Torr laughed and yanked her up against him. "So, Princess, it is a rutting stallion you want in your bed."

She smiled ever so sweetly and brought her lips a breath away from his to whisper, "The image your remark evokes turns me wet."

Torr grabbed her chin. "And your words grow me hard, so be careful or I will mount you as—"

"What do you wait for?" she challenged.

He took her hand and hurried her to the bed. They rushed out of their clothes and Wintra was quick to rest on her hands and knees on the bed. Her bare backside presented an enticing picture and Torr took a moment to enjoy the view, though not too long. He was hard and ready, and she was ready and eager.

He knelt behind her and slipped his hand between her legs, wanting to make certain she was as ready as she seemed to be and when his finger slid into her, she jolted and moaned.

"Do not tease me," she cried out. "Mount and ride me as you—ohhhh!"

Torr planted himself deep inside her. Her cry of delight let him know just how good it had felt. But then it felt damn fantastic to him. He took hold of her backside and kept a firm hand on her as he drove in and out of her, eliciting endless moans of pleasure from her lips with each forceful thrust.

It should have been a quick climax for them both, but it felt too good for it to end so fast. So Torr made sure they lingered in endless pleasure until it became unbearable and only then did he bring them to climax within seconds of each other. Then they collapsed spent and content in each other's arms.

"Do you think we can hide out here all day?" Wintra asked with a giggle.

"We could try, though Henry told me that he hoped to talk with you today."

"The emissary, I forgot about him." Wintra reached down and yanked the blanket over them, their heated passion having dissipated, leaving a chill to invade their naked bodies. "How did your talk go with him?"

"I found it a bit odd. He did not ask as many questions as I expected about you and me. He seemed more interested in my family."

"Did he not want to know if we loved each other?"

"I made that quite clear to him time and again. He would nod and ask another irrelevant question."

"Perhaps it does not matter. At least that is what Kellmara believes since Henry is beholden to Cree for saving his life. Therefore, his decision will favor what Cree wants for me, not Kellmara."

Torr rubbed his wife's arm, chasing away the chill that had settled there. "I still get the feeling that Henry had been intent on seeing to his mission. He was quite easy to talk with, his manner pleasant and jovial. It was not the difficult task that I imagined it would be."

"Are you suggesting that I make sure to talk with him?"

"I do not believe you will be able to avoid the man, though pleasant, there is a determination about him that has to be admired."

"I would imagine that determination is a necessary trait when it comes to his task. There are probably many who do not wish to speak with him, for fear of what his decision could bring."

"Do you still worry that I will be taken away from you?"

"I always wondered what my da was like and I had wished, with all my heart when I was young, he had not died before I had a chance to meet him. I prayed my mum would not be taken from me, yet she was. I begged Cree not to leave me at the abbey, but he did. And upon meeting the man who claims to be my true father, he tells me he is going to take me away from my husband, the man I love. So, yes I worry that you will be taken away from me, though I will tell you this. I would battle heaven and hell to get you back."

Torr kissed her gently. "And I would do the same if you were ever taken from me, which proves we will never be kept apart. So there is no need to worry. And while I would love to lie abed all day with you, I think it would serve you better to speak with Henry now and lay your worries to rest."

"Only if you promise me one thing."

"What?"

"That once I finish speaking with him, we will retire here and spend the rest of the day alone together."

"That is a promise I can easily keep and look forward to."

Chapter Thirty-one

Cree and Dawn entered the Great Hall the same time Wintra and Torr did, and Cree could not help but turn to whisper to his wife, "I have no doubt I will be told that I will be an uncle very soon."

She shook with soft, silent laughter and gave him a playful jab.

He loved when she laughed. Sometimes he would imagine what it would sound like if he could hear her. Lately, it was as if he heard her voice in his head and he liked the sound, gentle yet determined.

Dawn rubbed her stomach and pointed to her mouth.

"You are hungry and so am I. Let us feast and celebrate that things have finally settled down and life should be quiet now—hopefully."

Cree ordered extra food to be brought to the table and called out to Torr and Wintra to join them, and did the same to Henry when he entered. He sent Flanna to find Kellmara, so that he could join with everyone as well.

"I was going to talk with Wintra, but that can wait until later," Henry said, rubbing his hands together in anticipation of the delicious meal.

"I would prefer to speak with you now," Wintra said, approaching the man, after her husband gave her hand a reassuring squeeze.

Henry looked stricken, as if robbed of a great gift.

"I assure you it will not take long," she said and

walked across the hall to sit at an empty table far enough away that their conversation would not be heard. She had taken advantage of his enthusiasm for food, knowing he would not want to linger in talk, but then she had no intentions of them lingering.

Henry sat across from her, though his glance drifted to the dais where platters steeped with food were being placed on the table. He hurried to speak, his mouth already watering from the delicious scent.

Wintra spoke before he could. "What point is there in discussing this matter any further when your decision had been made or, I should say, the King's decision had been final the moment he had made it. He left my brother to deal with the consequences of those decisions."

Henry grinned. "You are as observant as your brother."

"Not until after I spoke with Cree did things seem to fall into place," she said. "Kellmara thinks that since Cree saved your life that you would rule in his favor and allow me to remain married to Torr. But after speaking with my brother and realizing his importance to the King it became clear why you were sent here. You were to determine if my brother had any objections to my union to Torr. If for some reason he did not favor it, the King would annul it. So the true reason you were sent here was to see if my brother approved of my marriage."

"Your wit is sharp. The King was concerned with his decision to wed you to Torr. He intended to annul your marriage if it did not please Cree. Unfortunately, the King did not count on Kellmara, which is why I was sent here to make certain Cree was satisfied."

"My brother must have served the King well, I imagine few if any know exactly how well, to allow him such choices."

"You have no idea the extent of Cree's service to the King," —Henry leaned closer—"or the respect and fear many have for your brother."

Guilt jabbed at Wintra. Here she had complained about being stuck in the abbey for all those years while her brother was off fighting endless battles and who knew what else to secure a good and safe home for them. He had sacrificed so much, and she had not appreciated it.

"My brother is a good and honorable man," she said with pride, "just as my husband is."

Henry nodded. "Torr impressed me. He is an honest man and his family means much to him. He will make you a good husband."

Wintra smiled. "I know. I am lucky to have him."

"Now that that is settled and everyone believes I have spoken with you to determine if you can remain wed to Torr, can we please go partake of that scrumptious food that awaits us?" Henry asked with a smile and a lick of his lips.

"My rumbling stomach agrees with you."

Henry chuckled as he stood and offered Wintra his arm. "And I thought that was my stomach."

Talk and laughter abounded around the dais as everyone enjoyed the bounty of food that was continually served.

Torr leaned close to his wife, resting his cheek near hers to whisper, "I will keep my promise and take us off to the cottage if that is what you still wish."

His remark brought a wider grin to her already smiling face. "I am enjoying the time with my family. Later we can enjoy each other, if you do not mind."

"Not at all. It brings me pleasure to see you

happy, though I can promise you that I will make you even happier later tonight."

"That will be quite a feat since I am *very* happy right now," she teased.

"Is that a challenge I hear?"

"Are you up to the challenge?" she asked with a laugh.

"Princess, you are going to be sorry you challenged me."

She laughed again. "Don't you mean that I am going to be extremely pleased that I challenged you?"

The suggestive banter had been slowly arousing Torr and if it continued he knew that they would not be remaining in the Great Hall for long. So with reluctance he whispered, "Later." And he turned away from her to turn and speak with—Kellmara. He had been so caught up with Wintra that he had forgotten that Kellmara had been seated on his other side. And it had not been by chance. He saw the look on Cree's face when he sent Kellmara to sit there.

Torr supposed he could not ignore the man forever. After all, he was Wintra's father, which meant he had little choice but to speak with the man.

Kellmara, however, made the first move. "You love my daughter."

Torr noticed it was not a question, perhaps Kellmara finally realized the truth. "I love Wintra very much."

"You will treat her well?"

"Always. You have my word on it," Torr assured him.

Kellmara smiled. "Wintra told me that you were an honorable man. I am beginning to see it for myself. I hope that you and Wintra will come spend time with me. What is mine, you and my daughter will inherit.

And hopefully there will be many grandchildren to carry on my legacy."

"Your legacy will surely pass to many generations since your daughter wishes many children."

"That would be so very nice. I never got to see Wintra grow. It would be wonderful to see her children—my grandchildren—grow. Something I thought I would never have in my life until Wintra."

"You do realize that if Wintra and I have a daughter that there is a good chance she will be born without a voice just like Dawn. It seems to be an inherited affliction in the women of my family," Torr said feeling the need to protect a daughter that had yet been born.

Kellmara looked taken aback for a moment, and then quickly said, "Well, then we will have to make certain she is well protected. I will not allow any harm to come to my grandchildren, though I must admit that if she is anything like Wintra, it might be more difficult than we think."

Torr had to laugh. "Getting to know your daughter, are you?"

Kellmara laughed along with him and shook his head. "I do not know how Cree did it, though he has done a fine job."

The two men continued talking, the conversation flowing more easily the longer they talked until anyone looking upon them would think them friends.

Wintra looked around her and her heart swelled with joy. She was home with family and she couldn't be happier.

Chapter Thirty-two

Lila stood with tears in her eyes. "You look so beautiful."

Dawn gestured, pointing to her friend, and then at the dress she wore.

Lila shook her head. "I stitched a nice dress for you, but you made it beautiful."

Dawn smiled, running her hand over the soft, deep blue wool. Lila may have thought that, but to Dawn her friend had made a gorgeous dress for her wedding day. The soft wool hugged at her neck and ran loosely down her arms to gather tight at her wrists. It also gathered just below her breasts leaving plenty of room for her growing stomach, which had rounded considerably in the last three weeks.

"I cannot believe today is your wedding day," Lila said. "The villagers had worried over the delay. Until they discovered you had delayed it until your father was well enough to attend. It is a shame that he took ill on his return journey here with his troop. He is well now?"

Dawn nodded and gestured how Elsa had taken good care of him.

"Elsa is a blessing to all here," —Lila giggled— "especially Neil. They are like two young ones in love."

Dawn smiled and agreed with a nod.

"They have been together ever since that day he took the arrow meant for you." Lila shook her head.

"I am glad those days are behind us. I worried so for your life. Now things have been good. The villagers are happy, food is plentiful, and today we all celebrate your union with Cree."

The door to the small sitting room opened and Cree walked in.

Lila was quick to bob her head and excuse herself, though not before giving Dawn a hug and having her thank Lila again for sewing such a beautiful dress.

Cree walked over to his wife and the sight of him never failed to catch her breath. This remarkable, handsome man belonged to her. He was her husband. The breadth, width, and strength of him stole another breath, and he stole yet another when he claimed a kiss.

"You are a beautiful woman and you are mine. You belong to me now and always," he whispered in her ear after kissing her. "And I will love you until my dying day and beyond."

She gestured that he belonged to her and slowed her gestures as she expressed how much she loved him.

Cree wrapped her in his arms and ran his hand over her rounded stomach. Something he had taken to doing a lot lately. He always loved touching her, but he loved it even more so now that he could feel his child growing inside her. "You grow more beautiful as our child grows within you."

She smiled, shook her head, and poked him.

"It is true," he insisted and smiled. "I decree it so."

Her smile grew and she shook her head again.

"Do not defy my decree, woman," he said with a teasing laugh. "You grow more beautiful and that is final."

She nodded, appeasing him and his good-natured teasing.

Wintra suddenly appeared in the open doorway. "Do I disturb anything?"

"What is wrong?" Cree asked.

Wintra had stopped wondering how he could tell when something troubled her. He obviously knew her well and could read her expressions easily. "Elsa insists that Old Mary is not well enough to attend the wedding ceremony or celebration and suggests that Dawn go see her so that the old woman does not attempt to attend."

Dawn nodded and gave her husband a kiss before walking over to Wintra.

"Go with her, Wintra," Cree ordered.

"I was planning to," Wintra said and playfully wrinkled her nose at her brother before taking Dawn's hand and tugging her along.

After collecting their fur-lined cloaks, the two women were out of the keep in no time.

"The air has a scent of snow to it," Wintra said.

Dawn agreed. It was an overcast day with a particular nip in the air that warned of snow. But she was not concerned with the weather or her wedding at the moment. Her only thought was of Old Mary. The old woman held a special place in Dawn's heart and she dreaded the thought of losing her. If Elsa felt she should stay abed, then Dawn wanted to make certain the old woman did so, though she would miss having her at the ceremony and celebration.

Elsa was just leaving Old Mary's place when the two women arrived. "She is a stubborn one. I wanted her to remain in my cottage where I could keep a close eye on her, but she refused. Several women are going to take turns watching over her so no one misses the celebration."

Wintra asked what Dawn was about to gesture. "Will Old Mary be all right?"

"With how old she is there is no telling for sure. Her chest seems clear, but the illness has left her a bit weak, so she needs rest and I do not want her out in the cold yet. If she listens to me, I believe she will be fine."

Dawn nodded and repeatedly patted her chest in thanks. She hurried into the cottage while Wintra remained outside talking with Elsa.

"What are you doing here? It is your wedding day and you have more important things to do than come here," Old Mary scolded from her bed.

Dawn smiled and gestured that she had wished to see her as she sat in the chair beside the bed.

"Elsa told you to come, the fool." Old Mary shook her head. "If I had wanted you to come here, I would have sent for you. Are you alone?"

Dawn shook her head, scrunched her brow and shrugged, asking what was wrong. Old Mary never snapped at her as she did now.

"You must return to the keep and stay close to Cree," Old Mary insisted. "For some reason there is no ceremony and no celebration today. I do not know why, though you will wed; it will not be today. Now go. I will be fine and will attend your wedding when it happens."

Dawn got upset and, with a quick nod to Old Mary, hurried out of the cottage to find Wintra there alone.

"Is something wrong?" Wintra asked, seeing how pale Dawn had become.

Dawn gestured for them to hurry.

With how upset Dawn appeared, Wintra did not

question her. She followed along toward the keep, though stopped abruptly after only a few feet. "Did you hear that? It sounded like a child crying."

Dawn shook her head and motioned for her to hurry.

Wintra heard it again. "A child in trouble." And with that Wintra hurried off.

Dawn grew frustrated. This was when she needed a voice to shout out for Wintra to stop and they would get help. But without a voice, the only thing she could do was follow her.

By the time Dawn rounded the cottage, it was too late. Wintra was struggling to break free from a large man who had his hand clamped firmly over her mouth. Another man grabbed her and was about to do the same.

"Not necessary," Owen said and stepped from behind a tree. "She has no voice and we have no choice but to bring her along or she will alert everyone to our presence."

Dawn looked to Wintra, who continued to struggle, and shook her head. She would tire herself out and be of no use if a chance came to escape. As if understanding, Wintra calmed. They were quickly dragged through the woods and planted on horses. Owen mounted behind Wintra and a large man behind Dawn. They took off without a word being said, while other men who were with them took off in the opposite direction.

Owen plastered the side of his face against Wintra's. "Your husband is going to pay dearly for foiling my plans. I do not take lightly to people who cause me to lose so much."

Curiosity had her asking questions that had been on her mind, but she had never gotten a chance to ask.

"What brought you to the abbey?"

"That simpering fool of a woman," Owen said with disgust. She actually thought that I truly loved her and the child and that I would save them. She believed every bit of drivel I fed her just as you did."

Wintra's brow creased. He could not be talking about— "Are you speaking about the pregnant woman at the abbey who died along with her child?"

"Yes, she lied to me about her family's wealth. They had little, though she told me they had much. By the time I discovered they were poorer than I was, it was too late. She was already pregnant. I did not want the burden of a child or her family's worthless land, so I refused to wed her. Her family insisted that I bring her to the abbey and, wanting to be rid of her, I did. Then I saw you."

"Do not think me foolish enough to believe you fell in love with me at first sight."

"I fell in love with what I knew you could bring me, more land than I ever dreamed possible of owning and a title. One look at you and I knew who your father had to be. I had seen him several times, though he did not know me, but the distinct color of his eyes is quite memorable and not seen often. I did some investigating and put all the pieces together."

"And you set your plan in motion. You made me believe that you loved me and wanted to spend your life with me. And like the naïve fool I was, I believed you. It was you who arranged for it to look as if my brother sent men to escort me home, wasn't it. Then you attacked those men, as if rescuing me, and let me know that they were not my brother's men. Tell me, did you do away with all those men so they would not tell anyone what you did?"

"I got rid of them so I would not have to pay

them," Owen said.

"As you will get rid of these men who help you now?" Wintra cringed when he pinched her arm hard.

"Keep your voice down," he warned and gave the pinch a twist. "We could have been wed by now and with your father's blessing if it had not been for Torr."

"I thank God every day for Torr and that the King decreed us wed."

"The King is a fool and since Torr ruined everything he will pay. I will enjoy you until your husband, your brother, and your father pay the hefty ransom I seek. Then I will leave Scotland never to return."

"I never loved you. You were simply a way for me to escape the abbey and find my way home. I would have never wed you."

"You would have had no choice," Owen insisted.

"At one time I may have believed that, but no more."

"You make no sense," Owen spat, "and I have the perfect way to fill your mouth with other than words."

Wintra recalled the scene in the cottage when he had almost forced her to take him in her mouth. She needed to escape and she had a good idea as to how to do it.

~~~

"Have you seen Wintra?" Torr asked Cree as he approached the large fireplace in the Great Hall where Cree stood looking as if he contemplated the day ahead.

"She went with Dawn to visit Old Mary," —Cree scowled— "though that was some time ago. They should have returned by now." Cree shouted to the warrior by the door to go see if Dawn and Wintra were still at Old Mary's.

"We cannot say we know each other well," Torr said, "but I want you to know that I am pleased that you are marrying my sister. You make Dawn happy and I am glad for that."

Cree smiled. "She makes me happy as well." He scowled again. "You better make my sister happy."

"I make her happy all the time," Torr said with a chuckle.

"Good, then I shall be an uncle very soon."

Torr laughed. "And probably many times over."

Cree grinned. "As will you."

"Then I say we are two lucky men," Torr said and held his hand out to him. "And I welcome you to our family."

Cree took it. "And I welcome you to mine."

The warrior returned, hurrying into the hall and speaking as he approached Cree. "Both women left some time ago and no one has seen them since."

Cree and Torr exchanged worried looks just before Cree ordered, "Gather some men and search the village." Cree turned to Torr. "Come with me, we will see if Old Mary knows what goes on."

Elsa stopped them before they could reach their destination. "I was just coming to see you. Glenda came to see me and told me that she had seen Dawn and Wintra a while back hurrying behind one of the cottages, though she said that Dawn had looked as if she thought twice before following Wintra. She thought it strange, which is why she mentioned it to me."

"Did she say which cottage it was," Cree asked.

Elsa pointed to their right. "Glenda also

mentioned that she was in the woods this morning, which is where she got the splinter she could not get out of her arm and thought she heard horses and voices. She told me that she was cautious, knowing how dangerous strangers can be. But she saw nothing, only heard what she believed were horses and voices, and then they faded."

Cree turned to Torr. "Owen?"

"The last report from my warriors was that he was well on his way home."

"But they did not continue on his trail?" Cree asked.

"They continued to follow, but Owen is a sly one. I would not be surprised if he made it only appear that it was he who led his troop."

"What is wrong?" Kellmara asked as he joined them.

Cree explained and Kellmara grew angry. "You think it is Owen?"

"If it proves the women are missing, then it would be the most likely explanation," Cree said, trying to maintain his own anger.

"I am going to kill the bastard," Kellmara said.

"No! That is for me to do," Torr warned as they hurried around the cottage.

Cree, Torr, and Kellmara stood staring at the ground where it was obvious an altercation had taken place. Henry the tracker was immediately summoned.

After looking over the area, he said, "The shorter one put up a struggle; the other one did not."

"Wintra must have put up a good fight," Torr said imagining his petite wife struggling desperately to free herself.

"She did," the tracker said with a nod as he remained on bended knee, observing the area.

"I am going to make the bastard suffer when I get my hands on him," Torr said before Cree could claim the privilege.

Chapter Thirty-three

They stopped what seemed like hours later, though Wintra prayed that it was not as long as it had felt. She and Dawn would then have a better chance of making it home perhaps by morning the latest once they escaped. She felt so foolish for not having thought better of simply running off to investigate a noise. But she had thought she had nothing to fear and the cry sounded so like a child in pain that she had not been able to ignore it. The worst part was that she had involved Dawn. Cree was going to be furious and she could not blame him. She had to make this right. She had to protect Dawn and get her home safely, though she hoped that their absence had been discovered by now and that Torr and Cree were on their way to rescue them.

She sent a silent prayer to the heavens. *Please, God, let it be so.*

Once they had dismounted Wintra went straight to Dawn, worried that the hard ride may have been too much for her and the babe. "Are you well?" she asked Dawn anxiously.

Dawn rubbed her back, though nodded.

Wintra lowered her voice. "We cannot let them take us any further. We must escape now before it is too late."

Dawn nodded and patted her chest.

"You feel the same. Good, I have a plan, but we must be quick about it." Wintra quickly whispered softly as she fussed with Dawn's cloak, making it appear as if she saw to her care.

Dawn squeezed Wintra's hand when she finished, letting her know that she agreed and was ready to do what was necessary.

"You will come with me, Wintra," Owen ordered.

The two women clung more tightly to each other's hand when they saw that the small troop had been divided in two. They were about to separate them and they both knew they could not let that happen.

"We need a moment of privacy in the woods," Wintra said, knowing they would never be sent alone, but hoping no more than two warriors would be sent with them.

"Later," Owen said impatiently.

Wintra bounced in place. "We cannot wait."

A sly smile came over Owen. "Fine, I'll escort the both of you." He turned to his warriors. "Do not disturb us."

Dawn saw the warrior who had captured her look with disgust on Owen. He had been kind to her while on the horse with him, asking if she fared well and telling her not to worry that no harm would come to her. He had insisted that she and Wintra would be released once the ransom was paid. The warrior obviously believed what Owen had told him. She, however, did not trust Owen.

The last she saw of the warrior was him slowly backing away from the small troop as the other warriors grinned, watching Owen disappear into the woods with her and Wintra. He was probably taking his leave, not wanting any part of what was to come, or could he possibly be brave enough to be going for help? She could only hope.

They walked a distance into the woods before Owen ordered them to stop.

He pointed to Dawn. "Go do what you must while Wintra pleases me. Then you can take your turn pleasing me." He grabbed Wintra's shoulder so hard that she winced and pushed her to her knees. He pulled out a dagger from the sheath at his waist. "And no tricks or I will leave you with a worse scar than your husband's."

Wintra had to stop herself from grabbing for his nose and ripping it off. She could not make any move that would bring the other warrior's to Owen's rescue. She and Dawn had no choice but to make a silent escape. It would give them time to put some distance between their captors. She purposely fumbled with the ties at his waist, trying to give Dawn time. She had not counted on it being Owen who would bring them into the woods, but at least he was only one man.

"Finished already?" Owen asked as Dawn approached. "Damn, what is wrong now?"

Wintra turned her head to see Dawn doubled over and vomiting. Good Lord, she was sick. She would have to see to this herself and get Dawn help.

Owen pushed Wintra out of his way. "Pregnant women are nothing but trouble." He walked over to her annoyed. "Get up and go back to the warriors. I will not have your disgusting mouth on me."

Wintra sprang into action and grabbed for the rock she had spied when she had gone down on her knees. She got to her feet and ran at Owen.

He heard her approach and turned too late. He never saw the blow coming. Dawn hit him in the head with a rock from behind and as he staggered forward, Wintra lashed out at him with the rock, catching him in the forehead before he reeled back and fell to the ground.

Wintra quickly dropped the rock and held her hand out to Dawn. "You are not ill?"

Dawn shook her head and patted her stomach, then pointed to what snow still remained on the ground.

"You used the snow to pretend you were sick," Wintra said with relief.

Dawn nodded and took Wintra's hand. Wintra grabbed the dagger from the ground where it had fallen and they both hurried off, knowing there was no time to waste.

They kept a brisk pace, Wintra silently berating herself for not killing Owen when she had the chance, then he would never be able to hurt another woman again. She hoped that they had done enough damage to him that he would be unable to chase after them when he came to, or better yet, it would be hours before he regained consciousness.

Wintra worried that Dawn would grow tired at the fast pace they were keeping, but then she was as determined as Wintra to return home. Wintra kept a watch on her anyway, ready to do whatever was necessary to make sure Dawn got home safely to Cree. And to make certain she got back to Torr.

~~~~

"The troop divided," Cree's tracker said after examining the ground.

Cree looked to Torr. "We will have to separate."

"You think they separated the women?" Torr asked, his worry for his wife mounting by the minute.

"If you can wait a moment, I may be able to

determine from the tracks if the women were separated," the tracker Henry said.

"A moment is all you get," Cree ordered, knowing the more time lost in following Owen, the longer it would take to find his wife and sister. And find his wife and sister he would. They had traveled hard. The tracker had confirmed that the tracks were fresh, which meant that they were not that far behind them.

Cree felt the ground rumble and heard the faint pounding of hooves before the tracker glanced up at him with wide eyes.

Torr looked to Cree. "I hear it?"

"A rider approaches," Cree said.

"Only one?" Torr asked.

"A single rider," the tracker confirmed. "Could be a scout that has been sent ahead."

Cree signaled his warriors, and they circled with weapons ready.

The lone rider slowed his fast gait when he caught sight of the mighty warriors prepared for battle, and he knew at that moment that he had made a wise decision. He approached the group at a quick pace and called out to Cree as he got close enough, "I have word of the women."

Cree ordered him forward with the snap of his hand and the circle of men parted to allow the man entrance.

"Speak and be quick about it," Cree ordered.

"First, please know that I wanted no part of this. Many of us didn't, but we had little choice."

"You are from the McBride clan," Cree said.

"Aye, my lord, I am Neville of the Clan McBride," he confirmed, "and there is no time to waste. I do not believe that once Owen gets what he wants that he will spare the women or the warriors' lives. He will take for himself and be gone. I will take you to where I last left the troop."

"Are the two women well?" Torr asked.

"We rode hard and the pregnant one seems tired. As for the petite one, Owen underestimates her, and I hope the two make an escape before he..." Neville let the words drift away. He could not speak aloud what Owen would do to the women.

"What?" Cree and Torr shouted in unison.

"Owen was taking the two women into the woods when I left and ordered that he not be disturbed. I am a farmer with little fighting skills, and there are a few of Owen's men that are just as ruthless and uncaring as he is, so I knew the only thing I could do to help the women was to leave and get help."

"We ride," Cree shouted and his warriors fell into formation and followed their leader.

Torr worried what Wintra must be going through and that he wasn't there to save her, but then she would know that he would come for her. And he knew that she would fight heaven and hell to get back to him. They would be reunited. He would have it no other way.

Cree kept pace behind Neville, though it could be a trap he was leading them into, he doubted it was. It did not actually matter since nothing would stop him from getting to his wife. He did not want to think of what Dawn might be suffering right now. If he did, the whole woods would tremble from the rage he would roar if he let loose his anger.

He wished his wife had gone for help instead of following after Wintra, but she would have never done that. And he could not fault her action. She was, after all, looking out for his sister. What concerned him more was that neither his wife nor his sister would simply submit to Owen without a fight. Knowing his wife and sister's tenacity, there was a chance they could very well escape. He prayed if they attempted such a feat that they would be successful, for if they were not the consequences could be deadly.

Cree also silently berated himself for not letting Dawn get more sleep last night, then she would not be so tired today. But he had come upon her just after she had finished a bath in preparation of their wedding today. Her body had been so shiny and soft, and her scent so enticing that he had not been able to keep his hands off her. They had spent time making love and when he woke in the middle of the night hard from a dream, he had made love to her again. Then she woke early this morning to prepare for the special day, so it was no wonder she was tired. And it was his fault—damn him to hell.

~~~

Owen held his head when he was finally able to sit up and shouted out to his men, then cringed from the pain reverberating through his skull. He would kill the two women for this and be done with them, though not before he got what he deserved. It had taken endless months to court Wintra and to convince her father that they were in love. He had been so close to succeeding in becoming the new Earl of Kellmara, having plans to do away with Kellmara soon after he wed Wintra, and now that was no more. His dreams had vanished in an instant when Cree had announced that Torr was Wintra's husband, though he had held out hope that had been dashed much too soon.

He would, however, have his revenge. They

would all pay for what they had done to him, even the mighty Cree.

Owen wiped the blood from his head, though there wasn't much. It was the two bumps on his head that caused the most discomfort, especially when he mounted his horse and began to ride. The throb in his head escalated, and he silently swore that the two women would suffer much more pain than he by the time he got done with them. He would make them suffer until they begged to die.

~~~

Wintra saw that Dawn's steps had turned sluggish, as if it was a burden for her to lift her feet. She needed to rest and though it was unwise for them to stop, Wintra felt they had no choice. She did not want to take the chance of Dawn losing the babe. Cree would never forgive her and she would never forgive herself.

"We will stop and rest," Wintra said.

Dawn looked ready to disagree, then her shoulders slumped and she nodded, as if she too realized that she could not go on. She silently cursed herself for not having gotten more sleep last night, but then she did not regret her time with Cree. She never did. Making love with him always left her feeling safe and cherished, and it made her all the more determined to return home to him.

Wintra searched the area for a secluded spot to rest. With it being winter, the trees were mostly bare, except for the pines, leaving the forest naked with few places to hide. The only spot that would afford them any cover was an old pine with a thick trunk and low branches.

"Over there behind the pine tree will be a good place to rest," Wintra said and once there she helped Dawn to sit. As soon as her head rested back against the tree trunk, she fell asleep.

Wintra stood beside the tree to keep watch. She would give Dawn a little time, and then wake her and they would go. She kept the dagger clutched tight in her hand as she kept her eyes and ears alert. However, her thoughts wandered to Torr and the joy they had shared these last few weeks. She had been so very happy, and the more intimate she and Torr had become, the more deeply she had fallen in love with him. He was a kind and generous lover and an attentive husband. He was not one to anger fast, at least not with her. He was patient with her, and she loved that about him. She actually loved everything about him and, at the moment, she missed him terribly. She feared she would never see him again, and she could not let that horrible thought take hold, or all would be lost.

Dawn stirred awake and when she took in her surroundings, she bolted up away from the tree and winced, though it could not be heard. Her legs and back ached, and she feared she would not be able to stand.

Wintra was at her side as soon as she had seen her move. "You are in pain?"

Dawn didn't want to admit it, but she would be foolish if she did not. So she gestured to Wintra that she ached and could not go much further.

"I thought that might happen. You look exhausted. I am going to find a place to hide you, and then I will keep watch. If Owen manages to find us, I will divert him and you wait here for Cree and Torr. I am sure they are on their way to rescue us. They will

339

find you."

Dawn shook her head adamantly.

"It is the only way," Wintra insisted. "You haven't the strength to help me."

Dawn shook her head more strenuously, insisting Wintra was wrong.

Wintra knew there was only one thing that would change her mind. "What of the babe? Would you endanger his life?"

Dawn's hand went to her stomach. She would do anything to keep her babe safe. But could she sacrifice Wintra's life to do that?

"There is no time to waste arguing," Wintra insisted. "There is no other way." She did not wait for Dawn to agree or disagree. She got busy searching for a hiding spot. She found a small cropping of rocks not far away that seemed the only possible choice. By adding fallen pine branches along one side, it just might work.

Dawn tried to protest again, but Wintra would not have it. Wintra made certain that Dawn could not be seen behind the large formation of rocks by scattering fallen pine branches on the sides in just the right places.

"You must promise me that no matter what you hear, you must stay put," Wintra said worried that Dawn would try to help her.

Dawn shook her head and with her finger crossed her chest, letting Wintra know that she could make no such promise.

Wintra took Dawn's hand. "Please, Dawn, let me do this for you and the babe and for my brother. Cree has protected and kept me safe all my life. Now it is my turn."

Dawn understood her need to be courageous. She

had experienced it herself and gave no thought to doing what had to be done. But she did not know if she could sit by and not help Wintra if it should prove necessary. There was the babe to consider, but he was safe inside her. And how could she ever face Cree and tell him she had sat by and done nothing to help his sister.

Dawn could make no promises and she was about to let Wintra know that when they both suddenly heard the pounding of hooves not far off.

"Please stay put," Wintra said and hurried off to meet her fate.

Chapter Thirty-four

"Blood," Cree's tracker said as he examined the area.

Cree and Torr were off their horses in an instant. Kellmara followed, staring at the rock smeared with blood as the tracker drifted off.

Torr's gut clenched with fear for his wife and his sister. He raged inwardly at feeling so helpless. He wanted his wife and sister back and he wanted Owen dead. And he would not rest until he saw that both were done.

Cree stepped away from the others and looked in the distance. He balled his hands into fists, needing to control his anger. Right now he had to focus on Owen and his men, not his wife and sister. He would lose all perspective if he allowed his fear for his wife and sister's safety to interfere. He was a warrior and this was a battle. And this battle was not going to end well for the enemy. He intended to slaughter every one of them.

The tracker returned smiling. "The two women escaped and from their footprints neither appears injured."

"Get us to my wife and sister, Henry, and you will live like a king," Cree said.

"I live better than a king, my lord, thanks to you. I would have never met my wife Greta if you had not freed her people from invaders, and now she and I will welcome our first child in two months. I have a good life and I am grateful. I will get you to your wife and sister," Henry said, "but we must hurry. Horses follow the tracks."

They all mounted their horses and followed the tracker.

~~~

Wintra waited until the riders came into view. Owen rode in the lead and after staring at him for a moment, she turned and ran. If she could put enough distance between her and Dawn before Owen caught her, there would be no way the stubborn woman could help her.

She had no doubt that Owen would catch her. What he would do when he did, she wasn't sure, but she did not think he would kill her—not yet at least. And, hopefully, that would give Torr and Cree time to find her.

The pounding of the horse's hooves grew louder and closer, no matter how fast she ran, and she knew it was only a matter of time before the riders caught up with her. She spied a clumping of trees and headed for them, knowing that it would be hard for the horses to maneuver around them.

She heard Owen spew a string of oaths as he drew near and a chill raced through her, knowing he was not far behind her. She had left the dagger with Dawn in case she needed to protect herself. As for herself, she would do whatever was necessary to stay alive until Torr or Cree found her.

The brutal shove to her back came suddenly and sent her sprawling to the ground face first. Her face no soon as smacked the patch of snow, then she was yanked up by the back of her hair and turned to face a furious Owen.

Wintra could not help it, she could not stop from smiling. The lump on his forehead protruded like a horn from his head.

"You bitch," he screamed and slapped her across the face so hard that the sting reverberated through her head. "Before I get done with you, you will beg for death."

"I would not be so quick to harm me," she warned. "Not only will my husband want to see that I am unharmed, but so will my brother and father before any ransom is handed over to you."

Owen grinned. "What I intend to do to you no one will be able to see, and do you truly believe I intend to return you to your husband?"

"No, never did I believe that."

"So you attempted a foolish escape." Owen suddenly gave a quick look around. "Where is the pregnant one?"

"Do you actually think I would tell you," she said mockingly.

Another hard slap sent blood running down the corner of her mouth.

"You do know that Cree will stop Torr from killing you fast. My brother will want to see you suffer for every injury you inflicted upon me, and I want to see you suffer for what you have done to those women."

"We will see who suffers," Owen sneered and hit her again. "Now tell me where the pregnant one is."

"You are wasting your time," Wintra said and felt the breath whoosh from her body as he landed a solid blow to her stomach.

"Go find the other woman," Owen yelled to one of his warriors.

"Now let's see how brave you truly are?" Owen said and turned his fist on her again.

~~~

Dawn had waited until all the horses had passed and the ground trembled no more. Then she got up and followed the horses' tracks. She did not care how tired she was, there was no way she was not going to help Wintra. She would not be foolish about it. She would stay hidden and wait for just the right moment.

She saw the warrior in the near distance at the same time he saw her, and she knew there was no point in running. She would tire herself out and he would catch her, and then she would have no strength left to fight him. She blessed Wintra ten times over for having left the dagger with her. She gripped it tightly in her hand, her cloak concealing it, and waited.

~~~

The tracker spotted the two bodies crumpled on the ground, a few feet from each other and yelled out.

Cree flew past him as did Torr and Kellmara. Cree was off his horse in a flash when he saw that it was Dawn lying face down in the snow, blood pooling at her side. He threw his head back and released such a roar that the birds and animals in the woods hurried off in fear to bury themselves from the terrifying howl. And Cree's men kept their distance, knowing all too well that Cree was about to release hell.

Cree stared down at Dawn, afraid to touch her, afraid to find out that his wife was dead.

Torr was not. She was his sister, and he dropped to the ground beside her.

"Don't touch her," Cree shouted when Torr reached out.

"Then see to her," Torr said angrily. "She may be able to tell us where Wintra is." He refused to believe Dawn dead. She couldn't be and neither could Wintra.

Cree went down on his knees beside her and as he gently turned her over, her eyes fluttered open, and she struggled to smile at him. Relief punched him in the gut, rendering him as speechless as Dawn.

"Where are you wounded? Who did this to you? Where is Wintra?" Torr asked anxiously since Cree had been struck silent, not that he could blame him. Seeing Dawn sprawled so lifeless on the ground had given the impression she was dead. He was grateful she wasn't and he hoped she could tell him where Wintra was.

Dawn raised her hand, though winced as she did.

Cree quickly and gently rested her hand in his and winced himself when he saw how her palm had been sliced across. He was also relieved to see that the wound was the reason for the blood that had been spilled.

"I found tracks," Henry called out.

Torr jumped to his feet, though gave a last look to Dawn. "I must go."

Dawn pointed and wagged her hand for him to hurry.

"I will leave you and Kellmara to return my sister safely to me," Cree said, knowing both men were more than capable of the task and also knowing there was no way he was going to leave his wife.

Torr was on his horse and gone before Kellmara

reached his horse.

Cree looked down at his wife, snug in his arms. "I am going to shackle you to me so that you never leave my side again."

Dawn grinned and shook her head.

"I am serious. I never want to feel again what I did a few moments ago when I thought you dead. It was as if all life had suddenly been drained from me, and there was no point in living without you or the babe in my life. Damn it, Dawn, I love you so much more than I ever thought possible."

She smiled at his loving declaration, and then with slow gestures, assured him that she and the babe were fine, with the exception of her hand.

"The fool I am," he scolded himself, "to talk with you when your hand needs tending." He got to his feet while keeping her snug in his arms and looked around to see that half his warriors had gone with Torr and the other half had remained behind. They were busy scouting the area, posting guards, while two saw to removing the dead man's body from sight, and two others had just finished preparing a pallet made of pine branches and were placing blankets on top.

His men knew well their jobs and he would see them rewarded for a task more than well done. He placed Dawn on the pallet and with relief saw to her care.

~~~

Wintra had managed to avoid the blow, though it cost her since her hair had been pulled when she yanked away from him, and she thought for sure that a portion of her scalp had been torn away with it. She was surprised, and relieved, to see only a few strands of her hair hanging in his hand.

Owen grew even more furious and lunged at her, and she came up with her hand just as he did and caught him hard in the nose.

Owen stumbled back as blood poured from his nostrils. He looked dazed and it took him a moment to regain his focus. He wiped the blood away from his mouth with the back of his hand, but it did not stop blood spittle from flying as he spoke. "You will pay for that, bitch."

He lunged at her again, catching her shoulder.

She swerved and released the ties at her neck, and her cloak slipped off along with his hand.

He cursed and rushed at her, but she was quick to step out of his reach. He grew more furious with each unsuccessful attempt. Until, in a blinding rage, he threw himself at her, knocking her down. He scrambled over her, her hands and arms flailing as she tried to deflect the blows he haphazardly threw at her.

Suddenly Owen was gone, and she turned her head to see Torr and him rolling around on the ground a few feet from her. She scrambled to her feet just as mayhem rained down upon them. Her father came charging in with Cree's warriors and attacked Owen's men. She hurried out of the way, though remained near, never taking her eyes off her husband as he and Owen got to their feet and exchanged vicious blows.

"I'm going to kill you, and then take your wife with your blood on my hands," Owen screamed at Torr.

"You do not have the courage. You sniveling coward," Torr challenged.

Owen lunged at him like a madman and in only minutes Wintra realized that he did not stand a chance against Torr. His punches staggered while Owen's appeared to glance off Torr. He sent Owen reeling time and again until the man could barely stand. Torr stood firm on his feet, his breathing steady, and his nostrils flaring in anger.

One of Owen's men tried to help him and Torr took him down with one quick jab in the face. At that one moment, Owen attempted to run. Torr was on him, grabbing his arm, and swinging him around, his fist connecting with Owen's jaw.

He went down on his knees and Torr circled him like a hunter closing in on his prey. "I really should let Cree have you. Your death would be slow and painful, but I want this done here and now."

He lashed out at Owen so fast that all Wintra could see was a blur, though she heard Owen scream and saw a bone protruding from his arm.

"That's for daring to abduct my wife and sister," Torr said circling him again.

Wintra heard it then—silence. She glanced around to see that Cree's warriors had won and they now stood watching Torr with respect. She also saw that her father stood looking upon Torr with admiration and pride.

Owen was on his knees, his face deathly pale, his head turned away from his broken arm unable to look upon it.

Torr struck him again, this time breaking his other arm. "That is for causing my sister harm."

Wintra gasped. Dawn had been hurt? How badly? That was why Cree wasn't here. He was with Dawn. She prayed for Dawn's well-being.

Owen cried out, "Enough, mercy, please mercy."

"You showed no mercy to others. You deserve none for yourself." Torr took Owen's head in his hands. "And this is for what you've done to my wife and all the other women you have so ruthlessly harmed." With a vicious twist, he broke Owen's neck.

Chapter Thirty-five

It was late, the keep quiet after a hectic night. Cree had shouted orders as soon as they had all returned, sending everyone jumping and running at his command. Elsa had hurried from her cottage to attend Dawn in her bedchamber, where Cree had insisted his sister wait so Elsa could tend her wounds as soon as the healer finished seeing to Dawn.

Wintra had tried to explain that she was fine, but there had been no winning against her husband, her brother, and her father. She did not know how she was going to deal with three strong men in her life, but she was happy to try.

She had been so relieved to know that Dawn's wound had not been as bad as first thought. Elsa had cleansed and bandaged it and ordered her to refrain from using it for a few days until the wound closed sufficiently.

Dawn had worried that she would not be able to talk with one hand.

Cree had shocked everyone when he told her, "You talk too much anyway. It will not hurt you to be silent for a few days."

Dawn's body had started shaking with laughter and all those in the room had joined in, their laughter reverberating throughout the room.

Cree had ordered everyone out and they had complied, laughing all the way.

Torr stopped after taking a few steps out of the

room and slipped his arm around Wintra's waist. "Are you sure you do well?"

"You have asked me that endlessly since first seeing my wounds. And I have assured you again and again that I am fine. And Elsa agrees. You have no cause to ask me again."

Torr eased her up against him. "And what if I have a particular reason for wanting to make certain?"

"That might prove interesting," she said and smiled, then winced.

"See," Torr said accusingly, "you are in pain."

"You trapped me," she insisted and gave him a shove, not that it did any good. He was too solid of a man to move with a shove from the likes of her. Then a thought hit her, a single thought, and she said, "My lips may be too sore to kiss, but the rest of me is feeling just fine."

Torr rested his brow to hers. "You tempt me, Princess."

A familiar tingle ran through her and she ran her hand over his chest. "I meant to."

"You have been through an ordeal—"

"That is done and finished thanks to you. We should celebrate."

"I will do all the work," he ordered.

"Now you tempt me," she said.

He smiled, though it faded slowly. "I thought I had lost you. I never want to feel that soul-wrenching emptiness again. I love you, Wintra."

"And I love you, Torr, forever and ever and ever."

"I wish I could kiss you right now, but since I cannot kiss your mouth," —he took her hand and his other hand went to rest at her back just above her backside—"let's hurry and go to the cottage."

Wintra and Torr rushed down the stairs and

stopped when they reached the Great Hall taken by the beauty of the wedding decorations. Pine garlands hung across the mantel with candles interspersed throughout. Garlands were also strung from the rafters as were clan color banners.

"It is a shame the wedding never got to take place and now it is postponed until Dawn feels well enough for a celebration. And another wedding dress must be stitched since hers got ruined," Wintra said.

Torr turned to her and said, "Marry me, Wintra, here and now."

"We are married," she said looking at him as if he had gone completely mad.

"Marry me this time because you choose to do so."

He gave her a choice, and she didn't have to think about it. Her heart swelled with joy. "Yes. Yes, I will marry you."

"Wait here. Do not move. Promise me you will not move," Torr said excited.

"I will sit at the table by the hearth and wait," she said, keeping a smile at bay so she would not disturb her wound.

Torr returned in no time with her father in tow, a huge smile on his face as he hurriedly lifted her off the bench to place her in front of him like a shield. "You need to protect me from your brother."

"I am going to beat your husband," Cree warned as he entered the Great Hall with his wife smiling beside him. Dawn gave him a jab when they came to a stop near Wintra and Torr. He scowled at her.

After a simple hand gesture and a touch to Cree's chest, his tone softened.

"We are overjoyed that *someone* is able to wed today," Cree said annoyed. He looked to his sister and a smile crept over his lips. "Truly, we are overjoyed for you and Torr."

Wintra went to him and gave him a hug. "I love you and I am glad you and Dawn will share this moment with us."

"I wouldn't miss it and I love you, little sister, and it is glad I am to have you home again." Cree said and kissed her cheek.

Before Wintra returned to Torr's side, she went to Kellmara. "I am glad you are here to see me wed the man I love, *Da*."

Tears sprang in Kellmara's eyes that she had called him Da, and he reached out and gave his daughter a tight hug.

Henry entered the Great Hall, yawning. Since he was sent by the King with the powers to annul the marriages if need be, he also had the power to wed those that had been joined by proxy.

Surrounded by family, those who loved her most, Wintra exchanged vows with Torr and sealed their love with loving words and a loving kiss.

Chapter Thirty-six

Summer

Wildflowers bloomed everywhere and fields were lush with growth as was Dawn as she prepared for her wedding day. Her hand went to her large rounded stomach and loving stroked it. The babe had been more active than usual of late, and she had wondered if he was eager to be born. She certainly was eager for the birth. She had grown uncomfortable in the last day or so and while she was excited about today, she wished it was over. But she had given Cree her word that they would wed before their babe was born, and she would not disappoint him. Besides, the villagers had long anticipated this day.

Everyone had joined in to make it extra special. Turbett had cooked for three days in preparation of this day. Flanna had worked with the servants and villagers alike to set up a lovely feasting area outside. The weather had even cooperated, the sky seeming to shine a more brilliant blue and the sun remaining bright and warming the land.

Lila had made three different dresses for her; a warm one for winter, a lighter one for spring, and her favorite, the one she wore now. Dawn ran her hand over the lovely pale blue dress that gathered just below her breasts and had sleeves that ended at her elbows. William, Cree's castle designer, had brought the material and much more back with him from his journey to Edinburgh. She had hoped for the drawing materials he had told her he would try and bring for her, but since he had never mentioned them, she had assumed he had been unable to acquire them.

Wintra and Lila had fussed over her and had just left her with instructions that Cree would be there soon to get her. The two women had laughed and joked about how Cree had planted a guard outside the bedchamber door. He had insisted that no one would interfere or prevent Dawn and him from getting married this day.

Dawn reached for the lovely wreath Lila had made for her out of pink heather and yellow gorse sprigs fresh from the land and winced at the pain that stung her lower back. She gave it a rub, then scooped up the wreath to place on her head. She was happy and would not let a little discomfit disrupt her day.

She had much to be thankful for, especially the news that Wintra would give birth late fall, though she would be leaving shortly after Dawn delivered the babe. They would return to Torr's home and Dawn would miss them both terribly.

She told herself not to think about that, but rather the good times she had shared with Wintra since her arrival here. Life had turned very good for all, and she prayed it would stay that way for a long time to come.

A knock sounded at the door and Dawn scrunched her brow wondering why Cree would knock. But it wasn't Cree who entered, it was Old Mary.

Dawn smiled, seeing the old woman spryer than ever walk toward her with a wide smile.

"I have something for you," she said holding a small, cloth-wrapped package in her hand. She stopped and held it out to Dawn. "It is a gift from your mother for your first child. She made me promise to give it to you."

Tears threatened Dawn's eyes as she reached for the package with trembling hands. She carefully unwrapped the cloth and though she smiled, she could not prevent tears from falling. She placed the wrapping on the table and held up the tiny linen garment embroidered with pale yellow flowers around the neck.

"It was yours," Old Mary said, tears stinging her eyes as well. "She stitched it for you from a favorite dress that was once hers. I remember the day she first put it on you. You smiled and grabbed the garment as if you were thrilled to be wearing it, and your mother and I cried at the joy it brought you just as we do this day."

Dawn could not stop the tears from flowing and she gestured that she wished her mum was here to share this day.

Old Mary took hold of her hand. "She is here with us in our hearts and happy for you. And I must tell you that you will have another gift this day, and it will come from the heavens."

Dawn wiped at her tears, though they would not stop falling and scrunched her brow and shrugged.

"I cannot tell you what it is. After all, it is a gift."

The door opened and Cree walked in with a smile that quickly turned to a scowl when he saw his wife crying. He hurried over to her and placed the package he carried on the table before he slipped his arm around her waist and demanded, "What's wrong?" Before she could respond, he turned to Old Mary. "What have you said that upset her?"

Dawn shook her head and pointed to the small garment and at Old Mary.

"Tell me," Cree ordered the old woman, not

happy to see his wife crying on their wedding day. He would not have joy for their wedding taken from her a second time.

Old Mary explained about the garment, though did not mention the gift that was yet to come this day.

Cree's scowl vanished. "That is lovely of you, Old Mary, and it will be the first garment our child wears, even though it has flowers on it."

Dawn smiled, a gentle laugh shaking her body, and Cree was glad he brought joy back to her face.

Old Mary laughed. "Yes, flowers." She continued laughing as she left the room.

Cree wiped Dawn's wet cheeks as she hugged the small garment to her chest. "I have a gift for you, but I doubt it will be as wonderful as the one from your mother."

Dawn's eyes lighted with excitement, and she placed the baby garment on the table.

"A wedding gift for you," Cree said and pointed to the package that lay next to the garment.

Dawn unwrapped the cloth-covered package and stared for a moment at the drawing material.

"I had told William to make certain he brought back what you needed to draw with and any new drawing implements as well. He has more to show you."

Dawn almost laughed at the thought that he had rendered her speechless, but how did she let Cree know how very much this gift meant to her? She took his hand and placed it on her chest and looked at him with what she hoped he could see—love and appreciation for him being such a wonderful husband.

"The love in your eyes tells it all," Cree said and brought his lips to hers.

The babe kicked hard just as they kissed, and

Dawn winced as her hand flew to her stomach, though Cree's hand got there first.

"He is awfully active today," Cree said, stroking her stomach in hopes of calming the babe.

Dawn nodded with a sigh.

"You will sit and enjoy the festivities, and we will retire early tonight while the villagers continue to enjoy the celebration."

She nodded and smiled, grateful that she would not have to endure a long night since she was already wishing for her bed.

Cree took her hand. "Let us go and be wed and enjoy this memorable day."

~~~

Dawn smiled and enjoyed, as best she could, the wedding festivities. It had been several hours since the brief ceremony and she wished she could take her leave. The pain in her back had returned until finally it had refused to go away. She wanted nothing more than to take to her bed and rest.

She wished she did not feel so tired so that she could participate more in the festivities. But then there had been too many years of hardship for the village and this wedding celebration was, in a sense, a celebration of freedom from misery for all.

Dawn watched as Lila and Paul danced happily to the music and how Dorrie was teaching a reluctant Elwin to dance, and then there was Elsa and Neil dancing more jubilantly than the young couples. Her eyes widened when she saw Wintra attempting to pull Cree away from the warriors, he was speaking with, to dance.

"Cree won't win against my tenacious wife."

Dawn turned a smile on Torr as he took a seat beside her.

"You look tired. Are you feeling well?"

She faked a yawn to let him know she was tired.

"Perhaps you should retire now. We will keep the celebration going," Torr said with a smile and concern for his sister.

Dawn was about to gesture that she would go soon when a stabbing pain hit her so hard that she grabbed her stomach and doubled over, her head almost hitting the table.

Torr stood and shouted, "Cree!" Before he could see to Dawn, Cree was there going down on one knee beside her.

"Dawn," Cree said softly, slipping his hand under her chin to lift her head and when he did, his stomach clenched at how pale she was.

She grabbed Cree's hand and patted her stomach.

"It is time," Elsa said from behind Cree.

"Now? The babe is ready to be born now?" Cree asked as if he did not believe it.

Elsa reaffirmed with a smile. "Now. And it would be wise to get her to her bedchamber right away."

Cree stood and eased his wife into his arms.

Cheers rang out for good luck and good fortune for the child that was about to be born and the celebration continued as Cree rushed through the keep to their bedchamber.

He sat Dawn on the bed once in the room, though did not let go of her hand.

"You may leave now, my lord," Elsa said, Lila, Wintra, and Old Mary following her into the room.

"I am not leaving her." He held up his hand, stopping Elsa from speaking. "I will not repeat myself."

Elsa nodded. "As you wish, but I must ask you not to get in our way."

He nodded. "I will sit beside the bed and hold her hand."

Elsa looked none too happy, but she had no choice but to obey.

Elsa instructed Wintra as to what to do, but Lila knew what needed doing and went about doing it. Old Mary remained by the fire, Cree having heard her say that she was present for Dawn's birth and she wanted to be present for Dawn's babe's birth too.

As the pain worsened so did Cree's concern for his wife. It tore him apart to see her struggle in silence to give birth to their child. And he did not know how he would be able to put her through this again. But it would be inevitable, since he knew he would never be able to keep his hands off her. He promised himself that if she had to suffer then so would he. He would be with her through every birth, and he would endure the pain as if his heart was being ripped from his body as he watched his wife suffer through childbirth.

It was only a couple of hours later when a surprised Elsa announced that delivery was near. "A short labor," she said with a smile.

Cree glared at her. How could she think this was a short labor?

Dawn was relieved that the babe would soon be born, the pain having been more than she had imagined, though it was nothing compared to the pain she saw in her husband's eyes as he held her hand and spoke softly and encouragingly to her. She knew of no man who stayed with his wife during delivery of their child. Cree was truly a remarkable husband.

"All right, Dawn, it is almost time," Elsa said.

"When I tell you to push, push hard."

Lila stood beside Elsa, a towel in her hand ready to take the babe. Wintra stood behind them, her eyes wide and her face pale.

"Push!" Elsa said.

Dawn gripped Cree's hand tightly and pushed with all her might.

"He is slipping out with ease," Elsa announced with a pleased laugh. A sharp cry pierced the air, and Elsa laughed again. "The lad's not even all the way out and already he's crying."

Dawn smiled and looked to Cree. He smiled and kissed her forehead, relieved that this ordeal would soon be done and thrilled to welcome a son.

"He is a good size and looks fit," Elsa announced as she held him up for all to see.

Cree felt his chest tighten with pride at the sight of his son. He had barely a sprinkle of light fuzz for hair and he was long and solid in weight with a cry on him that rivaled his father's roar. He did not think he could ever know such joy, and he leaned down and whispered to Dawn, "Thank you for giving me such a fine son."

She smiled and her face suddenly contorted in pain.

"Oh good Lord, there's another one in there," Elsa said.

"What do you mean another one?" Cree asked.

"Twins," Elsa said, handing the babe over to Lila.

She wrapped the wailing babe in the blanket and took him to the table to clean him up, a basin of warm water waiting there for her. Wintra remained next to Elsa in case she needed help.

"Twins?" Cree repeated as if trying to comprehend that there would be two babes.

"Yes, now leave me be," Elsa snapped and looked up at a scowling Cree. "This one is having some difficulty. She needs my attention." Elsa did not wait for a command. She got busy seeing to the babe.

Cree felt his chest tighten again, though this time with worry. He looked to his wife and saw the same worry mirrored in her eyes. "It will be all right." But she cringed in pain, her head tilting back and he could only imagine the scream that echoed so silently inside her.

Old Mary was suddenly at the bedside. She patted Dawn's head. "A gift, my child. A gift from the heavens." She drifted away then.

"You need to push, Dawn, and hard," Elsa ordered.

Cree held her hand. "You can do it. You are strong like my warriors."

Dawn gave him a weak smile and pushed with what strength she had left.

"That's it, that's it—" Elsa suddenly turned silent and no cry was heard.

Dawn looked frantically to Cree.

"What's wrong," Cree demanded.

"You have a daughter," Elsa said.

Dawn's head fell back, and she wanted to scream for her daughter who would never be able to do so herself, just like her mother.

Cree felt as if his chest had been gripped by a mighty hand, the pain was so intense and when he looked at his wife, tears falling from her eyes on a day that should hold such joy for her; he wanted to roar out his anger. But he held it back like a dam trying to hold back an angry sea.

He took hold of his wife's hand and she squeezed tight, her tear-filled eyes looking to him as if she was sorry. It tore at his heart and he leaned down and kissed her wet cheeks. "I love you and I love the babes you gave me this day."

Wintra, fighting back tears, took the wiggling child from Elsa and held her high for Dawn to see. "She is a beauty like her mother."

Elsa cut the cord while she fought back tears.

Cree let go of his wife's hand and walked over to his sister who was wiping the babe clean. She had a thatch of dark red hair like her mother and the prettiest face he had ever seen, and she was so tiny, though wiggled fiercely in Wintra's arms as if she was trying to break free. He took his daughter from her and her squirming calmed as he lifted her to rest her cheek against his. "I love you, little one, and I will hear you as clearly as I hear your beautiful mother."

Tears fell from the women's eyes as they watched the mighty warrior pay homage to his voiceless, new born daughter.

The tremendous wail echoed off the walls, startling everyone in the room, including the mighty warrior Cree. His daughter cried out more heartily than his son had.

Old Mary patted Dawn's shoulder. "A gift from the heavens."

~~~~

Cheers of joy rang out through the village when the births were announced and good fortune was claimed for years to come with the birth of a daughter who was born with a voice. It brought tears to many and hope to all.

That night Cree lay in bed with his wife, she cradling their sleeping son and he their daughter.

Dawn never felt so content. She was blessed, so very blessed. She smiled at her husband and pressed her one hand to his heart than pressed it to hers, letting him know how much she loved him.

"That fateful day you entered that hut I thought you nothing more than a weak, frightened lass. But you proved me wrong, and in so doing, you stole my heart. I belong to you and always will." He kissed her gently. "And make no mistake, wife, you are mine; you belong to me now and forever."

The End

Titles by Donna Fletcher

Single Titles

San Francisco Surrender
Untamed Fire
Rebellious Bride
The Buccaneer
Tame My Wild Touch
Playing Cupid
Whispers on the Wind

Series Books

The Wedding Spell (Wyrrd witch series)
Magical Moments
Magical Memories
Remember the Magic

The Irish Devil
Irish Hope

Isle of Lies
Love Me Forever

Dark Warrior
Legendary Warrior

The Daring Twin
The Bewitching Twin

Taken By Storm
The Highlander's Bride

Return of the Rogue (Sinclare brothers' series)
Under the Highlander's Spell
The Angel & The Highlander
Highlander's Forbidden Bride

Bound To A Warrior (Warrior King series)
Loved By A Warrior
A Warrior's Promise
Wed To A Highland Warrior

Highlander Unchained (Highlander Trilogy)
Forbidden Highlander
Highlander's Captive

About the Author

Donna Fletcher is a *USA Today* bestselling romance author. Her books are sold worldwide. She started her career selling short stories and winning reader contests. She soon expanded her writing to her love of romance novels and sold her first book SAN FRANCISCO SURRENDER the year she became president of New Jersey Romance Writers. Donna is also a past President of Novelists, Inc.

Drop by Donna's website www.donnafletcher.com where you can learn more about her, find out Book News, get a printable Book List, and read her blog.

Want to be alerted to Donna's book releases? Sign up for Book Alert. Send Donna an e-mail at donna@donnafletcher.com with Book Alert in the message box and you're all set.

71026487R00221

Made in the USA
Columbia, SC
18 May 2017